THIRST

for

JUSTICE

THIRST

for

JUSTICE

A Novel

DAVID R. BOYD

Published by ECW Press
665 Gerrard Street East
Toronto, Ontario, Canada M4M 1Y2
416-694-3348 / info@ecwpress.com

Editor for the Press: Susan Renouf
Cover design: Michel Vrana

This is a work of fiction. Names, characters,
places, and incidents either are the product of
the author's imagination or are used fictitiously,
and any resemblance to actual persons, living or
dead, business establishments, events, or locales is
entirely coincidental.

LIBRARY AND ARCHIVES CANADA CATALOGUING IN
PUBLICATION

Title: Thirst for justice : a novel / David R. Boyd.

Names: Boyd, David R. (David Richard), 1964–
author.

Identifiers: Canadiana (print) 20200248340
Canadiana (ebook) 20200248359

ISBN 978-1-77041-240-8 (softcover)
ISBN 978-1-77305-492-6 (PDF)
ISBN 978-1-77305-491-9 (EPUB)

Classification: LCC PS8603.O983 T45 2020
DDC C813/.6—dc23

The publication of *Thirst for Justice* has been generously supported by the Canada Council for the Arts which
last year invested $153 million to bring the arts to Canadians throughout the country and is funded in part by the
Government of Canada. *Nous remercions le Conseil des arts du Canada de son soutien. L'an dernier, le Conseil a investi
153 millions de dollars pour mettre de l'art dans la vie des Canadiennes et des Canadiens de tout le pays. Ce livre est financé
en partie par le gouvernement du Canada.* We acknowledge the support of the Ontario Arts Council (OAC), an
agency of the Government of Ontario, which last year funded 1,737 individual artists and 1,095 organizations in 223
communities across Ontario for a total of $52.1 million. We also acknowledge the contribution of the Government
of Ontario through the Ontario Book Publishing Tax Credit, and through Ontario Creates for the marketing of
this book.

PRINTED AND BOUND IN CANADA

PRINTING: MARQUIS   5   4   3   2   1

MIX
Paper from
responsible sources
FSC® C103567

This book is dedicated to Médecins Sans Frontières.
A portion of the author's royalties will be donated to MSF.

"A man does not have to be an angel in order to be a saint."

—ALBERT SCHWEITZER

"It has long been recognized that among the public utilities, water supply facilities offer a particularly vulnerable point of attack to the foreign agent, due to the strategic position they occupy in keeping the wheels of industry turning and in preserving the health and morale of the American populace."

—J. EDGAR HOOVER, DIRECTOR OF THE FBI

"Individuals have duties which transcend the national obligations of obedience. Therefore individual citizens have the duty to violate domestic laws to prevent crimes against peace and humanity."

—NUREMBERG WAR CRIMES TRIBUNAL

PART I

The

ATTACK

CHAPTER 1

MICHAEL TOOK A DEEP BREATH before turning to his next patient. She was the size of a two-year-old American toddler, although her head was disproportionately large. Big brown eyes, but vacant. Skin stretched over bones. Legs like two sticks hinged, with a golf ball in the middle. He looked at the chart. Kapinga Kabobo was seven years old. Nineteen pounds. She should have weighed at least forty. The latest cholera outbreak had tripled the number of people seeking medical attention at the International Medical Assistance Foundation field hospital in Goma.

Michael had quickly become a staff favorite, his quiet confidence and warmth revealed in a broad smile and the crow's feet at the corners of his eyes. He opened the girl's mouth gently and used a tongue depressor to take a quick look. "Let's get this girl on a rehydration program. If she can't swallow, then use intravenous glucose and electrolytes." Perhaps startled by the foreign sound of Michael's voice, the girl defecated onto the dirt floor of the medical tent. The watery diarrhea contained flecks of mucous and epithelial cells the size of rice grains, a telltale sign of cholera.

"We also need some metronidazole. Add it to the IV drip please." He scrawled instructions onto the chart.

The girl's listless eyes fluttered and closed. She was fading fast.

"Come on, sweetheart, don't give up on us now," Michael pleaded, unwilling to admit that she was probably too far gone. He checked her pulse. Rapid, way faster than it should have been. He took her blood pressure. Low and falling. There was nothing he could do.

He held her hand and stroked her cheek, trying to offer some small comfort as he heard the last, rattling breath. Biting back grief and frustration, Michael closed her eyes. Back in Seattle he could have saved her life. Then again, back in the U.S. he'd never seen a case of cholera and probably never would.

He knew that it wasn't really the disease that had killed her. It was the fact that she had no clean water to drink, and no latrine for going to the bathroom. There were no parents or other relatives to notify; the girl was an orphan and a refugee. Michael would fill out the death certificate later. There were living, breathing, laughing, crying children needing his help.

"I'm going to step outside," he said to no one in particular. "Back in five."

He walked slowly out of the operating tent, stripping off his mask, hairnet, gloves, all drenched in sweat. He suppressed the urge to scream, cry, tear out his hair, curl up on the ground in the fetal position. In his third month in the Congo, Michael desperately wanted a hot bath, the feeling of his wife Maria's skin against his, even two mindless hours in an air-conditioned movie theater distracted by Hollywood flash and glitter. None of these luxuries were available. Instead, inside the secure compound, he circled past the bile-green rehydration and recovery tent and stopped to fill a red plastic cup at one of the faucets on the giant bladder flown in from Europe. Clean water poured into his cup.

Michael walked around the perimeter of the compound with deliberate slowness, stretching every moment of his break. The night was young and the casualties were endless. To the north, despite the lights of the city he could still see the glowing cauldron of Mount Nyiragongo, one of the world's most active volcanoes, smoldering away. To the south it was much darker, thanks to Lake Kivu.

A piercing shriek from inside the medical tent interrupted the night. Michael ran back inside to see an agitated woman burst into the cordoned-off surgery, oblivious to the orderly's restraining hand. She carried a bloody bundle of rags and raced forward to thrust it into Michael's hands, screaming and gesticulating wildly. Behind her trailed a wizened man, looking at the ground. He murmured quietly and nodded, as though embarrassed by all of the commotion but compelled to confirm her story.

The orderlies were shouting apologies to Michael and trying unsuccessfully to restrain the woman. Michael joined the din, yelling, "What's she saying?" as he cautiously peeled back the rags. He'd picked up some French during his months in the Congo but remained flummoxed by the myriad local languages and dialects.

"She says she had six children but this is the last one alive. She is begging you to please save her child." Daniel, one of the local Congolese who worked as a nurse's assistant, translated from Kiswahili, the lingua franca of the Great Lakes region.

The rags contained a young boy of indeterminate age. He was either sleeping or unconscious, and he was missing his right hand. Machete or land mine? Machetes made a clean cut, although sometimes the blade was deliberately smeared with shit to increase the odds of an infection. Land mines, in contrast, tended to rip and tear, leaving jagged wounds. Severed body parts were shockingly common, usually hands or feet, occasionally ears or even lips and tongue. Michael was tired of the amputations. He himself had removed so many limbs that he felt a lurking complicity, as if he was becoming a silent partner in the atrocities inflicted by the warring factions—Hutu ex-militia, the Congolese army, outlaw Mai Mai, and child soldiers from the Lord's Resistance Army. Every day he dealt with the aftermath, the evidence of evil that corroded his belief in the goodness of human beings.

What kind of person could hit a child with a machete? As there were no satisfactory answers to this kind of question, Michael tried to avoid dwelling on them. He cast a quick glance at the woman. She looked back at him, her eyes making it clear that he was her last hope. She herself was in terrible shape, painfully thin and covered in sores.

One look at Michael's solemn face and she collapsed onto the ground, clawing the dirt and hitting her head with bony fists. From somewhere deep inside her came a powerful ululation, incongruously melodic. The man also fell to the ground, struggling to wrap her tiny figure in his arms.

Jesus H. Christ, thought Michael. Children. The kids could pierce his emotional armor. He lifted the child toward his face and sniffed like a drug-seeking customs dog. The smell was a relief. It wasn't exactly pleasant, but there was no sign of the putrid and inimitable odor of rotting flesh. Michael looked up. "Hakuna matata," he said to the woman, exhausting his Kiswahili vocabulary with a phrase from Disney's *The Lion King*. No problem.

"This kid has lost a lot of blood. He needs a transfusion, stat. Get me at least 500 ccs of O negative, and let's get the intravenous rehydration running too. Daniel, I want his name and any medical history you can gather."

Daniel rattled off several quick questions and passed the information on to Michael. "His name is Étienne Tshisekedi. He is in his eighth year. His hand was amputated by soldiers near Bunia when he refused to join them."

"Michael?" Anna, the young Danish nurse, came into the tent. She was striking despite trying to look nondescript to avoid unwanted attention. She dyed her blond hair brown and kept it short. But even a bad haircut, an ill-fitting T-shirt, and the inevitably disheveled condition produced by eighty-hour work weeks couldn't disguise her beauty. With the high adrenaline and the long shifts together, it was easy to sit too close in the lounge, to slide into the casual contact that opened the door to more. But Michael had sensed himself on the precipice and had pulled back to cool professionalism in the OR and nothing more friendly than a game of cards after a shift.

"Yes?"

"The fridge is empty. We're out of blood."

"You've gotta be kidding!"

6

"No. I'm so sorry. Jean-Claude says that the next shipment should arrive on Thursday."

Normally JC worked miracles keeping the facility stocked with essential supplies, from antibiotics to vaccines. Michael wondered how the only remaining surgical facility in the entire city could run out of blood. "This kid isn't going to make it through the night without a transfusion, never mind surviving forty-eight hours until Thursday. Hook up one of the locals with blood type O neg for a direct transfusion."

Anna cringed. "We cannot do that."

"This kid is dying!"

"Yes, but some of the people here might be HIV positive. Giving the child blood from one of them would be like playing Russian roulette." Anna held her hands out, palms up, as if to say there's nothing we can do.

She was right. Michael looked at Anna, then the boy, and finally his eyes came to rest on the mother, now sitting on the floor watching him intently. They had little in common, the American doctor and the Congolese refugee, but an understanding passed between them.

"Okay then, hook me up. My blood's O neg and it's clean. It's almost the end of my shift anyway." Michael would have twelve hours to recuperate before his next shift. It was breaking most of the rules, and it would push Michael closer to, or possibly over, the edge of exhaustion. On the other hand, it was the only hope the child had. Anna knew from experience that there was no point in arguing with him when he decided to do something.

"Is that needle new?" Michael asked.

"Of course! I just unwrapped it myself."

Anna squeezed Michael's arm, found a vein, and inserted the needle. Soon blood was flowing through the one-way shunt. Anna used Michael's phone to record the moment. In seven years as a nurse, she'd never seen a doctor take such a step.

Michael opened and closed his fist. "Okay, let's go. We need a full amputation kit, bactericidal solution, a local anesthetic, and something strong to sedate him—ketamine or diazepam. Daniel, secure the patient." The boy was nearly catatonic from shock but he would start thrashing when the operation began unless he was sedated and restrained.

Michael stood up, tubes still attached to his arm, and hunched over the boy, visualizing the operation, the steps he needed to take. Although amputations were grueling, Michael excelled at them, quarterbacking his small team. He was pleasantly surprised at the lack of infection in the boy's arm. It looked like the machete had been sharp, and the assailant strong.

"We'll cut it back here," he said, quietly talking through the procedure. He marked the incision midway up the boy's forearm, leaving as long a stump as possible while removing the damaged tissue to minimize the risk of infection.

Anna and Daniel gathered the equipment, unfazed by the oppressive heat and humidity. Michael cleaned the wound and used a piece of surgical tubing to fashion a makeshift tourniquet, minimizing further blood loss. "Anna, be ready with clamps and suction. Here we go. Bear with me, Étienne!" He used a scalpel to cut quickly through the skin, muscle, and other soft tissue. Anna rotated the boy's wrist and Michael made a similar incision on the anterior side of the arm. Crimson gushers spurted from the radial and ulnar arteries but were quickly arrested as the blood vessels and nerves were ligated.

"Saw, please."

Daniel passed Michael the oscillating surgical saw. It whined when Michael clicked it on. He carefully sliced through the two bones in the boy's lower forearm. Michael then used the saw to bevel the edges of the bones, preventing sharp edges that could cut through the skin during the healing process or as the boy grew. He performed a myoplasty to connect the transected muscles to the bone, necessary to prevent atrophy and allow the forearm muscles to maintain function. The whole procedure took about thirty minutes, and Michael was soon using absorbable sutures to sew the two flaps of skin back together. He inserted a small drain, closed the wound, packed the area with gauze, and then pulled a sterilized stocking over the stump. The operation was complete.

"Brilliant!" Anna said.

"Thanks. Great team effort. I'm wiped out." Michael's green surgical gown was drenched in sweat and spattered with blood. He smiled and laugh lines appeared at the sides of his mouth and around his eyes. His face was too long and thin and his ears too large to be described as handsome, but Maria always told him he had kind eyes. "Any sign of Henri?"

"He's already here," Anna replied, "checking patients in the supplemental feeding tent."

"Good. Tell Henri to keep a close eye on Étienne, and call me if anything goes wrong with him. I'll see you tomorrow." For now, the boy's vital signs were weak but stable.

Michael undid the intravenous hookup, put a bandage on his own arm, changed out of his filthy scrubs, and washed up. He walked out of the tent into the darkness.

CHAPTER 2

THE FOLLOWING DAY WAS A FIELD DAY. Laurent, a young Congolese who'd become one of Michael's friends, drove him and Anna northwest of Goma to medical outpatient clinics scattered across a series of villages in Masisi province. They traveled in an aging Toyota Land Cruiser with bald tires, no windshield wipers, and one reliable headlight. A Cadillac by local standards. On the door were two faded decals, the Red Cross sign and a red circle around a Kalashnikov assault rifle with a red line through it, intended to emphasize that the vehicle was not carrying any weapons.

The villages were all within a 100-kilometer range of Goma but the drive could take up to five hours because the roads were cratered moonscapes, unrepaired since the Belgians withdrew in 1960. There were always people walking along the roadside, carrying bags, bundles, bananas, corn, onions, blankets, mattresses, saucepans, wood, jerry cans, and clothing. Refugees flowed like rivers, their homes destroyed, fields burned, families torn apart by rape, assault, murder, and forced recruitment into militias and gangs. They moved into tent cities of wretched squalor, living under sticks and strips of plastic. In some places, you could still see remnants of the beautiful countryside, once speckled with small farms, forests, and tea plantations. Occasionally they passed skeletons at the side of the road, bodies and vehicles picked clean by different kinds of vultures.

It had been a long day. Michael had conducted almost one hundred exams. Without blood tests or x-rays, his diagnostic abilities were limited but he did what he could, listening carefully to each individual's story, handing out antibiotics, and even stitching up a few cuts and gashes. Anna met dozens of women, offering them vitamins, contraceptives, and AIDS-prevention advice. The villagers whom they visited were kind and disarmingly generous, offering to share their meager food with the team. Laurent translated, chatting with people he met for the first time as if they were old friends, discussing the ever-shifting political landscape, the loyalties that changed direction as effortlessly and as often as the carrion eaters riding the thermals above them. They kept going until all the vaccines, infant formula, nutritional supplements, and medicines in the Toyota had been dispensed.

As they drove back to Goma, Michael and Anna argued about his decision to donate blood to Étienne. Michael leaned forward from the back seat to argue his case.

"I still think it was the right move. I'd do it again."

"It was impulsive, and it put you in danger. Worse, it put the boy in danger too!"

"How?"

"The operation went smoothly and yet you were completely exhausted by the end. I saw your hands beginning to shake. What if there were complications? You could have hit a wall."

"I hit the wall in marathons, and guess what? I just keep going. It's more mental than physical."

Anna shook her head at his stubbornness, his conviction. She put in a CD, cranked up the volume, and turned to look out the window. The gorgeous voice of Mali's Rokia Traore filled the vehicle.

Michael enjoyed making snap decisions in the face of adversity. It was a large part of the reason he had become a surgeon and also underlaid his decision to join IMAF. He'd become increasingly frustrated in the emergency ward at Seattle's Harborview Medical Center. Renowned as one of the best trauma surgeons in town, he had an ability to envision the violent geometry of bullets as they entered the human body and ricocheted off bones, deflected off tendons, and pierced soft tissues. What had finally pushed Michael over the edge was the return of a bullet-riddled teenager named

DeShawn. The kid had been in the wrong place, at the wrong time, with the wrong skin color. According to the paramedics who brought him in, he'd been shot by Seattle police on the fringes of a peaceful protest. The America he knew and loved was coming apart at the seams.

Michael went for a long run after his shift that day and came across a demonstration refugee camp set up in Volunteer Park. After several conversations with volunteers about their experiences overseas, he decided that he would join IMAF for a tour of duty. He needed the change. He would happily go wherever they wanted him to go. When they assigned him to Goma, in the Democratic Republic of the Congo, he had to look it up on Wikipedia. Maria, understandably, had been less than thrilled by his radical change of course.

Michael was jolted from his memories when the speeding Land Cruiser hit a deep pothole. There were less than five hundred miles of paved roads in the entire Congo, a country the size of Western Europe.

"Hey Laurent. Slow down a bit would you, please."

Laurent was taken aback, and took his eyes off the road to glare at Michael. "It is too fast?"

"Yes."

"All right." He lifted his foot imperceptibly from the accelerator. "It is better?"

Michael grunted ambiguously. The two men had dueling fears. Michael was afraid they would crash. The roads were in dismal condition, rules and enforcement were nonexistent, and driver's licenses required passing a bribe, not an exam. Particularly unsettling were the hand-painted signs, hung on bent poles, which said "DANGER—LAND MINES." The crucifix dangling from the rearview mirror and the plastic Jesus glued to the dashboard were no consolation.

Laurent's fear, on the other hand, had nothing to do with driving. He didn't want to be on the road after dark because he was familiar with the Congo's three Rs: roadblocks, rebels, and robbers. They were already behind schedule. Both men's fears were well founded. One man's were about to materialize.

"Can you pull over? Sorry, Laurent, but I need to take a leak."

"Vous ne pouvez pas attender quelques minutes?"

"No, I can't wait."

"Merde!" Laurent abruptly stopped the vehicle at the side of the road. Michael climbed out to relieve himself. The sunset above the volcanic peaks was an apocalyptic sight, the blood red sky darkening to a livid purple, like a fresh scab congealing. Congolese sunsets happened fast, as if the sun itself shared people's paranoia about the dangers of night and was eager to escape.

A gang of children appeared from nowhere, surrounding Michael. Palms extended, begging, but also curious, the children slipped their roaming quicksilver hands into the pockets of his shorts, seeking something to eat, something of value, or an item that could be ransomed back to its owner. Michael chuckled at the sight of a bright-eyed boy, barefoot but wearing a Harvard University T-shirt like a tunic, with a string tied around his waist. Another boy was shirtless, wearing only acid-washed blue jeans and a straw fedora.

"Bonjour, mes amis," said Michael loudly, prompting a chorus of giggles. Coming up empty in their informal frisking, the boys turned their attention to the Toyota. Laurent stood, leaning on the hood of the car, having a quick cigarette break.

"Allez, allez. Let's go!" Laurent licked his thumb and index finger, pinched the half-smoked butt, and put it in his shirt pocket.

Michael shooed the children away. Like Laurent, he knew the road was a poor place to spend time at night. Soon they were back to a foolhardy speed on the narrow, winding road. The potholes were nearly invisible in the fast encroaching darkness. Laurent navigated as best he could, swerving and veering in a futile attempt to avoid the bone-rattling impacts. The concept of a centerline was foreign to Congolese drivers. The only observed rules of the road were that smaller vehicles had to give way to larger vehicles, and slower vehicles had to make way for faster ones.

It began to rain, a heavy pulsing downpour. Without functioning wipers, they had no choice but to slow down. It was now pitch black outside. Although the Toyota's sole headlight was on, many of the other vehicles on the road had no running lights, bulbs long smashed or burned out, or wires pirated to fix something else. Darkened vehicles appeared without warning, as in a video game. Every approaching corner made Michael take a deep breath, exhaled only when it became clear that there was no oncoming traffic.

Anna awoke from an intermittent nap and bent down to change the CD.

"How about some King Sunny Adé?" Michael asked.

"Merde!" Laurent cursed.

Michael was momentarily confused. He thought that Laurent was a fan of the Nigerian band and their exuberant drumming rhythms, but the vehicle was skidding to a jerky stop.

"What the—" Michael saw the makeshift roadblock, a tree trunk and two 45-gallon fuel drums. Standing on the road was a ragtag band of about dozen men and children, armed and bizarrely dressed.

"Merde," Laurent repeated, softer this time.

"Rebels?" whispered Michael.

"No, c'est pire."

"Worse? What do you mean?"

"Mai Mai."

The Mai Mai, meaning "water, water" or "strong water," were a legendary group of warriors, sorcerers, and priests. Rooted in a long history of animism, superstition, and secret societies, the modern Mai Mai struck fear wherever they appeared. Their reputation for unwavering courage made them popular mercenaries, and they'd become even more deadly when assault rifles supplanted bows, arrows, and spears. It was rumored that the Mai Mai ate the flesh of their victims, particularly the warm hearts and livers, to bolster their courage.

In the solitary headlight filtered into flickering prisms by the rain, the Mai Mai appeared ethereal, like dark spirits of the forest. Some wore long blond wigs, while others sported grass skirts or sequined dresses.

"We need to stay calm," Anna said.

"Can you handle this, Laurent?" Michael asked.

He didn't answer. His hands were still clenching the steering wheel.

"Laurent! Are you okay?"

Still no response. Michael slowly opened the door, raising his empty hands above his head. One of the children approached the Toyota, casually propping the duct-taped stock of a Kalashnikov against his shoulder with one hand while smoking a cigarette with the other. Decked out in a military uniform several sizes too large, bandoliers over both shoulders, wearing a beret at a rakish angle, and with a showerhead dangling around his neck to ward off evil spirits, the boy was almost a comical sight, but Michael, Anna, and Laurent were not laughing.

As he came closer, it became apparent that he was not a child at all, but a short man, less than five feet tall, perhaps in his mid-thirties. He had a thin, sparse mustache and bloodshot eyes.

"Donnez-moi votre identification! Passeports!" the man demanded.

"I am a doctor," Michael replied, "with the International Medical Assistance Foundation, and these are my colleagues."

The man switched to English. "I am the General. Where are you going?"

"We're on our way back to Goma."

"We'll see about that. Where have you been?"

"We spent the day in Masisi, distributing food, vaccinating children, and checking for outbreaks of cholera, measles, and other diseases."

"Do you work for the Hutus or the inyenzi?" The General used the Kinyarwanda word for cockroaches to refer to the Tutsis. It was a loaded question. The Hutus and Tutsis, the most populous ethnic groups in Central Africa, are blood enemies. The Mai Mai belong to a different ethnic group, the Hundes, who were perpetually at war with both Hutus and Tutsis. There were so many feuds, so much hatred, that the aid organization's neutrality was challenged every time they visited a new community. A decision to begin a therapeutic feeding program in one village meant that people might continue to go hungry in villages down the road or over the hill.

"IMAF is neutral," Michael answered. "Our mandate is to help all people in need of medical and humanitarian assistance. We do our best to treat everybody that comes to our clinics."

"Very well, you may proceed."

Michael exhaled and started to relax, allowing his shoulders to fall and his fists to unclench. The General watched him closely, then added, "Of course first you must pay a road tax."

Michael frowned. "We can't do that, General. Such a payment would compromise our neutrality. Please accept my apologies and permit us to continue."

"You will pay." It was a statement, not a question. The Mai Mai leader lay his Kalashnikov on the hood of the Toyota and pulled a handgun from its holster.

"No." Michael stared at the gun but held his ground.

The General's red-rimmed eyes flashed from bemused to angry. He sneered at Michael and turned his head, shouting orders. Two teenagers with acne-pocked faces and gangly limbs hurried toward the vehicle, where Laurent and Anna remained in their seats. The soldiers brandished pangas, the flat-bladed machetes that were used to conserve bullets. The taller one knocked aggressively on the driver's side window with his blade, motioning for Laurent to get out.

"Please leave the driver alone." Michael spoke firmly.

"No. Pay the road tax or face the consequences."

Michael bit his lip and shook his head, refusing to be black-mailed. He didn't want to show weakness. Paying a bribe would violate IMAF rules and if the Congolese government discovered that IMAF gave money to the Mai Mai, it could spell the end of their operations in the country. Laurent was dragged from the vehicle to stand beside Michael. The General dismissed his two soldiers with a nod, and they melted back into the shadows beside the road. The rain was easing off.

Through the open door Anna whispered, "Take your money and hand it over."

The General leered at Anna before returning his focus to Michael. "Listen to your friend, and do it now. This is not a negotiation!"

Michael looked down at his feet, wondering if he should offer what was in his wallet, or try to disarm the smaller man. There was an earsplitting explosion. For a nanosecond he thought it was odd that a spray of warm raindrops struck only the right side of his face. Time ran in slow motion. He looked up and saw the General blowing on the end of his gun's barrel. Then Michael turned toward Laurent, whose face had become a bloody mask. His body toppled backwards, glancing off the side of the Land Cruiser as he fell. Michael instinctively knelt down and put his fingers on Laurent's neck, checking for a pulse. A glance at the gaping entry wound in the middle of his forehead confirmed that it was futile. He turned to look up at the General and slowly rose to his feet.

The pistol wavered less than a foot from his face, pointing up at him. The General's gun hand was shaking. Michael could smell an acrid miasma of body odor, marijuana, and sex emanating from him. He could hear the other soldiers, out of sight, laughing and swearing. He could feel his own heart racing.

Sweat dripped from the General's temples, rolling down his face as he ranted. "You have no idea what it's like to live here. Every day, guns pointed at our heads. Every day, death all around us. Congolese lives are cheap. You think you can come in, save a few lives, and puff out your chest? Do yourself a favor and go home. You're putting Band-Aids on machete cuts."

Michael was outnumbered, outgunned, out of his element. He had unwittingly sacrificed one friend. Continue to refuse to pay, and who knows what they would do to Anna. He, too, would probably be shot in the face. Run, and he'd be shot in the back. He lifted his shirt to reach into his money belt.

Then the General's arm swung in an uppercut motion, smashing his pistol on Michael's temple. Anna's scream was the last thing Michael would hear before he blacked out.

When consciousness returned, Michael thought he was waking from a nightmare. But his vision was blurred, and he was lying on a road, not in bed. His head throbbed and when he reached up to touch it, he saw stars. His fingers came away sticky with blood.

It all came roaring back. Laurent, dead, on the ground beside him. "Anna," he cried, pulling himself up on the Land Cruiser and looking inside. Empty. In the soft light of the moon he swung his gaze left and right. The Mai Mai were gone, the roadblock dismantled. Michael walked around the vehicle and an animal cry was wrenched from his throat. Anna was on the ground, blood on her face, shirt ripped open and pants around her ankles. "No," he moaned, kneeling beside her. His hand flew to her neck. There was a pulse, steady and strong. He did a quick check for further injuries, found none, pulled up her pants, closed her shirt, and as gently as possible placed her in the backseat. He circled the vehicle, picked up Laurent's body and carefully laid it in the back. Michael knew he had to keep going. Shock and adrenaline would lend a hand, but soon he would crash.

He climbed into the driver's seat. All of their phones were gone but the keys, miraculously, were still in the ignition. He drove back to Goma, speeding recklessly through the dark and the rain, head pounding, vision still dodgy, flinching every time the vehicle hit a pothole. The events ricocheted in his mind. The gunshot. The spray of blood. The destruction of Laurent's face. Then the savage blow that knocked him out. He punished himself by imagining how he could have responded differently. If he'd handed the money over right away, maybe the General would have let them go. Who knows? The possibilities were irrelevant because only one outcome had occurred. Michael knew the night's images would haunt him forever.

CHAPTER 3

MICHAEL RETURNED TO THE STAFF COMPOUND, a sprawling villa abandoned by a colonial Belgian businessman. Although it was two in the morning, somebody would still be up. He leaned on the horn, stumbled out of the Land Cruiser, and opened the back door so he could sling Anna's body over his shoulder. He staggered to the surgical tent and slid her onto an operating table.

"What's going on? We couldn't reach—" Jean-Claude asked as he ran in, stopping as he recognized Anna, who was beginning to regain consciousness, a low moan emanating from her that grew into quiet sobbing.

Through his shock, Michael tried to explain. "Mai Mai. Shot Laurent. Think they raped Anna. She needs help. And call the police."

Jean-Claude absorbed the cascade of catastrophic news and turned to run back to the vehicle. It was his job to be unflappable, but this was bad. "I'll go get Laurent."

"No!" Michael couldn't meet Jean-Claude's eyes. "It's too late for him. Get Henri."

He turned to Anna. She flinched as he placed his hand on her shoulder.

"Shh. You're safe now. We're back."

Anna didn't say anything, just rolled onto her side and pulled her legs to her chest. Michael had carried out many examinations of sexual assault victims, but never on a close friend. Henri could do it, but he might be half drunk, and Michael felt a sense of responsibility. He would have to distance himself, carry out the physical examination, collect evidence, and provide Anna with preventive medications to deal with possible infection or pregnancy. He could feel his pulse slowing as he slipped into the medical routine. First, he needed to wash up. As he scrubbed his hands, he remembered Laurent's body in the back of the vehicle and felt weak in the knees. But nothing could be done for Laurent now. Anna came first.

"Anna, I'm sorry. So sorry. But can you tell me where you are in pain?"

Almost imperceptibly, Anna shook her head. There was a lot of blood matted in her hair. Michael would need to clean that up, see if stitches were needed, and test her for a concussion. His own head hurt like hell and his vision was still blurred around the edges, but he shrugged it off.

Jean-Claude was back. "Henri will be here in a minute." He hesitated. "He's in good shape, Michael. When we couldn't reach any of you on your mobiles we stayed up waiting. He only had one or two beers. And the police will be here in a few minutes."

"Okay, thanks, JC. Now give me a hand. I need warm water, sponges, and some cloths. And a pair of scissors. I want to start with her head wound."

"Of course."

Henri entered the tent, wearing scrubs and ready to work, and took in the scene. "Are you okay, Michael?"

"No, I'm . . . Yes, fine. It's Anna that needs help. Head wound, lost consciousness, and pretty sure she was sexually assaulted."

"Mon dieu! Anna, I'm terribly sorry. But Michael—you are bleeding."

"I'm fine."

"Let me see your 'ead—"

"No! Leave me alone. We need to help Anna."

"Look at me, Michael." The two doctors locked eyes. "You need 'elp too. And where is Laurent?"

Michael looked at the floor. "He's in the back of the Toyota." He paused. "Dead."

Henri dropped his head to his chest for a moment and took a deep breath. "Okay, so sit down, and if I need your 'elp, I'll ask for it."

"Let me see your hands," Michael replied.

Henri scowled but held out his hands, palms down. They were rock steady.

"All right." Michael pulled up a chair on the far side of the operating table and held Anna's hand. Her grip was tentative at first and then fierce.

As Michael suspected, Anna had a severe concussion and there was evidence of sexual assault. With her consent, Henri took swabs and photographs, collected hairs and fingernail scrapings. Jean-Claude made sure the samples were properly packaged, labeled, and sealed in an evidence collection kit.

When the police arrived, Michael took them to the house, where they sat in the living room while he recounted the attack. They took notes but explained that their jurisdiction was limited to the city of Goma itself. They assured Michael that they would pass his information along to the federal police. It was frustrating, but there was no use in blaming them.

Michael returned to the surgery. Henri had done everything he could, but because of the concussion could not prescribe Anna a sedative. She lay on her side staring into space. Jean-Claude had put Laurent's body in the morgue.

"I'll stay with Anna," Jean-Claude volunteered. "You both need to get some sleep for tomorrow."

"What the 'ell 'appened out there?" Henri asked.

"Tomorrow," Michael replied curtly. Henri nodded, and the two men walked in silence back to the house.

Michael walked into his bedroom and lay down, fully clothed, on his bed. As soon as he closed his eyes, the replay of the night's events took over. While some aid workers occasionally used drugs or alcohol to numb themselves into a state where sleep was possible, Michael had a different addiction. He'd convinced

IMAF to transport his old Cervélo racing bicycle and wind-trainer to Goma. The wind-trainer converted the Cervélo into a stationary bike. Giving up on sleep, he slipped into a pair of threadbare spandex shorts, inserted his ear buds, picked a playlist, checked his musty cycling shoes for scorpions, slipped the shoes on, and swung his leg over the seat. He clicked his shoes into the pedals and was soon pedaling about thirty kilometers per hour. He tried to visualize the training route he had done hundreds of times back home. North from Seattle, across the flatlands, into the foothills, and then up and down the highways that cut through the North Cascades. The mountain roads were narrow, but the scenery was breathtaking, traffic was scarce, and the air tasted alpine fresh.

The sweat began to run, welling out of his pores. In its exodus, some of the frustration, and fear began to leave him. His legs pumped and whenever thoughts of Anna or Laurent intruded, he put the hammer down, pedaling furiously. The combination of fatigue and throbbing punk music temporarily banished the demons. Cycling was his daily salvation, cleansing his mind, body, and spirit. It was an act of obsession and meditation. After an hour on the bike, Michael dismounted, toweling the sweat from his face. It reminded him of the Mai Mai general, and he shuddered. He changed T-shirts and went to the kitchen for a bottle of water before crawling again into bed. He lay there, conscious but almost comatose, until dawn arrived.

Without changing or washing up, Michael trudged into the kitchen.

"'ello, Doc Mac. I am so sorry," came the greeting of Mbake Sivha, the compound's cook. She was an imposing woman, always swathed in bolts of bright material and a matching scarf in her hair Today she wore red, green, and yellow stripes, the national colors of the Congo. With her vibrant clothes, her huge smile, and her fabulous cooking, she was a boon to the often exhausted and sometimes discouraged medical staff.

"Bonjour, Mbake," Michael replied in a monotone.

She wrapped him in a hug, but stepped back moments later. "Doc Mac, I t'ink you still have the blood on you." She swept her fingers across her right cheek.

Michael put his fingers to his cheek. Something had hardened on his skin. He flaked a piece off and looked at it. Definitely blood. He collapsed into a chair at the kitchen table and put his hands over his face.

Mbake wiped her hands on a tea towel and, not knowing what else to do, ladled a giant portion of hot cereal into a tin bowl. It sat untouched in front of Michael as he began to cry.

As he calmed down, Michael started to explain the previous night's disastrous events to Mbake. "It was my fault! I should have just given him the money right away."

"No. You did not know what would happen. There was nothing you could do."

A phone jangled on the kitchen table. They both looked at it, fearing bad news.

Mbake picked it up. "Bonjour." She listened briefly. "Oui, un moment. Michael?" Mbake held out the phone. "It's Henri."

Michael looked at the phone before taking it, worried about Anna and also suddenly remembering Étienne.

"Michael here."

"Michel, mon ami, je veux dire . . ."

"English, Henri, tell me in English." There was a pause. "Is it Anna?"

"No, she is doing well. A strong woman, our colleague. I wanted to tell you—the boy, Étienne. 'e is doing very well. Stronger. No fever. 'ungry."

"Good." Michael struggled to respond with the appropriate enthusiasm. The boy would not yet join the hordes of dead African children whose ghosts already haunted his nights. Michael took a deep breath and then said, "Thank you, Henri. That's really great news. Merci."

Mbake hugged him and stepped back. "Go see Étienne, Michael."

"Thank you, Mbake. I'm so sorry, about everything."

Étienne was recovering nicely. Kids, he thought. Such remarkable powers of recuperation if given half a chance. Étienne was smiling and looked like he'd already gained five pounds. Henri had changed the dressing on his arm and there was no sign of infection. But this small victory was overshadowed by last night's losses. He walked over to see Anna and was relieved to see that she was finally asleep.

As Michael was leaving the rehab tent he ran into Jean-Claude.

"I've been in touch with HQ."

"Why?"

"You know the drill. When something like this happens, we have to file an incident report. It's a sure thing that they're going to send you home early."

"What? No! There's still so much to do. You need me."

"It's routine, Michael. When our people are victims of violence or other major traumas, they get pulled out. IMAF has to protect its people, and itself. Anna's going home too."

"When?"

"As soon as she's medically cleared to travel."

"And me?

"As soon as I can get you on a flight."

Michael was stunned. He was supposed to work in Goma for another three weeks. On autopilot, he brushed his teeth and took his anti-malaria medication. Although it was mid-morning he went back to bed, lying under the mosquito netting, trying not to think about Laurent and Anna. He needed to call Maria but wasn't ready. He wondered for the umpteenth time what he was doing in Africa, eight thousand miles from his wife, home, and friends. How could he return to a normal life in Seattle after everything he'd experienced here?

Insects hummed and lizards darted, the walls moving with life. The air was heavy and warm. From the moment he had first stepped down the shaky steps of the single-prop plane, two things had struck Michael. The piercing clarity of the light, and the intensity of the smells. The pong of nervous sweat and the odor of decay were pervasive, unpleasant, foreboding, and would be stuck in Michael's nostrils until he left. Occasionally there was relief—the aroma of a roasting goat or chicken, or a bush exploding with fragrant blossoms. But the stench of decomposition—living things on their inevitable trajectory toward death—was ubiquitous.

He put on his headphones, choosing Rostropovich playing Elgar's cello concerto. Eventually the music lulled him to sleep. Despite his exhaustion, it was not a peaceful experience. He tossed and turned, thrashing the mosquito net. Drenched in sweat, he awoke with a start, pushed the light button on his watch, and saw that it was 3:47 p.m. He had somehow slept through his alarm and the hottest part of the day. He reached for his water bottle on the floor beside him, acutely aware, even in the haze of his grief and guilt, of the luxury of having a secure supply of clean water.

Michael wanted to talk to Maria. He wanted to call Dominic, his best friend. He longed to hear the voices of the people who meant the most to him. But for now, he had patients waiting, children who needed his help. Michael pulled on his running shoes, yanked the elastic laces tight, and ran toward the surgical tent. Time for another shift, and another, until it was time to go home.

CHAPTER 4

MICHAEL FLEW TO SEATTLE FROM Goma via Entebbe, Addis Ababa, and Frankfurt, finally touching down at Sea-Tac Airport. Less than forty-eight hours earlier he'd been living in the midst of a humanitarian crisis, in a city of abject poverty, in a nation embroiled in a perpetual civil war. And it was only a few days since the vicious Mai Mai attack. He was returning to a middle-class neighborhood in a cosmopolitan city in the world's wealthiest nation. Instead of worrying about violence, hunger, and disease like Goma residents, folks in Seattle were worried about whether the Seahawks would make the playoffs, whether the Mariners should trade their ace pitcher, the twists and turns of the latest Netflix hit series, and the yo-yoing price of gasoline.

Maria met Michael at the airport. She was short but not petite, with long black hair and smooth tawny skin. Her big brown eyes were magnified by a stylish pair of bright red glasses. Tears welled as she saw how haggard he looked. He smiled and opened his arms to hug her, but she could see that the familiar sparkle in his eyes was missing.

Maria burrowed into his embrace. He lifted her off the ground and they held each other tight, breathing each other in. She stood on her tiptoes and gently pulled his head down so she could give him a long, soft kiss on the lips.

"Hey, you're supposed to be happy to see me! What's with the waterworks?"

Maria looked up at him, shaking her head. "I *am* happy. I missed you terribly! These are tears of happiness that you're back safely."

"Well, it's great to be home."

"But how are you? You look so . . ." she searched for a kind way to put it ". . . thin! And why won't you tell me why you came home early? What happened?"

"It was crazy. The time went so fast. It seems like I just left yesterday but also as though I've been gone for years. But last week—" Unconsciously he rubbed the right side of his face where he'd been spattered with Laurent's blood. "I'll tell you all about it. I promise. But let's get out of here."

"Yes of course, let's go home." Maria took Michael by the hand and led him toward the exit.

They spent the evening together, overcoming the awkwardness of almost three months apart. For one night, at least, they implicitly agreed not to discuss the storm clouds that hung over them. Michael's obvious trauma. Seven years of frustrated efforts to become parents. Their window of opportunity was closing. Michael was forty-two and Maria thirty-nine. Neither had mentioned the subject of children while Michael had been in Africa, but they would have to face it soon.

When they went to bed, naked, their lips and hands roamed freely, finding and caressing each other's sweet spots. Neither spoke as Michael rolled on top and Maria guided him inside her. She placed her hands on his hips, setting the pace as they moved together. For a few precious minutes, all of their trials and troubles were a million miles away. Michael closed his eyes only to see an image of Anna's battered body, lying prone on the dusty road. His erection deflated, and he rolled back onto his side of the bed.

"I'm sorry," he said, unable to make eye contact. He wanted to scream.

"It's okay. We're just out of practice." Maria stroked the side of his face, but he turned away from her. She frowned but put her arm around him anyway. "Good night, my love."

"Good night, Maria," Michael managed to say, his throat constricted with grief.

He woke early from a fractured sleep in which he had cried out several times, waking Maria each time. The birds were welcoming the new day, although it would be another hour before the sun poked over the treetops and shone into the bedroom window. There was a slight whiff of salt in the air, meaning the breeze was blowing onshore.

Maria was still asleep, her rhythmic breathing music to Michael's ears. He listened for a while, then carefully untangled his arms and legs and sat up. Through the French doors he could see the small garden, surrounded by wild blackberries and towering cedar trees. Finches, chickadees, and nuthatches jockeyed for position at the bird feeder. Michael marveled again at how far he'd come, how fast, and how different were the two worlds. The transition back to his old life in Seattle would be challenging. He was struggling with what to say, what to share.

Maria stirred, and draped her arm across his waist. "Buenos días," she murmured.

"You mean good afternoon."

"No."

"Yes. You're going to be late for class," Michael warned.

"No. It's Saturday."

"Nice try. It's Wednesday. But if you want to skip school, I could give you a doctor's note."

Maria stayed in bed until the last possible moment, then dashed off to teach her international law class at the University of Washington. Michael wandered around the house, struck by the relative luxury they lived in. To reboot he called Dom, his best friend, campaigner for the National Wildlife Federation and fellow endurance sports enthusiast.

"Hey, Dom, it's Michael."

"Hiya, stranger! I was wondering when I'd hear from you. Maria told me you were coming home early."

"Well, here I am, sitting at home with an Americano and a blackberry scone. Not my usual breakfast in Africa, I can assure you."

"Welcome home to the land of soy milk and organic honey. How was your trip?"

"It was a trip all right—gut-wrenching, heartbreaking, unbelievable, insane. They say Africa gets in your blood—not just the malaria and the dysentery—but the magic of the place. How are you doing?"

"Same old same old, you know. Saving the planet isn't getting any easier. The environmental crisis seems to worsen week by week, and too many Americans think climate change is a hoax invented by the Chinese so they can sell solar panels. It's just about enough to make a guy move to Canada!"

"You're still a fountain of good news. Win any races while I was gone?"

"Nope. Gettin' old. Hey, listen, I've got a conference call coming up in about five minutes. Can I call you back this afternoon?"

"Sure. I was hoping we could go for a run sometime this week. We can catch up better in person."

Over a supper of Mexican lasagna and green salad, Michael and Maria talked about friends, family, and the dismal state of American politics, but the conversation was stilted, awkward. Michael couldn't bring himself to describe the events that led to his early return. After dinner, Maria embraced Michael from behind as he stood at the sink washing dishes. She nuzzled the nape of his neck with the soft skin of her cheek.

"Are you sure you're okay?" Maria had noticed him rubbing the right side of his face during dinner, an odd new habit he'd brought back from Africa.

"I'm fine. Just tired."

She gently turned him around, examining his bloodshot eyes, the circles underneath so dark it looked like he had two black eyes. She gave him her skeptical look. "You've got to talk to me."

Knowing she wouldn't relent, Michael raised his dripping

hands in surrender. "It's a long story. Let's finish that wine while I fill you in."

Maria poured the last of the cabernet sauvignon into two mugs and took them out onto the deck. There was a new moon, and despite the lights of the city, the Big Dipper and other constellations glowed faintly. She had spent many evenings out here while Michael was in Africa, making wishes on the first star she saw. Maria swore she wouldn't have been as lonely while he was away if they had a child. But after three miscarriages and one stillborn baby, she wasn't sure she could cope with trying again. Still, she had desperately wanted to become a mother, and so her anguish continued.

"Sure is beautiful here," Michael said as he joined Maria on the swinging loveseat, rubbing lotion into his dishpan hands.

"You have to tell me your story now," said Maria. "No more small talk. I know something terrible must have happened for you to come home early."

Michael hesitated. He didn't know where to begin. He loathed the thought of talking about what had happened to Laurent and Anna. Maria slipped an arm around her husband and rested her head on his shoulder.

"I don't know what I'm doing here—back home. I'm supposed to be a medical professional. I'm trained to cope with trauma and death. But I really wasn't prepared for the Congo. The endless, senseless violence. The horrific regularity of sexual assault. The astronomical child mortality rate. I felt so helpless seeing children die from illnesses that could easily be prevented by access to clean water or treated for about fifty cents' worth of medicine." Michael's voice was cracking now. "I watched so many kids die under my care. Too many! I failed them. We all failed them."

"But that's simply not true. What about all the lives you saved or improved? You must have made a difference, Michael. A huge, positive difference. I'm sure that you helped so many people while you were there. Organizations like IMAF win the Nobel Peace Prize for a reason, and it's because of people like you."

Michael placed his hands over his face, as though he could block reality, and then let his hands fall to his sides. "Maybe you're right. But our little victories are dwarfed by the losses. They seem insignificant. And it's so bizarre to return to this other world, where people have so much wealth and so little compassion. There's so much food in the grocery store, drinking water is used to flush toilets, there's an epidemic of obesity, and our back alleys have fewer potholes than their highways." He hesitated. "Sorry, I'm ranting."

"No, don't worry. It's healthy to talk about how you feel."

"I thought I'd develop a thicker skin, like when I started working emergency here. But that didn't happen. There were so many people I couldn't save. So many kids! African parents are so demonstrative. Their grief. Instead of suppressing their emotions, they just let 'er rip. Screaming, moaning, groaning vectors of pain and sorrow. It was contagious, devastating. I felt gutted every time. I let them down, failed them, over and over."

Michael sobbed, tears and snot running down his face. He howled, deep guttural moans that left him gasping for breath. Maria held him, gently swinging the loveseat back and forth. She'd never seen Michael like this, and it filled her with fear for their future.

Eventually he resumed. "I'm having insomnia and nightmares, but complaining about it seems weak, so trivial compared to the suffering of the Congolese.

"And there's more. Something terrible did happen." He recounted the Mai Mai attack that left Laurent dead and Anna brutalized. He heaped blame on himself for his arrogance, his errors in judgment.

Maria was horrified, both by the story and by what these events had done to her partner. It was a painful reminder of her own terrible experiences growing up in Nicaragua, experiences that she still struggled to cope with. They were silent for a time. Then she quietly asked, "Does IMAF offer counseling? Maybe you should talk to someone."

"Yeah, they recommended that I see a shrink when I got home. Henri even suggested that I might end up suffering from post-traumatic stress disorder." Michael waved a hand dismissively as if shooing away a fly. "I'll be fine. I'm exhausted, for sure, so I just need some rest. That's all."

It's so true, Maria thought, the cliché that doctors make the worst patients.

CHAPTER 5

DAYS DRAGGED BY. MOST MORNINGS Michael felt more tired when he got up than when he'd gone to bed. Some days he went back to bed as soon as Maria left for the university. She thought maybe he'd brought back some kind of parasite or illness from the Congo, and urged him to go for testing. He refused, sticking with his theory that he just needed some time to recuperate. He was restless and easily irritated. He would soon be back at the Harborview Medical Center, but he had to wait for the locum they'd hired to replace him to finish her contract. He brooded endlessly about the mistakes he'd made that had caused Laurent's death and Anna's assault. It seemed irredeemably unfair that all he got was a whack in the head, and worse yet, an early release home.

Michael went for a couple of short bike rides but found that he tired quickly. He spent an unhealthy amount of time online, emailing Anna to see how she was doing, checking with JC and Henri about Étienne, other patients, and the state of the hospital, and voraciously reading news about Africa. He was relieved when Saturday rolled around, the day he was to meet Dom for a run. It was a gray Seattle morning, not actually raining but with so much humidity that water drops seemed to be suspended in the air.

"Good to see you, man!" Dom, tall, dark, and *GQ* handsome, was cheerful despite the fog.

"You too."

"Beautiful morning," Dom said as he embraced Michael in a bear hug.

"For fish!"

"C'mon, Michael, we live in a rainforest."

"I know, I know. It rained in Goma most days too. I can't get away from it."

"So what do you think? Warm up on the Swordfern trail?" A system of paths crisscrossed the University of Washington campus, through regenerating second-growth forest and along Union Bay.

"Sounds good."

Michael and Dom had met in college, running together on the cross-country team. Dom had more natural talent, but Michael was willing to dig a little deeper. Dom got the girls while Michael got the medals. After university, they both got into the triathlon scene but neither was interested in the volume of training needed to pursue it as a potential career. Michael's fitness had eroded with the busy life of an ER doctor and then declined more while he was in Goma because it simply wasn't safe for running. Back home, Dom was still in terrific shape, training incessantly with the Seattle Triathlon Club.

He ran like a wolf—lean, tireless, predatory—and soon Michael was struggling to keep up. His competitive streak pushed him past the threshold where most runners would have quit. According to his monitor, his heart was going at almost 180 beats per minute, well past his anaerobic threshold. Desperate, he found a little extra reserve and surged to catch up with Dom.

"Uncle, uncle." He gasped and slowed to a walk.

"What's the matter, bro?" Dom was breathing easily, smiling.

"Gonna burst a lung!"

"Did Africa make you soft?"

"Land mines," Michael wheezed.

"Mmm."

"Machete-wielding rebels."

"Uh-huh."

"Child soldiers with AK-47s."

"Right. Your point?"

"Suboptimal running conditions."

"Ah. Good excuses, except for one small problem. Africans are the best runners in the world. Olympic champions in all of the track and road running events."

They paused at a water fountain. Michael slurped greedily, then wiped a handful of cold water across his face as he struggled to catch his breath.

"Maybe they get fast running away from all of those hazards. Seriously though, you'll note that it's Kenyans, Ethiopians, and Moroccans who take home Olympic gold medals and world championships. Not Congolese, Rwandans, or Liberians. You can't outrun mosquitoes, bullets, or bacteria."

Michael sketched the situation in the eastern half of the Congo for Dom, the interminable civil war, the recurring disease outbreaks, and the hundreds of thousands of refugees streaming into North Kivu province trying to escape even more wretched conditions elsewhere.

"Jesus," Dom said, when Michael stopped talking. "Makes our problems seem pretty minor. But we're here to burn some fast-twitch muscle fibers. If you can't keep up on the way back, I'll meet you at the parking lot. Loser buys coffee."

Dom took off, running at a clip that Michael simply couldn't match. By the time he got back to the parking lot, Dom had put on some warm-up clothes and was lying on a yoga mat in the grass, stretching his hamstrings. "So how come you're back from the heart of darkness a few weeks early?"

Michael gritted his teeth and rubbed his cheek at the prospect of telling his brutal story again. But he gave in and told Dom.

"Holy shit. That's unbelievable. You're lucky to be alive!"

"To be honest, it doesn't feel that way. I'm the one who fucked things up."

"Dude! Don't lay that guilt trip on yourself. The whole situation was fucked up, and you aren't the killer or the rapist. You've gotta get that straight in your mind."

"It's not only the person pulling the trigger who's responsible for the crime. There's often a chain of causation, and I was definitely a link in that chain."

"But you're a human, not a superhero. Who can say what the right thing to do is in those circumstances?"

"Well, what I did was the wrong thing."

"I can tell I'm not going to change your mind. But are you okay? I mean going through something like that . . ." Dom shook his head.

"Yeah, I'm fine. A little burned out maybe. A little pissed off at the world for letting such massive suffering go almost unnoticed. I mean when was the last time the Congo made the news here?"

"Look, Michael, I hear you. Clearly Africa needs help. But that's exactly what you and IMAF were doing. Using your expertise to save lives and improve the situation."

"Dom, we're not even a drop in the bucket. IMAF runs a couple of medical centers in the Congo, co-manages a hospital, and operates a few mobile health care buses. But we rely on donations and can help maybe one or two out of every hundred people who desperately need assistance. We spend millions when what's needed is billions. Tens or even hundreds of billions."

"You've been there and you're probably right. But that kind of money doesn't just appear. Such a huge investment would require years of concerted effort by philanthropists, governments, and businesses. It takes time to change the world."

"We don't have time. Millions of African kids will die this year! Easily preventable deaths. Easily treatable diseases. Millions more next year. It's a fucking emergency. A humanitarian crisis that dwarfs almost anything the world has ever seen."

"I'm sorry, man, I really am. But Africa's challenges will probably take decades to resolve."

Fuck that, Michael thought. There has to be a faster way.

"Let's go refuel. I need a hit of caffeine and sugar, and you're buying. Let's head to the Bakery Nouveau for espresso and twice-baked almond croissants."

"All right." But at the bakery Michael did some quick math. Two coffees and a couple of sugar-laden treats cost more than the average monthly income in Goma. For the price of their morning snack, he could have bought forty vaccines for measles or several cases of the dehydration tablets that prevented deaths from diarrhea. The inequality hit him like a hammer every time he pulled out his wallet.

CHAPTER 6

AS WEEKS PASSED, MICHAEL'S DEPRESSION only deepened, and Maria's concern grew. During another silent breakfast, Maria made a bold suggestion. "I think it's time for us to spend a few days in North Cascades National Park. Pick a hike, any hike."

"I don't think now is a good time. I've got shifts coming up at the hospital."

"Michael."

"Yes?"

"You need to get out of the house. And out of your head. You can trade a couple of shifts at the hospital, and I'll find a couple of guest lecturers for my classes."

"Okay. You win."

Maria unleashed her dazzling smile. The North Cascades were Michael's heaven and haven. As a young man, he had explored their wilderness, seeking adventure far from the roads and clear-cuts that scarred so much of the state. It was in the North Cascades that he and Maria had first made love, in an alpine meadow under a moonlit sky. The memory always triggered smiles from both of them, not so much at the corny image or a recollection of the earth moving beneath them but because Maria had been frightened that a curious grizzly bear would make it a threesome.

"How about the Thornton Lake Trail?" Michael asked.

Maria had anticipated this suggestion. She knew her husband well. He loved to repeat their first backpacking trip. At the time, Maria had been very much a city person, and the thought of a night in the wilderness with only a thin tent between her and marauding wildlife had been terrifying.

"Is it safe?" she'd asked.

"Of course," he had replied. "No grizzlies have been seen in the North Cascades for decades." There were alleged sightings every summer, but there'd been no conclusive scientific proof of grizzly presence since an old silverback was shot in 1972, the year before grizzlies were put on the endangered species list. No scat, no tracks, no skulls, no skeletons. "Scientists call them the ghost bears of the North Cascades for a reason."

"I'm sorry if this sounds weak, but that's a relief."

"There's just one small problem with the absence of grizzlies."

"What is it?"

"More room for black bears and mountain lions."

Maria looked alarmed.

"I'm kidding." Sort of, he thought. "As long as we follow the three golden rules of hiking we'll be fine."

"What golden rules?"

"One, always hang your food from a tree. Two, make lots of noise when approaching blind corners. Three, always hike with someone you can outrun."

"You're awful!"

That first backpacking trip had cemented their relationship. Four magical days in a world of their own, seeing more wild animals than hikers, sleeping under more stars than Maria had ever seen, breathing the incomparably fresh alpine air. Maria broke a longstanding silence and talked about her troubled childhood in Nicaragua, when her family got on the wrong side of the Sandanistas. On Michael's side, on the final evening, as they lay with their heads sticking out of the tent, looking for constellations and shooting stars, he took a deep breath. Inhaling Maria's smell, fresh from lake swimming, he felt almost intoxicated, and looking her in the eye said for the first time, "I love you. You're the one."

The first available window that they could both pry open was about two weeks away. Maria hoped that the North Cascades would work their magic. She picked up the rental car, then stopped by REI to buy an assortment of dehydrated dinners, granola bars, and chocolate. The pile of food looked like it would feed a group of six for a week, but Maria had learned that that your appetite explodes when you walk up and down mountains with a fifty-pound pack on your back and bathe in lakes where the water temperature is barely above freezing.

At home, Maria pulled their camping gear together, laughing to herself at the so-called "two-person tent" that was a leftover from Michael's bachelor years. The tent was so tiny that any two persons who slept in it had little choice but to be intimate.

They took the I-5 north from Seattle. The traffic was light and they reached the rangers' station at Marblemount ahead of schedule.

"I'll get the camping permits," Michael volunteered.

"Thanks. I need to use the ladies'."

With Maria safely out of earshot, Michael was able to ask the young ranger if there'd been any bear problems in the Thornton Lakes area recently.

"Nope, but you should still be careful."

"Right."

The drive from the ranger station to the trailhead was uneventful except for a glimpse of two black bear cubs cavorting in the ditch.

"I hope they're going the other way. We don't want to run into their mother."

"I'm sure we'll be fine." Michael was an old pro at reassuring Maria that they would be safe. He told her, accurately, that the odds of being harmed by a bear in the USA were a small fraction of the likelihood of being assaulted by a human, and that bears lagged far behind wasps, cats, dogs, and ferrets in causing visits to American hospitals.

Just past Milepost 117, they turned left onto a rough old logging road. The gravel road was heavily washboarded, with potholes that looked like they could swallow a small vehicle. Michael had a flashback to the Congo and tried to banish his dark thoughts with a joke.

"Do you know what they would call this kind of road in Kivu Province?"

"A disgrace? A disaster?"

"No. A national scenic highway."

It was only nine miles to the end of the road but the drive took half an hour. There were no other cars in the small parking lot.

As they fiddled with plastic clasps and Velcro straps, Maria said, "Funny thing about putting on a heavy pack out here. I still feel lighter than in the city where I don't carry a pack."

"Must be something in the air," Michael replied, as he and Maria kissed.

"We aren't going to make it very far at this rate."

"It's kind of nice here. We could kick some gravel out of the way and pitch the tent just over there . . ." Michael winked.

"Come on, wilderness boy. Let's hit the trail." It was five grueling miles of switchbacks climbing uphill to the pass, and then a quick descent to lower Thornton Lake. Craggy peaks pierced the clear autumn sky. The mountains were covered in an evergreen blanket while valley bottoms had erupted in a riot of fall colors.

"Look! A marmot!" Maria exclaimed.

"Where?"

"Sitting on that big rock, just to the left of the trail. Perfectly camouflaged."

"Mmm-hmm," Michael mumbled and returned his gaze to the ground in front of him.

"Not a bad eye for a city girl!" Maria was unsettled by Michael's tepid response. Even out here he seemed distant, haunted by demons acquired in Africa. Would he ever again be the man she'd married?

They headed for the third Thornton Lake, the farthest away but easily the most beautiful. "Michael?"

"Yes?"

"A penny for your thoughts," Maria said as she took a swig of her water.

"Oh, I was just admiring that gorgeous alpine lake, full of seemingly clean water. Wait a second!" Michael looked from the lake to Maria's bottle. "I just had a crazy idea! Americans are the wealthiest people in the world, right? We drink billions of bottles of water, beers, soda pops, lattes, and cappuccinos every year. Imagine if one cent, just a measly penny, was charged on each of those drinks. It would add up to billions of dollars annually."

"Okay . . ."

Michael was as animated as he'd been since returning. "That money could be dedicated to African countries for drilling wells, building basic water-treatment facilities, constructing latrines and sewage systems. Billions of dollars per year . . . and who on Earth could possibly object to paying an extra penny for a Vitaminwater, Coke, Budweiser, or Starbucks coffee?"

"But most of those companies already donate to charities. You know, like McDonald's has Ronald McDonald House."

Michael scowled at Maria. "So what? I'm talking about a high-profile new initiative where they all raise their prices by one cent per beverage for everyone."

She raised her hands in surrender. "It's a cool idea, for sure."

"That's more like it." Michael shifted back to smiling. "What's the U.S. population these days?"

"About 330 million, I think."

"And how many drinks does each person consume each day, ballpark?"

"I don't know. Two? Maybe three?"

"That's a billion drinks a day! Times a penny?"

"Ten million dollars a day. Over three and a half billion dollars per year."

"And that's just the U.S. What if the program went global?"

Maria was heartened to see Michael engaged again. She knew there were big problems with his idea. But right here, right now?

43

The last thing she wanted to remind Michael was that Africa's situation is incredibly complex, with more than fifty countries still struggling to flourish decades after decolonization. Somebody else could tell him that the most important factors in reducing child mortality are providing education for girls, offering health care to women, and improving the socioeconomic status of poor families. Achieving those advances required tackling even more daunting challenges. Ending civil wars with deep historical roots. Finding a cure for endemic corruption. Nurturing weak democracies. The list was long. If the solutions were as straightforward as throwing money at the problems, they'd have been implemented long ago.

"Hey, what is it? Is there some kind of fundamental flaw, an Achilles heel that I'm overlooking?"

"No . . . I think you might be onto something. You should think it through, talk to Dom."

"Yes!" His eyes blazed with excitement. The idea seemed like a shot at redemption.

CHAPTER 7

THE WEEK AFTER THEIR TRIP to the North Cascades, Maria set up a dinner party. Michael had tried to talk her out of it, to no avail. Four other couples, mostly Maria's friends, but Dom and his new girlfriend, Amy, were the first to arrive. Like Dom, Amy was tall, lithe, and athletic. They brought organic beer from a local brewery and a bottle of Sea Star wine from a vineyard just across the border on Canada's Pender Island. Michael was chopping vegetables for gado-gado salad. The spicy peanut sauce was already prepared, and the basmati rice was steaming away.

"Oh no," said Dom, "rabbit food!" Amy looked at him in fake horror.

"New article in the *British Medical Journal* this week," Michael responded. "Vegetarians have higher IQs."

"There goes your theory about the caveman diet," Amy said to Dom.

"The caveman diet?" Maria asked.

"Sure. Mostly meat, and a few wild plants. The theory is that you get loads of protein and avoid all of the preservatives, pesticides, and stuff that's in contemporary food," Dom replied.

"And that's supposed to be healthy?" Maria looked skeptical.

"That's the theory. Not that I've tried it," Dom admitted.

"Hmm." Maria smiled. "Cavemen had a life expectancy of what, thirty-two, thirty-three years?"

"Yeah but they lived large." Dom smiled as he uncorked a bottle of organic wine from California. "Multiple wives. Roaming the continent. Killing animals with their bare hands. Connected to Mother Nature."

"Speaking of hunter-gatherers, could somebody get some blackberries for dessert?" Michael asked, not giving away the secret that while Maria was at the university, he'd spent the afternoon baking her favorite cheesecake.

"Sure," Maria said. "Hey Amy, why don't you join me? We'll leave the men in the kitchen."

"Is that safe?"

"Michael, we can trust. Dom, I'm not so sure."

"Hey, wait a second . . ." Dom shrugged. The truth was that his culinary skills were limited to can openers, barbecues, and microwave ovens.

Maria and Amy carried a pile of empty yogurt containers out into the unruly backyard. As the other guests arrived, they helped pick the Himalayan blackberries from bushes that covered the cedar fence on all three sides of the yard. Juicy dark purple berries pulled the branches toward the ground, but were protected by vicious thorns and marauding wasps.

Back inside, Michael grabbed Dom's arm and began describing the vision for his project, sketching out how just a penny per beverage sold in wealthy countries would put a major dent in the water and sanitation challenges afflicting some of Africa's poorest countries, including the Democratic Republic of the Congo.

"Twenty billion dollars in five years, Dom. Billion with a B. It would be a massive undertaking, like the Apollo Project, but focused on saving millions of children's lives."

"So you're going to collect billions of pennies? Like the way UNICEF used to raise money by handing out those little orange boxes at Halloween?"

"No! The plan would be to engage the big companies and get them to collect the money. They could raise their prices by a penny and nobody would even notice, let alone complain. They'd pass along the funds to the project, and we'd allow them to place some kind of endorsement on their products in recognition of their participation and contribution."

Dom looked curiously at Michael, as if reappraising his old friend. He took a few seconds to digest what he'd heard.

"Hot damn, Michael MacDougall! You may be on to something. You're right—it could actually save the lives of millions of children."

"I need to know if it could really work and if so, how to get started. I don't have a clue. That's why I'm asking you."

"Look. It's a hell of an idea. It really is. But I'm gonna give you the straight goods. You need to be realistic. The world is full of brilliant ideas that are being ignored. The peace dividend. The financial transaction tax. Green jobs. So the crux of it isn't whether it's a bright idea or the right thing to do—you're two for two there—but would people go for it and how do you implement it. Would powerful people support it, ignore it, or block it?"

"Well, that's why I'm asking your advice," Michael said, color rising in his cheeks. "I know it's a good idea. But I need help on the how."

"Okay, first of all you need to set up a charitable organization. With it you can issue businesses a tax receipt for their donations. Believe me, that's absolutely essential. Otherwise, you'll never get a dime from a corporation. You'll have to find start-up funds to set up and staff the foundation. A CEO, a fundraiser, an accountant, and communications people. Website, Facebook, Instagram, Twitter, all the social media. Oh, and you'll need a board of directors, the more high-powered and high-profile the better. And all that is just for the United States. Going global multiplies the complexity by at least a factor of ten."

"Whoa. Does it have to be that complicated?"

"All I'm saying is that turning your dream into reality won't be easy. But on the other hand, it's not rocket science. As you say, the solutions exist and the kind of money you're talking about would go a long way to making them happen."

"What kind of timeline are we talking about, roughly?"

. "Well, it definitely won't happen overnight. It'll take years of hard work, determination, and persistence."

"Years?"

"Yes. And we haven't even discussed the challenges of getting the beverage companies onboard, distributing the funds to the right organizations, and ensuring that projects get implemented in places where they're needed the most. I mean look at the Gates Foundation. It has an endowment of something like $50 billion. They're doing incredible things but are only beginning to make a tiny dent in Africa's gargantuan problems."

"Okay, I know it won't be easy. But we don't have years and years. Like I keep saying, millions of kids are dying this year!"

"Michael! I hear you. I'm on your side already. But—"

"Dom it's a fucking emergency—"

"I know, but—"

Maria, Amy, and the rest of their friends came back in with overflowing baskets of juicy blackberries, ending their conversation.

"I hope everybody's hungry," Maria said. "We've got enough food here to feed a small army."

Michael bit his lip, turned, and went down the hall to the bathroom to regain his composure before dinner. He felt like punching a hole in the wall, not sitting down to a meal of obscene abundance. As he washed his hands, he was transported back to Goma, prepping for another futile surgery. He looked in the mirror and thought about smashing his face into it. Never in his life had he felt this magma of anger bubbling so violently and close to the surface.

CHAPTER 8

MICHAEL WAS SPLINTERING. One part of him was plagued by flashbacks, nightmares, and emotional turmoil. His thoughts even spiraled to considerations of suicide, quickly suppressed. Another side was relieved to be back to work, pulling four or five twelve-hour shifts a week at the medical center, and being on call every weekend. Surrounded by highly qualified staff, and with reliable access to the best diagnostic and surgical equipment money could buy, he found patients flourished under his care. If they were alive when paramedics, police, or family members brought them into the emergency ward, odds were good that Michael would pull them through.

Nonetheless, Michael suffered flashes of asphyxiating rage. Despite their immense good fortune, Americans complained incessantly and vociferously. If cellphone reception at the hospital was fuzzy or the Wi-Fi signal was intermittent, people griped about it. If room temperature deviated from a narrow band, people thought it was too cold or too hot. Doing his daily rounds, patients bitched about the food. Compared to what the field hospital could feed people in the Congo, the hospital kitchen was cranking out food worthy of a Michelin-rated restaurant.

His best moments were when he was in surgery, figuring out when to cut and where, what to prescribe or not, which tools he needed. All the steps in the medical process occupied his full attention, leaving no room for despair.

When he wasn't at the hospital, Michael either worked compulsively on what he had named the Blue Drop Foundation or was paralyzed by depression he continued to misdiagnose as fatigue.

49

He had incorporated the foundation as a non-profit society and applied for official charitable status so that it could issue tax receipts to donors. The government's estimated processing time was twelve to eighteen months, another source of acute frustration. A friend of Maria's volunteered her graphic design expertise and came up with a striking logo, an aquamarine water droplet resting on a rainbow of colors from African flags.

Dom had suggested that the idea could take years to build, but Michael was determined to have the project running in a matter of months. He sent introductory letters to the chief executive officers of every large beverage corporation in the United States, introducing the Blue Drop Foundation and requesting a meeting at their earliest convenience.

Michael also sent letters to the president, vice president, secretary of state, secretary of commerce, Washington State senators, and his local members of the House of Representatives. Weeks rolled by without a single response. Michael stewed, simmered, and grew increasingly distant. Maria watched his deterioration with alarm and despair. She suggested that Michael see a therapist or another physician but this prompted dismissive, surly reactions, so she stopped nudging him.

Remarkably, the president was the first to reply. Michael carefully opened the envelope. On impressively weighty stock, embossed with a golden White House logo, it said:

Dear Dr. MacDougall,

Thank you for your recent correspondence. The president is pleased that Americans such as you take such an active interest in the affairs of this great nation. Rest assured that your opinions are highly valued by our administration.

The United States will continue to demonstrate international leadership in bringing freedom, democracy, security,

and economic prosperity to the rest of the world, including
the struggling nations of Africa to which your letter refers.

God Bless America.
Sincerely,
A/Director of Correspondence
The Office of the President of the United States

Empty rhetoric. Michael barely refrained from tearing the letter into small pieces. More weeks went by. More form letters arrived. "Thank you for your interest. Blah, blah, blah." Not a whiff of genuine interest in the Blue Drop Foundation or a hint that a meeting might be in the cards.

Michael called Dom. "I wanted to ask you a couple of questions about Blue Drop. I'm not getting much in the way of responses to my letters."

"Have you followed up with phone calls?"

"No, not yet."

"Get on it, doc! Remember that these are busy people, and they've never heard of you. You need to be like a rabid pit bull that bites them in the leg and refuses to let go until they capitulate and agree to a meeting."

"Rabid dogs are not really my style."

"Oh, come on! Dr. Michael 'Ironman' MacDougall? You're as persistent as sea lice on farmed salmon."

"Yeah, thanks. It's just that I don't like being pushy, hassling people."

"Don't think of it as hassling them. You're offering them a chance to share in the spotlight of a brilliant idea, to be a part of history. People want to do the right thing. Leaders want legacies. You need to push those buttons to sell them on this."

"All right." But he felt that he was play-acting in a world he didn't understand. He was a doctor, not a pitch-maker or mover and shaker. He felt at home in the operating room, scalpel in hand, not sitting at a desk with a mouse or a phone. But what other choice did he have?

Michael tried cold calls next but could never talk his way past the corporate gatekeepers. The wall between elected representatives and the constituents whom they purportedly served was no more permeable.

The rejection letters piled up, a tangible symbol of failure. His depression deepened, and fury festered in his heart. Despite his medical training he failed to recognize the symptoms of post-traumatic stress disorder in himself.

And then a tiny crack appeared, a fissure in the world's wall of indifference.

After reading the email twice, Michael banged his fist on the desk and grabbed the phone. "Dom! We finally got a break."

"Whaddaya mean?"

"Senator Piatkowski has agreed to a meeting. His chief of staff just emailed me to schedule it. Hallelujah."

"Piatkowski, eh? I've met him a few times. Former head of the state Cattlemen's Association. Not exactly a bleeding-heart liberal."

"No, but he's been a senator for what, twenty years? He knows D.C."

"Yeah, true, but he's a Democrat in a Republican Congress. He can answer your questions, but he can't solve your problems."

"I don't expect him to solve my problems. I just want some answers, and I'm hoping that you'll come to the meeting with me. As a founding director of the Blue Drop Foundation."

"Sure I'll come."

"One strange thing—his chief of staff asked if I could bring along a stethoscope. Do you think he's looking for some free medical advice?"

"Of course not! He wants a photo op." Dom continued to be amazed at his friend's political naiveté. "Do you think he just wants to shoot the breeze with you? He's a politician. There has to be something in it for him. The quid pro quo."

More weeks passed, more waiting for the meeting day to arrive. Dom and Michael met for coffee beforehand to plot their strategy. Michael was vibrating with excitement.

"No coffee for you, my friend!"

"Don't worry, I've developed an immunity to caffeine."

"Yeah, right. That's why you can't stop tapping your toes. Look, this is how we'll play it." Dom walked Michael through meeting tactics.

"Sounds good. Let's go."

They called an Uber and were soon whisked to the senator's office in a heritage building on the edge of downtown. They signed in at security, skipped the elevator, and ran up the stairs to the top floor.

The receptionist, a young woman wearing a wireless headset, sat behind a gleaming Scandinavian-style desk bearing nothing but a coffee mug and an iPad.

"Hi." Dom flashed his winning smile. "We've got a date with Senator Piatkowski at eleven."

"I'm sorry, sir, but the senator is running a little bit behind schedule this morning. Please have a seat, and I'll let you know when he's ready."

Michael sat down in a well-worn green leather chair, picked up a newspaper, scanned the headlines, and put it back down. Then he fidgeted with his briefcase. Dom got acquainted with the receptionist. Part of his strategy was to befriend the gatekeepers. Soon a door opened and two burly men emerged, chomping on cigars. Michael recognized only the senator. Dom, on the other hand, swore under his breath.

"What's the matter?" Michael whispered.

"That's Steve Mason, CEO of the biggest clear-cutter left in the USA. He's totally old-school and has never seen a forest that he wouldn't happily turn into toilet paper."

"Save that lecture for another day," Michael warned and stood as the senator approached. He was six-foot-six and weighed close to three hundred pounds, his body wrapped in an expensive-looking charcoal suit.

"Gentlemen, welcome."

"I'm Dr. Michael MacDougall, nice to meet you, senator."

"Dr. McDonald." They shook hands. The senator's grip belied his advancing years, but he had become hopelessly addled with names.

"Dominic Fiore, good to see you again, sir."

"Ah yes, Mr. Ford, still tilting at windmills, are we? Come on in," the senator said, waving them into his office. "This is my chief of staff, Robert Mills, and my senior policy advisor, Janine Werbach." Mills and Werbach were young, both dressed sharply in black, clutching their smartphones. "Now, Dr. McDonough, your letter mentioned that you have some questions regarding American foreign policy."

"Yes, sir. I spent almost three months in Africa earlier this year, working as a trauma surgeon for IMAF."

"A fine organization. Didn't they win some award a few years back?"

"That was actually a different organization. Same type of work though, providing free medical services."

"An honorable endeavor. Now whereabouts in Africa were you posted?"

"The Democratic Republic of Congo."

"Jesus. Hell on Earth."

"In some ways Hell and in other ways Heaven. Have you been to Africa, senator?"

"A few times. Egypt, South Africa, Kenya. Not the Congo. The folks who amaze me are the Masai. As fellow cattlemen, of course. Walking miles and miles in the blazing heat to find waterin' holes and some decent grass to graze on."

The Senator rambled on. When he paused to take a breath and a pull on his cigar, Michael could hear the distinctive rumbling of chronic obstructive pulmonary disease in the big man's chest. He leapt in. "Senator, the places you visited in Africa are in good shape compared to the Congo. As a physician, I was horrified by the poverty, the human suffering, the pointless deaths of young children. AIDS. Malaria. TB. Kids blown apart by land mines. Most of this misery is avoidable, if the resources were available."

"We pour more money into that bureaucratic black hole called the United Nations than any other nation in the world."

"And what about our low level of foreign aid?"

The senator violently stubbed out his cigar. "Same damned thing. When you look at foreign aid as a percentage of our GDP, we're at the bottom of the heap, with South Korea, Greece, and Portugal. But that's because our economy is so huge. In terms of the actual George Washingtons leaving our country to lend a helping hand to poor countries, we're number one."

"Number one? Really?"

"Janine? Pull the numbers for Dr. MacDonald."

"Yes, sir. I'll get them printed out."

Michael looked at Dom, who shrugged, a "don't ask me" look. "All right, let's not get bogged down in the numbers. The fact remains that whatever we're doing, it's not enough. There are hundreds of millions of people in Africa without clean drinking water. And millions of kids dying each year because of illnesses that we could easily prevent or treat. For pennies per child. We're the richest nation in the world. The richest in the history of human society. Don't we have a moral obligation to help those who are in desperate straits?"

"Look, son. You remind me of a passage from the great book—'Blessed are those who hunger and thirst for justice.' And personally, I agree with you." The senator had been re-elected five times, and one of the reasons was his ability to agree convincingly with anyone on any issue. "Yes, we're punching below our weight. But what am I supposed to do about it? If you're asking me to push for increases in our foreign aid budget, I can't do it. There are folks right here in Washington State who are starving, living in the streets, dying of preventable diseases. Maybe they don't make campaign contributions, but they can still vote. They're my constituents. Desperate people elsewhere, well, they don't donate and they can't vote.

"America's already running the biggest deficit of all time. Trillions of dollars. Should we raise our taxes so we can send more money overseas? Hard-working Americans just don't see the sense in that. They want tax cuts, better health care, better education, and a military with the resources to get the job done."

"But—"

"No buts, Doctor. I'm just telling it like it is. The plain truth. Unvarnished. And nothing you or I can do will change it. Either you produce oil, purchase a lot of American goods and services, or have a nuclear weapons program. Otherwise you're not on our radar screen."

"What about the Sustainable Development Goals that the world pledged to achieve? To reduce global poverty and hunger by half, to achieve universal access to clean water and primary education, to tackle global pandemics like AIDS, all by 2030. The U.S. signed on to those goals, right? But at the rate we're going, the world will never make it. And yet we spend trillions of dollars on our military so we can knock countries backwards instead of moving them forward."

"I like your bullheadedness, but you don't appear to be hearing me. You have to understand how the world works, not just how you want it to be, or think it ought to be. Change doesn't happen overnight. It kind of flows along like a big ol' river. You can build a dam and block it, although you have to let some water through or it'll burst. You can divert it, so that it carves a new channel. You can contaminate it in a hundred different ways. But the one thing you cannot do is speed it up. Frankly, Doc, you've got a tougher challenge than the Greek fella, what was his name, Oedipus? Syphilis? The guy who was pushing the rock up the hill, and it kept steamrolling him."

"Sisyphus," the chief of staff, Robert, chimed in.

"Right. Sisyphus. What I'm saying is this: you have a big boulder to push and a high mountain to climb. American altruism is going through a tough patch right now."

As the senator prosed on, a whirlwind of images and thoughts blew through Michael's mind in an incoherent, incomprehensible storm. The only unifying element was rage.

Dom took advantage of Michael's heated silence and leapt in with his own shopping list. "Let's talk about something a little bit closer to home. Salmon." Michael glared at Dom for shamelessly hijacking the agenda.

Janine interrupted. "You've got five minutes. The senator has another meeting at eleven-thirty. Dr. MacDougall, I'll go get your information."

"Five minutes is plenty." Dom made a pitch for removing some old dams along tributaries of the Columbia River that were no longer serving any purpose but continued to block Pacific salmon from reaching their ancient spawning grounds.

The senator listened halfheartedly, calculating the energy required of him in units of elbow grease against the vote-gaining potential, the horse swapping, the photo ops, and the possible backlash.

Janine returned, bearing a plain manila file folder that she passed to Michael. "Levels of official development assistance for the twenty largest donor nations, going back a decade. We're number one."

And then their time was up. Handshakes and platitudes all around. A couple of quick photographs. On autopilot, Michael managed to maintain a semblance of manners. Once he and Dom were safely out of the building, he erupted.

Dom let Michael vent for a few minutes, then put a hand on his friend's shoulder. "Welcome to the real world."

Michael did a double take. "The real world? This is fantasyland. And what was that tangent about salmon? How did that help?"

"Just trying to save some fish and the old-growth ecosystems they depend on," Dom said.

"Save some fish? We're supposed to be saving people!"

"Hey, man, we're all related. Part of Mother Earth." Dom's attempted levity failed to placate Michael. "Okay, let's both give this some thought. We can talk about next steps during our run on Saturday. Do a long slow one so it's easier to talk."

"All right. Sorry. I'm just frustrated."

Now there's an understatement, Dom thought. His best friend seemed primed to explode.

CHAPTER 9

THAT NIGHT, MICHAEL HAD ANOTHER NIGHTMARE. In it, Maria was pregnant. He was delivering their child. The labor was long, complicated, painful. She gave birth to dozens of misshapen, undersized, and stillborn babies. He woke up drenched in sweat, wondering if it was an omen or whether it symbolized the failed birth of the Blue Drop Foundation.

Nine months had passed and he'd been unable to persuade a single beverage corporation to express even a modicum of interest in his proposal. Nor did the American government have any interest in promoting the interests of the world's poor. No amount of public protest, lobbying, international humiliation, diplomacy, multilateral pressure, or litigation had made a difference in the past three decades. What hope was there that somebody would listen to a nobody like Michael?

One night, lying awake in bed, obsessed with his failure, a dark and malignant idea arose, like the evil brother of the one that had jumpstarted the Blue Drop Foundation months ago.

Only one avenue offered the potential for an ordinary individual to create a significant short-term shift in America's national priorities. The powers that be could ignore the Blue Drop Foundation, but they could not ignore the threat of an attack on America. September 11 was irrefutable evidence of that. Terrorism provoked a response. A big response. What if he threatened to poison the drinking water supply of an American city? He'd heard media reports about the vulnerability of public infrastructure, the physical impossibility of protecting it all without creating a police state. He would have to figure out how to create a realistic, credible threat without actually harming anyone. He was still a doctor after all, bound by the Hippocratic oath to do no harm.

Part of Michael was horrified by his own wayward thoughts. Where had they come from? Was he willing to risk everything on such a wild gambit? Would he actually have the balls to go through with it? Would it actually make a difference? Part of him became obsessed by the idea.

"It's only curiosity," Michael told himself. "I just want to know how much information is out there." Some nights he was up until three or four in the morning, unable to sleep, researching the unthinkable. Maria thought he was still working on the foundation, but he realized now that idea was at a dead end. Without the knowledge, ability, or resources to move things along, Michael was stuck.

It took less than ten minutes of Google searches to learn how to create Ricin, the toxic nerve gas that had been used in several terrorist plots. All you needed was a handful of castor beans and access to a kitchen. There were thousands of websites describing other chemical and biological weapons. The advice offered was often contradictory, a testament to either the dubious quality of the information or the success of FBI counterintelligence programs. The former seemed more likely. Opinions were divided on the most effective means of delivering a biological or chemical attack. It seemed that the most potent weapons were those capable of aerial delivery, so that people breathing the air would become afflicted. Nerve gases, pesticides, anthrax, industrial chemicals, viruses, bacteria. Each of these deadly substances had been used or modified for use in modern warfare. It seemed only a matter of time before terrorists used them too.

Michael wondered if some of the websites he'd visited were monitored by security and intelligence agencies. It seemed likely, and he was uncomfortable about the prospect of having his searches traced back to him. Although he hadn't done anything illegal, yet, maybe it would be a good idea to do some of the woolier research from an internet café or one of the public computer labs at the university.

He did some digging into the vulnerability of urban water supplies to contamination. Post–9/11, governments talked a lot about strengthening security measures at water reservoirs and treatment plants. Yet there were over 50,000 large community water systems in the USA, and an additional 100,000 systems serving smaller communities. Properly protecting them would cost hundreds of billions of dollars. In the North Cascade Mountains east of Seattle lay the Chester Morse Reservoir, downstream from the headwaters of the Cedar River. North of the Cedar River lay the Tolt reservoir, on the south fork of the Tolt River. Water was sent westwards from both reservoirs in large pipelines, passing through filtration and chlorination plants en route to people's homes in downtown Seattle and the suburbs. Both watersheds were reportedly protected by regular air and road patrols.

A topographical map of the Cedar River watershed posted online showed that it was crisscrossed with dozens of old logging roads. "Mountain biking country," Michael mused. He ordered a twenty-four- by thirty-six-inch copy of the map online, with free delivery.

He was doing another advanced search about security at the Chester Morse Reservoir when his cellphone rang.

"Michael MacDougall."

"Dr. MacDougall, it's Simone Levesque from IMAF. How are you today?"

"I'm fine," Michael lied. "How are you?"

"Swamped, to tell the truth. Have you heard the latest news from the Congo? Mount Nyiragongo near Goma erupted again, just like in 2002, burying a large swath of the town. The volcanic activity beneath Lake Kivu released a giant bubble of carbon dioxide during the night, suffocating hundreds of Congolese who were sleeping outside. Subsequent contamination of the lake has led to a cholera outbreak. To makes matters worse, Goma has had its first cases of Ebola. And the conflict in the Eastern Congo shows no signs of abating. We are very short of doctors."

"Oh" was all Michael could say. He had been hoping for this phone call, and dreading it, for months. Part of him hungered to return to the mind-numbing frenetic activity of aid medicine. Part of him was terrified by the consequences of returning to Africa. Would he ever be able to sleep? What if he encountered another roadblock? How would he respond when a child died in his care? How would Maria react?

"We are hoping that you might consider another rotation. We wouldn't normally ask this of you but we are in dire straits."

"How soon?"

"Assuming you can pass a physical exam, as soon as you can get your affairs in order—visas, vaccinations, and so forth. We can take care of your air travel arrangements."

"Back to the Congo?"

"Mali, the Sudan, and the Congo are all in crisis. In the circumstances, Dr. MacDougall, we would leave the choice open to you."

"Can I call you back?"

"Yes, of course."

"Okay. I'll get back to you in a few days."

CHAPTER 10

MICHAEL AWOKE BEFORE HIS ALARM WENT OFF. It was still dark and he could hear rain pounding on the deck outside the bedroom. He slid stealthily out of bed. He was going for a long bike ride today, and maybe a run, depending on the access situation in the forests north of the Chester Morse Reservoir.

He pulled on a battered pair of cycling shorts with a chamois added that gave a little extra cushion and reduced chafing. Over top he wore another pair of fast-dry shorts with an absurd number of pockets. A long-sleeve polypropylene shirt, a lightweight fleece, and a Gore-Tex windbreaker would keep the rest of him dry and warm.

The night before he had swapped his super-skinny urban bike tires for a pair of hybrids that would be slightly slower on the highway but would offer more traction when he got onto the rough forest service roads north of the reservoir. He packed two peanut butter and jam bagels, two granola bars, two Fuji apples, and a chocolate bar into one pannier, along with spare tubes and a repair kit. He mixed up two bottles of lemon-lime Gatorade and filled his CamelBak with water. In the second pannier he put his topographical map, a compass, and a pair of binoculars.

He ate a huge bowl of muesli and two sliced bananas for breakfast, washing it down with two glasses of orange juice. He wrote *I love you* on a post-it note and stuck it on the toaster where Maria would place a bagel in about an hour. He stepped onto the back porch, buckling his helmet. Despite the rain, the sky was suffused with tendrils of light as the sun rose, and the day appeared to have some potential for dry periods.

Michael's mountain bike was an ancient steed. He'd always believed that it was worth spending as much as you could afford on a bike because a high-quality one will last a long time. Despite some epic crashes, the Gary Fisher bicycle was still in good shape. He'd gone through a lot of brake pads, tires, and tubes, even replaced the wheels and derailleur, but the frame was the original.

Michael clipped the panniers onto the rear rack and saddled up. He smiled, as he always did when first mounting the bike because several Christmases ago Maria had given him two new bike seats, ergonomically designed to take pressure off certain parts of the male anatomy. One for his racing bike, one for his mountain bike. She'd been spooked by a news story about lower sperm counts and even sterility among men who rode too many miles on rigid bicycle seats.

Michael hit the road, riding against the tide of morning commuters. Soon he was on the Mountains to Sound Greenway, a network of multi-use trails stretching over 100 miles from Puget Sound all the way to the west Cascades. He pedaled east along trails that ran parallel to Interstate 90, crossing the Lacey V. Murrow Memorial Bridge onto Mercer Island, and passing through Factoria, Eastgate, Lake Sammamish State Park, and Issaquah before reaching rural Washington. There was a long stretch of forests, mountains, and desert between here and Spokane. It was fantastic not having to ride on the highway on a rainy day, holding one's breath as trucks roared past belching carcinogenic diesel fumes, and being drenched with sheets of dirty water. The trail wasn't as direct, as it sometimes veered off to avoid private property or a natural obstacle like a wetland, but the safety and comfort were worth the trade-off, and the miles rolled by.

He crossed the old wooden bridge over the Cedar River on 436th Ave. Southeast, known locally as the Cedar Falls Road. It was thirty miles, as the crow flies, from Seattle to the Chester Morse Reservoir. Michael knew he couldn't cycle up the main road to the reservoir, where he would encounter a manned security gate and an extensive perimeter fence. The watershed was 90,000 acres though, and there was no way the whole area was fenced.

The Cedar River valley had been carved by retreating glaciers thousands of years earlier, and 4,000-foot mountains rose up on both sides of the river. In decades past, a rat's nest of logging roads had carved up the mountains, and exposed the forests to relentless rounds of clear-cutting. Seattle owned the entire watershed now, so the days of cut-and-run logging were over. But hundreds of miles of rough gravel roads remained, some melting back into the forest, others looking more like trails. Michael hoped he could use these to navigate his way to the north shore of the reservoir.

The odometer on his handlebars indicated that thirty-six miles had passed since he left home. According to the map, he was now directly north of the reservoir. He spotted an old logging road, sep-arated from the highway by a deep trench. Beyond the trench was a closed metal gate that sported a No Trespassing sign riddled with bullet holes. He pulled over and pretended to fiddle with his chain while checking for passing vehicles. Seeing none, he hefted the bike onto his shoulder, grunting as he dashed through the trench and around the gate intended to dissuade off-road vehicle users. Once on the logging road, Michael pedaled hard for a minute before stopping to look back over his shoulder. The highway was invisible, blocked by the thick regenerating forest, stout Douglas firs straining upwards and competing for the sun's rays.

He was trespassing in the no-go zone of Seattle's primary drink-ing water reservoir. Keeping people out protected water quality. If caught, he could face steep fines and even jail time. He would try to play the role of the innocent mountain bike aficionado, looking for new terrain to conquer. In truth, however, today's trip was a dress rehearsal for an event that could not be explained away so easily.

The old logging road was in rough shape. There were no other visible human tracks—no footprints or tire tracks. There were deer droppings, and one pile of bear scat. Michael stopped and poked the scat with his foot. It was dry, old. No cause for concern. Then the hairs on the back of his neck stood erect. He was being watched.

By whom, or by what? He stood, legs straddling the bike, eyes scanning the forest, looking for movement.

Not more than twenty feet from where he stood, a doe and two speckled fawns had stepped out of the woods. The fawns couldn't be more than a couple of months old. All three of them had sensed Michael and frozen, their big dark eyes watching him warily, ears pivoting like satellite dishes trying to pick up danger signals. He burst into nervous laughter and the deer bolted, springing effortlessly back into the forest and out of sight.

Michael took a deep breath and resumed pedaling. Saplings, fallen trees, and thick clumps of salal occasionally blocked his way. Some he rode over, some he rode around. Twice he had to stop, dismount, and push his bike through a narrow gap while ducking branches. Although his watch read 9:22 a.m., it seemed like twilight because the tree canopy had closed overhead, filtering out most of the day's weak sunlight. The road was mostly a descent, down toward the reservoir. Easy pedaling.

He noticed a change in vegetation. More cedars, alders with new leaves unfurling, and even patches of skunk cabbage as the microclimate grew damper. As he crested a small rise, the reservoir came into view. It was beautiful. There was no fence, no patrol, nothing between Michael and the water. He dismounted, leaning the bike against the armored bark of an impressive Douglas fir. Before leaving the cover of the forest, Michael took a good look through his binoculars. No sign of security. No sign of other humans. He was struck by the gap between the government's rhetoric and the on-the-ground reality. Municipal websites boasted that the Chester Morse Reservoir was protected by an armed security force. And yet here he was.

Michael sauntered out of the forest for a closer look. With eighty or ninety years of growth healing the logging scars, the watershed was truly striking. Whereas old-growth forests were an unruly patchwork quilt of trees—different species and different ages—the second-growth forest was a sweeping, gorgeous blanket of fir and hemlock with the luxuriant look of velvet. To the east was magnificent Meadow Mountain, the tallest peak in the watershed. The reservoir's water looked crystal clear, inviting. He could see the sandy bottom.

Michael heard a low droning noise behind him. He turned and sprinted back toward the shelter of the forest. A small single-propeller airplane was zigzagging back and forth in a grid pattern, clearly patrolling the watershed.

CHAPTER 11

MICHAEL CYCLED HOME, unsettled by the close call with the aerial surveillance. Days passed, and he could not seem to let go of his idea, which was quickly evolving into an actual plan. He avoided people, getting up before Maria to do research, ducking most of Dom's invitations to go for coffee or runs. He needed to shock people in a manner that caused maximum effect with minimal risks to public health. That was the key. He dimly realized that he was coming to think of the unthinkable as the only way forward. On some level, he understood that he was in trouble, that he had been damaged by his experiences in Africa, but he was unwilling to seek help, stubbornly determined that he could work through his anguish himself. He threw himself into the planning for his attack, believing that he could stop and pull the plug at any time, that he had not yet reached the point of no return.

Two weeks later, Michael was on the brink of breaking the law for a second time. This evening's plan involved a more serious offense than merely sneaking around in an off-limits watershed. He was about to steal from the hospital where he worked.

As an emergency room physician, Michael had a key card that allowed him to open just about any door in the hospital. When a doctor in scrubs or a white lab coat opened doors, nobody batted an eyelash. As always, Michael traveled between floors by taking the stairs. He rarely saw anyone else in the stairwell, apart from the occasional physiotherapist working with a patient, and today would be no exception.

The hospital laundry facilities were in the basement, along with the backup generator and the main supply room. His shift was over, but he was still wearing green scrubs and a hair cap. His stethoscope dangled around his neck like a charm, not unlike the Mai Mai general warding off evil spirits with a showerhead. He slid his key card through the slot adjacent to the door of the supply room. The motion-activated lighting system silently turned on as he entered, illuminating the rows of cleaning supplies—paper towels, toilet paper, antibacterial hand soap. Michael pulled on a fresh pair of thin plastic surgical gloves to avoid putting fingerprints on anything he touched.

He couldn't see any video cameras on the walls or suspended from the ceiling. Satisfied that nobody was watching, Michael walked up and down the aisles, looking for one of a series of trade names. PerSec. Perklone. DowPer. Dr. Google had provided names and images. Michael slowed down as he came to a row that housed a variety of laundry products.

And there they were. A shelf of plastic jugs, each bearing the skull and crossbones. Perklone. Each jug contained five liters of perchloroethylene, perc or PCE for short, also known as tetrachloroethylene. An industrial solvent used as dry-cleaning fluid, a spot remover, and a degreaser. Nasty, frightening stuff. Tests on laboratory animals indicated that long-term exposure to perc caused respiratory difficulties, liver damage, kidney failure, reproductive abnormalities, and cancer. At high concentrations, acute health effects could result from breathing it, swallowing it, or allowing it to come into contact with the skin.

Perc was one of the most toxic chemicals to emerge from a biohazard laboratory in the twentieth century. A single liter would dry-clean about ten thousand suits and dresses when diluted to proper concentrations. For years, environmental groups had called for a ban, but millions of pounds of the chemical were still produced annually. In recent years, it had started to show up in the groundwater and drinking water of a few communities, as it leaked out of contaminated industrial sites. From his research, Michael knew that the Environmental Protection Agency had established a limit for the maximum permissible concentration of perc in drinking water of five parts per billion. That meant just one gallon of perc could contaminate almost 200 million gallons of water to the point where the concentration of the chemical exceeded the EPA's maximum permissible level.

Sweat beaded on Michael's forehead and stained the armpits of his scrubs. He took one jug down from the shelf and put it into his duffel bag, covering it with a ratty old Washington Huskies T-shirt. He added a second jug and stuffed another T-shirt between the jugs so they didn't make odd noises. He headed for the door, eager to get out of the hospital and get home and stash his perverse booty in the garage.

Just as his fingers touched the doorknob it started to turn. Someone was on the other side of the door.

"Hola, señor," said the smiling orderly who opened the door. He was a man whom Michael often saw buffing the floors and washing the walls. They had a cordial tradition of exchanging greetings in Spanish. "Hola," said Michael. The orderly didn't seem the slightest bit curious as to why a doctor was in the supply room. He held the door open, and Michael walked away, carrying about ten kilograms of a toxic chemical in his gym bag.

Dom finally convinced Michael to join him for another trail run. They met at Discovery Park. Between his work at the hospital, his obsessive efforts to launch the Blue Drop Foundation, and his chronic sleep deprivation, Michael wasn't exactly rounding into racing shape. Once again it was more a case of meeting Dom, warming up together, and then doing separate runs along the same trails followed by a conversation over coffee and croissants.

"Any progress on the project?" Dom asked, stirring two teaspoons of sugar into his Americano.

"Nope. Just a growing stack of rejection letters. Let's not talk about that, okay?"

"Well, you don't seem interested in small talk anymore. Football? Baseball? Basketball? Or are sports no longer interesting to you?"

"I just don't have time—"

"You used to be a Mariners fanatic! You knew everything about that team, from the earned run average of Félix Hernández to the best prospects in the farm system. You loved baseball, and now you don't have time? That's a bit sad, my friend."

"Haven't watched a game since I've been home. And there's no ESPN in the Congo."

"Come on, ESPN is everywhere!" The sugar and caffeine were amplifying and accelerating Dom's voice.

"There's just other stuff on my mind these days."

"No kidding! What do you want to lecture me about today?"

"No lecture—more like questions. I was wondering what you think about terrorism."

"I knew it! Another light topic for our Saturday morning chat. You're killing me, Doc! Terrorism? Really?"

"I was just reading an article about Indigenous people in Latin America being described as terrorists for trying to defend their land, water, and culture from industrial development. So, I wonder if you think terrorism is inherently evil? Or can it sometimes be justified?"

"First of all, those Indigenous people you're describing are not terrorists. The real terrorists are the politicians and CEOs still inflicting genocide more than five hundred years after Columbus."

"I agree. But the article made me wonder where we draw the line. Was dropping atomic bombs on Nagasaki and Hiroshima an act of terrorism?"

"Nope. To me, those were acts of war."

71

"What about national liberation movements, like the IRA in Ireland or the Tamil Tigers in Sri Lanka?"

"Not as clear. They thought they had legitimate causes."

"But they killed innocent people."

"That's true. So, it's complicated."

"Can you imagine an ethical act of terrorism? I mean, what if nobody really gets hurt?"

"That seems oxymoronic. Although somebody wrote a book called *The Good Terrorist*. Give me a second here . . ." Dom thought for a minute. "Lessing. Doris Lessing. One of my girl-friends read it."

"What was it about?"

"I don't know. It was just a memorable title."

Michael made a mental note to read the book. "What about eco-terrorism? Disabling logging equipment or pounding spikes into trees in order to protect old-growth forests?"

"I think those kinds of actions often do more harm than good, but so-called ecoterrorists only cause property damage, they don't kill or hurt anyone. To me, that's still a crime, but I wouldn't call it terrorism."

"I guess it boils down to your definition. What the president sees as terrorism may be different from what Congress views as terror-ism. And the courts may have an entirely different interpretation."

"Uh-oh, now we're talking about lawyers and legal opinions. Out of my league, but you could ask Maria about it. Wait a minute. You're not planning something crazy, are you?" Dom winked but Michael missed it.

"No fucking way! Of course not! Don't be an idiot." Michael rubbed the side of his face.

"I was just kidding. Lighten up! Sheesh."

"All right. Sorry. Enough about that." Michael forced a smile and said, "So what about those Seahawks, anyway?"

"Well, they're undefeated so far."

"Opening day is next week, wiseguy."

"Exactly."

Dom started talking about the team and its promising outlook, but Michael was thinking about whether his plan constituted terrorism. Was he planning something crazy? A terrorist attack? Not by Dom's definition, because nobody was going to get hurt. Except, according to a small voice in the back of Michael's brain, Maria. Louder voices, however, drowned out that dissenting opinion, clamoring for justice and the interests of millions of African children.

CHAPTER 12

OVER THE NEXT FEW WEEKS, Michael continued to probe his plan for weaknesses. He found a series of helpful documents on the internet to guide his planning and ensure his threat was taken seriously. The Environmental Protection Agency had published a "Response Protocol Toolbox: Planning for and Responding to Drinking Water Contamination Threats and Incidents." Knowing the other side's strategies in advance was useful.

He was confident that he'd chosen the perfect chemical for the job. While perc was extremely toxic and capable of causing terrible health effects if consumed in large quantities or over a long period of time, the amount of perc he planned to put in the Chester Morse Reservoir was too small to cause any significant short or long-term health impacts. The chemical would be too diluted. He wanted to shock, not harm.

He still had moments when the old Michael resurfaced. Then he would recoil from the prospect of committing what would be widely viewed as a terrorist act against the people of the United States. He recognized that many would see his actions as reprehensible. If caught, he'd potentially spend the rest of his life in prison despite not actually harming anybody. Even if he wasn't caught, his life would never be normal again. Every phone call, every knock on the door would ignite a brushfire of fear. Yet he kept coming back to his conviction that it was the only effective means he had to force the government to act to save children's lives. One person's freedom, even if it was his own, seemed a small price to pay for the prospect of saving the lives of millions of kids.

But what about Maria's life? What would his actions do to her? He was able to rise out of his obsession enough to see that their relationship was already in deep trouble. He'd told her nothing of his plans, justifying his secrecy by telling himself that it protected her, prevented her from sharing any criminal responsibility, should that arise. Would she be frightened? Horrified? Appalled? Would it in fact, be the thing he did that finally drove her away?

The morning after he stole the perchloroethylene, before Maria awoke, Michael slipped out of bed and went to the kitchen. He picked up his phone and dialed the number. It felt predetermined, inevitable.

"Hello, Dr. MacDougall. I'm pleased that you called back. Can you join us again?"

"Yes, count me in. I passed my physical, took my shots, and my passport is good for another three years."

"Fantastique! That is wonderful news. Thank you so much."

"Will I be working in the Congo again?"

"I cannot say for certain just yet, but it appears quite likely. And you can stay how long?"

"How long do you need me?"

"Well, Doctor, you know Africa. Perhaps forever."

"Forever seems a little long. How about a couple of months?"

"Two months? Three?"

"Let's start with two, for now."

"Okay. You can start how soon?"

"I need a few days, to sort things out at home and finish a few shifts at the hospital. Oh, and can you make the same arrangement as last time for my bike?"

"Ah yes, of course. Dr. MacDougall and his bicycle. We'll make your flight reservations, email the details to you, and await your confirmation before finalizing the booking."

75

He had no choice but to tell Maria that he was leaving. He steeled himself for an unpleasant breakfast. He ground some super dark coffee beans and prepped the Italian stovetop espresso maker. Maria would be coming into the kitchen any moment for a bagel with cream cheese and an Americano.

Michael put his empty bowl and spoon in the dishwasher. "Good morning. Coffee's on and bagel is in the toaster."

"Thank you. Looks like I'm actually going to be on time today."

"Maybe."

"What do you mean?"

"There's something I have to tell you."

Maria added hot water to her espresso and sat down.

"I need to go back to the Congo. A volcano near Goma erupted, buried part of the city and messed up the water supply. There also appears to be an Ebola outbreak. IMAF needs me."

These were words that Maria had dreaded, yet anticipated. "If you go back again, the Michael MacDougall that I know and love may never return."

"That's a bit melodramatic. Of course I'll come back."

"That's not what I mean. I think we both know that part of you never came back from your first trip. You've already changed. If you go again, I'm afraid that you'll be changed beyond recognition. And you may never stop going back."

"It's a crisis."

"There'll always be another crisis. And there are other doctors out there, doctors who aren't broken like you are."

"Broken?"

"This isn't about IMAF, it's about us. And you're showing me that they're more important to you than I am. More important than our life together."

"It's true that Africa changed my life. But Maria—"

"Listen to me, Michael, please. You know how badly I've wanted to have a child with you. Our child. A child that I carry within me for nine months and give birth to with you beside me in the delivery room. I've been through living hell four times trying, but . . . you know. When you came back I wanted to try one more time, but I'm forty now. You're forty-two. And we don't even make love anymore." Her eyes shone with tears.

There was a long silence. "You could come to Africa with me." Maria glared at him. "It's the middle of a school year. I'm teaching two courses. Leaving now would be irresponsible. It's impossible." She paused. "If you have to go, then go. But stop pretending that you don't have a choice." She pushed back from the table, grabbed her purse and shoes, and slammed the front door behind her.

Michael sat heavy in the chair. He'd failed Laurent, Anna, and countless Africans, and now he'd failed the person he loved most in the world.

Maybe I don't deserve to live, he thought. He pictured capsizing his kayak in the squalls, of Puget Sound. Hypothermia would develop almost immediately, and his weighted body would sink to the bottom of the sea. Or maybe an "accident" in the mountains. Falling hundreds or even thousands of feet onto rock would almost certainly be fatal. In the absence of a suicide note, either would look like an unfortunate accident.

A few years earlier it had seemed that he was on top of the world. A talented young doctor. Nationally ranked amateur triathlete. A wonderful, brilliant, and beautiful wife. But in the last year all of his dreams had crumbled to dust.

It had been months since he'd had a decent night's sleep. Every time he closed his eyes, harrowing images would leap up. Catatonic, emaciated children. Women and girls, beaten and raped. People missing limbs. Laurent's face, the red hole blossoming in his forehead. Anna violated, unconscious, lying on the dusty road.

He'd wake up sweating, heart racing, jaw clenched. He'd tried melatonin, over the counter sleep meds, powerful prescription sedatives, tonics, tinctures. Nothing could keep the ghosts away. It didn't matter that he'd saved hundreds of lives. He never dreamed of the lucky ones' faces. Being a doctor in Africa had stretched him to the breaking point. Murder and rape had pushed him over the edge.

Back home he was faced with more painful demons. His disintegrating marriage. Their lack of a child. Far from making a baby, they slept on opposite sides of the bed like there was still an ocean between them.

But he would not give up so easily. He would suck it up and go through with his plan. Do the unthinkable. Take one last shot at making a difference, being the game-changer he'd set out to become. If it worked, he could be the catalyst for saving millions of lives. If not, well, what else did he have to lose at this point?

Several days later, Simone phoned back.

"Dr. MacDougall, I'm just calling to let you know we had a bit of trouble getting you a flight from Seattle to London. Everything from Sea-Tac is booked solid. We've booked you a flight from Vancouver. And a train ticket, with Amtrak, to get you there. I hope that the inconvenience, it is not too much?"

Michael took the call but kept looking at his computer screen. "No. That's fine."

"Excellent. British Airways Flight 48 leaves Vancouver International Airport at 5:00 p.m. Pacific Standard Time. You arrive in London the next day at 10:30 a.m. You have a bit of a wait before leaving London at 7:00 p.m. the same day and arriving in Addis Ababa at 6:30 a.m. Your next flight leaves at 10:00 a.m. and arrives at Goma at 10:20 a.m. We will arrange for a driver to pick you up at the airport."

"Sounds good," Michael replied, though when Simone mentioned a driver Laurent immediately came to mind.

"I will send your tickets via email immediately. Bon voyage, Michael." She paused. "Et bonne chance."

CHAPTER 13

CHARLIE BOYKINS AND BART JOHNSTONE were two portly loggers who had grown up in Forks, on the Olympic Peninsula, surrounded by giant trees that they cut down. The forests fell and eventually the environmentalists came to town, talking guff about spotted owls and salamanders. The lumber jobs petered out and Charlie and Bart found themselves retired.

So much had changed, but by God, Charlie still loved to fish. His knees were gimpy but standing in a stream with the water flowing around his legs made him feel young. Of course, the goddamned government was trying to take away the pleasure of fishing too. Licenses for this and that, seasonal restrictions, stream closures, daily quotas, catch-and-release rules, certain species protected. Jesus H. Christ, he just wanted to put a line in the water. "The next thing ya know," Charlie liked to say, "the government will be telling you how much butter to put in the frying pan with your rainbow trout."

Charlie and Bart had a secret spot, one where the yuppie fly fishermen of Seattle never ventured. One where the fish still rose to the fly on a misty morning. The stream was always quiet. Charlie laughed. It was his way of getting back, just a little bit, at the government he felt had let him down. Seattle might have bought up the whole watershed and closed it to public access, but a few old-timers still stayed in touch with their favorite hangouts.

There were bull trout in some of the streams above the reservoir. Charlie could wax poetic about the allure of the bull trout. The government made his small act of rebellion even sweeter by placing the bull trout on the list of endangered species. "Endangered species, my ass," he'd say, "there's thousands of those damn fish out there, but federal bore-o-crats cain't see them from their cushy offices in the city."

Charlie wore his old falling suspenders, holding up a pair of filthy blue jeans under the hip waders that he used against the chill of the cold, clear water. Charlie and Bart were having a slow day. Bart had a couple of trout that were below the legal size but they'd fry up nice and tasty anyway. Charlie was being shut out.

"I'm freezing my ass off here," Charlie complained.

"Wimp!" Bart replied.

"Aw hell, nothin's biting anyways. I'm gonna walk down to the lake for a smoke in the sun."

"Sure. Piss off. I'll keep working on catchin' us a decent meal."

Charlie set his rod down on the bank, grabbed the coffee thermos from his pack, and set off, splashing down the stream. It was a hell of a lot easier than slogging through the forest. He soon emerged from the woods and stood overlooking the gorgeous vista of the reservoir.

It was almost too easy. Michael pedaled along like an ordinary cyclist. The morning sky was light although the sun had not yet risen above the peaks to the east. In roughly twenty-four hours he would be on a different continent and could well be one of the most wanted men in the world. The potential consequences of his actions were not lost on him, but he believed that he had weighed the moral implications and reached a decision that he could live with. His plan would terrify some people, yes, but cause no physical harm. And weighed against those modest costs were life-changing improvements for millions of people.

Michael retraced the route he'd taken before. Highway I-90 out to North Bend, and then the road along the northern side of the reservoir. His legs felt heavy as he pedaled, as if the gravity of what he was about to do was manifesting itself physically. He could smell his own sweat, not the clean, fresh scent of exercise but the acrid, malodorous sweat of nerves and tension. There were no excuses now, no alibis, no fast-talking stories to be swiftly invented and embellished. He was about to commit a serious federal felony.

He reached the turnoff. There was no traffic, so he darted down the road until he saw the Iron Horse trail marker. He didn't want to be seen here today by anyone. He wanted to get in, do it, get out, and get home.

The trail was deserted. There didn't appear to be any fresh tracks, human or otherwise. Michael was on edge. Maybe over the edge. For a moment, he felt that he no longer knew himself, and it occurred to him that maybe Maria and Dom were right, that maybe he was suffering from post-traumatic stress. But he shook his misgivings away; he was committed now.

He found the spot where the old logging road wound down to the reservoir. Time compressed. Once he could see the reservoir, he dismounted and leaned the bike against the same magnificent Douglas fir.

He didn't even bother to remove his helmet, but he did pull on another pair of thin surgical gloves to avoid fingerprints. He unbuckled the straps on the panniers, lifted a fleece jacket and a rain jacket out and unwrapped the jugs of perc. He tucked a plastic bottle under each arm and ran like a running back through the shrubs down to the water's edge. He paused, placed one jug on the gravel, and glanced skyward to search for the surveillance plane. Nothing but blue sky dotted with a few clouds, for now. If Michael went ahead, there'd be no turning back, no putting the genie back in the bottle.

He unscrewed the cap, cut the seal with his jackknife and froze. He couldn't breathe. He felt paralyzed. He thought of the children he was trying to help, and life returned to his limbs. He poured the first gallon of the exquisitely toxic perc into the reservoir that provided drinking water to the city of Seattle.

The perc was clear and merged with the water. It had a sickly sweet smell that made Michael instinctively hold his breath. He bent down and rinsed the jug out several times. His quadriceps were tight from the ride and complained about being in a crouch. He repeated the process with the second jug, then stood, stretched, and felt a strange combination of awe and horror at what he had just done. His stomach felt tight, as if he might throw up.

After returning to his bike, he left the trail and bushwhacked through the understory for two or three minutes until he found a hiding place for the perc jugs and plastic gloves under a salal bush. A fine for littering was the least of his worries. He closed the bike panniers and began his journey back to Seattle.

Charlie was just enjoying the view and puffing on a Marlboro when a man burst out of the forest and ran down to the edge of the reservoir. Charlie rubbed his eyes. He and Bart had never seen anyone else in here. Shit, he thought, the binoculars are back upstream in my pack. The man was quite a distance away but was clearly wearing a bicycle helmet and shorts. It looked as though he was rinsing out or filling up a couple of large jugs of some sort. Then he jogged back into the forest. Maybe he was a government bureaucrat, carrying out some kind of goddamned test on the water or a science experiment. Either way, Charlie wasn't about to introduce himself. He turned around, trying to minimize his own splashing sounds, and reentered the forest, walking back upstream to where Bart had doubled his output, catching two more undersized trout.

"Bart," Charlie hissed, "there's a guy down there."

Bart frowned. "What?"

"Shhh. There's a guy down at the lake."

"Who is he?"

"I dunno, but he could be with the government. It looks like he's taking water samples or something. We gotta get outta here."

"Aww, shit. I'm just getting warmed up. The rainbows are starting to bite."

"Bart, if we get caught here, we're up shit creek without a fishing rod."

"Come on. What's this guy going to do, arrest us?"

"Maybe. Remember awhile back on the news, they said you could be fined something like ten grand for trespassing in Seattle's watershed. And we're not just trespassin,' we're fishin' too. Double whammy."

"Shee-it. Okay, let's get outta here."

Charlie and Bart packed up their gear, returned to their truck, put the trout on some ice in a repurposed beer cooler and headed back to Sara's Coffee Shop in Kent, where they routinely spent their afternoons shooting the breeze with other retired loggers, fishermen, and farmers. Their brush with the law was about to transform into an unexpected bonanza.

CHAPTER 14

MICHAEL'S BIKE RIDE HOME WAS SLOWER, the adrenaline replaced by foreboding. He was going to have to rush to get ready, say a painful goodbye to Maria, and catch his train to Vancouver. He put his bike back in the garage where he always kept it, taking out his water bottles, wallet, and phone but leaving the panniers still attached. The garage was a mess. It hadn't been cleaned for years.

He packed his duffel bag and said a quick, tearful goodbye to Maria. They were both overcome by emotion but so traumatized that they were unable to articulate their feelings or even look each other in the eye. Maria realized that Michael had changed irreversibly. They no longer wanted the same things. Michael was exhausted, exhilarated, and plagued by guilt. He took an Uber to the Amtrak station, alone. The train ride was uneventful, although Michael had an uncomfortable moment when the Canadian customs agents boarded the train at the border.

Michael disembarked at Heathrow Airport outside London. Announcements on the public-address system came in a dozen languages. London, once the lily-white center of empire, had come a long way. Heathrow was a miniature version of the global village and everybody was in a hurry. Michael collided with a short brown-skinned man pulling an immense wheeled suitcase.

"Sorry," Michael said instinctively, although the collision was not his fault. He smiled, the man smiled back, and each of them went on their way.

The customs agent was a rotund Sikh with a blue turban and a handlebar mustache. Michael focused on keeping his hands as steady as in surgery as he passed over his passport. The agent looked Michael up and down, and then squinted at the computer screen. "What's the purpose of your visit?"

Delivering a virtual bomb to the government of the United States. "I'm just going to do a little bit of shopping. My next flight isn't scheduled to leave for about seven hours."

"What do you intend to purchase?"

"Nothing specific. I'm going to browse through the used bookstores on Charing Cross Road. See if I can find any gems."

"Very well. Please be sure that you return at least two hours in advance of your scheduled departure. By the way, sir—" He paused, leaned toward Michael and spoke softly as though imparting a secret. Michael unintentionally held his breath. "It will be very much faster if you take the Heathrow Express. This train is much faster than the tube."

"Thank you." Michael exhaled. "I appreciate the tip."

Michael strode through the wide entrance hall, following signs to the Heathrow Express. He purchased a ticket and joined hundreds of people who were dragging luggage onto the train. The seats filled quickly, but Michael found standing helped ground him.

Michael exited the Heathrow Express, which had whisked him downtown in just seventeen minutes. The Paddington Tube Station was about a ten-minute walk away. It was a moderately cloudy day, but he wore a baseball hat and sunglasses and tried to act normal. He forked over the metro fare, descended the stairs, and waited for a train on the Hammersmith and City Line. He was headed for Barbican Station. The tube trip chewed up another sixteen minutes.

He rode up several long escalators from the depths of the underground to the city's surface. The streets were jammed with traffic. Although he looked like an ordinary tourist, he wasn't shopping or looking for used bookstores. He was looking for the City of

London's Barbican Library, where he would find computers with free public access to the internet.

The Barbican Library was London's newest and largest. Michael took off his sunglasses and entered the library, where he put on a cheap pair of reading glasses. There were dozens of computer terminals, a feature that seemed to attract as many people as the books themselves. Today there was a short lineup of young people waiting for their turn. The line moved quickly, and soon he was at the front. Then an uninviting wooden chair with faded orange upholstery worn smooth by a diverse array of derrieres was vacated.

Michael sat down and clicked his agreement with the notice warning patrons not to use the terminal for viewing pornography, sending spam, or other illicit activities. He had fifteen minutes, according to a pop-up notice, before the computer would automatically shut down and restart so that another patron could be served.

He opened a browser and went to the Hotmail website. It took less than a minute to sign up for a free email account, with the address endpovertynow@hotmail.com. Michael typed in fake information—name, address, password, name of favorite pet, etc. He would never use this address again.

He began typing the first of three emails that he had memorized, including the email addresses that he needed. There would be no paper trail. The first email was to the Seattle Water Utility.

> *To: info@seattlewaterutility.wa.gov*
> *Re: Urgent Warning: Contamination of Seattle water supply*
>
> *Please be advised that within the last twenty-four hours, the Chester Morse Reservoir was contaminated by perchloroethylene.*

Michael reread the note. The recipient, probably a receptionist or intern in the communications department, would pass it on to his or her supervisor and the firestorm would grow from there. He clicked the send button.

The second email was equally terse.

> To: *breakingnews@cnn.com, newsdesk@foxnews.com*
> Re: *Contamination of Seattle Water Supply*
>
> *The main water supply of the City of Seattle has been contaminated by a highly toxic industrial chemical called perchloroethylene, also referred to as perc or PCE. Exposure to PCE can cause respiratory problems, liver damage, kidney damage, birth defects, and cancer.*

Michael couldn't believe that he was actually doing this. But he'd already taken the big steps, and now he was compelled to continue. Deep down, beneath the fear and the nagging doubts, he still thought he was doing the right thing. The third email was the most important in terms of attaining his ultimate objective, which was saving lives, not sowing panic.

> To: *president@whitehouse.gov*
> Re: *The Contamination of the City of Seattle's Water Supply*
>
> *The Chester Morse Reservoir, the main water supply for the four million residents of Seattle, has been deliberately contaminated with the industrial chemical perchloroethylene. The level of contamination was carefully calculated to avoid reaching concentrations that could cause either acute or chronic health effects from consuming the water. In other words, there is no danger to human health.*
>
> *However, this event is a warning. The next action to contaminate the drinking water of a major American city will result in significant mortality and morbidity, unless the following commitments are made and implemented:*

The Government of the United States must announce,
within the next forty-eight hours, the creation of a major
new initiative to combat poverty in Africa's poorest nations.
Key elements of this new initiative should focus on ensur-
ing access to clean water, educating girls, and preventing or
treating the diseases that cause the unnecessary deaths of mil-
lions of children under the age of five each year.

The Government of the United States must publicly
allocate $25 billion in additional funds over and above
existing foreign aid and debt relief programs, each year for
the next four years, for a total of $100 billion. The money
must be targeted exclusively to alleviating poverty and dis-
ease in Africa.

If these actions are announced, we will take no further
steps and we will never publicly connect the contamination
of water supplies with the $100 billion African initiative.

Michael hit send. There. He had done it. The infusion of $100 billion over the next four years into a war on global poverty could change the course of human history. It would be like a Marshall Plan for African countries. Millions of children's lives could be saved, changing their fate, improving the prospects for their families, communities and countries. The accelerated progress in combating poverty and disease would provide a powerful antidote to the wretched conditions producing legions of desperate terrorists who believe they have nothing to lose. The outlay of $100 billion would provide a much-needed boost for America's flagging reputation. And the cost, in relative terms, would be minimal. One hundred billion dollars was a big number to most people but a small number in the U.S. budget. Michael fervently hoped that they wouldn't call his bluff. He would never be capable of following through on the threat that he'd made.

Michael had four minutes left before his time at the computer terminal expired. He suppressed an urge to drop a quick note to

Maria. Instead, he signed off early. He stood, took one last look around, and saw that a short, stout woman was standing several paces away, peering at him intently through thick-lensed, black-framed glasses. Michael felt his heart accelerate and his breathing turn shallow as he pushed back the chair. She was walking directly toward him. He stood, rooted to the spot, unable to move. She stopped, close enough to reach out and touch him. She couldn't possibly be police, thought Michael, but she could be a librarian.

"All done, sir?" she asked.

"Yes. All done." Michael repeated her words, thrusting his hands deep into his pant pockets to stop their shaking.

"Thanks." She pulled the chair back further so that she could step past Michael to take her turn at the computer. She was just another library user.

PART II

The

DEADLINE

CHAPTER 15

NANCY BRADSHAW, A COMMUNICATIONS ASSISTANT with the Seattle Metropolitan Water Utility, was nursing a decaf chai latte, trying to make it last the morning. Before the internet came along, she answered phones, opened mail, and typed a few letters each day. Now she also had to deal with hundreds of emails, trying to weed out spam, viruses, and lunatics. The latest was from some kooks calling themselves "End Poverty Now" who claimed to have poisoned the Seattle water supply.

Yeah right, she thought. There were one or two of these every month. The protocol was that Nancy would forward the email to her boss, Communications Manager Alistair Gryzbowski, and make contact by telephone as well, so that the threat didn't fall into a virtual black hole. Big Al would follow the rigorous, paranoid process put in place post–9/11. There were three thick binders on the shelf behind Nancy detailing the new procedure for responding to terrorist threats. She'd skimmed the first one, but it was full of acronyms, tech talk, and Byzantine diagrams. Boring, she'd thought, and left it to gather dust. She dialed Big Al's extension.

It rang three times. Big Al never answered quickly. It was how he asserted his importance. "Alistair Gryzbowski, communications manager."

"Yo, Big Al."

"Nancy." She could hear the distaste that Al felt toward all of his subordinates.

"Got another nutjob for ya. Says they dumped poison in the rez."

"The rez?"

Duh. "The Chester Morse Reservoir." You know, where our water comes from.

"Did the threat arrive via fax, email, or telephone?"

"Email."

"Please forward it to me immediately."

"Done."

Nancy hung up and groaned as her phone rang before she'd even placed the handset back on the charger.

"Seattle Water, Nancy Bradshaw speaking. How can I help you?"

"Hello, Nancy, it's Ariel Santana calling from CNN. We have a report that the City of Seattle's water supply has been contaminated. Can you confirm this for us?"

Whoa, thought Nancy. That was fast. Apply the protocol. "I'm sorry. You'll have to speak to my supervisor. Would you like me to transfer you now?"

"Yes, please."

"One moment." Nancy smiled at the thought of blindsiding Big Al with a call from CNN.

"Alistair Gryzbowski, communications manager."

"Me again."

"What is it now?"

"Ms. Ariel Santana from CNN on line three."

"CNN?"

"Apparently our whack jobs have been busy spreading the word about their little prank."

"Hell's bells." Big Al looked out his window. As a communications grad, he'd always wanted to be on CNN. It would blow his wife's mind. Maybe get her off his back about his stalled career path. He shook his head. The public would panic if CNN ran a "poisoned water" story without a calming response from the utility. Despite his yearning for fame, Big Al knew that he had to kick it upstairs. This was out of his league. "Get her name and phone number and tell her someone will call her back in a few minutes."

"Okey-doke," said Nancy. She cut the line to Big Al and picked up the extension where Ariel was listening to the soporific classical music inflicted upon callers on hold.

"Hello, Ms. Santana, it's Nancy again. Mr. Gryzbowski is tied up in a meeting right now but someone should be able to call you back in a few minutes."

"Nancy, have you heard anything about the Chester Morse Reservoir being poisoned?" Ariel was well aware that the story couldn't run without some kind of confirmation from the authorities. However, even an unofficial source, like Nancy, would suffice, so she was appealing to Nancy's sense of sisterhood, giving her a chance to bypass The Man.

"I can neither confirm nor deny that report." Nancy quoted the words from the cheat sheet she kept on her desk by the phone. Sisterhood or not, she needed this job.

"All right. Let your boss know that the story will run as an unconfirmed breaking news report at the top of the hour if he doesn't call me back."

Ariel gave Nancy her cellphone number and hung up. Standard empty threat. Worked often enough to warrant trying it again. Ariel tapped her fingernails on the wall of her cubicle in CNN's Seattle office. She knew that the likelihood of the email from endpovertynow being accurate was next to nothing. But journalism was like a lottery. Every day she chased the wildest leads, the longest odds, hoping for a break. And then she'd have to fight off the buzzards, senior reporters with no qualms about scavenging stories and stealing the glory from the up-and-comers like her who did all the legwork.

She picked up her phone and dialed. "Hey Jim, Ariel here. I may need a camera crew and a van sometime in the next half-hour or so." Jim Dunlop was the van man, the dispatcher who controlled CNN's camera crews in Seattle.

"Headed for?"

"The Chester Morse Reservoir."

"A floater?"

"No, nothing like that. Just another wild goose chase. Don't hold your breath." Ariel played it down, worried that Jim was tipping off the senior guys whenever she called in with a hot story.

"All right. I'll see if I can line something up for you."

Ariel had already sent an email to endpovertynow@hotmail.com asking them to contact her immediately. Now she started frantically Googling the phrase. No website, no Twitter feed, no Facebook page, no Instagram account. Nothing at all on social media. What the hell? A nonexistent group claiming to have carried out a terrorist attack?

At the Seattle Metropolitan Water Authority, Big Al was working the phones, implementing the protocol for alleged water contamination events. He called the engineering department, asking them to switch the water supply on a precautionary basis so that Seattle residents would receive all their drinking water from the Tolt River Reservoir. He phoned the water quality testing lab, informing them of the need for urgent sampling and analysis. He called the Seattle Police Department, notifying them of the threat and the possibility that it had been carried out. He called the Washington State Department of Health, putting them on notice that there was a potential problem with Seattle's drinking water.

Finally, Big Al called the regional office of the Environmental Protection Agency, the lead federal agency in protecting American water supplies from physical, chemical, and biological attacks.

The investigative wheels were in motion while Michael slept fitfully on a crowded airplane high above sub-Saharan Africa.

CHAPTER 16

THE WHITE HOUSE, Department of Homeland Security, Pentagon, National Security Agency, FBI, CIA, and other government agencies have to filter through hundreds of threats, demands, pleas, conspiracy theories, false accusations, false confessions, and other deluded ravings daily. These missives come from all over the world. Letters, phone calls, faxes, emails, tweets, blogs, even homemade video recordings. Each federal agency has employees, usually receptionists or similar frontline staff, specifically assigned to monitor the "nut lines" and "c-mail"—emails from crazies, cranks, and crackpots. Some of the communications are anonymous but the majority of correspondents feel no inhibitions about signing their real names, guaranteeing their immediate addition to no-fly lists, watch lists, and various federal law enforcement databases.

If the initial recipient of an incoming communication feels there is even a shred of plausibility in the threat, then it is routed to the FBI's domestic terrorism unit and relayed to the Department of Homeland Security. It triggers an immediate credibility assessment—under federal supervision but conducted by local law enforcement authorities. If the threat is deemed viable, then several federal agencies leap swiftly into action. Only in the rarest of cases, if there is solid information, an imminent situation, and a genuine threat to national security, does it result in a presidential briefing.

Because of this, there was no immediate response to the email sent to the White House by endpovertynow@hotmail.com. The email just sat in an inbox, unread, waiting.

Although the events in Seattle were not yet on the radar screen at 1600 Pennsylvania Avenue, Big Al's phone calls set off a ripple effect of communication up the bureaucratic chain of command at the Environmental Protection Agency. Cassie Harden-Hernandez was its head. Democrats had attacked her appointment two years before, labeling her an industry flack and a token woman. At the same time, there was a firestorm of opposition among the Republican old boys. As far as they were concerned, Cassie had three strikes against her—female, Hispanic, and a self-described environmentalist. In fact, Cassie wasn't Hispanic, despite her appearance and her hyphenated last name. Despite the initial uproar, Cassie had gradually earned grudging bipartisan respect for being tough but fair.

She was constantly swamped. Yesterday, Sunday, she'd worked from dawn until dusk catching up on the tsunami of paperwork so that the week could start with a clean slate. The days when weekends were for hiking and skiing were a fond memory, ended by her promotion to America's top environmental cop. Happily married, she'd heard the groundless rumors on Capitol Hill that she was romantically involved with the president and had slept her way to the top. She also knew that her nickname, probably propagated by the same slimy sources, was Hard-on Hernandez. These insults made Cassie even more determined to do her job with unimpeachable integrity.

Her cellphone chimed. Abdullah Ali, her executive assistant, and the only person Cassie knew who worked longer hours than she did, was on the line. If he was calling her while out on a falafel-hunting mission, then it had to be important. She sighed audibly and answered. "Hi Abby."

"Cassie, sorry to bother you."

"It's okay, what's up?"

"Bad news. CNN is reporting a possible chemical attack on Seattle's drinking water. The local utility just notified our regional office about receiving an email indicating that perchloroethylene has been dumped into Chester Morse Reservoir."

"Any confirmation?"

"Not yet. The utility has taken water samples, and their lab is running tests as we speak."

"I want those test results ASAP, and I want a copy of the email sent to the utility."

"I'll text you if I hear anything before I get back to the office."

Cassie switched on the flatscreen TV in her office that was permanently tuned to CNN. After a few minutes of international news coverage, the news anchor mentioned that they would be going to Seattle for a live update on a breaking story. An attractive young reporter stood in front of a forested backdrop.

"CNN has obtained an unconfirmed report that the main source of Seattle's drinking water, the Chester Morse Reservoir, has been intentionally contaminated with a hazardous chemical called perchloroethylene, or PCE. CNN is seeking confirmation and further details from local and federal authorities, who have thus far refused to comment."

Cassie exhaled loudly. The possibility of an attack on a major American city's water supply was something she'd been briefed on during her first week on the job. The day after being sworn in, she'd read almost a dozen black binders filled with terse memos on everything from the disappearing glaciers in Glacier National Park to flame retardants in women's breastmilk. A planet in crisis. Pretty bleak reading material. She tried not to worry about attacks on America's drinking water but it was one of many potential disasters that gave her nightmares.

Ten minutes later Abby was back with two falafel pitas, his with extra hot sauce. He tucked a cloth napkin between his neck and shirt to protect his silk tie from dripping tahini. Abby was a natty dresser partial to tailored suits that fit his slender build.

Cassie wolfed down her food, then paced around, thinking about how to respond if the threat was confirmed. She set her phone to buzz for incoming emails and placed it in the front pocket of her pantsuit. Unfortunately, she was getting so many emails that it felt like a vibrator. She put the setting back on silent and sat down at her desk. It would be hard to concentrate on other problems until the claim of an attack was validated or debunked.

After two long hours, an email arrived from the Seattle Metropolitan Water Utility with a header that shouted CONFIDENTIAL TEST RESULTS. The body of the email simply read *Please see attachment.* Cassie hit download and the PDF popped open on her screen. She scrolled down past a useless cover page. The second page explained the abbreviations, units, and measurement techniques involved in chemical testing of municipal water supplies. More scrolling down. On the third page, the magic numbers appeared. The tests confirmed the presence of significant levels of perchloroethylene in the Chester Morse Reservoir. One sample showed 6 parts per billion (ppb), while one showed 10 ppb and another 11 ppb. All three exceeded the EPA's maximum acceptable levels for safe drinking water, and there was no effective way to remove the perc from the reservoir or filter it out at the water treatment facility.

"Holy shit." This wasn't an empty threat. For an American public permanently on edge about terrorist attacks, stress levels were about to jack into the stratosphere.

"So CNN's right?" Abby asked.

"Sure looks like it. Tests on three separate samples confirm perchloroethylene contamination."

"Stormy waters ahead." Abby reveled in bad puns.

"Yup. This could turn into a real interagency cockfight. FBI, CIA, DHS, they're all going to want a piece of this. I need you to call CNN, track down that reporter, and find out everything she knows."

"On it. Cassie, I'm not a chemist. How poisonous is this stuff?"

"PCE is highly toxic, but there are two pieces of good news, to use that phrase loosely. The first is that those levels of perc aren't going to kill anybody in the short term. They're too low."

"Right. Unless there's a flood of car accidents during the rush to buy bottled water." Abby smiled.

"Not funny. The second bit of good news is that Seattle has reservoirs on two rivers, the Cedar and the Tolt. So far, it looks like only one reservoir has been contaminated. The local water utility is taking steps to ensure that all residents are being served by water from the Tolt. It's the public perception of the risks that will be harder to manage."

"What are you going to do?"

"I'm tempted to head for Seattle right away. Then I could oversee the investigation myself. But first I need to get the word out so that the rest of the government doesn't get blindsided. Can you book us overnight flights and hotel rooms downtown for at least a couple of nights?"

"Will do."

"And give our Northwest Regional Office a heads-up that we're coming. We'll need to borrow an office." Cassie picked up her phone and sent a quick text to the directors of the CIA, the FBI, the acting head of Homeland Security, and the new director of National Intelligence. It was faster, and a hell of a lot less painful, than having to talk to the pompous pricks.

Cassie's message simply said, "Confirmed contamination event at Seattle watershed. PCE > EPA drinking water safety standards. No immediate health risks. Suggest conference call at 4:00 p.m. today. Call-in details to follow."

Within seconds, her phone was beeping and vibrating as the men in charge of protecting America from terrorists responded with a barrage of texts and emails.

"Have you advised the White House? We need to get to the president before he sees this on the news." Billy Joe Stryder, the director of the Central Intelligence Agency, was acutely aware that his position hinged on keeping the president informed, as the failure to do so had resulted in the swift dismissal of his predecessor.

"Raise terror alert to Code Red, national and now!" Roger Osborne's message sounded almost enthusiastic, as though he was stoked about the prospect of leaping into action. Things had been quiet since his appointment to head of Homeland Security. If the level of perceived threat to America jumped, so would his budget and relative importance in the administration's pecking order.

"Anyone claiming responsibility? Any suspects?" Randall Tierney, the veteran director of the FBI, focused on the investigation.

The messages were edgy, aggressive. Knowledge was power in the intelligence community and these men didn't like it when others had information before they did. Let them stew, Cassie thought. Moments later, her phone rang.

"Cassie, it's Roger Osborne. Any updates?

"No." Not since I emailed you forty-five seconds ago, Cassie thought.

"Who'll be leading the investigation?"

"I will."

Her blunt assertion of control made him pause. "Have you spoken to the president?" he asked.

"Not yet. We just confirmed that Seattle's water is contaminated. Although preliminary tests indicate perc is present at levels that violate EPA's standards pursuant to the Safe Drinking Water Act, the level of the chemical is not an acute danger."

"I don't understand—you said the level exceeded national drinking water safety standards. It must be dangerous."

"Those standards are based on exposures to toxic substances arising from cumulative consumption over the long-term. You wouldn't want to drink water contaminated with PCE at these concentrations for years or months, but for a few days it's unlikely to hurt anybody. We're going to craft our key messages for the media carefully on this one, play it low key, reassure the public that there's no serious threat to their health or well-being."

"Reassure them? It's a terrorist strike on our homeland! This whole country is about to go on red alert."

"Why? There's no immediate danger. With all due respect, you'll just create panic in Seattle and paranoia everywhere else."

Cassie paused, digesting what Osborne was saying. "Who said anything about this being the work of terrorists?"

"Poisoning a big city's water supply is an act of terrorism. Ergo the act was committed by terrorists. It's obvious. Our country continues to be assaulted by radicals for whom there are no boundaries, no rules, no morality."

Spare me the speech, Cassie thought. "I think we should hold off on the red alert for a few hours to gather some evidence before we jump to conclusions about the nature of the attack."

"That's the president's call. We also need to notify the Federal Emergency Management Authority. ASAP."

"Okay. You inform FEMA. I've got to go. Talk to you at four." Cassie hung up before Osborne could pontificate any further.

She sat down and made a quick list of the leads that needed to be followed up. The main crime scene at the Chester Morse Reservoir. The email to the utility, which could be tracked and analyzed. How CNN picked up the story so fast. The source of the PCE. The organization End Poverty Now, which she'd never heard of. The local police would have to do a door-to-door sweep of the surrounding area to try to dig up eyewitnesses. And Cassie had a potential ace up her sleeve in the form of a comprehensive database of attacks on watersheds and water treatment systems across America, compiled by the EPA over recent decades. If there was any kind of similarity or connection to a previous crime, she was best situated to find it.

"Abby?"

"Yes?"

"Can you get Seattle's police chief on the phone?"

"Will do."

Abby worked his usual magic, and Cassie was soon patched through to Seattle.

"Jack Gilhooley here. I'm on the speakerphone and I've got two of my bureau commanders with me—Assistant Chief Jim Metz, who looks after emergency preparedness, and Assistant Chief Clark Pierce, who supervises investigations and major crimes."

"Good morning, gentlemen. Thanks for taking the time to brief me. Why don't you sketch where the investigation is at so far? Then I'll give you a sense of what the federal involvement will look like."

Chief Gilhooley spoke first, in a low soothing baritone. "We're obviously treating this as a major crime. We've mobilized as many crime scene techs, detectives, and patrol officers as we can muster. Out of a total of 1,200 law enforcement officers with the Seattle PD, we've already assigned approximately 200 personnel to this case. Jim, over to you."

"Thanks, Chief." Metz began speaking quickly, as though worried that he'd be cut off. "The Seattle Water Utility has switched sources so that the entire city is being served by the Tolt River Reservoir. That limited the public's exposure to the contaminated water, although the utility isn't one hundred percent clear when the attack happened. We've put out a joint statement with the city's public health department reassuring citizens that their health is not at risk. However, several hospitals are already reporting a surge in cases of gastrointestinal illness. Retailers are being swamped by consumers buying large quantities of bottled water. Some isolated incidents of panicky people and the odd fistfight but no major chaos. Yet."

"Thank you. And the investigation? Any suspects or hot leads?"

"No. It's early." Assistant Chief Clark Pierce had a voice made for radio—deep, calm, and resonant. "We have two helicopters and two spotter planes currently sweeping the reservoir and surrounding watershed area. Within the hour we'll have four boats on the water with dive teams. Our efforts are being hampered by heavy rain, which is limiting visibility."

"The rain will also erase tracks and other potential evidence," Cassie said.

"Maybe. But our crime scene techs are used to dealing with the wet stuff. If rain always erased all the evidence, Seattle would be the crime capital of America." Pierce chuckled briefly. "The Chester Morse Reservoir is located in a fairly remote area, but we have officers talking to farmers, gas station attendants, coffee shop servers, and the like to see if anyone saw anything out of the ordinary in recent days. We're also contacting media outlets and calling for eyewitnesses."

"All right. Sounds like you have the bases covered. Please notify me of any significant developments right away. Call me on my cell and call my EA if you get my voicemail. Federal intelligence agencies will be meeting later today to discuss how we can be of assistance, and as soon as I have details I'll get back to you. The Centers for Disease Control could be helpful in assuaging public concern about potential health effects, so I'll get someone there to connect with you."

"Gilhooley here. Do you have any information indicating that this is an act of terrorism, as opposed to a local crime?"

"Not at this time, no. But we need to keep an open mind."

"This is already a huge media story out here. If there's a terror angle, it'll be gigantic, and we'll be grateful for all the help the federal government can provide."

Abdullah popped his head into Cassie's office. His wide eyes and raised eyebrows told her that he had important information.

"Thank you for the briefing, and good luck. I've got to go, but as I said, keep me in the loop. I'm flying to Seattle tonight so I'll probably meet you tomorrow." Cassie ended the call but did not put the phone down, tapping it against her jaw as she waited for Abby to speak.

"The White House is on lines one and two. On line one, the president's chief of staff, Jeremy Chan, wants a briefing on the situation. On line two, an intern with the White House correspondence unit apparently has new information related to the Seattle attack."

"I'll take the intern first. Ask Chan if he wants to hold for a minute or have me call him back. And Abby, can you put together a dossier on PCE for me? What it's used for, where it comes from, where it ends up, and a comprehensive review of the short- and long-term health effects."

"Okay."

"Thanks." Things were moving fast. She pressed the button for line two. "Cassie Harden-Hernandez."

"Good afternoon, ma'am. Katie Cornett over at the White House. Just wanted to let you know that we received a detailed email earlier today claiming responsibility for the contamination of the Seattle water supply. There's no name included but it's from an email address called endpovertynow@hotmail.com And they're threatening to do it again unless the U.S. announces $100 billion in funding to tackle poverty in Africa.

Cassie sat back in her chair, silenced by the nature of the demand and the dollar figure.

"Ma'am?" the intern asked.

"I need you to forward that email to me right now. Do you have any other information related to the events in Seattle?"

"No, ma'am. Not yet."

"If you receive any further emails please notify me immediately. And thanks—good work."

Cassie quickly read the email when it hit her inbox. Holy shit, she thought. One hundred billion dollars in four years. And the threat of a follow-up attack within forty-eight hours. Six hours had already elapsed since the email was sent.

CHAPTER 17

WITHIN AN HOUR, a meeting was convened in the White House Situation Room, built by President Kennedy after the failed Bay of Pigs invasion that many in the intelligence community had blamed on a lack of real-time communications. The latest reno had added six large flatscreen monitors for secure video conferences and replaced the echo-inducing mahogany wall panels with fabric coverings.

Cassie had been to the White House several times but never to the Situation Room. Arrayed around boardroom table were ten of the most powerful people in the world, including the president, his chief of staff, the secretary of defense, the secretary of state, the attorney general, the national security advisor, and the intelligence directors that Cassie had been in contact with earlier. The only woman in the room besides Cassie was Eleanor Stein, the secretary of state. One of the men approached Cassie, bent down, and began to whisper in her left ear. "Ms. Harden-Hernandez, Billy Joe Stryder here. We haven't had the pleasure of working together but it looks like we're about to. Don't get in my way and we'll get along fine."

Cassie anticipated this kind of crap from the CIA. "Hi Billy Joe, remember Presidential Decision Directive 63?"

He straightened up. She didn't wait for the wheels to stop turning. "The EPA is designated as the lead agency responsible for protecting the American water supply from physical, chemical, and biological attacks."

"Out of date. PDD 63 was issued in 1998. Before 9/11," Stryder smirked.

"Ah, yes, but the EPA's role in safeguarding the water supplies of the nation was reinforced by Title IV of the Public Health Security and Bioterrorism Preparedness and Response Act." Cassie paused. "After 9/11."

"Come on, Ms. Harden-Hernandez. This is a terrorism investigation, not a case about spiked trees, smuggled parrots, or leaky pipes. You may be in on this meeting, but you're out of your league." Stryder narrowed his hooded eyes, and his gleaming shaved head added to his air of menace. He strode back to his seat before Cassie could respond. He might have been a good ol' boy from rural Texas but he wore the finest tailored Italian suits that money could buy. Today it was a charcoal Armani, with narrow lapels and a tailored fit.

The president, wearing his trademark blue poplin dress shirt with the sleeves rolled up, started the meeting promptly. He believed he was still handsome, although the years in the oval office had deepened the wrinkles, pushed back the hairline, and forced him to use hair dye. He was notoriously impatient. "Ladies and gentlemen, we are taking this attack on America, and the threat of a future attack, very seriously. I've decided that the FBI will coordinate the investigation. Personnel from the CIA, White House, National Security Agency, Department of Homeland Security, and the EPA will form the investigative team. I want the director of each of those agencies to be part of a task force that will hold meetings at the beginning and end of each day. I want all briefings, memos, and notes generated by the task force to be shared with the heads of the U.S. Marshal's Service, the State Department's Bureau of Diplomatic Security, U.S. Customs, the Secret Service, and the Department of Defense. Let me be perfectly clear. Our intelligence and law enforcement agencies have botched the investigations of Oklahoma City, 9/11, and more mass shootings than I can count. You can't allow any leads or any suspects to slip through your fingers this time. We can't put America through another tragic catastrophe. Not under my watch."

The president was tired, as usual. No human being could do the job properly and not be perpetually exhausted. Unlike some of his predecessors, he governed by gut instinct. "Now I thought we had top-of-the-line security in our watersheds. So would someone please explain to me how terrorists were able to drive up and dump a truckload of poison in the water supply of one of America's greatest cities?"

"Mr. President, that watershed is 90,000 acres. There are two security guards at the dam, video cameras at the water treatment plant, and the perimeter is partially fenced where there is road access. There's also periodic aerial surveillance," replied Randall Tierney, veteran director of the FBI.

"Why can't the greatest country on earth, the richest country in history, protect its water supplies?" the president spat. "What good is a partial fence? Terrorists can just walk around the end, dump their poison, and go home? Is Seattle an outlier in terms of its weakness? What about New York? Washington? Los Angeles?"

Stryder jumped in. "Sir, every major urban area in America is vulnerable, and the jihadis know it. If the terrorists had used a different, deadlier chemical, or struck a different part of the water supply system closer to the end users, then we could be facing a large number of civilian casualties. The only way to alleviate the threat and protect Americans is to catch the goddamned maniacs who did this. Even if there are multiple cells operating on our soil, we'll catch them and make them tell us what we need to know. Throw the book at them, set an example, discourage others from taking similar actions."

"Cassie, do you agree?"

"There are chemicals hundreds of times more toxic than perchloroethylene. But I'm very concerned by the threat of a follow-up attack and by the prospect of copycat events. If we don't nail those responsible pretty quickly, we could be facing a wave of water supply poisonings."

Tierney was shaking his head and the president noticed. "What is it, Randall?"

"Sir, all American communities that get their drinking water from surface sources like lakes, rivers, and reservoirs face more or less the same level of vulnerability. Communities that depend on groundwater are more secure because it's harder to contaminate underground aquifers. The FBI has been working with state and local governments to strengthen the ·security of our water systems, but it's a massive undertaking. We have nowhere near the resources—"

"Save your breath. I know you want a bigger budget. You're all telling me the same thing. America is currently incapable of defending its water supplies from terrorist attacks. It is unacceptable to me that the richest nation in the entire world is so weak. I want a memo on my desk by tomorrow morning estimating the costs of securing, and I mean seriously securing, all American water supplies. No partial fences or wishy-washy bullshit."

"Sir, there are roughly 100,000 water systems serving at least 5,000 Americans each."

"Put it in the memo. I need a ballpark figure so that I can make a deal with Congress."

"Yes, sir."

"I plan to make a national television address this evening at 9:00 p.m. to reassure the American people. I've already spoken with Elaine about this. We agreed that the Rewards for Justice Program will offer a $25-million reward for information leading to the arrest or conviction of the people responsible for this attack. Now, I've got more questions. Did we have any warnings about this attack? Any intelligence? Roger?"

"Sir, I'm afraid this incident came straight out of the blue. No warnings, no rumors, nothing. No chatter in recent weeks, either domestically or internationally. I strongly recommend putting the nation on red alert, in light of the threat that the next attack could be even deadlier and could occur in less than two days." The Department of Homeland Security, in theory, was supposed to create a more integrated approach to intelligence and security. However, Osborne was somewhat of a lame duck, often left out of the loop and prone to reckless decisions in the hope of making a lasting impression.

"Affirmative on the red alert," the president agreed. "We've got to assume that there's a serious risk of further attacks. Two days is a tight timeline, and the clock's already running. We have to nail these bastards fast and stop them from following through on their threat. I may have to call up the National Guard to defend the water supplies and treatment facilities of all major American cities. Randall?"

Tierney spoke so quickly and quietly that he was almost hard to hear. "With respect, sir, I hope it doesn't come to that. We've done threat assessments, and there isn't enough manpower in the entire U.S. armed forces to adequately patrol all of those places, even if we brought all of our troops home from overseas and called up the reserves. We've dispatched more than four hundred agents and crime scene analysts as well as a dozen of our best canine units to Seattle to make sure the locals don't screw up the physical side of the investigation. We have agents on the water, in the water, in the air, and on land. We have aerial reconnaissance units sweeping the entire perimeter of the watershed for possible entry points. The agent in charge of our Seattle field office is one of our best men. Unfortunately, it has been raining heavily since investigators hit the ground. The most promising lead so far is several recent sets of unauthorized off-road vehicle tracks on the northeastern edge of the reservoir. Preliminary indication is that they're from within the last forty-eight to seventy-two hours. We have a mobile evidence processing unit at the reservoir and are attempting to identify the tread patterns and specific make of the vehicles."

"Any eyewitnesses? Are you getting full cooperation from the local authorities?"

"Cooperation yes, but no witnesses. We're hoping the $25-million reward jogs a few memories or loosens a few tongues."

"Make it $50 million," the president interrupted. "Money talks. Now what were you saying, Randall?"

"We've had no jurisdictional hassles. The Seattle police department recognizes that this is a potential terrorist attack, so we call the shots. The watershed is off limits to the public, so evidence of recent human activity stands out, but it's 90,000 acres of densely forested wilderness with a network of old logging roads. Local law enforcement officers are doing a door-to-door sweep of residents living in proximity to the reservoir, mostly farms and recreational properties. I've got our computer experts working double-time tracing the emails. That'll give us our first clear indication about who's really behind this mess. In sum, we're working every lead with due diligence. But my honest assessment is that we have a long way to go and not much time to get there."

Stryder scoffed. The directors of the FBI and CIA hated to cooperate. "Look, we've already figured out that this is a terrorist attack. It's obviously jihadis, though we don't know if it's ISIS or a breakaway group. We're monitoring Al Jazeera for claims of responsibility and checking with our agents in the Middle East. Right now we're focusing our attention on Iraq, Syria, Pakistan, and Afghanistan."

"What makes you certain it's jihadis?" Cassie asked, skeptical about going on a wild goose chase before more facts were known.

"Seriously?" Stryder responded with thinly disguised contempt.

"Why would they attack Seattle?" Cassie kept probing.

Stryder rolled his eyes. "Sources embedded in Pakistan, Afghanistan, and Africa consistently tell us that American water and energy infrastructure are priority targets."

The Director of National Intelligence, General Orrin Matthews, weighed in. "It's not necessarily ISIS. There are all kinds of splinter groups, copycats, and homegrown terrorist cells. They all have one thing in common—a big hate-on for America."

"It also fits the profile of a disgruntled employee, a jilted lover, or a single lunatic like the Unabomber. Why don't we gather some evidence before we jump to conclusions?" Cassie wasn't backing down. Stryder, Tierney, and Matthews reminded Cassie of a trio of bloodhounds, baying uncontrollably in their hard-wired enthusiasm for the hunt, stumbling over each other to be in the lead.

"We also shouldn't rule out the possibility of domestic terrorist groups," Tierney added. "Ecoterrorists are number two on our domestic terrorism priority list. The Animal Liberation Front and the Earth Liberation Front are both highly active in the Pacific Northwest. ELF burned down a research lab and destroyed the Center for Urban Horticulture at the University of Washington a number of years ago. And torched two buildings and several vehicles at Clatskanie, Oregon, the same day."

"Randall's got a good point, sir," Matthews agreed. "Ecoterrorists are armies without generals, bases, or equipment. Their command structure, strategies, and communication techniques remain shrouded in mystery despite years of persistent counterintelligence efforts to penetrate their organizations. As far as we can tell, there are sleeper cells scattered across America. Instead of frustrated Muslims, these are radical environmentalists disenchanted with the capitalist system, paranoid about the future of the planet, and eager to stick a wrench in the wheels of progress."

"Poisoning Seattle's water supply seems like an odd choice for radical environmentalists," said Cassie. As a younger woman, she would have been so inflamed by Orrin Matthew's polemic that her tongue would have been tied. Now she found his posturing almost comical. What was not funny was that these close-minded reactionaries were in charge of national security.

Tierney stood up. "I'm getting an update. Back in a minute."

"We need to get in touch with our Canadian counterparts. Remember Ahmed Ressam, the millennium bomber?" Stryder continued to push the terrorist angle.

"Who was that?" the president asked.

"He was planning to bomb Los Angeles International Airport on New Year's Eve, 1999. Trained in Afghanistan, lived in Montreal.

We caught him with a car full of timers, detonators, and explosives as he came off a ferry from Canada entering Washington State." Catching Ressam was one of the biggest victories in the American war on terror, and Stryder mentioned it whenever he could. He also made it sound like his agency deserved the credit when it was actually a random inspection by a U.S. Customs agent in Port Angeles.

The president switched topics. "Let's talk about the poison, this perc that was used in the Seattle attack."

"Nasty stuff. Really bad," Osborne piped up.

"How nasty?"

"Well, you wouldn't want to drink a glass of it. Or inhale a lung full of it. It's acutely toxic, carcinogenic, screws up your internal organs, and may cause birth defects." It was Cassie's turn to roll her eyes.

"That does sound really bad," the president said. "Are people getting sick in Seattle? Any deaths yet?"

Cassie had to jump in. "Mr. President, all of the test results from water sampling so far indicate that the perc was diluted to a level ranging from six to eleven parts per billion. While this slightly exceeds EPA standards for drinking quality, both toxicologists and epidemiologists at the Centers for Disease Control have assured me that there is virtually no short-term health risk."

Osborne objected. "That's junk science. Despite Ms. Harden-Hernandez's assurances, we are receiving reports of increased visits to doctors' offices, walk-in clinics, and emergency wards in Seattle. People are suffering from stomach ailments, nausea, dizziness, headaches, etc. The public has gone into a bottled water buying frenzy."

"If people are getting sick, Cassie, then maybe those scientists you mentioned need to get out of their labs into the real world."

Cassie squared her shoulders to face the president directly. "Sir, every expert with whom I've spoken agrees that the levels of PCE in the water supply are too low to cause acute health effects. But people don't always listen to the experts. They overreact when an event like this occurs. These are psychological reactions, not physiological responses. Like spikes in crime during a full moon."

"All right. Either way, we need to keep people calm. Cassie, I want statements about the safety of Seattle's drinking water from the head of the Centers for Disease Control and some independent doctors. I'll quote them in my speech to the nation."

"Yes, sir."

"Now can we trace this perc back to a specific source? Where did the terrorists get it from? I'm sure that it's not sold at Walmart."

"No, not at Walmart, but it's not like this stuff is sold under lock and key or treated like nuclear waste. You can order huge jugs of it online with a credit card. Free delivery and no security check needed.

"Here's a brief synopsis of what we know about perc. There are four American manufacturers: Dow Chemical, in Midland, Michigan; Occidental Petroleum, in Los Angeles; PPG Industries in Pittsburgh; and Vulcan Materials Company in Birmingham. The stuff is heavily regulated. The Occupational Safety and Health Administration issues permissible exposure limits for employees working with perc. The EPA enforces a variety of regulations and guidelines for perc discharges, including air quality standards, drinking water standards, pollutant discharge permits, and emergency reporting."

"I know we've got a lot of red tape. But I don't want to become an expert on PCE. Just tell me what I need to know." The president was fidgeting with his pen, growing restless from listening to technical information he would not retain.

Cassie accelerated her delivery. "Under the Emergency Planning and Community Right-to-Know Act of 1986, all releases of more than one hundred pounds of perchloroethylene into the air, water, or land must be reported annually and entered into the national Toxic Release Inventory (TRI) database. That gives us a comprehensive overview of where the perps might have got the stuff."

"How much perc are we talking about here, nationally?"

"In 2019, roughly 200 million pounds of perchloroethylene waste were managed, mainly through recycling, treatment, and energy recovery."

"Wait a minute. Are you kidding me? Two hundred million pounds? Of a toxic substance!" The president's eyebrows jumped halfway up his forehead.

"Sir, we've reduced perc releases into the environment by more than eighty percent in less than two decades."

"But you're still talking about hundreds of millions of pounds pumped into our air, water, and soil."

"Yes, sir. As you know, we're working hard to reduce all forms of toxic pollution, including perc. A couple more facts and then I'm done." Cassie tapped lightly on her keyboard and a chart popped onto the large wall-mounted screens. "This chart lists the ten states in which the largest amounts of perchloroethylene were released in 2006. You'll note that Washington isn't on the list.

"The next chart shows the ten facilities releasing the largest amounts of perc last year. Again, nothing in Washington State."

"But the stuff is everywhere. How the hell are we going to get a handle on it?"

"These large corporations all have high-tech pollution monitoring systems and sophisticated security. We're contacting all of the companies that report to the Toxics Release Inventory to determine if any recent thefts have been reported. Unfortunately, that's the easy part. Perc is also used by thousands of smaller businesses and institutions that are not legally required to report. Dry cleaners, gas stations, mechanic's garages, and the like. In Washington State alone we estimate there are at least 5,000 of these small businesses using perc, in addition to government facilities such as schools and prisons."

There was a stunned silence around the room. Hundreds of millions of pounds of this highly toxic chemical were being used annually in America by tens of thousands of businesses, large and small. The odds of tracking down a few missing pounds were astronomical.

"All right." Tierney had returned, taking charge and speaking at his usual lightning pace. "We need to contact police throughout Washington State and see if there've been any thefts reported by the kinds of small businesses that use perc. Now can we wrap that discussion? I have new information about the source of the emails."

CHAPTER 18

TIERNEY MANAGED TO LOOK SMUG without smiling. "I just spoke to the director of the Forensic Computer Lab. Tracing emails to specific computers isn't exactly rocket science anymore. As you all know, every computer, tablet, or smartphone that's connected to the internet requires a unique IP address. Although not foolproof, in that they can be faked, IP addresses usually point us in the right direction. We've got software programs that make tracing emails a piece of cake. They can analyze an email to determine the sender's IP address, penetrating most efforts at misdirection and working equally well with seemingly anonymous emails sent through free service providers. Plus, they can tell us which country and which city the email originated from, the registered owner of the domain, and contact information for the company providing internet access through that domain."

He paused for effect. "The three emails were sent from one computer at the City of London library. London, England, that is."

"Are you sure?" The president leaned forward.

"Reasonably sure."

"I knew it." Stryder slapped his palms on the table. "ISIS has several active cells based in London." He had a facial tic, Cassie noticed, a fluttering of his left eyelid that acted up when he was excited.

The president nodded slightly and shifted in his chair. "Orrin?"

"I agree with Billy Joe. The London angle rules out the domestic explanations that Ms. Harden-Hernandez was speculating about."

"All right. Let's get some of our agents to this library in London, on the double," the president ordered. "Better yet, get the Brits to close it down, right now."

Matthews glanced at his watch. "Actually, sir, it's probably closed already. London is five hours ahead of us."

"Let's make sure it stays closed."

"Yes, sir," Stryder jumped in enthusiastically. "We'll get right on it. The library will get immediate crime scene treatment. We'll seize the computer that was used, and the seats beside it, and dust them for prints. The hard drive will go to the nearest forensic computer lab to see what they can extract—other messages the perp sent, websites they visited, even books they looked up."

"Do they have user identification systems on the computers?" Matthews asked. "Do they have videotape surveillance at the library? We know when the email was sent. You'll want to interview the librarians who were on duty, see if they can remember anybody or anything unusual."

"This opens up another line of inquiry," Tierney added. "I'll get copies of all of the passenger manifests for flights between Seattle and London for the days and weeks prior to the attack. Run background checks on any passengers with Arabic names. Run all of the names through the Terrorist Screening Center, the National Crime Information Center, the Violent Criminal Apprehension Program, and the White House correspondence database. Maybe make a quick connection." Like sharks sensing blood, they fed off each other's excitement.

Attorney General Leon Bynum intervened. "Normally we'd need judicial authorization to intercept oral and electronic communications among potential suspects and suspect organizations. But in these circumstances . . ." Bynum was a ruthless lawyer who felt no trepidation about exploiting the legal system's inherent ambiguities to further the administration's political agenda.

"We don't need a judge to give us the green light. Just do it. This is a national emergency." Stryder also never let the rules get in the way of the investigation.

The president interrupted. "Somebody mentioned closed-circuit televisions and that reminded me of something else. Do we have any satellite coverage of the Seattle watershed?"

Stryder frowned. "Yes, sir, but the resolution isn't sufficiently fine to pick out an individual."

"What about a vehicle?"

"Unlikely."

"Double check. Otherwise why are we spending billions every year on a fancy satellite network? It sure isn't predicting the weather."

Now Stryder winced. "Yes, sir."

"Does the aerial reconnaissance of the watershed collect video?"

Stryder was shrinking in his seat as the president peppered him with questions. "No, sir. The planes are manually operated and not equipped with cameras."

"Talk to the pilots, then. See if they remember anything out of the ordinary in the days and weeks leading up to the attack. If not, we should fire them and replace them with drones."

"What about the demand for $100 billion to address poverty?" Cassie asked.

Tierney spat out a response. "It's outrageous. Sounds to me like the terrorists hired a PR firm to give their image a makeover."

Stryder jumped on the bandwagon. "Ludicrous. As if we're just going to fork over one hundred billion dollars!"

Cassie was the lone voice of dissent. "That's substantially less than one-fifth of last year's defense budget."

All the attention turned to Cassie. Like wolves attacking a crippled deer, they pounced on Cassie, talking over each other in hostile, offended outrage. "The citizens of America are being held hostage by despicable scum. Are you suggesting that the greatest country in the world bend over and pay the ransom?"

The president intervened. "I don't negotiate with terrorists. Period." The wolves shook their heads and grumbled.

Cassie was undeterred. "But they didn't go public. A smart move on their part. They've left the door open."

"How so?" the president asked.

Cassie felt her face flushing. "As you said, sir, there's no way that the USA would ever publicly capitulate to blackmailers' demands. We all agree on that point. The floodgates would open. But in the Seattle case, whoever did this created a situation where we can meet their demands without the public connecting our actions to their threat. Just as importantly, their demand asks for something that's positive rather than negative. They don't want us to give them money to buy weapons or release a bunch of thugs and murderers from jail. They want the U.S. to take an unprecedented step in the global war on poverty, an action that would enhance our international reputation and actually diminish the anti-American attitude fostering terrorism around the world."

Cassie could feel Osborne, Matthews, Stryder, and Tierney looking at her in horror. Bad enough that there was a woman involved in the investigation at this senior level, but she was such a raging and unrepentant liberal. A tree-hugging, cappuccino-sucking bleeding heart. No doubt they were wishing she could be more like the secretary of state: Stein was as conservative and hawkish as they were, maybe even more so. An honorary member of the old boys' club.

The president smiled. "Interesting perspective. We've got less than two days to make that decision and, as I said, we will consider all available options. Back to you, Billy Joe."

"I've issued a worldwide alert instructing our people to contact and question international sources for information about the attack. The FBI's counterterrorism unit should do the same. We'll pull together a list of names of possible groups who may have been involved and check where key individuals were most recently located."

"Have any specific terrorist groups claimed responsibility?"

"Not yet. The emails are signed 'endpovertynow.' You've put your finger on a troubling anomaly, because usually these Islamic fundamentalists aren't shy about taking credit. And they never ask for anything like this."

"Do we know anything about endpovertynow?"

"We have zero on them. There's no organization in our surveillance database using that phrase as a name or slogan. Internet searches are coming up empty. It's probably just a front. Agents are investigating an international group called Make Poverty History, but at this point we have no reason to believe they are involved."

Cassie bit her tongue. These buffoons were obsessed with Islamic terrorists. Sure, it was one explanation. But to go tearing down that path and write off all other possibilities was poor judgment. Her dad had been a policeman in Tampa Bay. Nothing fancy, just a patrolman who never got promoted because he was a bit of a hothead. But he taught her that good investigators worked methodically building up evidence, not fitting the evidence to preconceived notions.

"All right. Is that it?" The president stood up. "At the risk of stating the obvious, if there's any kind of news, good or bad, I need to hear about it immediately. I'm flying to Seattle this evening after my address so I can be on the ground there tomorrow. Can I give anyone a lift?"

What the hell, Cassie thought. Why not? "I was planning to fly to Seattle tonight, sir. With my executive assistant."

"Good. Be at the Andrews Air Force Base by nine-thirty p.m. We leave at ten sharp."

CHAPTER 19

THE OVERNIGHT ETHIOPIAN AIRLINE FLIGHT from London
to Addis Ababa departed three hours late and carried no liquid
refreshments, just salty, thirst-inducing peanuts. It was as though
the airline was providing passengers with a sneak preview of the
chaos and dysfunction that awaited them.

Every time he passed through airport security or customs on his
journey, Michael wondered if he would be pulled aside. Every time
he saw someone in a police or military uniform, he felt as though
they were staring at him, planning his arrest. Every time he saw a
TV or computer screen, he feared seeing his face prominently dis-
played above a Most Wanted sign.

Now that he was in African airspace, the adrenaline and paranoia
began to dissipate. Part of him remained in a state of suspended ani-
mation, unwilling or unable to process the magnitude of what he'd
done or the risks he now faced. Part of him was filled with electric
anticipation about whether the U.S. government would accede to
his request and finance a Marshall Plan to combat poverty in sub-
Saharan Africa. He tried not to dwell on his relationship with
Maria. Going back to Africa was probably the last straw. He
also began to contemplate what would happen if he was caught.
He'd been so obsessed with carrying out the action that he spent
little time considering this possibility. His missionary fervor had
suppressed thoughts about being hunted down, arrested, and
imprisoned. What if he hadn't done the right thing after all?

He thought of all the amateurish clues he'd left behind. His
Google searches on terrorist topics and toxic substances. The emails

sent from London. The Mexican cleaner at the hospital. Tire tracks at the Chester Morse Reservoir. The bicycle in his garage, with an incriminating map of the watershed tucked away in a pannier. Yet Michael couldn't imagine any series of investigative steps that would lead the authorities to him, especially in less than two days. And he would know soon if the whole effort had been worthwhile or a quixotic, self-destructive disaster.

While waiting for his final flight to Goma, Michael found an internet terminal in the airport bar. He ordered a Coke, paid for it with American dollars, and received change in Ethiopian birr. He fed some coins into the machine and typed cnn.com. It took forever for the page to load, and none of the photographs or graphics worked.

The text was in microscopic print. The lead story on CNN was about a small earthquake in the Ring of Fire near Indonesia. But near the top of the CNN homepage, the headline read "Seattle Water Poisoned." He clicked on it, holding his breath.

Seattle, WA. Authorities suspect terrorists are behind the contamination of the Chester Morse Reservoir, Seattle's drinking water supply, with a toxic chemical called perchloroethylene. Although medical experts believe that exposure to the water will not cause short-term health effects, area hospitals have been inundated with citizens complaining about stomach pain, headaches, and difficulty breathing. There are no reported deaths at this point.

Stores have already run out of bottled water and isolated violent incidents have occurred. A Joint Terrorism Task Force led by the FBI is investigating the attack. The president will address the nation later this evening, and a source at the White House indicated that the president will likely upgrade the Department of Homeland Security's threat status to Code Red, suggesting that more attacks are anticipated.

A senior source inside the White House would not specify a particular terrorist organization but acknowledged that radical Islamic groups and domestic ecoterrorists were at the top of the suspect list.

Counterterrorism experts point toward foreign responsibility for the attack. The focus of terrorist attacks up until now has been on the East Coast, and the prevailing theory is that by striking the West Coast, terrorists seek to ensure that all Americans taste fear. According to Dr. Jay Martin, of the think tank U.S. Center for Terrorist Information, circumstantial evidence suggests that ISIS or one of the other large, decentralized Islamic organizations with sleeper cells throughout the U.S. is the likely culprit.

Michael stood up, stunned. The CNN story finally broke through his fog. He was a wanted man, a suspected terrorist. What on Earth had he done?

Michael wandered around the airport. By sheer luck he was passing the departure gate when a crackling, fuzzy announcement indicated that his flight was ready for boarding. He walked out onto the tarmac to the plane.

The paint was flaking from the fuselage and although the plane was traveling between Ethiopia and the Congo, the faded logo on the tail still said Air Zaire, using a name abandoned years ago by both the airline and the Democratic Republic of the Congo. It didn't foster confidence in the level of repair of the rest of the aircraft. An elderly African man waiting in line in the suffocating heat poked a bony elbow into Michael's ribs.

"Air Zaire," he rasped. "Air peut-être." Air Maybe. "C'est la seule chose au Congo qui ne vole jamais." He convulsed with laughter while Michael tried to translate the joke. The Google Translate app on his phone helped him figure out that it was a play on the verb "voler," meaning both to steal and to fly. The airline was the only thing in the Congo that didn't steal or fly.

Michael walked up the rickety steps, folded his lanky frame through the doorway, walked hunched down the center aisle, and squeezed into the window seat of an empty row, knees pressed into the seat ahead of him. Other passengers jammed themselves into the ramshackle seats, and some who didn't get to the plane fast enough were sent back into the terminal to await the next flight. A man in mechanic's overalls climbed the steps onto the plane and ducked into the cockpit. He fiddled with the instruments then started the engines, producing a sound similar to that of an old Volkswagen van in need of a tune-up. Moments later, the mechanic guided the small plane toward the runway. Nobody else on board showed the slightest indication of concern as the plane rattled and shook its way into the air. Michael tried to clear his mind and focus on the landscapes below—green hills juxtaposed with ochre soil.

They landed in Goma in the middle of a sweltering afternoon. As he wandered out of the airport, a familiar honk startled him. It was the same Toyota Land Cruiser. The driver, never again to be Laurent, introduced himself as Issama Masuaku, one of three drivers at the Goma medical clinic. He helped Michael load his bike and backpack into the back of the vehicle. Then Michael climbed into the passenger seat and his thoughts shifted to Anna. She had recovered from her physical injuries and was working at a hospital in Copenhagen now, having told Michael in an email that she would never return to Africa. As the vehicle began thumping along Goma's battered roads, he wondered if coming back was a mistake.

CHAPTER 20

BART AND CHARLIE WERE SITTING in Sara's Coffee Shop, as usual. The poisoning of the water supply was the talk of the town. Theories about who did it, and why, were rampant, flourishing like mold and mushrooms in the damp climate. Charlie razzed Gracie about the coffee. "Are you sure it's safe to drink?"

"My coffee's the least of your problems," she shot back.

"Probably safer than most of the swill you pour down your gullet." Bart howled at his own wit, although the laughter quickly morphed into a body-rattling cough.

"You okay? Sounds like you're about to cough up a lung."

Bart still couldn't speak, but he waved his hand in a way that said "No big deal." Then he managed to whisper "Caught." Cough. "A goddamn." Cough. "Cold."

"At least you caught something," Charlie replied.

"Fellas. Can you keep it down? The president is about to begin." Sara, the septuagenarian owner, ran the café with an iron fist. She turned up the volume on the TV mounted above the red Formica counter.

Seated behind his desk in the Oval Office, the president looked straight into the camera but did not smile.

"Fellow Americans, it is with a heavy heart that I must inform you that our great nation is once again the target of a terrorist attack. The Chester Morse Reservoir, Seattle's main water supply, has been contaminated with a chemical substance called perchloroethylene, or PCE for short. Although this is listed as a toxic chemical, the country's leading medical authorities at the Centers for Disease Control in Atlanta have assured me that it will not cause negative health effects for residents who drink it, because the chemical is too diluted.

"Dr. Elaine Carswell of the Massachusetts Institute of Technology said that if you put a teaspoon full of rum into an Olympic-sized swimming pool full of Coke, you'd have a higher concentration of rum than the concentration of this chemical in Seattle's water supply. So your tap water continues to be safe to drink." Now the president smiled, showing his even, white teeth, thousands of dollars well spent.

"However, as a nation we must exercise caution. I am going to place America on a Code Red state of alert for the next seven days, in light of the possibility, however remote, that there could be more attacks. Americans returning home from abroad can expect delays at airports and border crossings. We will also be stepping up inspections and patrols along the Canadian and Mexican borders and at all ports. I regret the stress and inconvenience this state of affairs may cause to honest, hard-working individuals and their families, but our national security is of paramount importance.

"These are difficult times for our great nation, but we will remain strong and we will get even stronger through our experiences. Adversity builds character. We will not rest until we've brought the perpetrators of this terrorist attack to justice. Federal, state, and local law enforcement agencies are cooperating in an intense investigation. The United States is fortunate to have the world's finest criminal investigators. Every lead is being pursued. Every resource necessary is being provided. If we have to go to the ends of the Earth and back we will. We will not tire, we will not quit, we will not fail. We will capture the evil criminals who attack our health, our security, and our great American quality of life.

"I'm also announcing tonight that the State Department will pay $50 million for information leading to the arrest or conviction of those responsible for these reprehensible crimes, through our Rewards for Justice Program. If you believe that you have valuable or useful information, please contact your local law enforcement agency immediately.

"You can be confident that I am doing everything in my power not only to catch the terrorists who walk in our midst but also to ensure that these people never strike again. I'm on my way to Seattle tonight to support the fine people there. Good evening and God bless America."

After the president's address went off the air, the rewards information scrolled across the screens.

Bart looked at Charlie, wide-eyed, after the president's speech.

"Smoke break," Charlie said, nodding toward the door.

They headed out onto the deck where smoking was allowed and nobody could hear them.

"You saw that guy. You know, down at the reservoir. Fifty million George Washingtons. Holy mackerel. We could hit the jackpot here!" Bart could barely contain his excitement.

"Whoa now. Slow down. First of all, I just saw some guy in a bike helmet and shorts. I didn't see any ragheads or terrorists."

"Jumpin' Jesus, Charlie. Have ya ever seen a spy movie? They wear disguises, so nobody will suspect them. These terrorists musta dressed up like cyclists."

"If we report it then we're in trouble too. We were trespassing in the reservoir."

"Do we look like terrorists for God's sake? We could pay all the fines they give us for trespassing and illegal fishing and still have $49 million and change left over."

Charlie looked down at his feet. "I just need to think about the best approach, that's all."

"Well, hurry up and think. Some other clowns might grab the reward while we sit around scratching our butts!"

"Let's go over to Gators and grab a beer." Charlie needed a shot of liquid courage.

"Now you're talking. A brewski or twoski to celebrate."

It was only a four-minute drive over to Gators, a rundown sports bar on 84th. The Boston Celtics were playing the Portland Trail Blazers on the big screen, and about a dozen fans in varying states of intoxication were cheering the teams on. By the sound of it, Portland was on fire. Bart and Charlie sat at the back, where they could still see the television but hear each other without shouting.

"What would you do with your half?" Bart asked.

"I'd get a big fishing boat, tricked out with sonar and all that computer stuff, get a mail-order bride and a box full of Viagra, head for Mexico, load the boat with Corona, limes, Cuban cigars, nacho chips, and salsa. Eat, drink, fish, and fuck every sunny day till I die. How about you?"

"I dunno. Never thought about bein' rich before. Get the truck fixed up, I guess. Maybe get some new hip waders and a big new TV—one of those fancy flat ones you can hang on the wall."

"Jayzus, Bart! Don't blow the whole wad all at once, going on a spending spree like that! You crazy mallard."

"Maybe we should talk to an attorney."

"An attorney? That'd be pissing money down the drain. They'd figure out some way to swindle us outta the dough. Nope. Your gut instinct was right. Let's get on the phone."

Bart downed the rest of his beer and released a savage burp. "Yes! Easy Street here we come."

There was a decrepit payphone in the back near the bathrooms. Charlie dialed the number he'd written down on the back of a napkin back at the coffee shop.

"U.S. Rewards. How can I help you?" The voice was female, calm, and soothing.

"I think I saw the guy who poisoned Seattle's water."

"All right, could I get your name please?"

"Charlie Boykins."

"Thanks. Please go ahead with your information."

"I saw a guy at the Chester Morse Reservoir on Saturday. He was down at the shore of the reservoir near the Iron Horse Trail across from Meadow Mountain, puttin' something in the water. It was pretty early in the morning."

"What did he look like?"

"He looked like he was just riding a bike. You know, wearing a helmet and tight clothing. I think maybe he was one of them terrorists."

"Hello?" The operator was momentarily silent. Charlie thought he'd lost her. "Hello?"

"All right, sir. It sounds like you might have some good information. We need you to report to the nearest law enforcement facility as soon as you possibly can. If you tell me your location, I can give you directions."

"Law enforcement facility?" Charlie didn't like the idea of going to a cop shop.

"They'll just take down the details of your information and tell you how to file your claim for the reward money."

"Okay. We're at Gators, that's a bar in Kent. Just outside Seattle."

"Have you been drinking, sir?"

"No—well yes, oh shit . . . I can still drive."

"I could send a local squad car over to pick you up."

"It's all right. I only drank one Bud. Honest. Now where am I headed?"

"The Kent Police Station is on 4th Ave. When you get there, identify yourself to the desk sergeant. He'll take care of you."

"Thanks. Can I bring my friend? He was with me at the reservoir."

"Of course."

"Okay, we'll be there shortly."

The news about potential eyewitnesses moved rapidly up the investigative chain of command. Keyvan Gushue, the local FBI agent, was on the line to Randall Tierney within minutes.

"Are they credible?" Tierney asked.

"Maybe. Two old-timers in the watershed saw some suspicious activities at the reservoir."

"What kind of activities?"

"Someone possibly putting something in the water. Two agents from our Seattle office are headed to the Kent Police Station to do the intake interview."

"This could be our first real break. Look, I want to be patched in to that interview—preferably by videophone. Audio as Plan B. And get our best sketch artists on a plane to Seattle, see if we can get some images of the perps to circulate."

Forty-five minutes later Tierney was staring at two men who looked and talked like characters in a Coen Brothers movie. He watched with mounting disbelief as they heard Charlie's story about seeing a lone cyclist at the reservoir's edge. Tierney hit the mute button and spoke into Gushue's earpiece. "Are you kidding me? One guy on a bicycle? Some thirsty, trespassing, mountain bike–riding, West Coast hippie is in a boatload of trouble." He rubbed his temples with both hands. The clock was ticking. What were the odds that a guy on a bicycle singlehandedly poisoned Seattle's water? These two old geezers looked about as reliable as a cheap umbrella in a torrential downpour.

"All right. Put out the word that one or more terrorists may have been disguised as a cyclist, and they would have to have been riding a bike with some means of carrying cargo. Let's see if we can reel in some more witnesses. And get those old farts over to our Seattle field office. Show them some mug shots. Put them with the sketch artists. And check their vehicles to see if they match the tire patterns we found at the reservoir."

Maria was marking term papers when the phone rang. She answered the phone with trepidation these days, fearing bad news. "Hello?"

"Hey, Maria, it's Dom. How're you doing? Do you miss the doc already?"

"Of course. Life goes on, but what can you do? I didn't want him to leave."

"Why didn't you go with him?"

"Dominic! What is it with you men? It's the middle of the semester. I'm teaching two courses and supervising eight graduate students. I'm on more committees than I can count. Women don't simply drop everything and follow their husbands to the ends of the earth anymore."

There was a brief, awkward pause. "Right. Sorry. I understand. Well, if there's ever anything I can do for you while the doc's away, just let me know."

"That's nice. Thank you."

"Hey, the other reason I was calling is that I was wondering if I could borrow Michael's mountain bike for a week or so. A bunch of folks from the Sierra Club are going down to Moab in Utah to blow off some steam by biking around on the red rock, and they asked me if I wanted to tag along."

"He took his road bike with him but his mountain bike is in the garage. The spare key to the garage door is taped to the bottom of the hummingbird feeder."

"Awesome! Thanks, Maria. I meant to ask Michael before he left, but it slipped my mind."

"No problem. Keep it as long as you like." Keep it forever, Maria thought bitterly.

CHAPTER 21

CASSIE GRABBED AN EARLY BREAKFAST with Abby at the hotel restaurant's pricey buffet and silently apologized to taxpayers. She filled a large plate with fresh fruit and spooned some yogurt and granola on top. Abby was reading the *Seattle Post-Intelligencer* on his phone.

"How's the story playing out today?" Cassie asked.

"About what you'd expect. Saturation coverage. People are upset but mostly not panicking. The initial surge in visits to doctors and hospitals seems to have abated. There was a run on bottled water but the Canadian government is sending a fleet of trucks full of water down from Vancouver. The president is getting good reviews for his speech and for flying out here right away. Speaking of the president, he'd like you to join him at nine a.m. for a meeting with the mayor and the governor."

"Damn. I was planning to meet with Chief Gilhooley at nine."

"I can bump the president."

"Yeah right. Can you call Gilhooley's office, try and reschedule for ten?"

"Sure. And you have the morning briefing at eight. Find anything interesting in our database?" Abby had printed a summary of hundreds of incidents involving water supplies and treatment systems in the U.S. over the past decade and given Cassie the two-inch-thick binder on their flight to Seattle.

"A couple of long shots. The number of incidents is stunning, but it's mostly small-scale vandalism, theft, petty misdemeanors. Teenagers partying, disgruntled employees and ex-employees, jilted lovers, and people suffering from mental illnesses. Not a single terrorist attack, confirmed or even suspected, in the entire database." Cassie had tasked two of her top investigators to follow up on a handful of incidents that she'd flagged. She'd keep an open mind while the boys chased after ISIS and its sleeper cells. Let the chips fall where they may.

Stryder kicked off the Tuesday morning briefing with a terse update. "We've heard back from London."

"And?" The president was prickly and looked tired.

"Not much to report. A security guard at the City of London library said that he saw several young men wearing traditional Muslim garb on Saturday afternoon, using the internet and whispering to each other."

"Whispering? That's what people do in libraries, for Christ's sake. Come on! We've got less than twenty-four hours to catch these creeps."

"Well, it lends credence to the jihadist angle but doesn't get us very far. There are hundreds of thousands of Muslims in London, and millions of them in England."

"Is the security guard still being questioned?" Tierney asked.

"No, he went home," Stryder answered.

"Well bring him back," the president snapped. "I want him to look through mug shots of Islamic jihad suspects and their known associates. See if he recognizes any faces. What about the closed-circuit TVs?"

"The Brits have handed over thousands of hours of recordings from different locations including the library, a five-block radius around the library, and the airport. We've got people reviewing them. A couple of assaults and lots of small fry drug deals, but nothing that helps us move forward. We're getting cooperation from British Intelligence to help interview all library users who signed out books or used the internet within two hours of the emails being sent. The Brits are also doing criminal record checks on all library personnel and running their names through Interpol's terrorist databases."

"Anything else in London?" asked the president.

"Just a series of dead ends. No hits on the fingerprints we collected at the library. Nothing incriminating on the computer. No eyewitnesses with any useful recollections. It looks like the perp just walked in, sat down, sent emails to the water utility, CNN, and the White House, and walked out."

"We could canvass local hotels, taxi drivers . . ." Tierney suggested.

"But we have no idea who we're looking for. Seven million people live in London, and hundreds of thousands more pass through every day," Matthews added.

"That trail is cold," the president concluded.

"Ice cold," Stryder piled on.

"All right, let's not waste any time. I need results and I need them now. Who's next?"

Tierney spoke up. "Apart from London, there've been a number of promising developments overnight and this morning, sir. Almost every domestic agent is working on this case. Regular investigations and cold cases are all on hold. Even the Kennedy assassination team has been reassigned." Nobody laughed. "Sorry, FBI humor. We're much more optimistic than we were at this time yesterday."

"Get to the facts."

"Yes, sir. Three main items. First, we have two pairs of eyewitnesses who saw suspicious behavior at or near the Chester Morse Reservoir. Second, our Behavioral Analysis Unit has come up with preliminary profiles of the perpetrators. Third, we cross-checked the names of all airline passengers who flew from Sea-Tac to London after the reservoir was contaminated against the names of known terror suspects and individuals that have written threatening letters to the President or the White House. No hits."

"Let's hear about the eyewitnesses."

"First, a local couple called the Rewards for Justice hotline claiming that two men of Middle Eastern extraction—'Arab types,' they said—were seen repeatedly in the neighborhood of the Chester Morse Reservoir in recent months. They were observed in a blue Toyota Tercel, leaving from the water treatment plant at approximately six p.m. on the day of the contamination event. We're tracking down the vehicle, and sketch artists are working with the couple."

"Sounds promising. And?"

"Second, two fishermen saw an individual whom they allege was pouring an unknown substance into the reservoir on Saturday morning."

"An individual?"

"Yes. A Caucasian male carrying containers of some kind and wearing cycling gear—a helmet and shorts. The timing fits, but they're not able to provide a more detailed description."

"Why not?"

"Unfortunately, these eyewitnesses are seniors and were a substantial distance away. We've confirmed the presence of bicycle tracks and footprints to the water's edge in the location they identified. We believe it's the primary crime scene. Local police are searching the area for additional physical evidence. People at our computer lab are running some quick modeling exercises to confirm that this is the point where the PCE entered the reservoir. We've also confirmed that it was the witnesses' trucks whose tracks we found trespassing in the reservoir. So that's no longer an active lead."

"All right. The Arabs sound promising, but the cyclist? Probably just filling up a water bottle."

"Possibly, but he could still be a material witness."

"Okay, then find him fast. Now what about the profiles?"

"We've got Alex Kharlamov connecting with us from the Behavioral Analysis Unit in Quantico. He'll outline the preliminary profiles for us. It'll just take a minute to patch him in on a secure video feed."

While they waited for Kharlamov to join them, Matthews said, "There's not much for the profilers to go on, so don't get your hopes up."

"They've surprised us before, pulling rabbits out of their hats," Tierney replied. "Descriptions that sound crazy and end up fitting to a T. This case is getting cold fast. We have to try pretty much anything, even the long shots." The phone beeped. "We've got Agent Kharlamov on the screen." Kharlamov looked like a retired Russian hockey player. His face was pockmarked with scars, and his nose was slightly off-center, as though it had been badly broken and poorly repaired. "Alex, please proceed."

"Yes, sir. Something unusual has occurred. Normally we strive for, and achieve, consensus on the profile of an unknown subject, or unsub. But today we have a divergence of opinion among senior members of our profiling team. As a result, I'll provide you with two very different, even contradictory, profiles, both of which enjoy equal support. All we have to go on is minimal information about the crime committed in Seattle and psycholinguistic assessment of the three emails sent by the unsub from London."

The president interrupted Kharlamov. "What the hell is psycholinguistics?"

"Forensic psycholinguistics is a new field of scientific study that looks at the psychological basis of linguistic competence and performance. It's used primarily in identifying criminals who threaten their victims in writing or correspond with police, government, or the media about their crimes. To be frank, these are early days, and this is more art than science."

"Caveats duly noted. Now hurry up and tell us what you've got."

"Yes, sir. Here's the first profile. Neither the crime nor the emails are believed to be the work of one person. The timing, professionalism, and geographic dispersal of evidence suggest that a team of highly organized, educated, and motivated individuals is involved.

The emails appear to have been written not by a single author but by several authors, based on internal inconsistencies in grammar, vocabulary, and tone. At least one of the authors probably has some type of medical training or education.

"There is no identifiable signature associated with these crimes that would lead us to believe that a single individual is responsible. Those involved are willing to put many people at risk in order to achieve their goals, indicating a degree of fundamentalism and fanaticism that is consistent with the approaches of major international terrorist organizations."

"That profile does nothing to advance the investigation." Osborne sat back and crossed his arms.

"Of course it does. Closes off all of the cockamamie dead-end guesswork that the EPA is wasting their time on," Stryder replied.

Cassie sat quietly, resisting the urge to roll her eyes.

"Let 'em waste their time. It's our investigation I'm worried about," Tierney added.

Kharlamov coughed to clear his throat.

"Go ahead, Alex. What else have you got?" Tierney asked.

"The second profile that our team has developed is viewed as equally plausible, despite the fact that it contradicts the first profile. There are reasons to believe that this is the work of a single individual, likely a white male in his thirties or early forties. He will be fit and healthy. He is a high school graduate and there is a strong likelihood that he has some college education, possibly in chemistry, biology, or political science. He may also have some type of medical training or education. Unsubs who harm many people without seeking publicity are motivated primarily by anger, severe depression, or failures in school, jobs, or relationships. There is a significant probability that the unsub has a history of psychiatric treatment."

There were grunts, gnashing of the teeth, and other audible signs of displeasure from Stryder, Tierney, and Matthews.

"It's highly probable that the unsub has made similar threats in the past but not carried them out. It's also likely that he has written letters to people in positions of power on issues related to global poverty and/or American foreign policy. The tone of these letters probably progressed from polite to angry over a period of time, with an acceleration of acrimony and possibly deteriorating rationality toward the end. It is highly likely that he experienced what we call a precipitating stressor, some kind of negative event in his life, adding sufficient fuel to his anger to move him from rhetoric to action.

"He's likely a resident or former resident of the Seattle area. Possible occupations include teaching, research, social work, or something in health care. He will likely be perceived as successful by peers and coworkers, although those who know him well may be aware of his frustration at not being important or not doing the kinds of things he believes he is capable of doing or deserves to be doing.

"The lack of detail regarding the follow-up threat makes it difficult to evaluate. It's clear from both the unsub's actions and his language that he has sufficient knowledge to identify the type of contaminant that would pose a high risk of acute short-term health effects. However, the fact that his demand is for socially positive government action raises questions as to whether this particular individual would be willing to follow through on the threat. His initial attack appears to have been very meticulously planned and carried out in a deliberate effort to avoid causing any short- or long-term health impacts."

"The lone gunman theory, except you think that our kook may be a compassionate crackpot," Stryder snorted.

"Regarding the second profile, how would we use this information to advance the investigation?" asked Cassie.

"There are several tactics that have been used successfully, including vigils for victims, placing some kind of bait, or putting forward a sympathetic shrink that the perp may contact. We've also had success establishing a civilian task force to receive and process anonymous tips, as perps fitting this profile are tempted to volunteer. In a similar vein, perps like this often attempt to engage in the investigation, attending funerals, revisiting crime scenes, contacting authorities with evidence or insights, etc. He may find that the publicity provides the ego boost and attention that he was previously lacking. He may keep a scrapbook of media clippings. It's important to avoid describing him using words like madman, lunatic, or other pejoratives, because doing so may raise his anger level and provoke him into acting again. If we can get the media to humanize the victims of the Seattle attack, it will decrease the likelihood of a second attack."

"Any other questions for Agent Kharlamov?" Tierney asked.

There was silence. "Good work," the president said. "Next?" Tierney pressed a button to end the videoconference.

Cassie jumped in before the men could control the discussion once more. "I've also got new information, regarding two potential suspects, although to be honest they're long shots. I went through the EPA database last night, looking for similar crimes or threats, parallels, any connection between past attacks and the attack in Seattle. Most of the cases are clearly irrelevant. However, I identified two previous events that involved perchloroethylene."

Everyone's eyes were on Cassie now.

"Both events were carried out by disgruntled former water utility employees. Both men served time for their offenses but are free. These two perps—Scott Fuller and Clinton Ray Franklin—have never given any indication of having the sophistication or political interest necessary to carry out an attack like the one in Seattle."

"Do these lowlifes have any London connections?" Stryder asked.

"Not that we're aware of," Cassie replied. "We're also exploring a number of events in large cities—places like Chicago and Detroit—where there were watershed break-ins but no contamination occurred. In retrospect, given what happened in Seattle, these could have been training runs. And finally, we're reviewing a case in Greenville, South Carolina, where a vial of deadly ricin was mailed to the local water utility. I want to stress that these leads, however promising they may seem in light of the lack of progress in other areas of the investigation, are extremely preliminary at this point."

"I don't give a shit if they're long shots. I'm putting out a national APB on Fuller and Franklin right now," said Tierney.

"And you should circulate information on all of those cases to the whole task force," Stryder added.

Cassie smiled. "Check your email, Billy Joe. I already sent it."

CHAPTER 22

MICHAEL WAS RELIEVED TO BE BACK IN GOMA. The last few weeks in the U.S. had been self-inflicted torture, as he agonized over whether to proceed with his plan and watched the light fade in his marriage. At times, his plan seemed eminently reasonable and rational. At other times, it seemed completely crazy.

Back at the staff villa, almost all of the faces were new.

"Hello, good people!" Michael called out as he walked through the front door and into the living room where staffers often hung out.

"Bienvenue! Bonjour! Comment ça va?" Mbake was the first to greet him, still handing out effusive, heartwarming hugs along with her food.

"I missed those hugs," Michael said.

"Welcome back, Michael." Jean-Claude was still there, making sure they had the requisite medicine, food, and other supplies to do their jobs. He was really the glue that held the mission together, and he jumped up from a chair to shake Michael's hand.

"Thanks JC. Good to see you again."

"You look—" Jean-Claude paused, searching for the right word "—tired." He looked like he wanted to say more, but held back.

"That's what thirty hours of traveling halfway across the world will do to a guy. Enough about me! How are things here? When can I get started?"

"Hang on, let me introduce you to your new colleague." A woman who'd been seated next to Jean-Claude stood up as well. "Dr. Michael MacDougall, meet Dr. Chantal Parizeau from Canada. Chantal is an infectious disease specialist and is on her third mission, after serving in Iraq and Syria." Chantal was a few years older than Michael, hair halfway to gray, with a no-nonsense demeanor offset by a warm smile.

"Nice to meet you," Michael said as he and Chantal exchanged traditional European pecks on each cheek.

"I've heard great things about your surgical skills, and I look forward to working together," Chantal replied.

Michael repeated his earlier question, aimed at Jean-Claude: "Okay, so how are things going in Goma?"

"You'll see tomorrow. We're busier than when you were here before. As you know, Ebola has arrived in the region. And politically, things are worse. Several of our colleagues in North Kivu were abducted three months ago and are believed to be dead." JC wasn't one for sugarcoating the truth.

"It's not all bad," Chantal objected. "At least we have an experimental vaccine for Ebola that seems to be working."

"That's encouraging, but how could the political situation possibly be worse than when I left?" Michael asked.

"Ahh. There is a new gold rush," Mbake said.

"A gold rush? Where? At Shabunda?"

"Not for gold, Michael," JC said. "For coltan."

"Never heard of it."

"Colombite-tantalite is apparently indispensable for cellphones, laptops, pagers, and other high-tech equipment," JC explained. "About eighty percent of the world's known supply of coltan is in the eastern Congo, not far from here. So the Ugandan, Rwandan, and Burundian armies are all trampling around. They buy coltan or steal it from small-scale miners, then sell it to buy guns and other weapons. I read that the Rwandan army made over $250 million last year from coltan, even though it's not mined in Rwanda."

"Incredible!" Michael shook his head. The Congo somehow never managed to benefit from its own wealth of natural resources.

"The Congolese army is trying to push them out but they're

outnumbered and outgunned. And of course, there are rebel factions trying to claim a piece of the pie. To make things interesting, there are now private militia on the scene too. Well-trained, well-armed mercenaries working for international mining companies. They've greased palms in Kinshasa and have papers suggesting that they were granted mineral rights and concessions over vast areas of the eastern Congo."

Michael sighed in resignation. "If I'm counting right, that's at least four different armies in our region. Who's winning?"

"The winners are the officers whose regiments can get coltan out of the Congo and onto the marketplace. They rapidly become rich beyond their wildest dreams. The losers are the people who live here. They're seen as pawns—men to enlist, women to rape, children to enslave, villages to burn. And the icing on the cake is that the Congo is also absorbing hundreds of thousands of Ugandan refugees fleeing from the Lord's Resistance Army. All in all, the country's infrastructure, which wasn't in great shape to begin with, is just getting shredded."

"Okay, now I understand why we might be busier than ever."

"Can you work tomorrow morning?" Jean-Claude asked.

"Of course," Michael replied.

"Excellent. I'm really glad you've returned but apologize because I need to leave—I have something planned this evening."

"Jean-Claude has a girlfriend. A beautiful, charming girl." Mbake was beaming.

"Really? JC, is this true?" Michael wondered how his colleague found the time for romance.

Jean-Claude merely shrugged, in typical Gallic fashion. "L'amour est fou. Love is crazy."

He left and Mbake went back to the kitchen, leaving Michael and Chantal alone.

Chantal looked Michael in the eye. "I heard about the terrible events that happened here last year." Michael looked at the floor. "How are you doing, really? We've got to have each other's backs, so I need to know that when the crunch comes you'll be right there beside me."

Michael met Chantal's eyes. "I've been working at Harborview Medical Center in Seattle for months. It has been going really well."

"I'm glad to hear it, but as you know, this is not an American hospital. To the contrary, and I'm sorry for being blunt, but this is where you lost one friend forever and where another friend was badly traumatized. My question is how traumatized were you, are you?"

Michael looked down at his hands, his feet, the grimy floor. "I'll be honest. I went through a rough stretch. But I'm much better now." Michael was attempting to convince himself, as well as Chantal. "So when IMAF called and said there was a crisis here, I couldn't turn my back."

"But it's always a crisis here, no? For almost fifty years, since the start of independence. For hundreds of years, beyond the era of Belgian exploitation to the slave trade. If you stay here until the crisis is over, you'll be here for the rest of your life!"

"Well, it's just a short contract. Two months."

Chantal shook her head.

"Look, Chantal, I'm here, I'm fine, I want to get back to work. To helping, healing, and saving people's lives. But I've got to get some sleep if I'm going to work tomorrow."

Chantal shrugged and sighed at the same time, like a lawyer who had failed to get the answers she wanted from an evasive witness. "Please tell me if you're having a hard time. You've got the same room as before, apparently. They've replaced your cot with a new bed." She paused, smiled, and said, "Good night, sleep well. I'm off to see our patients."

CHAPTER 23

DOM DROVE TO MARIA AND MICHAEL'S house in his battered, mud-spattered Subaru Outback. The roof rack was rigged to hold a bike, a kayak, skis, even a sailboard. Life in the Pacific Northwest was complicated for outdoor enthusiasts like Dom: there were so many choice activities, all requiring expensive equipment. Because he'd always worked for non-profits, Dom had to scratch around for gear, haunting the used sporting goods stores, borrowing from friends, and shelling out his hard-earned cash for new equipment only when all other avenues were exhausted.

He parked on the street right in front of the house. As promised, the key was taped to the bottom of a red hummingbird feeder hanging from the eaves of the garage. The door unlocked grudgingly, unleashing a smell of mildew and dust. The garage was cluttered with outdoor equipment, gardening tools, dilapidated furniture, and garbage bags overflowing with old clothes.

The only bike that Dom saw was Maria's gleaming, nearly new Giant. Michael had bought her the bike years ago, but she'd never taken to cycling and rarely rode it, preferring public transit. He wandered once around the garage looking for Michael's bike before noticing some plywood that, judging by the disruption of accumulated dust, had been moved recently. Michael's mud-spattered mountain bike was leaning against the wall behind the plywood and an electric lawnmower. Dom moved the plywood and pushed the lawnmower to the opposite side of the garage.

The rear panniers were still on the bike. Bonus, thought Dom. Another piece of gear he didn't own and didn't want to buy for this trip. Michael kept all of his sports equipment gear in tip-top shape. It made him a reluctant but excellent source of borrowed gear.

The Gary Fisher bike sported skinny hybrid tires, so Dom would have to poke around looking for the fat knobby ones that would get traction on the slick rock canyons of Moab and Arches National Park. One of the panniers looked like there might still be gear in it. Maybe something edible, given his friend's appetite when he was cycling. Dom leaned the bike against his leg and bent over to open the pannier. The first thing he saw was a see-through waterproof pouch containing a map. Curious to see where Michael had been riding, he opened the pouch to reveal a high-resolution U.S. Geological Survey topographic map of the area surrounding the Chester Morse Reservoir. That's weird, thought Dom. Then he remembered his unusual conversation with Michael about terrorism. "No," he said. No, it couldn't be. He tried to conjure up competing explanations, to fight against the obvious conclusion: his best friend was involved somehow in the contamination of Seattle's water supply. Feeling instantly queasy, Dom put the map back in the pannier, left the bike, locked the garage, returned the key to its hiding place, and got the hell out of there. He needed to think this through and figure out what to do.

Cassie walked a block to the headquarters of the Seattle Police Department. She passed two coffee shops but resisted the temptation, not wanting to be late after already changing the time of her meeting with Chief Gilhooley. She showed her ID to the desk sergeant and was escorted straight to Gilhooley's office. He was a bear of a man, matching the voice she'd heard on the phone. Late fifties or early sixties, broad shoulders, large head, brush cut, huge hands but a friendly smile. One huge hand gestured to the seat across from him, and Cassie sat down.

"Coffee?" he asked.

Cassie hesitated.

He sensed her concern. "You're in Seattle. Even cops drink good coffee."

"Sure, then. Black, thank you."

"I'll be right back." Gilhooley returned almost immediately with two steaming mugs.

"Any breaks in the investigation?" Cassie asked. She sipped the coffee and was pleasantly surprised.

"Lots of leads but no suspects so far. We have the eyewitnesses and the mystery cyclist, the emails—"

"And the two Arab-looking individuals seen in the vicinity," Cassie added.

"Nope. The report of Arabs in a Toyota Tercel turned out to be Hispanic-American janitors doing a weekly cleaning of the water treatment facilities at the Chester Morse Reservoir. We checked them out. Rock-solid alibis. I'm confident that they're innocent."

"I'd like to see the reservoir, get a feel for the scene."

"Of course. I can have an officer take you out there. About a half-hour drive, depending on traffic. How about you folks? Anything you're not sharing with the local yokels?" Gilhooley smiled but his eyes told Cassie he was concerned.

Cassie trusted Gilhooley, but she couldn't tell him about the threat of a second attack and the $100-billion demand. To avoid lying, she answered a slightly different question. "The intelligence guys are pretty keen on the Islamic terrorist angle. How do you see it?"

"Just between you and me? Doesn't seem to fit. But I've been wrong so many times over the years that I don't make predictions anymore. I stick to what I know."

"Just like my dad," Cassie replied. "He was a cop in Tampa Bay for twenty-five years. Taught me to focus on the evidence." She was interrupted by her cellphone. It was Abby.

"I'm sorry. I need to take this call."

Gilhooley held up his huge hands. "I understand. The office next door should be empty."

"Thank you. I'll try to be quick." Cassie stepped into the hallway, was momentarily confused, looked back at Gilhooley and saw him point to the left. She nodded, turned, and walked into the vacant office.

"Abby?"

"Big break, Cassie. The DNI got a hit on the NCTC's TSC."

"Too many acronyms," Cassie pleaded. "A hit from what?"

"The National Counterterrorism Center's Terrorist Screening Center has identified two prime suspects."

"Who?" she asked. The hair on her neck tingled.

"Two brothers. James and Mustafa Ujaama. Converts to Islam. Formerly known as James Ernest Thompson and Jon Thompson. Seattle connections. Al-Qaeda connections. Previous plots involving water supplies. They've issued a nationwide all-points bulletin for these guys. Mustafa Ujaama founded the Dar es Salaam mosque in Seattle in 2001 and served as its imam. Mustafa was heavily influenced by an imam in Atlanta named Jamil Al-Amin, a former Black Panther who called himself Rap Brown back in the 1960s."

At the mention of a Black Panther named Rap Brown from the sixties, Cassie began to doubt this so-called break in the case. It sounded wildly implausible.

"Any more on the Ujaamas?"

"Mustafa Ujaama spent several months in London, England, studying with the radical cleric Al-Masri before becoming an imam. The mosque in Seattle is closed now, but there are unconfirmed reports suggesting that it was recruiting and fundraising for Al-Qaeda a few years back. Mustafa Ujaama has been under surveillance off and on for many years and is still living in Seattle. Agents are executing a search warrant on his home as we speak."

"Doesn't seem to fit," Cassie said, lifting a paperweight from the otherwise empty desk, noticing the hole in the dust she'd made, and quickly replacing it.

"Several former members of the mosque are in custody at federal institutions. They are being questioned right now. And APBs have been issued for six other individuals of interest known to be associated with that particular mosque."

"And the other brother?"

"James Ujaama worked as a courier for Al-Qaeda, delivering laptops full of technical information to them in Afghanistan. As far as we know, he first trained at an Al-Qaeda terrorist camp in 2007. Like his brother, he spent time living in London, where he also knew Al-Masri. British Intelligence believes he helped design a website that Al-Masri uses to preach jihad against the U.S. government. And here's the kicker. James Ujaama was arrested in Denver in 2012 carrying a computer that contained extensive files related to poisoning water supplies."

Now Cassie gasped. Maybe these brothers *were* a good fit. For the first time, she wondered if the leaders of the American intelligence community, whom she'd dismissed as fools, were actually smarter than they looked. If the Ujaama brothers had done this, she would never live down her skepticism about the Islamic angle.

"Is he still in jail?"

"No. He entered a guilty plea on charges of conspiring to provide goods and services to the Taliban, in violation of the International Emergency Economic Powers Act."

"That's an odd indictment."

"Apparently it was the only thing that the government was sure it could nail him on. As a result of a plea bargain, James Ujaama was sentenced in 2010 to five years in federal prison plus three years of supervised parole."

"Just five years? Something else was going on there—"

"Yes. He provided a wealth of information on bigger fish—especially Al-Masri. James Ujaama was released almost immediately after sentencing on the basis of time served."

"Where is he now?"

"We don't know. He violated his parole conditions in late 2017 and hasn't been located since."

"These brothers sound like our first real suspects. Thanks for the heads-up, Abby. I'm going to pass this information to Chief Gilhooley right now."

Cassie rushed back into the chief's office. He was just hanging up the phone and had a stunned expression on his face.

"You heard about the Ujaamas?" Cassie asked.

"Yes."

"Do you know them?"

"Not personally, but I certainly know of them. Hold on a minute." Gilhooley picked up the phone and said, "Get me the files on the Ujaama brothers, James and Mustafa. Double time."

A young woman knocked on Gilhooley's door moments later. "Here you go, Chief," she said, handing over two thick manila folders.

"Thanks, Amy."

Gilhooley placed the folders side by side on his desk and flipped them open before turning them around and pushing them across to Cassie. "I know that paper files are old school. We're working on digitization. But here, have a look."

Cassie was initially taken aback. "He looks familiar . . ."

Gilhooley agreed. "Yes. Mustafa Ujaama bears a striking resemblance to the actor Forest Whitaker, although Ujaama is probably twenty pounds lighter at six-foot-two, 220 pounds. Mustafa has the facial hair of a devout Muslim. James is taller, at six-foot-four, but slimmer. He grew his hair and beard long while in prison. Of course, they may have altered their appearance since these photos were taken."

"Do you think they're involved?"

The chief leaned back in his chair. "As I said, I don't like to make guesses. But there appears to be at least some compelling circumstantial evidence. They have motive, they have means. Maybe they had the opportunity too."

CHAPTER 24

AFTER RETURNING HOME, Dom went for a long, slow run to think through his situation. Why did Michael have that map? Was he just looking for some good mountain biking trails? Was there another reasonable explanation that Dom was missing? Could the doc really be involved in contaminating Seattle's water supply? What was that odd phrase Michael had used during their recent conversation? Ethical terrorism. Dom wrestled with whether he should call this in. He didn't have much evidence, but his gut told him that Michael's obvious post-traumatic stress and frustration at the failure of his plans for the Blue Drop Foundation might have driven him to do something crazy. He didn't want to accuse his best friend, but if Michael had actually done this, he needed serious counseling and treatment. Dom got on his road bike and pedaled around until he spotted a rare pay phone. He looked up the number on his cellphone, fed coins into the slot, and punched the buttons. He held the filthy receiver a safe distance from his mouth.

"Good morning, EPA, Northwest Regional Office."

"Hi there. I need to speak to Cassie Harden-Hernandez. It's urgent."

"She's based in Washington, D.C."

"I know that. But my understanding is that she's currently in Seattle. Can you put my call through to her or give me her cellphone number?"

"Can I say who's calling?"

"No. But you can tell them I have information about the poisoning of Seattle's water."

"Oh! There's a 1-800 number—"

"I know. But I have evidence that might reveal the identity of the—"

"I can't put you through to Ms. Harden-Hernandez. That's not the proper procedure. You need to call the 1-800 number to report your information."

"Listen up." Dom struggled not to shout, as he gripped the receiver. "You'll be in a shitstorm of trouble if you don't put me through. You'll be responsible for stalling the investigation into a terrorist attack and possibly allowing the bad guys to escape." He laid it on a bit thick, but it worked.

"Okay, okay. I'm putting you through to Abdullah Ali. He is Ms. Harden-Hernandez's executive assistant."

"Hello, Mr. Ali?" Dom thought about trying to disguise his voice but decided it might make him seem like a flake.

"Yes, Abdullah Ali here. Ms. Harden-Hernandez is out in the field. If you've got information, tell it to me, and I'll pass it on to her directly."

"Mr. Ali, I can give you the identity of one of the people involved in poisoning Seattle's water, as well as physical evidence connecting him to the crime."

"So tell me."

"Well, as I'm sure you can understand, I'm not comfortable doing that on the phone. And I want some assurances as well."

"Assurances?"

"That I won't be arrested, that my identity will remain confidential, and that you'll protect the safety and well-being of the person I identify."

"So you know this person? Wait. Were you involved? Why would you be arrested?" Abdullah was speaking quickly.

"Yes, I know him, and no, I was not involved. Not in any way, shape, or form."

"All right. Assuming your information is accurate, your requests should be doable. You'll have to talk to Cassie. But for now, give me something so that we know you're for real."

"I found a topographic map of the area around Chester Morse Reservoir in the pannier of a bicycle that could have been used to access the reservoir. And I have information regarding this individual's motive."

"All right. That's good. We need the details of your information ASAP. Where are you calling from?"

"Seattle. And let me be perfectly clear. I talk to Cassie Harden-Hernandez or I don't talk. We talk alone or we don't talk."

"That's fine. You can meet her at the regional EPA office. I'll book a conference room and ensure that you can meet in private."

"Sorry, but I'm not willing to enter the lion's den. There's a Starbucks down the street from your regional office—"

"This is Seattle. There are probably five Starbucks in a three-block radius."

"The one at 2nd and Seneca. One o'clock. I know what Ms. Harden-Hernandez looks like."

"Fine. But let me make one thing perfectly clear. We're in the middle of one of the most important criminal investigations in EPA history, so if it turns out that you're feeding us crap, you'll be arrested for obstruction of justice and there'll be no Starbucks where you end up spending the next few years."

"It'll be worth it. I promise."

Dom hung up and grimaced. He could feel the stirrings of a massive headache, right behind his eyes. Turning in his friend wasn't going to be easy, even if it was the right thing to do.

Abby called Cassie immediately.

"Abby, I'm at the reservoir—what's up?"

"Another break!" Abby relayed the details of his conversation with the anonymous caller, trying not to let his excitement overwhelm him. After all, the 1-800 tip line had received hundreds of calls. A handful of publicity-seeking wackos had even confessed.

"He sounds legitimate," Cassie responded. "I'll get a lift back to the office right away. Great job, Abby." The only solid information they'd received from the tip line was from the two old fishermen who'd seen a cyclist at the reservoir. Their description matched this anonymous caller's story. But if the informant was a creep, or if he was involved in the poisoning, Cassie didn't want to meet him alone. She called Mitch Friedland, the EPA's regional head for the Pacific Northwest.

"Friedland here. What's up?"

"Can you go to the Starbucks at 2nd and Seneca for me?"

"You need caffeine so badly that you're asking me to be your coffeewallah? You should join Narcotics Anonymous."

"Shut up, Mitch. We might have caught a big break. Abby just talked to a guy claiming to know at least one of the perps and the location of some key physical evidence."

"Such as?"

"Topographical map, a mountain bike, and a motive. He wants to meet me at that Starbucks at one. I need you to go there now and hang out, backing me up in case things go off the rails."

"I'm your backup? I'm wearing penny loafers, have string bean arms, and only run to catch the bus. You want any uniforms? Suits? Men with guns? Muscle?"

"No. He wants to meet me alone, and I don't want to take the risk of scaring him off."

"Then I'm perfect."

"I'm sending Abby ahead of me as well."

"Great. A schleppy Jew and a Somalian refugee. Quite an intimidating posse you've got."

"Abby survived the anarchy on the streets of Mogadishu while he was growing up. Should be able to keep a source in a Seattle coffee shop under control if things turn ugly."

Friedland grunted his grudging agreement.

"Text me if you see anything suspicious," Cassie said. "I'll be there soon. And don't let on that you know me. I'm supposed to be alone."

CHAPTER 25

CASSIE TOOK HER TRAVEL MUG back from the barista and looked around. It was uncrowded. Mitch was at the counter by the door flipping through the sports section of *USA Today*. Abby was sprawled in an armchair near a faux fireplace, looking as though he owned the place. Both men were in good spots for watching people come and go.

There were two big armchairs empty near the back, on either side of a small coffee table, en route to the washrooms. Cassie sat down in one and pulled out her phone. Her inbox had seventy-two new messages. She clicked on the first message, from Stryder, but was interrupted before it could load.

"Cassie Harden-Hernandez?"

She looked up and then stood up. There was a handsome guy standing in front of her with wavy dark brown hair, a dimple in his square chin, and a bicycle helmet under his arm.

"Let me just turn this nuisance off." She appeared to fumble with her phone so she could turn on a voice-recording app to capture their conversation. She set it down on the table beside her coffee. "And you are?"

"A good citizen." Dom smiled nervously, revealing bright, beautiful teeth, then launched into the story about going to borrow a friend's bike and finding the topographical map.

"Is the evidence in your possession now?"

"No. I left it there. But I'll give you a name, an address, and a precise location at that address. Before I spill my guts, tell me how you'll protect my identity and ensure that the person I'm about to tell you about will get the help he needs."

"The success of the Rewards for Justice Program depends on our ability to maintain the strict confidentiality of our informants. If your information proves to be accurate and leads to the arrest and conviction of the people responsible then you'll be eligible for the $50-million reward we're offering. You can definitely remain anonymous if you choose."

"It's not about the money. I know this person. He's a good friend, but I think he's suffering from PTSD."

"Did he serve in the military?"

"No. But the media is saying that whoever did this is a terrorist, and I know how our government treats terrorists. This guy is a good person who needs help. I would really, really hate to see him killed or tortured, especially if I'm the one who turned him in."

"I'll do what I can. Everything I can. You have my word on that."

Dom sat back in his chair. Last chance to bail. He could withhold Michael's name, turn his back on Cassie, and walk out the door. Except now he'd probably be arrested for obstruction of justice. His best friend was a wanted man, a potential terrorist, and clearly ill. There was no alternative.

"His name is Michael MacDougall. He's a doctor."

"That doesn't sound Arabic," Cassie said, sotto voce.

"Pardon me?" Dom couldn't quite make out what Cassie had said.

"M-a-c or M-c?"

"M-a-c."

"M.D. or Ph.D.?"

"M.D."

"From Seattle?"

"Yeah."

"He did this himself?"

"I don't know. He sure as hell never mentioned it to me. I doubt he told Maria either."

"Maria?"

"His wife. Maria Morales. She's a law prof at the University of Washington."

It didn't sound like this guy fit either of the FBI's profiles. "Can you give me his address?"

Dom rattled off Michael's street and house number. "The bike is in the garage, and the map is in one of the panniers. But—"

"But what?"

"The doc's in Africa right now—"

"Africa?"

"Yes, working for the International Medical Assistance Foundation."

That rules him out if he did it alone, she thought, unless . . . "Where is he and how long has he been there?"

"He left on Saturday afternoon. He's in Goma, in the Congo."

"Do you know if his flight went through London?"

"I don't know."

This doctor fit the timeline, if not the profile. Some pieces of the puzzle were fitting together. Others were still missing. "Why would he be involved in something like this? Links to terrorist organizations? Anything like that?"

"God, no. Not the Michael I know. But he was a different person when he came back from his first stint in Africa. It was terribly stressful, and he was sent home early because of one of his colleagues was killed and another sexually assaulted. Michael felt that these awful events were somehow his fault. He hasn't been himself since."

"Okay. I need your name and contact information. It would be smart for you to stick around town for a couple of days, see how this pans out. We may need you to answer a few more questions."

Dom put his head in his hands. He felt like a rat, but he knew that if Michael really did this, then he needed help, and needed it now, before he did anything else that was even more dangerous.

CHAPTER 26

CASSIE GAVE A SURREPTITIOUS THUMBS up to both Mitch and Abby as she left the coffee house to run back to the EPA office. Abby arrived a minute later. "Abby, get the president and everyone else on the task force on a videoconference. Right now. It's urgent and can't wait for this evening's call."

Cassie was abuzz. She was about to break the case. In the nick of time. It would be beautiful to watch everyone's reactions. ISIS, my ass.

Five minutes later Abby poked his head in the door of the borrowed office. "Cassie. The videoconference is up and running. The White House is standing by. Some of the other directors will join the meeting on an 'as available' basis."

Their loss, Cassie thought as she logged on to the encrypted program on her laptop.

"Good day, Mr. President."

"Hello, Cassie. Give me some good news."

"I'm not sure if you'd call it good news, sir, but we've identified a prime suspect in the Seattle case."

"I thought we already had two jihadis in our sights. Have we caught those bastards yet?"

"Yes, sir," Tierney answered. "The Ujaama brothers are both in custody. Unfortunately, they both have airtight alibis for the Seattle attack and are no longer considered suspects. They were subjected to intensive interrogations and yielded no useful information related to our current investigation."

"Damn it! Cassie?"

"Mr. President, it appears that the person responsible for poisoning the Chester Morse Reservoir is a physician from Seattle by the name of Michael MacDougall."

There was a brief stunned silence, then everyone spoke simultaneously. Cassie watched with pleasure as Stryder's face turned purple. A heart attack did not appear to be out of the question.

"Shut up, all of you," the president stormed. "Is this doctor an American citizen? Is he in custody?"

"Yes, sir, he is American and no, he has not yet been apprehended. We just ascertained his identity minutes ago. We believe that there is physical evidence connecting this doctor to the Seattle attack. That evidence is apparently located in the garage behind his residence. We received a reliable tip from a confidential informant. I have lawyers on their way to the district court right now to get a search warrant approved so we can take a look at his house, get the evidence from the garage, and seize his computer. But the suspect—"

"Oh no," the president groaned.

"Let me guess. He got away?" It was Tierney's turn to sneer. "Why didn't you let the FBI handle the arrest?"

"The suspect apparently left the United States on Saturday en route to Africa."

"See? He is working with the jihadis!" Stryder wouldn't give up on his theory. "ISIS has strongholds in Nigeria, Mali, Somalia, and half a dozen other African countries."

"The suspect is working with a renowned aid organization in a city called Goma in the eastern region of the Democratic Republic of Congo."

"Good Lord. This is starting to sound like a wild goose chase," Tierney scoffed. "We should—"

"Shut up, Randall," the president interrupted. "Two things. First, forget about a search warrant. I want law enforcement officers at the suspect's residence within the next five minutes. Second, we need to pick him up right away. Who do we have in Africa?"

"Let me check my files, sir." Stryder's voice had lost its bluster.

"There are legats at the American embassies in Cairo, Lagos, Nairobi, Dakar, and Pretoria."

"What the hell is a legat?"

"Legal attachés. Special agents, usually with additional language expertise or extensive foreign experience."

"Okay. Scramble a team from wherever's closest. Pick this bastard up and take him somewhere close for interrogation."

"Yes, sir," said Stryder. "Rwanda or Uganda would be good options for that."

"Wherever. We need to know two things ASAP: who he's working with and what city they're planning to hit next. We're already dangerously close to the deadline."

"And if he's not in Goma?" Stryder asked.

"Then I want an immediate callout through Interpol to every police force on Earth. Arrest his family and his friends. Squeeze them hard. Seize computers and bring them in. We don't have a moment to waste."

"Assuming we bring him into custody, can we use enhanced interrogation techniques, sir?" asked Stryder.

"Do whatever's necessary to get answers. We desperately need that information."

Cassie recalled what she'd said to Dom and rebelled. "With all due respect, sir, are you giving the CIA the green light to torture an American citizen?"

"Did I say that? I'm telling them to use the tools necessary to get the job done. If finding out the location and timing of the next attack means bending the rules then screw the rules." The president slammed both of his fists on the table. "There are thousands of innocent American lives at stake here, and this guy is our best bet, maybe our only bet, for averting disaster."

Cassie made a calming gesture with her hand that was luckily off camera. She had no qualms with playing hardball, but torture was a line she was reluctant, and maybe unwilling, to step over. "I'm sorry for pushing this point, sir, but I need to remind you of the problems at Abu Ghraib and Guantanamo Bay. Those scandals would look like tempests in a teapot compared to presidential authorization of force against an American doctor working for an acclaimed humanitarian organization. We need to remember that this suspect is entitled to the presumption of innocence. All of our evidence thus far is circumstantial."

"Drop it, Cassie," barked the president. "This is your suspect, so don't go soft on me now. We're covered by the attorney general's legal opinion on torture; American law allows presidential authorization of force under compelling circumstances. Force probably won't be necessary. It's a last resort. This doctor may cooperate. Get him into custody and get him to talk, fast. Anything else?"

Nobody spoke.

"All right. Good work, Cassie. Billy Joe, I want to hear from you as soon as he's in custody."

Cassie's next call was Chief Gilhooley.

"Interesting development at the crime scene, Cassie. Our team just found two plastic perc jugs. Ten liters in total. Also a pair of thin plastic gloves, the medical type."

Bingo, Cassie thought. "Where?"

"About fifty yards from an old logging road that runs from the highway down to the reservoir. Right where our two eyewitnesses placed the lone cyclist. We're bringing the jugs to our lab for fingerprinting."

"That's great, Chief. Now let me share something that's strictly for your ears only. We've identified a prime suspect, as well as physical evidence, and are in the process of making an arrest."

"Here in Seattle?"

"No. We believe this individual left the United States soon after carrying out the attack and is currently in Africa. I wish I could tell you more but I have to run. Let's just say he should be flying home in handcuffs in a matter of hours."

CHAPTER 27

MICHAEL WAS WRAPPING UP HIS first operation of the day, a Cesarean section on a shy fifteen-year-old girl who refused to answer any questions about her pregnancy, her parents, her home, or the child's father. She turned her head away when Michael held the small baby boy up for her to see. Tears streamed down her cheeks as Michael cut the umbilical cord and worked to stitch the six-inch, sickle-shaped incision. The girl was HIV positive, but they had treated her with nevirapine and would administer the drug to the newborn within the next forty-eight hours. These simple interventions would reduce the odds of the baby being HIV positive by over fifty percent.

At least they could give the boy a fighting chance. But he would probably have to grow up an orphan. Maybe the girl was raped. Maybe she'd been forced into prostitution. Maybe she just didn't care. You could tie your soul in a Gordian knot trying to figure these things out. Michael needed to focus his attention on the next patient.

The intense pressure of performing an endless stream of emergency operations in the challenging circumstances of the Congo was a relief to Michael. He'd worried that his nerves would fray, that the rope connecting him to the world might finally snap. But he was feeling better than he had for weeks, months even. The medical work demanded his full attention, consumed all of his energy, and provided an unambiguous sense of doing good, without the endless and corrosive barrage of doubts, failure, and frustration that had haunted his life this past year. The events in Seattle were unreal here, like the remnants of a bad dream. He hadn't had a suicidal thought since he landed in Africa.

He paused as he heard a helicopter approaching from the east. The walls of the surgical tent billowed inwards. The chopper was landing inside the compound.

"What now?" he asked no one in particular. Helicopters seldom brought good news, except for the occasional overdue shipment of supplies.

Daniel burst into the surgery, eyes agog. "Doc Mac! Doc Mac! Men with guns, asking for you—"

Daniel was roughly elbowed out of the way by two burly men in military fatigues and mirror sunglasses, pistols drawn.

"Dr. Michael MacDougall?" Both men trained their guns on Michael.

Disconnected thoughts spiraled through Michael's mind, images of Laurent's bloody face and the Mai Mai general. He bit his tongue and said, "That's me. Who are you, and what's this about?"

"You'll find out if and when we want you to know. Now let's go. Pronto." The taller of the two men spoke.

Michael straightened. "I have to finish this operation. Please wait for me outside."

"No. You're coming now." The two men advanced toward him, walking in lockstep as though their intimidation was choreo-graphed. A hand clamped onto Michael's arm and almost lifted him into the air. The tip of the man's gun poked Michael in his Adam's apple. No one dared intervene.

Fear washed over Michael but he managed to bark a couple of instructions. "Daniel, get Chantal to finish the stitches and make sure the baby gets its shots. I'll be back as soon as I can." Michael tilted his head toward the Congolese girl as he was marched out of the tent and hustled toward the unmarked helicopter. There was no point in resisting. The two men were ripped like a pair of twin Rambos, muscles bulging out of their fatigues. They walked

166

on either side of Michael, each crushing one of his upper arms in their fists.

The shorter man climbed into the back seat of the chopper. The taller soldier lifted Michael into the middle of the three seats, sat beside him, and fastened both of their seat belts. Then he gave the thumbs up to the pilot and co-pilot, also wearing generic camo clothing. The men in front were smaller but equally stone-faced.

The helicopter revved up, lifted straight into the air, and headed northwest. Michael was wedged between the two behemoths and again sought some kind of explanation. "What's going on?"

"Shut up and hold your hands out." The tall soldier to Michael's left barked the command.

"Why?" Michael asked.

"Just do it," the man grunted, brandishing a pair of handcuffs.

They flew across mountains and forests for thirty minutes in silence, before landing in a clearing that appeared out of nowhere, an ephemeral breach in the jungle that would rapidly disappear unless constantly maintained.

Michael was unsure if he'd been kidnapped or arrested. He was taken from the helicopter and manhandled into a slapdash shack made of rusty corrugated iron. The floor was red dirt. There was a beat-up, sturdy-looking wooden table, and two decrepit folding chairs on either side of it.

"Sit." The taller Rambo did all of the talking.

Michael sat down. He was still handcuffed, clenching and unclenching his hands as the handcuffs slowly cut off his circulation. His ankles were then tied to the legs of the chair. The two men took up positions at the doorway, arms crossed and eyes vigilant, as if Michael might make a break for freedom, running hunched over and carrying the chair on his back into the thick jungle foliage.

A tall man in beige khakis entered the shack. He had close-cropped gray hair, a heavily tanned and deeply wrinkled face, and cold blue eyes. His face was all angles, and his lean body looked bereft of a single ounce of fat. He was the kind of man you would cross the street to avoid at night. If you saw him coming.

"Dr. MacDougall." It sounded like the man was from New York or Boston, the nasal drawl in the way he pronounced the name.

"Yes?"

"We need your help." The man folded his long frame onto the chair opposite Michael.

"With what? Who are you? Help?" he wondered. Maybe the leader of a rebel group or paramilitary needed medical attention? Were these men mercenaries? Coltan miners? Or was he going to be held for ransom, a bargaining chip in a kidnapping plot?

"We need you to answer a few questions."

"Okay."

"About Seattle."

Now Michael understood. The American government. How had they tracked him down so quickly? Why had he been brought to such a remote location?

"You're responsible for the poisoning of Seattle's water supply."

"Yes, that's true."

The man was momentarily quiet, as though surprised by the casual ease of Michael's admission. "How did you do it?"

"I placed several gallons of perchloroethylene in the Chester Morse Reservoir. Saturday. Early in the morning."

"Who are you working with?"

"IMAF, the International Medical Assistance Foundation."

The man leaned forward. "Not funny. I mean who were your co-conspirators in the attack on Seattle?"

Michael frowned. "Nobody. I did it myself. Who are you anyway? Has the United States publicly committed the money to the war on poverty?"

The man sprung up from his chair with the coiled power of a cobra. With his face about two inches from Michael's and his right hand wrapped around Michael's throat, he shouted, "I ask the questions. You fuckin' answer them. Who are you working with, or for?" Purple veins bulged in the man's forehead and along the sides of his neck. Spittle sprayed Michael's face.

"Nobody. I—" Michael's face began turning red as he struggled to breathe.

"Are you hooked up with ISIS?"

"No." The man's thumb was crushing Michael's larynx. Michael squirmed but the pressure was unrelenting. Any feelings of relief that Michael had experienced about being arrested rather than kidnapped evaporated.

"Okay, let's try a different question. Who's your next target?"

"No target," Michael wheezed.

"Bullshit." The man pressed harder on Michael's throat. "Let me refresh your memory. On Sunday, you and your accomplices sent an email to the White House saying that Seattle was just a warning, and your next attack will kill a lot of Americans. Unless your demands are met. Now let's try again. What city are you targeting?"

"None. A . . . threat." Michaels's mouth opened and closed like a fish out of water.

"Just a threat?" The man roared and released Michael's throat, now roughly grabbing his head by the ears. Michael gasped as oxygen flooded his lungs. "You've got the entire U.S. on red alert, you've got 330 million people scared shitless, you've got the government of the United States scrambling to beef up security at over 100,000 community water systems, and you're saying 'don't worry, be happy'? Your time is running out, you dumb fuck. What city?"

For the first time Michael saw the wider repercussions: he had been so obsessed with Africa's need that he had blinkered himself to the impacts on Americans.

"All right. You're not going to cooperate, we'll take this up a notch." The interrogator nodded to the men at the door.

The two guards left the shack but soon returned carrying a large galvanized tin tub that they placed on the table between

Michael and the man asking the questions. Water sloshed out onto the table.

The hairs on the back of Michael's neck prickled.

"You've heard of waterboarding?" the man asked.

Michael's eyes grew wide. His breath caught in his throat so he just nodded.

"You're about to experience a low-tech version of it. It's not much fun. I'd prefer to apply electricity to your testicles but that leaves a nasty burn mark, and my instructions are to avoid leaving any physical evidence of our conversation. So let's try the last couple of questions again."

Sweat ran down Michael's face, his sides, his groin. "I want to speak to a lawyer."

The man laughed, a short, rough bark. "You're speaking to one. Called to the bar in the state of New York and the District of Columbia."

Michael shook his head. "I want to speak to someone from a U.S. embassy."

The man laughed again. "I work at a U.S. embassy. Any other requests?"

"Believe me, please! I'm telling the truth!"

The man responded by lunging across the table, leaning over the tub, grabbing a fistful of hair at the back of Michael's head and asking, "Names of your accomplices?"

Struggling to free his head from the man's grasp, Michael said "No—" before his head was plunged into the tub. He opened his mouth to protest, to scream, and sucked water into his lungs. He tried to lift his head but it was impossible. Time slowed down. He opened his eyes and saw particles suspended in the water, rust streaks and nicks in the metal of the tub. He thought of the medical effects of hypoxia, the condition in which vital organs, particularly the brain, were deprived of oxygen. Hypoxia could lead to unconsciousness, seizures, brain damage, coma, and ultimately, death. His lungs were spasming and his vision was faltering when his head was yanked back out of the water.

Michael coughed up some water and gulped air greedily.

"You can't do this to me," he spluttered. "I'm an American citizen."

"Last chance," the man said, still gripping the hair at the back of Michael's head. "What city are you fuckers planning to poison next?"

Michael didn't respond. What could he say?

"Answer me," the man hissed.

Michael shook his head. "There's no plan. There's no we, only me. You—"

The man looked at his watch. "Let's see if he can go two minutes." Michael's head splashed in again.

The other men smiled. While Michael was drowning they made small talk. "I saw a guy on *Oprah* hold his breath for twenty-three minutes," the taller soldier said.

"That's bullshit," the boss replied as he held Michael's head under water. He was CIA now but he'd done a stint with the Navy Seals. "The world record is eleven minutes and thirty-five seconds."

"No, sir. This guy sucked pure oxygen for half an hour first. Super-oxygenated his blood and meditated to slow down his metabolism."

"Aah, so he cheated."

"Maybe," the soldier conceded. "According to Oprah, there's pearl divers in Asia who can hold their breath under water for fifteen minutes."

"It's incredible what the human body can be trained to endure. We'll see what this guy's made of in about sixty seconds. When I was with the Seals, I could almost get to five. But it felt like my fucking head and lungs were going to explode."

Michael was pulled back into the oxygen-rich air, coughing and gasping, taking huge gulps of air. He was beginning to think that he might die in this dusty metal shack. Who were these people?

What had he done to Maria with his actions? How had he come to this ending?

"You ready to talk?"

Michael looked the man straight in the eye, beseeching, pleading. "I'm telling the truth!"

"Bullshit. Three minutes this time." The man slammed Michael back into the water.

Michael began to thrash and the two guards moved in to hold him in place. At about two minutes and thirty seconds, Michael passed out. His head was jerked out of the water, flopping like a rag doll's, and dropped on the table beside the tub, neck at an awkward angle.

Michael slowly regained consciousness. He retched up water and blood. He heard the leader say, "While he's having his beauty rest, I've gotta make a quick call, see how far to take this interview."

Soon the leader reentered the hut, smiling. "We just got the green light. We'll go the distance with this guy. If he doesn't give us what we need then it's his problem. His life."

"Stop!" Michael screamed. "This is crazy. I'm an American doctor doing voluntary humanitarian work. You can't torture me."

The leader ignored him and approached the table.

"Names of accomplices and your next target. Or you go for the eternal swim."

Michael realized that this man was willing to kill him. Continuing to insist on the truth would be signing his death warrant. He shrugged his shoulders in resignation and gave them what they wanted.

"New York City." It was the first city that came to mind. Michael dredged his mind for accomplice names, terrified that he would involuntarily implicate family or friends. An unexpected drawer in his mind popped open. "Dave Fleming, Erik Hanson, and Chris Bosio."

"Say those names again."

Michael repeated the three names.

"You better not be fucking with me. You'd regret that more than death by drowning, I assure you."

CHAPTER 28

CARTER USED A SATELLITE PHONE to call his boss in Langley, Virginia. It was the middle of the night there, but everyone was pinned to their desks, waiting for the word from Africa.

"Stryder."

"Carter."

"Go."

"The Big Apple is on deck."

"Fuck! New York City?"

"Yeah. And I have three names. Co-conspirators."

"Give them to me."

"Dave Fleming, Erik Hanson, and Chris Bosio. Ring any bells?"

"A couple seem familiar, but I can't place them." Stryder was already entering the names into the National Criminal Information System, looking for prior arrests, convictions, and addresses or other contact information.

"Did he disclose this information willingly?"

"No, sir. This guy is almost as tough as a Navy Seal. He put up a hell of a fight."

"Any connections to ISIS, the Earth Liberation Army, or any other radical terrorist organization?"

"No. Nothing like that."

"Are you 110 percent certain about the information he gave you?"

"With respect sir, 110 percent certainty is mathematically impossible. Nothing's ever certain. But 99 percent confident, sure."

"You better be right. We can't afford to blow this one. A city other than New York gets hit and we're both going to be washing latrines at Guantanamo with our tongues."

"Well, this guy won't be out poisoning watersheds any time soon."

"Where is he now?"

"Air Force transport will get him back on American soil within in a few hours."

"Good work, Carter."

"Thanks."

"Lie low for a while."

Stryder's search of national criminal databases came up empty for two of the three names, Fleming and Bosio. These bastards were flying below the radar. It seemed odd, but then Michael MacDougall had a clean rap sheet. There were lots of hits for Eric/ Erik Hanson/Hansen. It would take time to sort out which was the right one. They'd have to focus their initial search for the trio in the Seattle and New York areas and work outward from there. There would have to be a massive effort to ramp up security in the Big Apple. It would be a nightmare, but New Yorkers would just carry on. Stryder wondered why anyone still lived in the cursed metropolis, besieged by one disaster after another.

He arranged an immediate conference call to explain MacDougall's confession. It was the middle of the night but no one on the task force was sleeping.

"Mr. President, we apprehended our prime suspect at 0900 local time in Goma. That's two a.m. Washington time. He was immediately interrogated and freely confessed to having carried out the attack on Seattle. He initially claimed to be operating alone and denied plans for a second watershed attack."

"But?"

"In the course of sustained questioning, he admitted that there was a second target, and that there were other persons involved."

"What's the target?"

"New York City, sir."

The president closed his eyes and buried his head in his hands. "Oh no."

"The suspect identified three men—Dave Fleming, Erik Hanson, and Chris Bosio—as his co-conspirators. Two of the three names garnered no relevant hits on the national crime or terror databases, and we're checking out a handful of Erik Hansons."

It was Cassie's turn to frown. She stood up from her hotel room desk and began pacing. This information didn't fit the picture she'd developed of Dr. Michael MacDougall. Based on MacDougall's profile, the information that Dom had provided, and the physical evidence regarding the contamination of the Chester Morse Reservoir, Cassie believed that the doctor was working alone, and bluffing about subsequent attacks.

The president drew a deep breath, as he prepared to issue orders for shutting down the largest city in the country. Law enforcement agencies would basically be imposing martial law in an effort to prevent the attack.

On an impulse, Cassie sat down and entered the three co-conspirators' names together into Google. She got 315 results, and as she scanned the summaries of the first ten, she clapped a hand over her mouth. All of the results were about the same subject: the Seattle Mariners baseball team of the early 1990s. Dave Fleming, Erik Hanson, and Chris Bosio were pitchers on the same baseball team. Was there any possibility that three retired baseball players were co-conspirators in a plot to poison New York City's drinking water? It was completely implausible. MacDougall must have lied. Why? Duress, Cassie guessed. And the CIA had swallowed the misinformation hook, line, and sinker.

She smiled and suppressed a laugh. "I have some urgent information on the three so-called co-conspirators." Silence. "Obviously there are no baseball fans here." Someone on the line cleared his throat but no one spoke. "Dr. MacDougall lied about having accomplices, meaning he probably also lied about targeting New York City for a second attack."

"What are you talking about?" Stryder asked. Noise bubbled up in the background.

"Dave Fleming, Erik Hanson, and Chris Bosio. Do I have those names right?" Cassie asked.

"Yes. What about them?" Stryder again.

"They played baseball together in the American League."

"They're relatively common names. Must be a coincidence." Cassie could tell that Stryder was reeling. She had more. "They all played for the Seattle Mariners for a number of years in the early 1990s. By my calculation, Dr. Michael MacDougall would have been a teenager at that time, and my guess is that he was a big Mariners fan."

"Maybe it proves that our suspects knew each other." Stryder was grasping at straws.

"Billy Joe?" The president was apoplectic, shouting instead of speaking. "I'm about to deploy the National Guard to New York City and set a city-wide curfew to prevent a terrorist attack. Law enforcement officials are going to launch a public manhunt of unprecedented scope. Are we seriously looking for a trio of retired baseball players?"

Cassie jumped in again with the results of her follow-up Googling. "Erik Hanson is a baseball coach with a community college in southern California. Chris Bosio runs a small business in Seattle. Give me a minute and I'll find out what Dave Fleming is up to these days."

The president continued to fume. "If this doctor lied about the identity of his co-conspirators, it's safe to assume he lied about New York. Agreed?"

"Yes, sir," said Cassie. The others mumbled muted agreement.

"All right. We'll maintain the red alert for the time being, but I'm not deploying the National Guard or declaring a state of emergency. And I have a question for Billy Joe, Randall, Roger, and Orrin." The four men braced themselves. "Why does the United States spend tens of billions of dollars a year on intelligence? Since the very beginning, you've all pointed the finger at various jihadists, and we've gone public with that theory. The perp is a goddamn American citizen. A doctor, no less. How do we spin this without looking like bumbling idiots? What do we do with Dr. MacDougall? I want to send a message to America that you can't get away with this kind of bullshit."

Stryder jumped in with his own spin. "The good news is that we nailed this guy and nailed him fast. We can work with this. He's the new face of terrorism. Fits with our domestic priority of fighting ecoterrorism. We can spin the ISIS angle as a misdirection that helped our agents close the noose on this guy without letting him know that we were on his trail."

Cassie marveled at how plausible Stryder's scenario sounded. Snatching victory from the jaws of embarrassment.

"As for what we do with the perp, that's easy," Tierney chimed in. "Death penalty. Send him to join Timothy McVeigh and bin Laden in hell. Right, Leon?"

Attorney General Bynum agreed. "Chapter 113B of the U.S. Criminal Code deals with acts of terrorism. One of the specified acts is the use of a chemical weapon. If the use of a chemical weapon causes a death, then the terrorist can be sentenced to death. This guy, this doctor, poisoned millions of people. Surely we can prove that somebody in Seattle died because of this guy's actions."

"The Seattle coroner's office can provide us with all of the death certificates from the days immediately following the contamination of the reservoir." Bynum sounded confident. "We'll have epidemiologists review them to determine whether we can link any deaths to the PCE. We can also pull data from hospitals, emergency rooms, family doctors, and poison control centers to tell us how many people became ill."

Cassie interjected, "Getting the death penalty in this case seems unrealistic. The levels of perc involved were insufficient to produce even mild acute or chronic effects. I don't think you'll find a credible toxicologist or epidemiologist to substantiate the allegation that the contamination of the reservoir caused anybody's death."

"We'll see about that," Bynum replied, his confidence unshaken.

"Okay, look. I've heard enough," said the president. "The spin we can put on this arrest sounds good to me. I'm going to call a press conference for first thing this morning to announce that we've apprehended the main suspect in the Seattle water poisoning. There'll be no mention of New York City or the so-called co-conspirators. Cassie, I want you to join the press conference via video link so you can describe how the investigation succeeded and help me answer questions. I want more information on the death penalty option. Let's get this rolling fast."

"Sir, my agents made the collar in Africa. I'd like to be at the press conference tomorrow too," said Stryder.

"Domestic terrorism is the Bureau's jurisdiction. We should be there too." Tierney wasn't going to pass this up.

"All right. We'll meet at eight a.m. to review our messaging." The president would make Stryder, Tierney, Matthews, and Osborne pay for their myopic incompetence, but not until it was politically expedient. Right now, it was more important to boost public confidence in the beleaguered law enforcement and intelligence communities and his administration's handling of the war on terror.

Cassie was staring out the hotel window at office buildings where the only lights were being used by workaholics and cleaners. A series of beeps and clicks signaled people leaving the conference call. Just as she was removing her wireless headset, she heard someone whisper, "Mr. President?"

"Yes, Billy Joe. Make it quick."

"I don't think we want this case to go to trial, sir. We'd be giving this homegrown terrorist a prime-time platform for spewing his anti-American views. The trial will last for weeks or maybe even months, and he'll be the headliner, spreading his subversive ideas like a virus. Plus, it's safe to assume he'll be a totally different kind of defendant. In contrast to nutcases like the Unabomber, this guy might come across as an intelligent, rational human being."

"You're suggesting that we offer a deal to avoid a public trial?"

"No, sir. We should never negotiate with this kind of scumbag."

"Then what are you suggesting?"

Cassie was listening, trying not to breathe, not to make a sound.

"We can make him go away. We already know he's guilty. He confessed. Why bother with an awkward trial? We could accelerate the death penalty process."

"How?"

"It's better if you don't know the details."

"Seems risky."

"We can minimize the risks. The stakes are so high. This would be a strong, decisive, preemptive move. We'd be in control, which we can't guarantee if this case goes to trial."

"It's your call. And Billy Joe, this conversation never happened," said the president, and abruptly hung up.

Cassie continued holding her breath, standing by the window, terrified that Stryder would realize someone else was still on the line. She tiptoed over to the desk, thankful for the lush carpet in her suite. It silenced her footsteps, and Cassie gently pushed the End Call button.

She contemplated the conversation she'd just overheard. The CIA wanted to kill MacDougall and avoid the unpredictable publicity of a high-profile trial. And the president basically gave Stryder the green light. Cassie was no longer sure she was on the right side.

CHAPTER 29

MARIA WAS SOUND ASLEEP AT FOUR A.M. when the phone began to ring.

"Hello?" she croaked.

"Is this the residence of Dr. Michael MacDougall?" The connection was faint and fuzzy. Maria covered her other ear and struggled to focus.

"Yes it is, but he's not—"

"Yes, I know he's not at home. My name is Jean-Claude. I work with Michael in the Congo."

Maria sat up in the bed. The logistics expert. Michael had spoken warmly of the man he called JC. "Dios mío! Is Michael okay? Did something happen to him?" Maria heard nothing but static. "Hello. Are you still there?"

"Yes. Hello. Can you still hear me?"

There was a delay on the line, and Maria wanted to scream. "Yes, please go ahead."

"Michael was taken away today by men in a helicopter. They held a gun to his head. We don't know who they were. It's dark now. He didn't return, and we haven't heard any communication from him or them. I'm terribly sorry."

Maria gasped and struggled to hold back tears. She worked with people whose families and friends had been abducted in Latin America. Her own family had suffered abductions in Nicaragua. Los desaparecidos. The disappeared.

"Have you called the police?" Maria asked, hoping if she sounded calm she would feel that way.

"Yes, of course. They'll do what they can. But—"

"But what?"

"The police here . . ."

"What?"

"The police are neither effective nor trustworthy. I've also contacted headquarters. They'll be in touch with you. But I felt it couldn't wait. You should contact the American embassy in Kinshasa. They may have greater resources at their disposal."

"Do you have any idea who took him? Did they hurt him?"

"No. There were four uniformed men in an unmarked helicopter. They spoke English and were heavily armed. Michael did not resist them. It would have been futile and might have endangered our patients and staff."

"Oh God. Has this ever happened before?"

"Unfortunately, kidnappings and killings happen far more often than we'd like. I'll call back if there's any news. Michael is a wonderful man." Jean-Claude's voice broke. "We hope that he will return unharmed. I am so sorry." The line went dead.

Maria's husband was ten thousand miles from home and had been kidnapped by unknown persons for unknown reasons. She realized that despite their deep troubles, she still loved Michael. Part of her always would.

She wiped the tears from her cheeks, took several deep breaths, and dialed o. She bounced around from operator to voicemail and back again, navigating the American and African telecom bureaucracies simultaneously. As she repeatedly reached dead ends, her frustration mounted but she pushed it aside, determined to speak to a real person who could help her. Finally, she reached a message at the American consulate in Kinshasa that provided a different phone number for emergencies.

She dialed the number and was surprised to get an answer right away.

"American consulate, Quinn speaking." A gruff voice barked at Maria.

"My name is Maria Morales. I'm calling from Seattle. My husband is a doctor working with the International Medical Assistance Foundation near Goma. I was just informed by one of his colleagues that he was kidnapped earlier today."

"An American? Kidnapped?"

"Yes."

"First I've heard about it. What's your husband's name?"

"Michael MacDougall. Dr. Michael MacDougall."

"Hang on a second."

The seconds ticked past and turned into minutes. Maria's teeth shredded what was left of her fingernails. She walked into the kitchen to put the kettle on for some coffee. She poured a heaping bowl of cereal but then only pushed the flakes around in the bowl. She was starting to worry that she'd lost the connection when Quinn returned.

"Ma'am?"

"Yes?"

"We don't have a file open on this yet. Can you tell me everything you know about your husband's abduction? I'll make some inquiries and get back to you as soon as I can. It's probably just a mix-up of some kind. There's a lot of fucking mix-ups in this country, if you'll excuse my French. So start at the beginning."

Maria told Quinn what she knew. It wasn't much. "Okay, I'm going to talk to the ambassador right now and either he or I will get back to you as soon as we have some news about your husband's situation."

"Please call me as soon as possible."

"Yes, ma'am. We will."

Maria jumped when the phone rang again. She prayed for good news and picked it up.

A senior vice president with IMAF in Paris was calling to apologize and assure her that the organization would do everything in its power to ensure that Michael returned home safely. Maria thanked him and quickly ended the call.

One long hour later, the consular official named Quinn called back. "Your husband wasn't kidnapped. That's all I'm authorized to tell you."

"What do you mean, not kidnapped? His colleagues saw it happen!"

"Further inquiries can be directed to the ambassador."

"I don't understand. What's going on?"

"I'm sorry, ma'am, but I'm not authorized to discuss this matter with you beyond what I've already said."

"Not authorized? Please. Please! Tell me what you're talking about. Is my husband—" Maria couldn't bring herself to ask if Michael was alive. "Is he all right?"

"I've said everything I can say. Goodbye."

"Wait! Put me through to the ambassador."

"He's not available right now."

"Then give me his phone numbers—home, cell, office, satellite, all of them."

Quinn complied. When Maria dialed the numbers, she reached voicemails and left a series of urgent messages. Ten minutes later, she called the numbers again. And again. And again.

The ambassador never answered and never called back.

At 5:45 a.m., Maria's house was silently surrounded by a dozen law enforcement vehicles from various federal agencies. There was a SWAT team, crime scene technicians, computer experts, the bomb squad, a hazardous materials team, and, at Stryder's request, a translator fluent in Arabic. The doorbell rang. When she opened the front door and saw two policemen standing there, Maria almost collapsed, assuming that they were going to inform her that Michael was dead. Instead, they threw Maria up against a wall, cuffed her, and dragged her, kicking and screaming Spanish swearwords, into a squad car with its engine still running.

CHAPTER 30

THE LANDSCAPE WOULD HAVE LOOKED familiar to Michael when the aircraft descended toward McChord Field air base in central Washington State, but he was still wearing a black hood. Although he'd never suffered from claustrophobia, there was something disconcerting about flying blind, not knowing the destination. Nobody had told him a thing. He'd been tossed, half-drowned, into a helicopter, then roughly transferred to an airplane somewhere in Africa, while in a state of shock. Aboard the plane, he slipped in and out of consciousness.

He came to with a start as the plane landed roughly. Still hooded and handcuffed, he was led down from the airplane to the back of a U.S. Army Humvee. After a brief drive, Michael was pushed out of the Humvee and led toward a low brick building. Muckraking journalists described the Northwest Joint Regional Correctional Facility at Fort Lewis as an Abu Ghraib on American soil. There were allegations of torture, extortion, and prostitution rings involving female guards. The administration denied all allegations of wrongdoing.

Michael heard orders being grunted and doors opening but could see nothing. His hood was finally removed as he was thrust into a small, dark, windowless cell.

"I want to—" he shouted.

The door slammed shut with a metallic click.

"—make a phone call!" His words echoed in the spartan cell. Illuminated by one bare bulb, it contained a cot, a toilet, and a sink, all metal. The cell was eight feet by ten feet with a high ceiling and a surveillance camera mounted in one of the upper corners, well out of reach. He gripped the sink with both hands, head bowed. The faucet dripped steadily. He tightened both taps but the dripping continued. The irony was not lost on him. Water. Taken for granted by most Americans, even in prison. A pipe dream for many Africans. The essence of life. A tool for torture. The focus of his obsession. And the cause of his downfall.

After being kidnapped, tortured, and flown halfway around the world, Michael was exhausted and disoriented. Yet he was also relieved to be back on American soil. Despite all the heated political debates in recent years, the Constitution was intact, the unassailable backbone of American democracy. Still, something strange was going on. I know I committed a serious crime, he thought, but what the hell happened to my basic rights?

He'd seen enough movies and television shows to believe something was amiss. Nobody had said to him, "You have the right to remain silent. Anything you say or do can and will be held against you in a court of law." Nobody had let him make a phone call or speak to an attorney. Nobody had told him what crime he was being charged with. Michael sat down on the cot to wait. Surely it wouldn't be long.

As the hours dragged past, Michael's mind oscillated between flashbacks to his recent torture and his growing guilt about Maria. Did she know yet? Was news of his arrest public? He desperately wished that he could apologize, try to explain, though his thoughts were so jumbled that he was barely making sense to himself.

Realizing that action could be an antidote to despair, Michael stood up and pounded on the door. Nobody responded. He did sit-ups, push-ups, and every type of exercise he could think of in a desperate effort to avoid sitting there and thinking about what he'd done and what was going to happen next. Eventually he collapsed onto the cot, physically and emotionally drained, all of the shock and adrenaline worn off. He couldn't sleep but had no way of measuring time.

Eventually a metal slot at the bottom of the door opened and a plastic tray was pushed in. The food was tepid and gray. Some kind of soup covered in a film of grease. A cold blob that might be meatloaf, along with soggy French fries and canned peas. No utensils. Although the food was unappetizing, Michael was famished and used his fingers to clean every morsel from both plate and bowl. Then he lay back on the cot, feeling the onset of a bad stomachache.

Without warning, the metallic door clicked and swung open. Two grim-faced men in dark suits looked at Michael like he was something unpleasant on the bottom of their shoes. They stood in the doorway but didn't enter the cell.

The larger man, whose nose looked like it had been broken several times, spoke. "Special Agents Moorhouse," he pointed at himself, "and Chang," turning a thumb toward his colleague. "Dr. MacDougall, we need to clarify a couple of things."

Michael backed up against the rear wall of the cell. Waves of fear and nausea racked his body. He struggled to keep his bladder and bowels under control.

"You poisoned Seattle's water?" Moorhouse asked.

Michael nodded.

"Part of a plot to blackmail the president?"

A half nod.

"New York is next?"

Michael hesitated, trying to determine what they wanted him to say but unsure of the right answer.

Chang stepped into the cell. Chang wasn't large, but he moved with a threatening grace, like a mountain lion capable of pouncing at any moment.

Michael threw up the meal he'd just eaten. Chunky gray muck gurgled out of his mouth as he tried to choke it back. His eyes watered, his throat burned, and he shrank further into the corner of the cell, squeezing between the toilet and the wall, sphincter clenched. "Stay away." His voice was tremulous and an octave higher than normal.

"New York's next, yes or no?" Moorhouse said.

Michael went with the truth, and shook his head.

"Plans to attack any other cities?"

"No." Michael scarcely recognized his own voice.

"Have you been acting alone?"

"Yes."

Moorhouse smiled. This was no consolation to Michael, who recalled the psychopath who had tortured him in Africa. "Here's a bonus question. Who are Dave Fleming, Erik Hanson, and Chris Bosio?"

"Seattle Mariners. Starting pitchers. When I was a kid."

"You know any of them personally?"

"No."

"Bingo. You win the prize. An all-expenses-paid trip for one to the penitentiary of our choice for the rest of your life."

Michael wiped a dangling thread of vomit from his chin with the back of his hand.

"Unless, of course," Moorhouse paused, "the judge prefers to reward you with a one-way trip to hell via lethal injection."

Chang laughed and they left. The door clanged shut with an intimation of finality. Michael washed his face and rinsed out his mouth. Then he lay down on the cot and wept. At some point the light overhead went out. Michael lay awake in the dark for hours before falling into a fitful, nightmare-plagued sleep.

When he awoke it was pitch black and it took a few seconds to remember where he was. He was in jail, and he might spend the rest of his life in a cell like this, never again walking free, never again riding his bike through the North Cascades, never again saving a patient's life, never again making love to Maria. There definitely would be no child now. He'd given up everything that he loved. And for what? There would be no $100 billion for Africa. The game was over and he'd lost.

The light in the ceiling came on. Michael assumed that it indicated daytime. He got up, relieved himself, and did a few cursory stretches. He rubbed his scalp, which still tingled from where the man had held his hair. There was light bruising on his wrists and ankles from the handcuffs and the rope that tied him to the chair. Otherwise there was no physical evidence to suggest that he'd been tortured. The bruises would disappear in twenty-four to forty-eight hours and only the psychological scars would remain.

The door clicked and swung open again.

"Put these on," a soldier said as he threw a bundle of clothes at Michael. Michael was still wearing his tattered and filthy operating scrubs. They'd taken his running shoes away in Africa and he'd been barefoot ever since. Not that he'd noticed.

"Now," the soldier said.

Michael turned his back on the soldier, stripped off his dirty clothes, and put on the sweatshirt, sweatpants, and flip-flops.

"Let's go." The soldier nodded at the door.

"Where to?" asked Michael.

"You'll see when you get there."

Michael was marched out of the building and into a small truck. There were metal benches in the back, welded onto the sides. Michael's right hand was cuffed to a ring attached to the bench. A black hood was again placed over his head and cinched around his neck. Not tight enough to hurt, just enough to cause discomfort. He wondered why, since there were no windows in the rear of the truck. Again, two military policemen rode in the back with him. Michael almost laughed out loud at the absurdity of being treated like a dangerous, violent criminal, but realized that to these people that's exactly what he was.

It was a quick trip, at first on a highway, then stop-and-go traffic punctuated by blaring horns that could only mean a big city. After less than half an hour, the truck stopped. The handcuffs were detached from the ring but quickly reattached, joining Michael's hands behind his back. A soldier yanked Michael down from the back of the truck, where he stumbled, struggling to regain his balance. When his hood came off, Michael looked around, half curious, half afraid. They were in an underground parking lot. It was nondescript, except for an unusual absence of graffiti.

One of the men swiped a card through a sensor that beeped and a door swung open, revealing a drab institutional corridor. Michael was steered down the hallway into a waiting room where other men were shackled, mainly in handcuffs but some wearing leg-irons as well.

"Welcome home," said the younger soldier, smiling for the first time.

"Where are we?" asked Michael.

"SeaTac Federal Detention Center."

"SeaTac?" Michael was astonished to be so close to home.

The older soldier ran his finger across his lips, indicating that the talkative private should zip up. The SeaTac Federal Detention Center was the only federal correctional institute for civilian inmates in the state of Washington. It looked more like a hospital than a prison, but the appearance was deceiving. SeaTac was designed to hold inmates in all security categories, from white-collar crooks to extremely dangerous, violent, or escape-prone inmates.

Michael was photographed, fingerprinted, and strip-searched, each step more humiliating and demeaning than the last. The prison system was just getting warmed up.

CHAPTER 31

MARIA HAD BEEN WHISKED DOWNTOWN and was being interrogated at the FBI's Seattle field office. Cassie watched from behind a one-way mirror. Maria was seated at a wooden table across from Special Agent Moorhouse, while Special Agent Chang leaned against the wall, watching. In DC, FBI Director Randall Tierney was watching on a live video feed with two-way audio.

Moorhouse and Chang, just back from Fort Lewis, began by double-checking her identity, confirming that she was still married to Dr. Michael MacDougall, and giving her the standard Miranda spiel about her rights. Then, without any context or explanation, Moorhouse dove right in. "Did you help your husband poison the city of Seattle's drinking water?"

Maria reacted like she'd been slapped in the face. "What?"

"Did you help your husband poison the city of Seattle's drinking water?" Moorhouse patiently repeated the question.

Maria struggled to understand what was being asked. "Of course not! My husband has been kidnapped, and—" Maria made the connection, as improbable as it seemed. "Did you kidnap him! Hijo de puta! Where is he? Where is Michael?" She stood up, anguish written all over her face.

"Sit down."

"No." Maria stood glaring at them. "I know my rights."

"Sit. Down. Now." Moorhouse spoke slowly and nodded to Chang who began moving toward Maria. She looked around wildly, then sat down before he reached her.

"Were you aware that your husband poisoned Seattle's water supply?"

"That's crazy! Michael's a doctor. He wouldn't do something like that."

"Ma'am, we have physical evidence from your residence and the Chester Morse Reservoir," Moorhouse said, placing photographs of the garage, Michael's bicycle, the pair of five-liter percholorethylene containers, and a topographic map of the Cedar River watershed on the table. "We have files obtained from the hard drive of a computer seized at your residence. And . . . we have a confession from your husband."

Maria looked at the photos in horror, lapsing into her mother tongue. "No lo creo. Es impossible. Tiene que ser un error."

"We don't make mistakes, ma'am. What we need to ascertain at this time is the extent of your involvement in these crimes."

Maria's head snapped up again. "I had nothing to do with any of this. And despite what you say, I doubt that Michael did either." The photographs could be faked. The evidence planted. The confession coerced. Michael could still be innocent.

"Are you close to your husband?"

"Of course."

"Really?"

"Yes. And it's none of your business, anyway."

"You expect us to believe that your husband plotted and conducted one of the most complex terrorist attacks in American history and never mentioned it to his wife?"

Maria shook her head but wondered about Michael's increasingly odd behavior in the weeks before he left for Africa. Could these crazy accusations possibly be true? Could Michael really have been involved in the attack on Seattle? "I want to talk to my husband."

"I'm sorry but that's not possible."

Maria felt like the bones in her body melted, and she had to fight not to slither out of her chair onto the floor. The wind was knocked from her lungs in an exhalation that was half choked cry. Michael was dead. She put her head on the table and sobbed.

"Ma'am?"

No response.

"Ms. Morales? We need you to answer some more questions."

Maria didn't even raise her head.

Cassie shook her head. Amateur hour. Where did these clowns learn to question a person of interest? Infuriated, she strode over to the door and knocked sharply. This was out of her jurisdiction, but she didn't care. She'd earned the right to break a few rules.

Chang opened the door and was surprised to see Cassie standing there.

"We're in the middle of a priority one interrogation here—"

"Thanks for the news flash. Get out and give me a minute alone with her."

Chang frowned. "No way. That's not Bureau procedure and—"

"Do it." The voice was unmistakable. Randall Tierney's baritone.

"Yes, sir."

Moorhouse and Chang skulked out of the room.

Cassie pulled a chair around the table so that she could sit close to Maria, and put a hand on her back. Maria flinched but did not look up, continuing to sob.

"Ms. Morales, my name is Cassie Harden-Hernandez. I am the head of the Environmental Protection Agency and I need you to listen to me. Your husband is not dead. He's not dead, he's in custody, and physically, he's fine."

Maria lifted her head and turned to look at Cassie, wide eyes beseeching her to explain that this was all some kind of terrible mistake.

"However, I'm afraid it's true that your husband is the prime suspect in the poisoning of Seattle's drinking water. He was arrested in Africa yesterday, confessed to an American intelligence agent, and is in transit right now. That's why you can't see him."

Maria reeled.

"You had no idea about any of this, did you?"

Maria shook her head and started sobbing anew.

The president kicked off the conversation at the teleconference later that day. "Nice job with the press, Cassie."

"Thank you, sir."

"You've done such a marvelous job throughout this investigation that I'd like you to continue to act as the administration's public face on this case as it moves forward. I've spoken to the attorney general and he concurs. I want our legal people to focus on the trial without being distracted by the media. Second, I want to downgrade the terror alert from Red to Orange. Roger?"

"Yes, sir." Roger Osborne was not going to disagree today.

Cassie didn't hear a single grumble of dissent. For once, the hawks weren't fear-mongering, though it was unlikely that they were feeling contrite. More likely they'd had their knuckles rapped by a president who realized how he'd been misled by their blundering.

"I've decided that we should pursue the death penalty," the president continued. "Any other choice sends the wrong signal to would-be terrorists. All right. I've got another meeting, so I'll leave you in Jeremy's capable hands."

The president's chief of staff, Jeremy Chan, took charge. "Leon, please brief us about plans for the trial."

"The trial will be held in the District Court for the Western District of Washington, in Seattle," said Bynum. "The defendant will be charged with use of a chemical weapon and committing a terrorist act. Other charges are still under consideration at this time, including theft, assault, and murder. The case is being prepared for a grand jury. That should happen within a matter of days. It will be open and shut. Then we'll take steps to ensure that the case is assigned to an appropriate trial judge."

"There are several excellent candidates in Washington's Western District," said Tierney. Both he and Stryder had files on every sitting judge in America. "A few of the older judges out west are liberals, but thanks to the current president we've had some real solid appointments. Law and order conservatives."

"I'll speak to the chief judge out there," said Bynum. "As you know, cases are usually assigned by random draw but the chief retains discretion to appoint judges to specific trials."

Chan asked, "What about the jury?"

"We'll take a close look at the jury pool," Tierney replied. "I think we can have confidence in our citizens to convict this kind of bastard. Especially after our jury consultants have done their job."

Cassie was about to ask an unwelcome question about the role played by FBI jury consultants in ensuring that defendants received a fair trial, but Chan cut her off. "That's enough for today. We'll reconvene again soon, as the preliminary legal proceedings get started."

Stryder immediately placed a call to Tierney. Being embarrassed by Cassie had brought the lifelong antagonists together to salvage their reputations.

"Randall, we need to ensure the right people are on this jury."

"We're already on it. Our office has the voters' rolls from western Washington. As soon as they draw the potential jurors, we'll have agents compile dossiers on each of them."

"Good. Every person in the jury pool will have vulnerabilities. Gambling debts. Stacked mortgages. Maxed-out credit cards. Kids in college. Affairs. Drug or alcohol use, past or present. Hidden family embarrassments. Their problems, our leverage. Time to put those deep-cover jury consultants to work."

"Exactly! Once the jurors are selected, we start with the honey. We offer to pay each of them one million dollars if they convict. A hundred grand up front and the rest when they deliver the verdict. We save the stick in case somebody starts to misbehave."

"You give them cash up front?" Stryder asked skeptically.

"Yeah, just a taste. It seals the deal, convinces them we're for real. The fact they're committing a felony by taking the money gives us an insurance policy."

"Nice. And I'm guessing your agents won't flash the badge when they make contact with the jurors."

"Uh no. That's where you can help me out." Tierney paused briefly. "If we could use intelligence agents from overseas for approaching jurors, it would minimize the risks of somebody being recognized."

"How many do you need?"

"Two or three."

"You've got them."

"Then we've got our jury."

"Yeah."

Tierney chuckled. "You've got to love America. Everyone has their price." He beamed: he was running an operation using CIA agents. If it blew up, the FBI would be far from the impact zone. But Stryder had his own covert operation underway and wasn't about to let Tierney in on the action.

CHAPTER 32

MARIA WAS RELEASED SOON AFTER Cassie's intervention in the interrogation room. Her home had been torn apart while she was in custody, and she found it difficult to know where to start picking up the pieces in the house or in her life. She retrieved the bottle from the cupboard above the fridge, poured a glass of rye, and added some diet cola. It took a few minutes for the alcohol to calm her enough that she could think.

She needed help. Maria decided to call two of her closest friends from the University of Washington law school, Consuela Jimenez and Peter Quarrington. Consuela was an expert in constitutional law. Peter was a nationally renowned criminal lawyer.

She called Consuela first. Not in her office, not at home, and not answering her cell. Maria didn't leave any messages, but sent a text, saying "Call me." Maria called Quarrington next.

When he answered, his voice was filled with sympathy. "Maria. I just saw the news about Michael. Please tell me that there has been some kind of dreadful mistake."

"No. I don't know." She fought back tears. "I haven't talked to Michael. I don't even know where he is."

"Has he not contacted you since he was arrested?"

"No."

"That is not like the Michael MacDougall I know."

"No."

"And the police will not tell you anything?"

"No."

"Let me make a call. I have a good friend in the Department of Justice. I will call you back right away."

"Thank you."

Maria sat by the phone, watching the kitchen clock. She rose to mix another drink, and was about to sit down again when the phone rang.

"Maria, my apologies for the delay. I can explain later. Michael is being held at the SeaTac Federal Detention Center. I have arranged with the warden for you to see him. Are you fit to drive?"

"Yes . . . no. I'm not sure. I'm on my second drink. Trying to calm down."

"Do not take any chances. Call a taxi and I will meet you there."

It was midafternoon when Peter arrived at the SeaTac prison. Maria was dropped off several minutes later. He was a tall, thin man, wearing a dark navy blazer and gray slacks. His left eye was milky with the cloud of a cataract but his right eye was still a piercing blue. Because of severe arthritis in his knees, Peter often used an electric wheelchair but he could still drive and could walk short distances with the help of two canes. While he appeared frail, those who knew him understood that he was still in full control of his considerable facilities and had a reservoir of courage that time could never drain.

"Why hasn't he called?" she asked. "I just can't believe that he wouldn't try to reach me."

"It is the bloody Patriot Act, a law that undermines the American constitution so badly that the Founding Fathers must be rolling in their graves. But look, we can discuss those issues later. They will only give us an hour, and a prison guard will be in the room with us at all times. You may be given a minute to hug Michael at the beginning and the end of the visit, but any physical contact beyond that is proscribed."

"Thank you, Peter. I really appreciate this."

Maria and Quarrington signed in. Quarrington showed his Washington Bar Association identification card to the guards, who waved him through. Maria showed her driver's license, went through a metal detector, and was patted down by a female guard who seemed to enjoy the experience more than was appropriate, running her hands slowly along the insides of Maria's thighs. Then the guard led the way through four sets of locked metal doors that slammed behind them.

The visiting room looked like a place where an interrogation might be held. There was a plastic table and three cheap, uncomfortable chairs. A yellowing American flag on the wall. Quarrington leaned his canes against the wall, pulled a chair to the back of the room, and attempted to be unobtrusive. Maria paced. Finally, the door opened and Michael shuffled in, leg-irons clinking, handcuffed, rubbing his eyes. The visiting room officer had a guiding hand on his elbow. Then Michael saw who was waiting for him.

"Oh my god! Maria!" He almost fell forward, caught his balance, and turned to the guard holding his hands in the air like a supplicant. "Please?"

"No way, José."

Maria approached Michael, sobbing. Michael was crying too. He lifted his arms in the air and awkwardly wrapped them around her. Maria rested her head on his chest.

"This is a nightmare, Michael!" Maria erupted. "Are you all right? You look awful! Are these crazy allegations true? Were you really involved in poisoning Seattle's water? Why didn't you call? Dios mío, they arrested me and destroyed our house."

Michael flinched. "Did they hurt you?"

"No."

"I'm so sorry, Maria. I don't know where to begin."

"Tell me what's going on!"

The guard interrupted them. "Break it up and sit down. You have fifty-four minutes left."

Michael noticed Quarrington sitting at the back of the room and gave an awkward two-handed wave. Then he told Maria everything.

It came gushing out, and Michael felt cleansed, even though he knew forgiveness was unlikely.

Maria cradled her face in her hands as she listened. "I can't believe it. You really did this? You did. What were you thinking?"

"I was trying to save lives—thousands of lives, maybe even millions of lives."

"That's not how the world works! I could have told you it wouldn't work. If you had just talked to me, I would have stopped you. And what about us? Why didn't you get some help?"

"I didn't want to get you involved. I was afraid that you would hate me for even thinking about it. I never wanted to hurt you. I never wanted to hurt anyone. You know that."

Maria leaned back in her chair and stared up at the dingy gray ceiling. "I'm not sure what I know anymore. But that you did this on your own, without ever confiding in me, that's what hurts the most. What happened to trust?"

"I'm sorry. So sorry. Please, can you forgive me."

"I don't know if I can. Or even if it matters. You could spend the rest of your life in prison. Or worse . . ." Maria's voice trailed off. "I wish you'd never gone to Africa."

"Time's up." The guard approached the table, arms crossed. Michael sought to hold Maria's gaze but she wouldn't look at him. He understood now that they couldn't recover from this. He had lost her.

As she and Quarrington left the prison, Maria thought about what Michael had done. It was inexplicable to her, despite his efforts to explain. He'd completely ignored the consequences of his actions—for the country, for himself, for her, and for any future they might have. She'd thought Michael was kidnapped or dead, had been arrested herself, and now had been reunited only to learn that the unthinkable accusations were true.

They arrived at Quarrington's vehicle, an ancient green Citroën with a hydraulic system that made it easier for him to get in and out. Ever the gentleman, he opened the door for Maria before stashing his canes in the trunk and gingerly hoisting himself into the driver's seat.

"I am so sorry Maria," he said. "It is hard to imagine, hard to believe, hard to accept. But there are further challenges ahead. Michael faces a trial and conceivably the death penalty."

Maria shook her head despondently. Quarrington turned to face her and placed his hand gently upon her shoulder. He'd had a different reaction to Michael's story, which was raw, almost biblical. The doctor was an impeccably honest man. Perfectly forthright. Not only willing to tell the truth, but to do so in an articulate and emotive way. Defendants like him were as rare as innocent men on death row.

"At the risk of seeming somewhat presumptuous, I would like to offer to act as Michael's attorney. I have two ideas that I think may challenge the government's assumption that he is guilty. This case is not what is euphemistically described as a slam dunk."

PART III

The

TRIAL

CHAPTER 33

AT AGE SEVENTY-ONE PETER QUARRINGTON, professor emeritus of criminal law at the University of Washington, had retired to a waterfront cottage on Orcas Island, just outside Seattle, but he kept a small apartment downtown. Every two or three years he'd give in to the itch and take on a case, usually involving an underdog defendant and a grievous miscarriage of justice. Much to the government's dismay, his success rate was close to eighty percent, and even higher when a jury was involved.

In his last case, he had defended Jorge Villalobos, a migrant worker accused of assaulting the farmer for whom he'd been picking fruit in an orchard near Spokane. After a grueling fourteen-hour day Villalobos had returned to the ramshackle trailers, rented from the farmer, where he lived with his wife and a dozen other workers from Mexico, El Salvador, and Guatemala. His wife was gone, along with their meager possessions. Friends in the neighboring trailer told him that they'd been evicted for stealing apples. Villalobos became incensed, as his wife was honest to a fault, and they were not short of food. When he knocked on the farmhouse door to complain, the drunken farmer answered with a shotgun in his hands, telling Villalobos to "Fuck off and go back to Mexico." Villalobos seized the gun, pumped out the shells, threw the weapon on the ground, and pushed the farmer, who reeled backwards into his house. Then he left to search for his wife. State police arrested Villalobos that night as he walked disconsolately along the highway, and charged him with assault. Quarrington turned the tables on the prosecution. He put the state's agricultural community on trial, highlighting the appalling treatment of vulnerable Latin Americans. The jury acquitted Villalobos after fifteen minutes of deliberation and issued a statement denouncing the exploitation of migrant workers.

Quarrington returned to the prison the next morning to meet with Michael.

He slowly lowered himself onto a cold metal chair, and struggled to find a comfortable position. "First of all, let us establish some ground rules. You will tell me the truth, the whole truth, and nothing but the truth, or I will withdraw my services faster than you can write a prescription. I must be your priest when you have the urge to confess, your best friend when you need to converse, and your psychiatrist when you hit rock bottom. Any facts that you have been holding back from Maria? You tell me. Any skeletons hiding in your closet? You reveal them to me."

Michael was frowning, and clenching his fists. "With all due respect, Peter, I don't see the point. I'm guilty and I have to face the consequences."

"Ah, the martyr complex. Listen—if you were feeling ill and I was your doctor, would you reach a diagnosis before consulting me?"

"No."

"Would you tell me how to perform an operation?"

"No."

"Right. A client who attempts to defend himself in a death penalty trial is, statistically speaking, as good as dead. So please defer to my wisdom on legal matters."

"Okay. As long as you consult me and get my consent on important issues."

"Of course. Despite what you may think of the legal profession, I have an ethical responsibility to do so."

"All right then," said Michael slowly. "I'm honored to have you on my side."

"Thank you. Let us dive right in, shall we?"

Michael nodded.

"The law requires any defendant who may be facing the death penalty to be represented by at least two lawyers. I have someone in mind to be the second member of your legal team. Shirin Yavari is one of the most gifted students that I ever had the pleasure of teaching, a young woman who went straight from medical school to law school at Harvard. With her combination of legal and medical knowledge she could negate both my shortcomings in dealing with certain kinds of evidence and my occasional memory lapses." Peter winked.

"Do you think she'd be willing to represent a guilty terrorist?"

"You must not think of yourself in those terms. Even if you committed the acts in question, that does not lead inevitably to a conclusion of guilt."

"Why not?"

"Because there are a great many defenses available in our justice system even when a criminal act has been committed. Consider a woman found holding a smoking gun with her husband dead on the floor in front of her, a bullet wound in his chest. She evidently killed him, but is she necessarily guilty of murder? No. It might have been an accident during the cleaning of the gun, with no intention to cause harm. Not guilty. It may be that she was abused, and he was threatening to give her a beating to end all beatings. She acted in self-defense. Not guilty. It may be that she suffered from a debilitating mental illness. Not guilty."

"Okay, point taken."

"Let us get the facts out of the way first. The events as you recounted them to Maria last night—was that a complete and accurate depiction?"

"Yes."

"Nothing missing or glossed over?"

"No."

"Any skeletons?"

"Arrested once for being drunk and disorderly when I was a freshman in college. Never charged though. That's about it."

"Good. Based on what I have heard so far, there are two defenses available that may be eminently suited to your situation."

"What are they?"

"The first is not guilty by reason of insanity, which would require us to provide convincing evidence from psychiatric experts that you—"

"No! Absolutely not."

"The defense has been used successfully in a number of cases involving soldiers suffering from post-traumatic stress disorder."

"I'm not crazy! I knew precisely what I was doing and why I did it. There's no way I'm insane."

"All right. We will set that option aside for now. The second possibility, which I think you may find more palatable, is called the necessity defense. Have you heard of it?"

"I don't think so."

"It has a long and colorful history, though it is rarely used. It is also called the lesser evil defense, in that the otherwise unlawful actions of the accused caused less harm than the consequences prevented. Consider a police officer who shoots a hostage-taker, or a Good Samaritan who commandeers a car and violates the speed limit in transporting an accident victim to the hospital. These are people whose actions we consider right, not wrong. For such actions people are often praised, rather than convicted, because they are motivated by noble objectives."

"Sounds promising. But what about the death penalty?"

"I was wondering when you would ask about that particular albatross. I suggest you try not to lose any sleep over it."

"Easy for you to say."

"I do not say it lightly. Despite what the public may think, the death penalty remains a very rare sentence in America—particularly for white men. Only sixty executions occur in an average year, eighty percent of whom are African-American, Hispanic-American, or Native American. Thus it seems highly improbable that you will be sentenced to death."

"It's hard to feel good about benefiting from institutional racism."

"I understand. However, our goal is to avoid your conviction entirely, rendering all discussions of sentencing, including the death penalty, moot."

Quarrington quickly outlined the stages of the trial, familiar to Michael from television and movies. "I will be back soon," he said, stuffing his notebooks into the battered leather briefcase that had been his father's in London, half a century ago.

"Thank you, Peter. I'm deeply grateful to have an attorney of your stature on my side." Michael felt slightly less alone as the guard pushed him back down one of the prison's long gray hallways. For the next few weeks, Quarrington and Shirin Yavari would be his only visitors.

One day, Shirin appeared at the prison without Peter. A second-generation Iranian American, she was short and stocky, with a round, attractive face highlighted by bright eyes. She'd been a Rhodes scholar at Oxford in her undergraduate years, and a competitive badminton player.

"Let's get down to business," she said. "Your first court appearance is tomorrow. We need to get you cleaned up. A shower, a shave, and, ideally, a haircut."

Michael ran his handcuffed hands over his shaggy head. "I'll do the best I can, but my options are limited. Can you walk me through the process?"

"Of course. The clerk of the court posts a schedule in the morning. Then we'll know what time your case will be called. Once we get in front of the magistrate, we'll learn exactly what charges the prosecution is proceeding with, and the judge will listen to arguments from both sides about setting bail."

"Is there any chance that they'll set me free?"

Yavari shook her head, almost reluctantly, as she prepared to deliver bad news. "It would take a miracle for our bail application to succeed, and there are no signs that any god is looking out for you. You'll likely be residing here at SeaTac until the trial is completed. We'll be able to sketch out our defense strategy once we know the charges. No more sitting around waiting, wondering, worrying. We can roll up our sleeves and get to work."

Michael sighed audibly. "It sounds like taking medicine—better to get it over with."

CHAPTER 34

THE DISTRICT COURT IN THE Western District of Washington was housed in a postmodern skyscraper, twenty-three stories tall. Security was strict but not over the top. U.S. marshals from the Judicial Security Division were posted at all entrances to the building, as well as at the doors to Courtroom B on the twelfth floor where the trial would take place. Michael was taken by bus, with other prisoners from SeaTac, to a holding cell in the basement of the courthouse.

The prosecution was confident, even cocky. They had motive, physical evidence, and a confession. The grand jury, a group of citizens convened to evaluate whether there was sufficient evidence to proceed to trial—without a judge, the defendant, or a defense attorney present—had returned a unanimous indictment in record time.

The arraignment took place before Federal Magistrate Judge Patricia Allan. With her granny glasses and hair pulled back in a tight gray bun, Judge Allan looked like a stereotypical librarian. She had a reputation as a fair but no-nonsense judge.

District Attorney Lisa Marconi commenced the proceedings by reading from the grand jury's indictment. "In the case of the United States v. MacDougall, the first count in the indictment is a violation of federal law prohibiting the use of chemical weapons. Pursuant to section 229 of Chapter 11B of the U.S. Code, it is unlawful for any person to knowingly acquire, use, or threaten to use any chemical weapon. A chemical weapon is defined so as to include all toxic chemicals that can cause death, temporary incapacitation, or permanent harm to humans or animals."

Michael flinched when Marconi mentioned chemical weapons. He looked over his shoulder at the gallery where media, government officials, and the public sat, mixed together. No sign of Maria, which was both painful and a relief.

"Mr. MacDougall, how do you plead?" Magistrate Allan asked.

"Not guilty, your honor," Michael said, standing beside Quarrington. Judge Allan raised her eyebrows ever so slightly.

There was a discernible buzz in the courtroom. Marconi continued. "The second count in the indictment is the federal crime of terrorism, which in this case includes two elements: the use of a chemical weapon in a crime that transcends national boundaries, and the intention of influencing or affecting the conduct of government by intimidation or coercion."

"Mr. MacDougall, how do you plead?"

"Not guilty, your honor."

Judge Allan did a better job of disguising her surprise. "On to the next order of business, the defendant's application for bail."

Quarrington made the best of a poor hand. "Dr. Michael MacDougall has no previous criminal record. He is a lifelong resident of Seattle, with a long record of community service. He has a family and a home here. He will voluntarily surrender his passport to the court, and is willing to post a substantial bond. Although Dr. MacDougall is entitled to the presumption that he is innocent until proven guilty, in the extraordinary circumstances of this case he would even consent to house arrest and twenty-four-hour electronic monitoring."

Marconi rose to address the court. "Your honor, as my friend acknowledged, this is an extraordinary case. The defendant committed one of the most serious crimes in Washington State history, deliberately poisoning millions of Americans. The damage to public health was immense, causing illness, death, and suffering. The defendant threatened to carry out a similar chemical attack on another American city, suggesting that there is a high likelihood of re-offending.

"This is a defendant who, within hours of poisoning Seattle's water, crossed the border into Canada, boarded a flight to London, England, and then transferred several more times en route to a remote location in Central Africa. In less than twenty-four hours, the defendant traveled halfway around the world. To set him free pending trial, even under strict conditions, would pose an unacceptable threat to the health and security of the American people. We ask you to refuse the application for bail."

"Application denied," Judge Allan ruled curtly. "Bail is clearly inappropriate in the circumstances of the case."

Michael's next visit from his legal team was several days after the arraignment. He was in a deep funk, reeling from the way Marconi had portrayed him as a cold and calculating criminal. A killer. A terrorist. The spin that Marconi put on the facts disturbed him because it contradicted his self-image and his good intentions. Her depiction forced him to see how the rest of the world would view his actions. Michael was particularly upset by the repeated allegations that the perc had killed or harmed anyone. He and Shirin had discussed that point in detail, and it would be of critical importance at the trial.

Quarrington appeared unfazed by the DA's confidence. "The pretrial process is moving quickly," Quarrington said. "Your case has been assigned to a trial judge, Justice Maximilian Klinsmann, which is a good news/bad news situation."

"Give me the bad news first."

"The bad news is that Justice Klinsmann is nicknamed Mad Max."

"Mad Max? As in the old Mel Gibson movie?"

"I am not familiar with the oeuvre of Mr. Gibson, but the sobriquet arose after the judge took part in one of these notorious judicial education conferences in Las Vegas about four years ago. His wife, whom he left behind in Seattle, was brutally beaten in a home invasion. Two of the young men subsequently apprehended by the police had appeared before Justice Klinsmann a year earlier on robbery charges. He'd given them suspended sentences because of their age and previously clean records. The experience transformed Klinsmann from a moderate liberal into a headhunting, defendant-loathing judge."

"So he's nicknamed Mad Max because he's angry?"

"Partly because of his newfound anger, partly to reflect the fact that he may be certifiably insane, and partly because the only sentence he has given out at criminal trials since his wife was assaulted is the maximum. Hence Mad Max."

"Yikes. What's the good news?"

"The good news is that the Ninth Circuit—"

"What's the Ninth Circuit?"

"The U.S. Court of Appeal for the Pacific region, based in San Francisco. The Ninth Circuit is aware of Mad Max's newfound zeal for punishment and has overturned several of his more excessive rulings."

"But it can take years for cases to work their way through the appeals process, can't it?"

"Unfortunately, yes."

Michael looked down at the handcuffs around his wrists and wondered if he'd ever experience the highs of successfully completing a complex surgical procedure again.

CHAPTER 35

MICHAEL KEPT HIS HEAD DOWN at the prison and said nothing unless spoken to. He'd heard that you needed to belong to a group to survive in prison. But there was no American Medical Association chapter or Sierra Club here. The options included the KKK, the Hells Angels, the Aryan Brotherhood, the Nation of Islam, and Hispanic gangs like the Norteños, Sureños, and Mara Salvatrucha. The air reeked of testosterone. Many of the inmates were enormous, jacked up on steroids, using every recreational moment to lift weights and pack on muscle.

Michael felt in constant danger whenever he left his cell. He'd seen the injuries inflicted on prisoners brought to Seattle hospitals for emergency surgery, injuries too severe to be handled properly at the prison's medical clinic. Like any group of humans, prisoners adapted to their environment. Dark ingenuity was used to craft deadly weapons. Razor blades were smuggled in and then welded to scraps of cans poached from the kitchen or recycling box. Spoons were pilfered and painstakingly sharpened into knives. Even plastic toothbrushes could be whittled to a deadly point.

So far, he'd defused several confrontations by leveraging his medical expertise. Inmates who learned he was a doctor trusted him far more than the prison's medical staff. And just about everyone had questions or concerns about their health.

One lunchtime, Michael was waiting in line for the daily special, which appeared to be fried baloney, white bread, a pale and gummy-looking macaroni salad, and some shredded iceberg lettuce. He tried, unsuccessfully, not to eavesdrop on the conversation of the Mutt and Jeff pair in front of him. A small, hyperactive man whose eyes flickered around the cafeteria was talking to a giant who kept popping knuckles embossed with tattoos that said *Fuck* on one hand and *You!* on the other. The big man's body was so enormous that the girth of his thighs forced him to walk with an unnaturally wide gait. His shaved head was disproportionately small, like the cherry on an ice cream sundae.

The little guy was complaining about his legal aid lawyer, as though it was the attorney's fault that he was in jail for the third time for breaking and entering.

"He looked like he was fourteen years old! Doogie Howser JD. Totally fuckin' clueless."

Knuckles grunted sympathetically.

"Never asked no questions on cross-examination. Not one! Read his closing argument from a piece of crumpled paper like he wrote it on the subway. And get this, he kept callin' me Gerald instead of Gerry. I ain't been called Gerald for twenty-five years."

"You should appeal!"

"Aw, what's the use? System's rigged. Guilty once, guilty forever. Anyways, I'll bounce on parole in a few months."

Michael had heard this story, or variations of it, dozens of times. If you believed inmates' stories, ninety percent of them were victims of miscarriages of justice. As the line inched forward, Michael caught a whiff of smoky, rancid grease from the old and overused frying oil. The hair on the back of his neck tingled as a fistfight broke out on the far side of the cafeteria. He watched out of the corner of his eye as several guards converged on the melee and started pulling combatants apart.

Then he sensed movement behind him. He turned. An enormous man was striding purposefully toward him, hands tucked close to his sides. He recognized Charley "Big Red" Barker, a biker facing multiple life sentences for gang-related hits. Barker sported scarlet pork-chop sideburns and looked like he'd been chiseled from stone.

"Fucking terrorist scumbag!" Big Red shouted as he closed in. Barker had been promised special treatment for the hit on Michael, told that it was revenge for the father of a child poisoned by the PCE in Seattle's water.

Michael heard someone else running hard toward him from the opposite direction. He was knocked to the floor, tray flying, as something metallic flashed past his face, connecting with Big Red's throat. The behemoth crumpled to the ground in a heap, gurgling. A sharp piece of metal tied to a spoon with dental floss, its handle wrapped in duct tape, clattered to the floor. The weapon's owner melted back into the gathering crowd as quickly as he had appeared. Winded by the impact, Michael didn't get a good look at him, just a glimpse of brown skin, tattoos, and khaki clothing.

As he regained his breath, Michael's instinct, hard-wired by almost twenty years of medical training and practice, was to crawl over and feel Big Red's wrist for a pulse. It was there but it was faint. Blood was leaking from Big Red's neck but not gushing, meaning the jugular and the two carotid arteries were probably intact. Michael looked around for something he could use to stop the bleeding. In Barker's hand he saw a deadly-looking piece of wire, a weapon for garroting him. Seeing nothing else useful, Michael picked up the shank that saved his life and slashed a strip of fabric from his own sleeve. He wrapped the makeshift tourniquet tightly around the man's neck, applied pressure, and elevated his head.

"Get some help!" Michael shouted.

A swarm of prisoners looked on, confused.

A pair of guards violently pushed and elbowed their way through the crowd, pistols drawn, screaming at Michael to lie down on the ground.

"I can't! This man's bleeding to death!"

"No shit," said somebody in the crowd. Others cheered and clapped.

"Let him go!" said one of the guards.

"No," said Michael. "I can't, bec—"

The gun didn't waver. "You're choking him. Let go now!"

"He's got a hole in his neck. If I—"

"For the last time, put him down and back up slowly! Or I'll put a hole in your neck too."

Michael reluctantly lowered Big Red back down to a prone position, releasing the tourniquet.

One guard approached, crouching down over the fallen man while his partner kept a gun trained on Michael. The blood oozing out of Big Red's neck had soaked through the tourniquet.

"Apply pressure to the wound or he'll die," Michael said.

"Do I look like a nurse to you?" the guard snarled. "Shut the fuck up."

Gun still aimed at Michael, the other guard used his shoulder mic to call for more backup. "Get a medic to the cafeteria. Double time."

Michael was handcuffed and put in the Special Housing Unit, otherwise known as protective custody, solitary confinement, or just "the hole." A tiny cell without windows. A toilet, a narrow cot, and a sink. He could cover the length of the cell in three strides. What the hell had just happened? Big Red had tried to kill him. That was clear. But why? Another man had stepped in and saved Michael's life. Again, why? Had he unknowingly violated some kind of jailhouse ethic? Was it simply a case of being in the wrong place at the wrong time? Did it have something to do with the terrorism charges? Michael was descending through Dante's inferno, each level of purgatory worse than the last.

CHAPTER 36

JUDGE KLINSMANN CALLED A MEETING of counsel to lay down
ground rules for the trial. Klinsmann had a great, hooked nose that
would not have been out of place on a bald eagle. His face was
tanned, thanks to weekends in Nevada, and he reluctantly wore
bifocals that made him look and feel old. Klinsmann shook hands
with both of the attorneys and then launched into a tirade.

"I don't want a circus here. While I appreciate that the general
public may be inflamed by the notion that there are terrorists in our
midst, I will not tolerate chaos in my courtroom. The prosecution
will follow both the letter and the spirit of the rules, and will avoid
trying this case through the media."

"Of course, Judge."

"Not just the letter of the law, Ms. Marconi. The spirit as well."

"Yes, sir."

"Nor will there be any emotional blackmail in the form of an
endless parade of victims and their families. Witnesses are there to
provide evidence of the crime and that is all. As for the defense, I
would like you to explain the contradiction between your client's
not guilty plea and the confession obtained by the prosecution. Are
you planning to challenge the admissibility of the confession?"

"No, your honor." Quarrington was the epitome of calm,
unfazed by Klinsmann's reputation or demeanor.

"Well then?"

"A confession does not necessarily equate to guilt, as your honor
is well aware. A range of exculpatory and justificatory defenses are
available to us."

"Is your client mentally fit to stand trial?" Klinsmann probed.

"Yes. We do not anticipate that Dr. MacDougall's mental state will be an issue."

Klinsmann glared at Quarrington. Only a madman would commit this kind of crime. "All right. I don't want a long stream of motions from either of you. I don't want to be snowed under with 500-page briefs. I expect counsel to be concise. I'm aware of the intense media interest, and I want all media contact to be preapproved by my office. I want to hear arguments from you directly, not read about them in the paper. I want a fair, expeditious trial."

"Those instructions are entirely consistent with Dr. Mac-Dougall's wishes, your honor. However, I would like to make one submission regarding publicity in advance of the trial." Quarrington leaned to his right and extracted a thick black binder from his briefcase. "This is just a small sampling of newspaper and internet coverage of the case to date. The media obviously are not bound by the presumption of innocence that is a cornerstone of American criminal law. One need only scan the headlines—'Perc Perp Popped,' 'All-American Terrorist', 'Shocker: Toxic Doctor'—"

"Are you laying the groundwork for a change-of-venue motion, Mr. Quarrington?" Klinsmann asked, eyes narrowed. "Because if you are, I can save you some time and effort. This trial isn't going anywhere."

"No, your honor. I do not take issue with the venue. But I am concerned that the case is already being prosecuted in the court of public opinion. I have advised Dr. MacDougall that he would be wise to present his side of the story in the media as well as in the courtroom."

"What do you have in mind?"

"We have discussed the possibility of inviting reporters from selected outlets for interviews with Dr. MacDougall at his prison."

Klinsmann waggled a finger at Quarrington. "That is completely unacceptable. As I said, this case will be tried in my courtroom, not in the media. End of story."

Quarrington held his gaze steady. "With respect, there have already been hundreds of one-sided stories portraying Dr. MacDougall as guilty. I am merely—"

"You are merely approaching thin ice," Klinsmann scowled. "Ignore my advice and you'll be charged with contempt of court. Now, are there any other issues either of you wish to raise at this time?"

"Yes, your honor," Quarrington said. "The defendant would like to relieve the prosecution of the burden of calling a long list of witnesses to establish proof of the facts. He openly admits having committed the actus reus of the alleged offenses and will sign a stipulation of the facts. The trial process would be substantially shortened."

Klinsmann looked at Quarrington over the top of his bifocals, as though reappraising his general opinion of defense attorneys. "That strikes me as a very generous offer. I favor any measures that expedite the trial without sacrificing due process. Ms. Marconi?"

"I appreciate the gesture, your honor, but must regrettably decline." Marconi wanted living, breathing, flesh-and-blood witnesses who could provide gripping testimony about Michael's misdeeds, not a dry recitation of facts on paper. Stipulation would diminish the impact of the evidence upon the jury. "Please rest assured, however, that we will keep our witness list and our examinations-in-chief as brief as possible."

"Mr. Quarrington, your offer to stipulate has been refused."

"You have the authority to compel my friend to accept my offer, your honor."

"I'm well aware of the parameters of my judicial discretion, Mr. Quarrington, and will exercise that discretion if and when I see fit. Any other questions?"

"Yes," Quarrington answered, "a minor issue."

"Make it quick then." Klinsmann closed his laptop roughly.

"Of course, your honor. I shall endeavor to be brief and compelling. My client is an American citizen, with no previous criminal record, no record of physical violence, no efforts to escape custody—"

"If you're attempting to reargue the bail hearing, forget it. There are no circumstances under which I would grant your client bail, period."

"Understood, your honor. That is not my intent. As I was saying, apart from the events forming the actus reus of the counts in the information, Dr. MacDougall has never been a menace to anyone, let alone a menace to society. I would simply like your honor to instruct the marshals to remove the handcuffs and leg-irons before ushering Dr. MacDougall into the courtroom. For him to be manacled like some kind of dangerous offender is a breach of justice and a disservice to all parties involved. Ideally, I would like you to allow him to appear before the court in civilian clothing."

There was a pregnant pause.

"That's it?" Klinsmann asked.

"Yes, your honor. It is, I submit, a modest proposal, but if granted will provide Dr. MacDougall with a modicum of dignity."

"Request refused. Your client is in no position to seek special favors from this court. He will receive the same treatment as any other defendant. Now is there any other pretrial business that we need to attend to today?"

Marconi and Quarrington both shook their heads. They could see that Klinsmann was in a bearish mood, likely to growl at whomever kept him in his office for an extra minute on this sunny day.

"Very well then, the trial date must be set in accordance with the Speedy Trial Act. I have space on my trial calendar beginning in one month. I assume that gives both of you adequate time to prepare? I don't want to set a trial date and then be forced to adjourn it because of heel-dragging by counsel. Once the date is set you will both be prepared. If you must move mountains to get ready, so be it."

CHAPTER 37

LIFE IN THE SPECIAL HOUSING UNIT was safe but miserable. Locked down for twenty-three hours each day. One hour alone in an exercise cage at 6:00 a.m. Escorted by two guards for a shower every third day. Repulsive food delivered through a slot in the door of the cell. Only one phone call per week permitted. Minimal access to books, paper, and writing instruments. And although it was cold, he had only one scruffy wool blanket and no pillow. Michael shuffled back into the visitors' room, having spent two hours enduring the pre-visit rituals. Shower, get dressed, be strip-searched, get dressed again, and then be left in another windowless room with no books, amenities, or personal items of any kind. As usual, his visitor was Quarrington, whose navy blazer and starched white shirt made Michael feel embarrassed by his crude uniform.

"Hello, Michael. I must apologize for being the bearer of bad tidings. The prosecution has filed a motion in limine to prevent us from presenting the necessity defense to the jury."

"Meaning?"

"I am sorry. A motion in limine is a pretrial application requesting that the court prohibit the other side from presenting, or even referring to, evidence on matters said to be so highly prejudicial that no steps taken by the judge could prevent the jury from being unduly influenced. The technical legal details are unimportant. What matters is that federal courts have a spotty record when it comes to protecting the right of criminal defendants to present evidence regarding the necessity defense during their trial. In essence, Marconi is launching a preemptive strike against the heart of our case."

Michael frowned. "What are the odds of them succeeding?"

"Ordinarily, minimal, but in light of our trial judge we cannot take anything for granted. There are two other pieces of disturbing information that I have no choice but to share with you."

"Maria?" Michael slumped in his chair.

"Yes. She has gone on stress leave from the university for an indefinite period and has requested that for the time being you refrain from attempting to communicate with her. I am terribly sorry, Michael. And the final piece of bad news is that Marconi served us with a Notice of Intent to Seek a Sentence of Death."

The motion in limine was argued four days later. It was Marconi's motion, so she went first, and wasted no time in going for the jugular. "There are persuasive reasons why the federal courts have been reluctant to authorize the use of the necessity defense. If the door were opened to this defense, it would be prone to terrible abuse. Do we want individual Americans to make their own choices about killing or harming innocent people, under the guise of necessity? Do we want anti-abortion protesters blowing up medical clinics and arguing that their actions were necessary to save the lives of unborn fetuses? Do we want ecoterrorists torching SUVs and arguing that their actions were necessary to protect the planet? Do we want to endow every individual in the United States with the power to unilaterally override government decisions whenever they disagree? Acceptance of the necessity defense in a case like this would be an invitation to anarchy."

Klinsmann was riveted by Marconi's argument, even nodding his head in agreement.

"Our courts have been particularly reluctant to allow defendants to take refuge in the necessity defense in political protest or civil disobedience cases. For example, time and time again anti-nuclear and antiwar protestors who committed criminal trespass or criminal mischief against nuclear or military facilities have unsuccessfully raised the necessity defense. Similarly, in cases involving everything from the disruption of naval exercises to the spray painting of government property, courts have ruled that the necessity defense is not available because of three factors. First, there is rarely a clear and compelling emergency that leaves the accused with no choice but to act. Second, there are almost always legal alternatives available to the protestors. Third, the actions of the protestors usually have little or no effect upon government or industry behavior or public policy. All three of these objections apply forcefully to the defendant in the present case. The courts have made it clear that acting upon self-proclaimed good motives is not sufficient to establish the necessity defense."

Klinsmann looked at the DA like a proud parent. "Thank you, Ms. Marconi. Mr. Quarrington?"

"Your honor, we have heard an impassioned rejection of the necessity defense by Ms. Marconi. While I found myself impressed by the U.S. Attorney's style and delivery, the substance of her arguments lacks merit. Worse, they display a stunning hypocrisy.

"In essence, Ms. Marconi argued that the defense of necessity should no longer be a part of the criminal law of the United States. Not only would this represent a rupture with hundreds of years of precedent under our common law system of justice, it represents a 180-degree reversal of the government's position on this issue. Our government repeatedly invokes the concept of necessity. It was used to justify extrajudicial assassinations of suspected terrorists. It was used to justify the torture of prisoners in Iraq, Afghanistan, Guantanamo Bay, and secret CIA interrogation chambers scattered across Europe and West Asia."

"Objection!" Marconi leapt to her feet. "Mr. Quarrington is presenting conspiracy theories as if they were factual."

"I share your concern, counselor." Klinsmann nodded toward Marconi. "Mr. Quarrington, you are walking a fine line. Do not cross it."

Quarrington continued, unfazed. "Our intelligence agents were frustrated by their inability to extract useful information from prisoners through the use of conventional interrogation techniques. So they crossed the line. A secret memo prepared for former defense secretary Donald Rumsfeld by the attorney general and the Department of Justice argued that the use of torture to aid the interrogation of prisoners was necessary, and therefore legally justified, to prevent the loss of American lives."

"Objection!" Marconi rose again. "That memo is a confidential government document, protected by executive and solicitor-client privilege from public disclosure. I urge your honor to maintain its secrecy."

"I'm inclined to agree. Mr. Quarrington, you will not—"

Quarrington interrupted the judge. "My apologies, your honor, but this allegedly secret memo was leaked to the *Wall Street Journal*, and the portions I intend to quote were published by that newspaper both in print and online, thus entering the public sphere. May I proceed?"

Now Klinsmann glared at Marconi, who'd led him into making a mistake in open court, in full view of the public and the media. He waved his hand, signaling that Quarrington should resume his argument.

"Thank you, your honor. I quote, from page twelve of the memo: 'Sometimes the greater good for society will be accomplished by violating the literal language of the criminal law. . . . In particular, the necessity defense can justify the intentional killing of one or more persons . . . so long as the harm avoided is greater.' The authors of the memo buttress their argument by citing the preeminent scholarly text on criminal law in the U.S., *Substantive Criminal Law* by W. LaFave and A.W. Scott, as well as a monograph on criminal defenses by another academic with a reasonably solid reputation." Quarrington was referring to himself.

"Move on," Klinsmann said. "You seem to be a long way from the facts at issue in this case."

Shifting slightly in his wheelchair, Quarrington continued. "The Supreme Court has described the essence of the necessity defense in the following terms: 'The peril must be so pressing that normal human instincts cry out for action and make a counsel of patience unreasonable.' That is precisely the situation that faced Dr. Michael MacDougall. As a medical doctor, he confronted a humanitarian disaster so horrific that his instincts cried out for action. As a volunteer surgeon, he could only save a tiny fraction of the lives that were needlessly being lost. He attempted to use a variety of legal avenues to persuade the government of the United States and this country's corporate elite to allocate the requisite resources to prevent and treat the diseases killing African children. His lawful efforts were unsuccessful, and the magnitude of death and suffering that he witnessed firsthand made 'a counsel of patience' utterly unreasonable.

"Consider what Dr. MacDougall was doing in Africa. He was caring for the world's most unfortunate, destitute, victimized people. Not for money. Not because of any contractual or employment obligation. Dr. MacDougall was there as a volunteer, providing essential medical services in brutal conditions because he valued the Congolese as fellow human beings. The doctor was trying to defend the right to life, the most basic and fundamental of all human rights. Without life itself, how can one enjoy all of the other rights, freedoms, and liberties?

"Contrary to the arguments of my friend Ms. Marconi, the necessity defense does not legitimize lawlessness or anarchy. Instead, it allows the jury to distinguish between necessary and unnecessary illegal acts, recognizing that the overwhelming majority of illegal acts are not necessary and cannot be reasonably justified.

"Establishing the necessity defense often requires the production of expert testimony to establish the underlying crisis or emergency and the presence of imminent harm. For example, when twenty-nine concerned citizens were charged with criminal trespass in their campaign against a plan to build a hazardous waste incinerator near a primary school in Ohio, they were allowed to present several public health experts. Experts testifying for the defense in that trial included the Chair of the School of Public Health at Boston University, a world authority on (or regarding) the impact of toxic exposures on young children.

"Two further points bear consideration. First, it is a fundamental principle of the American Constitution that a defendant has the right to be tried by a jury of his peers. This is a cornerstone of our legal system, to ensure that the people of America, not a single judge, are the final arbiters of freedom and justice. In the words of Thomas Jefferson, 'I consider the trial by jury as the only anchor, ever yet imagined by man, by which a government can be held to the principles of its constitution.' Precluding Dr. MacDougall's right to present evidence in support of the necessity defense would violate his constitutional right to a jury.

"Second, the case law is clear that the judge must allow the necessity defense to be presented to the jury whenever there is 'some evidence' to support it. And that evidence 'must be viewed in the light most favorable to the accused.' Applying these legal standards to the present case leads inexorably to one conclusion: the necessity defense must be presented to the jury for their consideration and judgment. Those are my submissions, your honor."

"Thank you both for your capable advocacy." Klinsmann was polishing the record in case his decision was appealed. "Having studied your written briefs and listened to your oral arguments, I am prepared to issue my ruling immediately, in the interests of expediting the trial."

Neither Marconi nor Quarrington was surprised. Mad Max was known for shooting from the hip.

"I am persuaded by Ms. Marconi that there is a very real danger of turning a formal criminal proceeding into a debate about politics. It is Michael MacDougall who is on trial here, not American foreign policy. At the same time, I am aware of the central importance of the jury in our criminal justice system and am reluctant to usurp their duties. Therefore, I will permit the defense to make arguments regarding necessity. However, I will impose a limit of two witnesses to provide supporting evidence, including the defendant himself."

"Your honor," Quarrington said, "such an arbitrary limit will hamstring the ability of the defense to make its case."

"You have the right to appeal, but rest assured you'll get nowhere arguing with me. My decision stands." In one crafty ruling, Klinsmann had managed to give the appearance of evenhandedness while sabotaging Michael's defense.

CHAPTER 38

AS WEEKS PASSED AND SHE commuted between Seattle and DC, Cassie became increasingly certain that American law enforcement personnel had tortured Michael MacDougall. Why else would he have made up the ridiculous story about former Seattle Mariners plotting to poison New York City's water supply? But if MacDougall had been tortured, was it justified in the circumstances? Cassie needed more information. But there wasn't anyone that Cassie could talk to about this—not Abby, not her husband, and certainly none of her colleagues.

Her other dilemma was worse. The snippet of conversation between Stryder and the president that Cassie had overheard suggested that the CIA was considering killing MacDougall before the trial.

Cassie realized that there was one person she could speak to who might be able to shed some light on these questions. Dr. Michael MacDougall. Talking to him would require breaking a few rules and taking a few risks, but in the circumstances, these seemed trivial. Cassie made a couple of phone calls and then left her hotel room, taking the stairs down to the lobby and striding into the street, where she ducked into the cab at the front of the taxi stand.

Within minutes, she was at the SeaTac prison. Having her picture all over the internet, newspapers, and the nightly news afforded more than just fifteen minutes of fame. The normally surly prison guards treated her like royalty, loosening the strict protocols surrounding prisoner visits. Cassie had been counting on this. She didn't want to sign in or leave any trace of her visit, if possible.

There was one awkward moment when the guard supervising the visitors' room asked if he could take a picture of himself and Cassie using his cellphone. Cassie imagined the photo going viral on social media and demurred, muttering something unintelligible about EPA policies.

Michael arrived in the visitors' room to see that his guest wasn't either Quarrington or Yavari.

"Who are you?"

"Cassie Harden-Hernandez. I'm the Director of the Environmental Protection Agency."

"What do you want?" The orange jumpsuit worn by inmates in the Special Housing Unit made Michael's skin appear sallow. And because it was two sizes too large, it made him look as if he was underweight. He certainly didn't look dangerous.

"I have some questions for you."

"More questions. All right. Go ahead."

Cassie had expected at least some concern about being questioned by a federal official without having his attorney present.

"I know you poisoned Seattle's water supply. But why did you make up the story about New York City and the Seattle Mariners?"

"I was trying to save my life." Michael looked directly at Cassie as he spoke. He had nothing to hide, no reason to resort to subterfuge.

"Trying to save your life from what?" she asked, holding his gaze.

"From the men who were drowning me." Michael shuddered. "Men whom I presume were working, directly or indirectly, for the government. Our government."

"How were they drowning you? I'm sorry to ask you to dredge up these memories. You don't need to answer if you don't want to."

Michael took a deep breath. He described his waterboarding experience in precise medical terms. And he explained being a baseball-loving kid who followed the Mariners' every move, especially the pitching staff, since that was the position he played in Little League.

Everything he said rang true and fit with her theory of what must have happened to him in Africa.

"Thank you for telling me this. Now I'll return the favor. Forgive me for being blunt, but I have reason to believe that your life may be in grave danger."

"What do you mean?"

"There are people who don't want your case to go to trial. People with a great degree of power and influence."

"Unbelievable," Michael said. "Well anyway, it doesn't matter now."

"Why not?"

"Your warning's too late."

"What do you mean, too late?"

"A man called Big Red tried to kill me with a wire that would have strangled me."

"What happened?"

Michael described the chaos in the cafeteria. "I had no idea why he tried to kill me. But what you're saying suggests that he was carrying out somebody else's instructions, somebody in government?"

"I don't have any evidence. But if they tried once they may try again."

"They've got me in solitary now, so I'm safe."

"I'm not sure that will save you."

"Well then, what the hell am I supposed to do?"

"You could go public. These people are like cockroaches—they don't like light. Shine a spotlight on what happened and hope it forces them back into their hole."

"But you said it yourself. There's no evidence."

"You're right. Sorry. There's one last question I'd like to ask."

"Fire away."

"Did you really think that blackmailing the U.S. government would work? It seems like such an extreme step for somebody like you to take."

"Yes, of course dumping perc in Seattle's drinking water was extreme. But there's an extreme problem, and nobody even talks about it, let alone does anything about it. Americans are bombarded with endless details about celebrities. NASCAR. Ultimate fighting. Game shows, soap operas, and reality TV.

"Yet more than 10,000 children die every day of preventable and treatable diseases. Unnecessary, indefensible deaths. Where are the headlines? Where are the radio and TV announcers saying, 'We interrupt our regular programming with an important news bulletin'? More than 10,000 children will die tomorrow: That's the real news of the world. A sold-out Madison Square Garden of kids dying every two days. Meanwhile, Americans sit on their sofas sucking sodas, watching boob tube bullshit, fooling around on the internet, and scratching their fat asses. We give our dogs cleaner water than a billion people give their families. It can't go on like this. We can't keep living in a bubble—deaf, dumb, and blind to human suffering. We can't live by 'out of sight, out of mind.'"

"But we spend billions on foreign aid."

"You've swallowed the Kool-Aid. We're the most miserly wealthy nation when it comes to aid. Fourteen cents out of every $100 in economic activity. It's like trying to cure cancer with herbal tea and aspirin. Think of the implications if America stepped up and pulled her weight. Instead of being one of the most loathed nations in the world, we'd be among the most loved. Billions of people in the world's developing nations would admire and respect us. American generosity would cripple the twisted aspirations of real terrorists as recruitment evaporated. It would create unprecedented economic opportunities and a new generation of immigrants to fuel the next stages of America's growth and prosperity."

Cassie found nothing to say.

"I'm sorry," Michael said. "That was a bit of a rant. Let me ask you a question. How did you find me so quickly?"

Cassie hesitated. He'd been open and honest with her. It seemed unacceptable to hide behind a wall of bureaucracy and rules in return. "I shouldn't tell you, but we had a CI—sorry, a confidential informant—who contacted us."

Michael inhaled sharply. "Who?"

"I can't tell you that. I've got to go," Cassie said, standing abruptly and turning her back to Michael, brushing away tears. He seemed like a decent, compassionate, intelligent human being, not a terrorist or a nutcase. Maybe, despite what he'd done, he was on the side of the angels. But that would put her on the dark side.

CHAPTER 39

MICHAEL'S DAYS AND NIGHTS IN solitary blurred together as he
awaited his trial. He was escorted once a day to a larger cell with a
metal grate ten feet up that faced outside and let in fresh air. Once,
he saw a crescent moon. Occasionally the rain passed through the
grate, and twice he could have sworn he smelled the ocean.

While Michael languished in jail, 184 prospective jurors completed a thirty-six-page questionnaire covering their personal
backgrounds, exposure to media coverage of the case, opinions on
terrorism, and position on the death penalty. The form requested
biographical data, including the jurors' names, ages, and marital
status; the educational level and occupation of each of their children; their religion and how often they worship; and whether they
supported groups such as the American Civil Liberties Union, the
National Rifle Association, and Amnesty International.

The jury questionnaire process was a key part of expediting the
trial, providing counsel with sufficient information to shape their
questioning of individual jurors during the selection process.

During their weekly meeting, Michael had quizzed Shirin
about the process. "What kind of jurors do we want?"

"Peter doesn't put as much weight on jury selection as most attorneys. He thinks we'll be fine with a good mix of Americans from all
walks of life, especially those who have young children. The only
people he plans to avoid are those who have already made up their
minds you're guilty or have a strong inclination in that direction."

Court commenced promptly at nine a.m. The bailiff said
"Please rise" when Judge Klinsmann entered. Two American flags

233

flanked the judge's seat and the wooden face of the raised bench was engraved with the Great Seal of the USA, a bald eagle holding an olive branch in its right talons and thirteen arrows in its left under the motto E Pluribus Unum. The deputy clerk called the court to order. Klinsmann addressed the potential jurors, who reflected the face of metropolitan America in the twenty-first century—a mixture of races, classes, and belief systems. Because of the large numbers, some would-be jurors watched the judge's speech on a large screen in a neighboring courtroom.

"Ladies and gentlemen, jurors perform a vital role in the American justice system. The protection of our rights and liberties is largely achieved through the teamwork of judge and jury who, working together in common cause, put into practice the principles of our great heritage of freedom. The judge determines the law to be applied in the case while the jury decides the facts. In a very important way, jurors become part of the court itself." Although Klinsmann had given this opening address many times, he still rose to the occasion with passion in his voice, embracing the legal institution to which he belonged.

"This is a case in which the defendant has pled not guilty to offenses that carry a potential sentence of death. For this reason, the case will proceed in two stages. During the first stage, the jury determines whether the defendant is guilty under legal criteria that I will define. If you reach a verdict of guilty, then during the second stage, you must decide whether the defendant should be sentenced to death or to life imprisonment. The jury's decisions shall be made on the basis of the evidence presented and the Court's instructions on the applicable law.

"We are here to select a jury for the trial of the defendant Michael MacDougall. We need a panel of twelve, with six alternates. The prosecution and the defense each have twenty peremptory challenges. Are counsel prepared to begin?"

Both Marconi and Quarrington nodded. Quarrington and Yavari sat with Michael on one side of the courtroom, while a team of lawyers, psychiatrists, and jury selection consultants backed up District Attorney Marconi. She was flanked by two assistant U.S. attorneys and a lawyer from the Criminal Division of the Department of Justice's Counterterrorism Section.

"Sheriff, bring in the first group of jurors," Klinsmann ordered.

The first prospective juror was Helen Dewitt of King's County. She was a mousy, nervous-looking woman with dyed blond hair and prominent roots who looked down at her hands, twitching for a smoke. U.S. Attorney Marconi was first up.

"Good morning, Ms. Dewitt. Can you tell me where you work?"

"I work with mentally challenged children at the Rosebud Center."

"Were you affected by the poisoning of Seattle's water supply?"

"No. Our water comes from a different reservoir."

"Do you believe that terrorism is a threat to America?"

"Yes."

"Do you believe in capital punishment?"

Dewitt hesitated, then asked, "You mean the death penalty?"

"Yes."

"Umm, not really."

"Not really as in not ever, or not really as in it should only be reserved for the most extreme cases?"

"Umm, not ever, I guess."

"Not even for terrorists?"

"No, ma'am. It's part of the Ten Commandments. Thou shalt not kill."

"This is a death penalty case as authorized by U.S. law. If you were to find the defendant guilty, would you be able to sentence him to death?"

"No, ma'am, I don't think so." Dewitt shook her head.

"Your honor, I challenge this juror for cause. This juror has a personal bias preventing her from executing her responsibility, so to speak."

"Mr. Quarrington?"

"Seems reasonable, your honor."

"Next juror? Your turn to go first, Mr. Quarrington."

"Thank you. Sir, do you have children?"

"Yes. Two sons and a daughter." Ron Thomson was an airplane mechanic with Boeing. His suspenders, Budweiser T-shirt, and handlebar mustache suggested he might tilt toward the redneck end of the spectrum.

"Do you love your children?"

"Of course. They mean the world to me."

"Do you think Dr. MacDougall is guilty?"

"Well, I don't know. The media thinks so, but in my mind, he's innocent until proven guilty."

"No further questions, your honor. This juror is acceptable to the defense."

Marconi asked each juror a battery of questions about their political views, their opinions on terrorism and the death penalty, and their personal experiences during the time when Seattle's water was contaminated. She sought to weed out liberals and parents with young children stack the jury with older conservatives who believed in the death penalty.

Quarrington sought to know whether they had children, loved them unconditionally, and were open-minded regarding Michael's guilt or innocence. When Quarrington encountered potential jurors with no children, he used his peremptory challenges, even if they were young and seemingly liberal.

By the end of the next day, the jury was chosen. Seven women and five men were sworn in, with three male and three female alternates.

Quarrington and Yavari had a quick debrief with Michael in the holding cell behind the courtroom. "How do you feel about the jury?" Michael asked.

"It is fine," Quarrington replied. "I have the utmost faith in our jury system, as long as there is no monkey business going on."

"Monkey business?"

"Tampering with the jury, bribery, intimidation. Although it pains me to say so, these shenanigans are not uncommon in high-stakes proceedings."

"You're not concerned that most of the jurors have conservative leanings?"

"No. The prosecution needs a unanimous verdict in order to find you guilty. We only need one juror with a conscience to set you free. If they are as open-minded as they claim to be regarding your innocence or guilt, then I expect we'll have more than one juror on our side by the end of the trial."

"I wish I shared your confidence."

"My confidence is the product of five decades of experience. Trust me."

Michael stared silently at Quarrington. "It's my life on the line."

"If I were facing a life or death operation with you as my surgeon, I would have legitimate fears yet still be confident in your abilities."

"You're right."

Yavari smiled. She'd been through a similar apprenticeship with Quarrington. "Might as well get used to it," she said.

CHAPTER 40

ON THE FIRST DAY OF THE TRIAL, Michael wore an ugly khaki jumpsuit and cheap blue tennis shoes without laces. His hands and ankles were manacled. His hair was longer than he liked it, but he was clean-shaven. Quarrington was in his wheelchair, radiating calm in a rumpled pinstripe suit. Yavari had tamed her unruly hair and looked more mature than her twenty-nine years. On the prosecution's side was an array of six attorneys, all dressed in well-tailored dark gray suits. Marconi was clearly in charge, whispering last-minute orders to her team. Maria was still absent, struggling to keep the rest of her damaged life together, and unable or unwilling to show Michael any support.

Sitting scattered around the public seating area of the courtroom were twelve shadow jurors, all residents of Seattle, with demographics closely matching the actual jury. They had been hired by an independent consultant with no traceable links to the U.S. government, and their job was to provide feedback, via text messages, about their perceptions regarding the style and substance of the attorneys' arguments.

Marconi had hired a PowerPoint expert to help prepare her visual presentations. Even the background colors for the slides had been the subject of discussions. Two psychologists, one of whom held a law degree, had been retained to monitor the jury's reaction to both counsel and witnesses.

Unlike courtrooms on television and in movies, Courtroom B was not a stately wood-paneled room. It was more like a large meeting hall, with utilitarian furniture and fluorescent lighting bouncing off drab walls. The public gallery was jammed, and another 150 spectators were in the courtroom next door, watching the trial on a large television. Cassie was in the front row reserved for high-ranking government officials.

Looking at Judge Klinsmann with his hunched shoulders, bushy eyebrows, large nose, and bald head, Michael was reminded of the vultures that swirled in the sky above Goma, looking for chunks of carrion. Klinsmann raised his arms to his sides and shook them to free his hands from the long sleeves. Draped in the black silk, his arms looked like a large pair of wings flapping.

The trial kicked off with Judge Klinsmann addressing the jury. "This is a high-profile criminal trial with the potential for you to be exposed to prejudicial publicity. For that reason, as you know, you'll all be sequestered for the duration of the proceedings until a verdict is reached. Fortunately, we're anticipating a relatively expeditious trial."

The jury had already checked in at the Best Western Plus Executive Inn, on the government's tab. For some it was an adventure, for others, a pain in the ass. They were all on the same floor, and U.S. marshals were posted at the elevators and stairwells to make sure there were no visitors or unscheduled departures.

"You must not talk about the case with others who aren't on the jury, even your spouses or families. You mustn't read about the case in the newspapers, and you should avoid radio and television newscasts. You must not conduct any research whatsoever on the internet about this case; do not use Google; do not email, text, or blog about the case. You may not use Facebook, YouTube, Twitter, or any other social network while the trial is underway. Your verdict must be based on nothing but the evidence and law presented in this courtroom.

"It appears that we're set to begin. Ms. Marconi?" He looked at the U.S. attorney with a warm smile, as though she were a close friend.

Lisa Marconi closed the binder on the table in front of her and stood, hands clasped behind her back. She had no need of a script, or even notes. This trial could make or break her career, and she was ready. She wore a crisply starched white shirt under a matte black suit, impeccably tailored to suppress but not eliminate the contours of her body. Professional. Attractive, but not quite sexy. Her long black hair, streaked with just enough gray to suggest years of courtroom experience, hung in a ponytail that fell halfway down her back.

"Thank you, your honor. Ladies and gentlemen of the jury, this is a very straightforward case. The facts are not in dispute. The defendant has admitted to committing the despicable crimes that he's charged with: use of a chemical weapon and terrorism.

"Both of the crimes have various elements. It is our burden to prove each element for both of the charges. We will meet that burden. In fact, we'll make your job easy by presenting ample evidence to convince you beyond any reasonable doubt that the defendant"—she paused, turned, and pointed a finger at Michael—"is responsible for these crimes." Marconi spoke forcefully, directly, implying she had no need for lawyer's tricks. The unvarnished facts were on her side and would suffice to compel a guilty verdict.

"Acting alone, like the Unabomber—"

"Objection!" The jurors all turned toward Quarrington, some of them looking startled. "Your honor, the reference to a convicted terrorist is highly prejudicial to Dr. MacDougall. This constitutes egregious prosecutorial misconduct." Although he appeared physically frail in his wheelchair, Quarrington still had a booming bass voice that commanded authority. Counsel was supposed to stand up to address the court but Quarrington sat in his wheelchair and merely waggled a raised finger between Marconi and Klinsmann. Several jurors looked at him with newfound interest.

"The objection is sustained. Jurors, you will disregard the prosecution's comment," said Judge Klinsmann, frowning.

Quarrington smiled. He had interrupted the flow of Marconi's opening and, in the judge's first ruling in front of the jury, he had sided with the defense.

Marconi resumed, unruffled. "Acting alone, the defendant single-handedly plotted, planned, and then poisoned the drinking water of the people of Seattle with an extremely toxic chemical. A chemical called perchloroethylene, or PCE. A chemical that the defendant stole from the hospital where he worked. A chemical that causes cancer, birth defects, kidney damage, and liver damage. That impairs the functions of the brain and central nervous system. In the hospital, this chemical is used as a solvent and for cleaning sheets, towels, and other linens. In the defendant's hands, PCE was transformed from a dry-cleaning fluid into a deadly chemical weapon. He illegally trespassed into the restricted zone of the Chester Morse Reservoir, which provides drinking water to millions of Americans. He poured gallons of this extremely toxic chemical into the reservoir and then fled the country, escaping through Canada and hiding in the Congo, deep in Africa, ten thousand miles from the scene of his crime. Millions of innocent people were exposed to a hazardous, potentially deadly substance. Mothers and fathers. Sons and daughters. Hundreds of millions more were terrified that this could happen in their city or town, no matter how big or how small. No one in America felt safe."

Marconi paused, letting the jury absorb her words. Michael squirmed in his seat, humiliated and shamed. He struggled to meet the eyes of the jury, the judge, the media, and the public as they scrutinized him. Quarrington had emphasized the importance of being himself, being alert, interacting with the defense team, and maintaining eye contact, especially with the jury. Jurors aren't supposed to make snap judgments based on appearances alone, but many ignored this unwritten rule. It all seemed surreal. He'd gone from being a heroic doctor volunteering for a globally renowned humanitarian aid organization to a defendant in a criminal proceeding that could result in the death penalty. Yet he'd done this to himself.

Marconi sketched the broad outlines of the prosecution's case. "Although we often take it for granted, drinking water is vital to life. More than half of your body weight is water. Human beings can't survive for more than a few days without it. Despite the best efforts of utility companies, public health authorities, police, and emergency workers, hundreds of thousands of Seattle residents consumed water contaminated by the defendant. Thousands of men, women, and children experienced gastrointestinal illness. You will hear testimony from medical experts that many people were hospitalized and several people died. In addition to the physical harm, the psychological damage inflicted not only on the people of Seattle but all Americans, in being afraid to drink water from their taps, in fearing more terrorist attacks, is incalculable."

"Objection," the booming bass of Quarrington's voice again resonated around the courtroom. "Psychological damage is irrelevant to these proceedings."

"Overruled," said Klinsmann. "I'm going to grant Ms. Marconi some leeway."

It was Marconi's turn to flash a quick smile at the jury. "Terrorism, as defined by the laws of America, has two components. First, it must involve one or more of a range of heinous activities, prohibited by federal criminal law, including the use of chemical weapons. Chemical weapons are defined as toxic substances that, through their effects on life processes, can cause death, temporary incapacitation, or permanent harm to humans or animals. The second aspect is that terrorism must include actions calculated to influence the conduct of government, either by intimidation or coercion. We will provide evidence proving that this is exactly what the defendant attempted to do.

"Why did the defendant poison Seattle's water? What was his motive? He was trying to blackmail the USA into spending $100 billion on foreign aid. One hundred billion dollars, during these economically challenging times, on top of the tens of billions America already dedicates to helping the world's poor. The defendant warned that he would poison the drinking water of another major American city with an even more toxic substance unless his demand was met within forty-eight hours. Only the truly extraordinary diligence of our intelligence and law enforcement communities in tracking down and arresting the defendant prevented even greater suffering."

Several of the women in the jury nodded every time Marconi made a point.

"The defendant's attorney will talk about the problems facing Africa, in a misguided and disingenuous effort to deflect your attention from his client's crimes. To be sure, the continent of Africa faces monumental challenges. Africans deserve our sympathy and support. However, this case is not about Africa. This case is about the laws of America, crimes that the defendant committed in America, and suffering inflicted by the defendant upon the American people. Justice demands nothing less than his conviction on both counts of the indictment."

Marconi's pace slowed as she hammered home her final points. "Quite frankly, to allow this defendant to go free, after the criminal acts that he committed, would deal a terrible blow to our justice system. An acquittal would encourage anarchy, chaos, and vigilantism. If every person with an ax to grind or a grudge against the government could take justice into his own hands without fear of punishment, then the rule of law would collapse, and the law of the jungle would return." Marconi hesitated, her eyes resting briefly on each of the jurors. "Your solemn responsibility, your sworn duty, is to listen to the evidence, apply the law to the facts, find the defendant guilty, and protect the American way of life from terror attacks. Thank you."

Marconi was a formidable orator, at the top of her game. The skillful way she told the story, although she twisted the facts, made even Michael almost want to agree with her. It was like seeing himself distorted in a funhouse mirror, grossly fat or absurdly thin, yet still recognizable. He glanced at the pair of attorneys in whom he was entrusting his liberty and his life. Compared to Marconi, Quarrington was over the hill and Yavari was an unproven rookie.

"Mr. Quarrington, would you like a recess before making your opening statement?"

"No thank you, your honor. On behalf of Dr. MacDougall, I would prefer to commence forthwith." Quarrington didn't want the jurors going out of the courtroom for a coffee break thinking about Marconi's version of how the trial would unfold. He rested his hand lightly on Michael's shoulder, a calculated gesture, before he slowly guided his wheelchair out from behind the counsel table and into position directly across from the jury.

"My fellow Americans, Dr. Michael MacDougall is an excellent surgeon, a humanitarian, and a man of unusual compassion. His constitutional rights have been repeatedly and inexcusably violated by the Government of the United States. He was arrested without charges. Denied access to counsel. Preventing from making a single phone call. His wife, who played absolutely no part in these events, was arrested and kept in the dark about his whereabouts. Indeed, she was unable to determine whether her husband was even alive.

"Dr. MacDougall was kidnapped by American law enforcement personnel, with the complicity of the highest levels of our government. He was tortured savagely in a foreign country by our very own intelligence agency, while senior government officials turned a blind eye." There was a cacophony in the previously quiet courtroom.

"Objection!" Marconi shouted over the din. "Your honor, counsel for the defense raised these groundless allegations in pretrial motions and pledged not to raise them at trial. This is totally inappropriate."

"I agree," said the judge with a frown. "The jury will disregard the last two sentences of the defense's opening statement. Mr. Quarrington, you are on notice. Proceed with caution."

Quarrington shrugged and continued. "Worse yet, an assassination attempt was perpetrated against him while he was in prison awaiting this trial."

"Objection. Same grounds, your honor." Like a jack-in-the-box,

Marconi popped up from her seat. Reporters took notes as fast as their fingers and thumbs could fly.

"Same ruling. Mr. Quarrington, any more of this nonsense and you will be bunking with your client tonight."

Quarrington bulldozed ahead. "Despite these egregious injustices, my client sits before you today with complete confidence in your ability to fairly adjudicate these proceedings. He trusts that you will not be swayed by the prosecution's siren songs of terror and vengeance. Dr. MacDougall anticipates that by the end of this trial you will understand why he felt compelled, as a human being, to undertake the seemingly inexplicable actions with which he is charged. He bore witness to human suffering and deprivation to extremes that few of us, mercifully, will ever see. The pain, the agony, and the anguish that Dr. MacDougall witnessed in the Congo is beyond our imagination, more horrific than our worst nightmares.

"I have practiced law for forty-seven years, including twenty-eight years teaching at Harvard, Yale, Berkeley, and the University of Washington. I retired eight years ago because of health problems but could not resist coming out of retirement to defend Dr. MacDougall. It is one of the most unusual cases that I have seen, and my client is the least likely defendant I have ever encountered.

"Most criminal lawyers will challenge all of the evidence brought forward against their clients, even if they know that the evidence is accurate, in hopes of being exonerated on a technicality. Dr. MacDougall has instructed me not to conduct his defense in such a manner. For example, we will not be challenging the admissibility of the confession referred to by my friend Ms. Marconi, despite the fact that it was extracted by torture and is therefore tainted. Most defense lawyers will seize upon any minor hole or flaw in the prosecution's case in an effort to sow doubt in the minds of the jurors. Dr. MacDougall has instructed me to refrain from using those legal tactics. We are not making a motion for transfer of the case to a different venue despite the prejudicial publicity this case has attracted. We waived the defendant's right to a preliminary hearing. We brought no pretrial motions to suppress evidence. I have complied with Dr. MacDougall's requests, and the result will be a highly unusual legal proceeding."

Quarrington paused. Contrary to conventional legal wisdom, Quarrington did not speak to the jury as though addressing a group of grade-school students. He used long words, extended sentences, and formal grammar. Although juries might be put off initially, by the end of a trial they would appreciate that Quarrington was, in effect, recognizing their intelligence. "Please bear in mind that we have not thrown in the towel by waiving and relinquishing these opportunities. Instead, we have expedited the judicial process in an attempt to focus on the fundamental purpose of this trial, indeed any criminal trial, and that is to seek justice.

"Dr. MacDougall is the kind of fellow who made his parents proud. He grew up in Seattle . . ." Quarrington sketched Michael's life history and his résumé in complimentary terms.

"Contrary to the assertions of Ms. Marconi, Dr. MacDougall was neither reckless nor cavalier in his actions. He did extensive research and relied on his medical expertise to select a chemical that would cause no serious harm to human health when a limited quantity was added to a massive reservoir. His intention was not to hurt people but to draw attention to the fact that millions of children are dying deaths that are out of sight and out of mind for Americans. He immediately notified the authorities about what he had done, and he asked merely that America fulfill its moral obligation to the children of the world.

"Despite the allegations made by Ms. Marconi, Dr. MacDougall is not a terrorist or even a criminal. Under our legal system, a person is innocent until proven guilty, and every person has the right to put forward a defense. Dr. MacDougall has a complete defense to the charges, and it is called necessity. In essence, the necessity defense means this: a person is justified in performing otherwise illegal activities in order to prevent a greater evil.

"This defense dates back to 1884. A British merchant ship was sunk in the Atlantic Ocean, and a number of sailors on board escaped in a life raft, only to spend weeks adrift, lost, without water, shelter, or food. Their efforts to catch fish proved futile and they were reduced to drinking their own urine. Finally, in their darkest hour, they made a pact to kill and eat the weakest among them, a cabin boy named Richard Parker." The majority of the jurors, engrossed in Quarrington's storytelling, looked horrified. He continued, undeterred. "The sailors carried out their dark agreement. Four days later their life raft was rescued, and their harrowing misdeeds came to light. The men were charged with murder, but pled not guilty, arguing that their actions, while admittedly illegal, were necessary for them to survive. The court acknowledged that the necessity defense existed in theory but held that the accused men had acted rashly by killing and eating the boy when they still had a chance of being rescued.

"In more recent times, the defense of necessity has been accepted by judges and juries in a wide range of cases involving political controversies. Protestors at nuclear power plants in Oregon in 1977, Illinois in 1978, and California in 1979 were arrested and charged with criminal trespass. All were acquitted based on the necessity defense. Students protesting the CIA's plans to recruit employees on the campus of Brown University were arrested and charged with trespass, mischief, and obstruction of justice. They argued the necessity defense, and brought in experts from across the nation, including former attorney general Ramsey Clark, to establish that the CIA was involved in actions that undermined American security. The students were acquitted. Most recently, a group of Greenpeace protestors were found not guilty of trespassing on the grounds of a coal-fired power plant based on their argument that their actions were necessary to address the global threat posed by the climate crisis. In addition to these cases, the Model Penal Code confirms that the necessity defense is an important element of American criminal law.

"The case before us today is perhaps more compelling than any of the examples that I have described. Dr. MacDougall didn't kill anyone. Not a single person. Dr. MacDougall didn't inflict any long-term injury or illness on anyone. But the evil that he sought to prevent is truly cataclysmic—the needless deaths of millions of children annually from preventable and treatable causes. His goal was to save their lives.

"The United States has the power, ability, and resources to accomplish that objective. Dr. MacDougall believes, and many Americans would agree, that America has a moral and ethical responsibility, rooted in the essence of our humanity, to save those children's lives. He himself saved hundreds of lives, one at a time in the Democratic Republic of the Congo, in the most grueling, difficult circumstances imaginable. But he saw that his efforts and the efforts of his compatriots were simply being overwhelmed. The flood of death continued, rendering their small victories insignificant. Who can be satisfied with saving one hundred lives, when a million are needlessly lost?

"Dr. MacDougall's African experiences transformed his view of the world. He returned to the U.S. and devised a brilliant way to raise money to help children beset by poverty. He created a non-profit organization called the Blue Drop Foundation to raise money to provide poor people in Africa with access to clean water. He spoke directly with his political representatives. He wrote to the president of the United States, urging him to address what history will regard as one of humanity's greatest failures. Sadly, his pleas fell on deaf ears.

"And so, badly traumatized by his experiences in Africa, frustrated but unwilling to accept defeat, and determined to do whatever was necessary to awaken America to the imperative of saving children's lives, Dr. MacDougall was seized by a second idea. He will admit that his initial reaction to the thought of contaminating a watershed was one of revulsion, as it may be for many of you. But eventually, as all other alternatives were exhausted and unsuccessful, the idea became irresistible."

All twelve jurors appeared to be riveted.

"Under American law, a defendant must satisfy four elements in order to rely on the defense of necessity. First, the harm to be avoided must be greater than the harm caused by the defendant's illegal activities. In the present case, that test is easily met. On one side of the scales of justice, the residents of Seattle had a few days of concern about the quality of their drinking water, and a small number of people may have experienced mild nausea. On the other side, we have the senseless and avoidable deaths of millions of babies, toddlers, and children.

"Second, the harm to be prevented must be imminent. The defense only applies in urgent situations—crises and emergencies. Again, who can argue that the death of millions of children each and every year is anything but a humanitarian crisis of the most compelling urgency?

"The third requirement is that it must be reasonable to believe that the defendant's actions will be effective in addressing the harm. The World Bank estimates that many of the most devastating aspects of African poverty could be eliminated in a few short years through an investment of $100 billion—the very amount that Dr. MacDougall was asking the U.S. to spend.

"The fourth element of the necessity defense is that there is no legal alternative to breaking the law. In this case, Dr. MacDougall pursued every lawful path to its ultimate dead end. He reached a point of desperation.

"We will provide you with incontrovertible evidence establishing all four components of the necessity defense. I must warn you that some of this evidence may be deeply disturbing. It may shock you to the core. Your hearts may be shattered by facts and images that describe human suffering on a scale that is almost incomprehensible to Americans living amongst the underappreciated daily luxuries of the twenty-first century. In the end, you will be able to understand what drove Dr. MacDougall to take the actions that initially may have seemed unthinkable to you. By the end of this trial, having reviewed all of the evidence, I believe you will agree with me that the man who sits before you acted to save lives, not take them."

CHAPTER 41

AFTER THE LUNCH BREAK, Marconi and her team began presenting their witnesses. The first was Stephen Carter, from the Central Intelligence Agency. Tall, slim, and radiating confidence, Carter strode ahead of the U.S. marshal and seated himself in the witness box, having performed this routine many times.

With his looks alone, Carter was magnetic. All eyes followed him, so nobody noticed Michael's intense reaction. Eyes wide, he scribbled furiously on the yellow notepad in front of him and shoved it toward Yavari and Quarrington. *He's the one who tortured me!*

The defense had received the list of prosecution witnesses in advance of trial, including the name Stephen Carter. But Michael had never learned the names of the men who'd tortured him.

Quarrington leaned over and whispered, "Maintain your composure." Michael gritted his teeth and nodded.

Carter was sworn in and began testifying. He explained that he worked as a legal attaché for the Central Intelligence Agency in Nairobi, Kenya.

"I received an urgent call from the Director of the CIA. He instructed me to charter a helicopter and fly to Goma, where I was to apprehend a suspect wanted in relation to the terrorist attack on Seattle. I followed the instructions and arrested the fugitive."

"Is that fugitive here in the courtroom today?" Marconi asked.

"Yes, ma'am. He's sitting right over there." Carter pointed toward Michael's chest.

"What happened next?" Marconi continued.

"We flew to a secure location made available to us by the Rwandan government. I began interrogating the suspect. To my surprise, he was highly cooperative and immediately admitted responsibility for poisoning Seattle's drinking water supply."

"What were the exact words he used?"

"One of my colleagues made an audio recording of the interview, and it was transcribed for use in these proceedings."

"Can you verify the accuracy and authenticity of the transcript?"

"Yes, ma'am."

"So the defendant's exact words were?"

"He said, and I quote, 'I placed several gallons of perchloroethylene in the Chester Morse Reservoir.'"

"Did he explain how the perc came into his possession?"

"Yes. He admitted to stealing it from the Seattle hospital where he was employed."

"And did he disclose any motive for this criminal terrorist act?"

"Yes. The suspect advised me that he was attempting to blackmail the United States of America into revising its foreign policy."

"Did the accused, at any time, express any remorse about the fact that his actions had killed and injured innocent Americans?"

"No, ma'am."

"Thank you, Mr. Carter. No further questions." The prosecution's strategy was to make an immediate and lasting impression on the jury. The defendant did it, he admitted it, and therefore he's guilty.

"Over to you, Mr. Quarrington." Judge Klinsmann bared his teeth in what passed for a smile.

Quarrington rubbed his hand on his chin for a minute, then said, "We have no questions for this witness, your honor." There was no way to raise the issue of torture. It would be Michael's word against Carter's, and the prosecution could, if it needed to do so, buttress Carter's testimony with the other agents present at the interrogation.

Klinsmann pushed his glasses up his long nose and fixed his

gaze on Quarrington. "The defendant does not wish to contest the admissibility of his confession?"

"No, your honor, nor do we wish to distract the jury's attention by raising the issues of kidnapping, coercion, and torture associated with the defendant's treatment at the hands of Mr. Carter and other representatives of the American government."

Marconi flashed to her feet, her posture perfectly straight. "Objection! Counsel for the defense cannot raise such outlandish and unsubstantiated assertions after pledging not to make an issue of them."

"I agree. The objection is sustained and the jury will disregard Mr. Quarrington's remarks. The witness is dismissed."

The next two witnesses were brief. Alistair Gryzbowski of the Seattle Watershed Authority provided evidence about the email notifying the utility of the PCE contamination and the emergency response it triggered. Katie Cornett, a communications intern at the White House, described the receipt of the email claiming responsibility for the poisoning of Seattle's reservoir and threatening a deadlier attack on another American city unless certain demands were met. Text versions of the emails were entered into evidence. Quarrington declined to cross-examine Gryzbowski or Cornett.

Marconi introduced the next prosecution witness. "Dr. Andrew Wright is a toxicologist with the Agency for Toxic Substances and Disease Registry." Dr. Wright was a wisp of a man with unkempt gray hair and Coke-bottle eyeglasses. He wore an ill-fitting blue suit, and it was easy to imagine him more at home in a white lab coat.

"Dr. Wright, are you familiar with a chemical called perchloroethylene?"

"Yes. Perchloroethylene is a manufactured chemical consisting of four chlorine atoms and two carbon atoms. It is also called tetrachloroethylene and is commonly referred to as PCE or perc."

"Could you please tell us about its chemical properties?"

"Certainly. At room temperature, perchloroethylene is a clear, non-viscous, nonflammable liquid. It evaporates easily and has a sweet odor. It is persistent, meaning it does not break down easily in the environment, and it bioaccumulates, meaning it builds up in the bodies of living organisms and in the food chain."

"Now, most importantly, what are the adverse health effects of exposure to PCE?"

Dr. Wright bit his lower lip before answering. "PCE is a potent neurotoxin, a reproductive toxin, a developmental toxin, and a probable carcinogen. The adverse health effects of exposure to PCE depend, er—" He paused. "The adverse health effects of exposure to PCE include dizziness, headaches, sleepiness, confusion, nausea, vomiting, difficulty speaking and walking, ocular and respiratory irritation, unconsciousness, coma, and death. PCE damages the liver and kidneys and increases the risk of heart attacks. Women exposed to PCE suffer menstrual problems and abnormally high levels of spontaneous abortions. Recent studies indicate that PCE also crosses the placental barrier in pregnant women, causing as-yet-unknown health problems in fetuses."

"Is there any known antidote to PCE poisoning?"

"No."

"None?"

"None."

"I see. And because of these hazardous properties, PCE is subject to extensive federal and state health, safety, and environmental legislation?"

"Oh yes. PCE is regulated by the Environmental Protection Agency and the National Institute for Occupational Safety and Health. Applicable laws include the Clean Air Act, the Safe Drinking Water Act, the Toxic Substances Control Act, the Comprehensive Environmental Response, Compensation, and Liability Act, and the Emergency Planning and Community Right to Know Act."

"So PCE, in your expert opinion, and I am quoting the United States Criminal Code here, is clearly a substance which, 'through its chemical action on life processes, can cause death, temporary incapacitation, or permanent harm to humans or animals.'"

"Yes, definitely."

"No further questions."

"Thank you, Ms. Marconi." Klinsmann continued to be solicitous towards the DA. "Mr. Quarrington?"

Quarrington wheeled his chair toward the witness box. "Dr. Wright, you have provided us with an exhaustive catalog of the potential health effects of exposure to perchloroethylene. I must admit that I have no formal training and no experience in the field of toxicology. I am a lawyer, not a scientist. So you must forgive me if my questions strike you as elementary, or even ill informed. However, there is a phrase, an old chestnut if you will, that has stuck in my mind for many years and which seems to have some bearing on your testimony here today."

Dr. Wright fidgeted on his seat, bit his lower lip again, and glanced at Marconi.

"The phrase," Quarrington continued, "dates back to the German Renaissance. Coined by a scholar by the name of Paracelsus, if memory serves me correctly. And the phrase is 'the dose makes the poison.' Is this a basic principle of toxicology?"

"Yes."

"Would you be so kind as to illuminate the repercussions of that basic principle in the context of perchloroethylene?"

"Well, you need to understand that the effects of exposure to any hazardous substance depend on the dose, the duration of the exposure, the physiological pathway through which you are exposed, your personal genetic traits, and whether other chemicals are present."

"Thank you. Let us focus on the dose for a moment. How does the dose to which a person is exposed relate to the disturbing catalog of adverse health effects that you articulated in your earlier testimony?"

"The higher the dose, the greater the likelihood that a person will experience adverse health effects."

"Yes. And the longer the period of exposure?"

"Again. The higher the dose and the longer the period of exposure, the greater the likelihood that a person will experience adverse health effects."

"And sir, are you aware of the level of contamination of the Chester Morse Reservoir as a result of the actions of my client, Dr. Michael MacDougall?"

"Yes."

"What were the levels of contamination?"

"My understanding is that the levels of PCE in Seattle's drinking water exceeded the health-based standard set by the Environmental Protection Agency."

"Can you elaborate on that by providing the court with a numerical figure?"

"The EPA standard is five parts per billion."

"And the levels of PCE detected in the Chester Morse Reservoir?"

"As high as eleven parts per billion, or more than twice the EPA standard."

"Parts per billion?"

"Yes."

"That is a difficult term to understand in the abstract. Could you try to describe it in layman's terms?"

"I'm not sure I understand the question."

"Can you provide us with an explanation of parts per billion, or perhaps a comparison so that we have a better grasp of the concept."

Dr. Wright rubbed his chin, perplexed.

"Let me endeavor to provide some assistance. Imagine that you were pouring me a gin and tonic. How much gin would you add to my glass to make it eleven parts per billion?" Quarrington cast a smile toward the jury box, hazarding a guess that at least one juror would be sympathetic to the choice of comparisons.

"Ah, I see what you're getting at. You certainly wouldn't be able to taste the alcohol. It would be akin, roughly, to placing a teaspoon of gin into an Olympic-sized swimming pool of tonic water."

"Thank you. And the adverse health effects that you described to the court earlier—brain damage, cancer, spontaneous abortions, and so forth—are those effects likely to be caused by short-term exposure to PCE at levels of a few parts per billion?"

Wright's answer was mumbled.

"Would you be so kind as to repeat that answer, sir?"

"No, not likely. But possible. You see, the health effects of consuming water contaminated by low concentrations of PCE for a short period are not known with certainty."

"Thank you. Let us move on. If my rudimentary understanding is correct, the adverse health effects that you described earlier are based on two kinds of studies. Occupational studies, in which individuals in the workplace are unintentionally exposed to elevated concentrations of PCE over a period of years, and animal experiments, in which mice and rats are deliberately exposed to extremely high concentrations of PCE, albeit for shorter durations. Is this basic summary correct?"

"Yes."

"Can you summarize the exposure levels associated with occupational and animal studies?"

Wright looked at Marconi, silently beseeching her to somehow extricate him from this situation.

"Sir?" Quarrington pressed.

"Would the witness please answer the question?" Judge Klinsmann glared at Wright.

"Most occupational studies involve prolonged inhalation of PCE at levels between 75 and 300 parts per million."

"I have to apologize, as I am not strong at mathematics. Did you say 75 to 300 parts per million, or billion?"

"Million."

"Could you convert that to parts per billion, since that is the measurement being used in the prosecution of Dr. MacDougall?

Wright winced. "It would be 75,000 to 300,000 parts per billion."

"Fascinating! So occupational studies involve concentrations more than one thousand times higher than in the case at hand. And animal studies?"

"Animal tests involve exposure to PCE at levels another order of magnitude higher."

"Again, I must apologize for my ignorance. Please explain what you mean by an order of magnitude."

"If two numbers differ by one order of magnitude, then usually one is about ten times larger than the other. So the levels of PCE in the animal tests range from 1,000 to 3,000 parts per million."

Quarrington raised his eyebrows and asked, "In parts per billion, please?"

"One to three million parts per billion," Wright said quietly.

"Thank you. In other words, the evidence of adverse health effects that you described in your earlier testimony is based on exposures to levels of perchloroethylene that range from thousands to millions of times higher than that which occurred in Seattle?"

Wright looked like he wanted to disappear. Yavari was smiling because she'd taught her legal partner Toxicology 101. The old guy was a pretty quick study. Wright's eyes flitted about the courtroom but found no avenue of escape.

"Dr. Wright?"

"Yes."

"Would you please be so kind as to answer my question?"

"Yes, the adverse health effects I referred to earlier were based on levels of exposure significantly higher than the people of Seattle experienced."

"And you mentioned that the duration of exposure is an important factor. For example, an individual exposed to low concentrations of a hazardous substance on a daily basis for many years would face an elevated risk of adverse health effects, correct?"

"Yes."

"And the duration of potential exposure of Seattle residents to PCE-contaminated drinking water, because of Dr. MacDougall's direct notification of the water management authorities, was how long?"

"Less than forty-eight hours."

"And in toxicological parlance, does forty-eight hours constitute long-term or short-term exposure to a toxic substance?"

"Short-term."

"Your testimony has been very illuminating, Dr. Wright, thank you. Given its complexity I would like to ask a few more questions before you leave to ensure that we fully understand what you've told us. Seattle residents were exposed to very low levels of perc for a very brief period of time, correct?"

"Yes."

"From a toxicological perspective, making conclusions about adverse human health effects based on extrapolations from animal and occupational studies involving far higher exposure levels is inadvisable, is it not?"

"Well—"

"Is it not mere guesswork?" Quarrington, feisty now, glowered at Wright.

"Objection! Counsel is badgering the witness." Marconi was in damage control mode, seeking to shift the jury's attention from Wright's botched testimony.

"Withdrawn. No further questions for this witness, your honor."

"Ms. Marconi? Any redirect examination?"

Marconi took a deep breath. She needed to salvage something from the wreckage of Dr. Wright's testimony, do it quickly, and move on. "Dr. Wright, could you review the adverse health effects associated with exposure to PCE for us?"

Wright's shoulders, which had ratcheted up close to his ears during Quarrington's cross-examination, relaxed at Marconi's return. He repeated his earlier evidence about health problems ranging from dizziness to death.

"Now, without going into great detail," said Marconi, "I would like to know one thing. Could those adverse effects potentially arise from short-term exposure to low levels of PCE?"

"Potentially? Yes. An important consideration for chemicals like PCE is that for some health outcomes there is no known threshold below which there are no observable adverse effects."

"Can you give us an example in layman's terms?"

"Of course. With many carcinogens, exposure to even a small dose increases the risk that an individual will eventually develop cancer."

"Even brief exposure to low concentrations of substances like PCE can increase the risk of cancer?"

"Yes."

"Thank you. That's all, your honor."

"All right. We'll take the lunch break now." Klinsmann glowered at Marconi, not impressed with Dr. Wright, and laying the blame squarely at her feet.

With his back to the judge and jury, Quarrington winked subtly at his client. Michael felt an unfamiliar frisson of hope flutter in his chest.

CHAPTER 42

CASSIE WAS ON THE VERGE of going outside the playbook. If things went south, it could end her career and possibly land her in prison, but she couldn't bear the thought of being complicit in government actions that included torture and the attempted murder of an American citizen. She believed what Dr. Michael MacDougall had told her, and she had to move fast in case there was another attempt on his life. The doctor wasn't innocent, but he was no terrorist. Cassie would call him a naive and misguided idealist. Badly misguided, likely due to his traumatic experiences, but well intentioned. She, in contrast, understood the system, the rules, the games, and the players. She called Abby into her borrowed office in Seattle.

"Hey boss, what's up?"

"I need to reach our best undercover agent. They have to be a wizard at electronic surveillance. And they have to be one hundred percent trustworthy, but ideally with a maverick streak."

"There are almost two hundred agents in our Criminal Enforcement Program, but only one fellow I know of who matches that description. Alan Jones."

"Thanks. Can you pull him off whatever he's working on and get him to Seattle by tomorrow?"

"Will do."

Less than twenty-four hours later Cassie met with Alan Jones in person. He was average height, medium build, brown-haired, nondescript in every way.

"Congratulations for nailing the guy who poisoned Seattle's water supply," Jones said.

"Thanks, Alan. I appreciate your coming here on short notice. You're the best we've got, and I need you to plant some bugs. On phones."

"Okay. Where?"

"Two in DC, two in Virginia."

"Can you be a little bit more specific?"

"I can, but you need to swear that this will remain buried forever."

"Done." Jones leaned toward Cassie.

"Randall Tierney and Billy Joe Stryder."

Jones smiled. "You're kidding, right?"

"Nope, I'm dead serious. Tierney and Stryder are the targets, but security at the J. Edgar Hoover Building and CIA headquarters is more or less impenetrable. So we'll settle for tapping their phones."

"Why?"

"That's classified. You'll have to trust me when I say it's a matter of national importance."

"If I get busted—"

"Don't. I'll personally help put together your cover—plumber, electrician, cable guy, whatever. I'll pull strings if you need the latest whiz-bang electronic gizmos from our National Computer Forensics Laboratory in Jacksonville."

"An undercover surveillance op on our own guys?"

"Happens all the time. You'd be surprised."

"Yeah, right. You know that text messages and emails will be encrypted."

"Can you break the codes?"

"Yup," Jones answered confidently.

Cassie smiled. "Are you in?"

"Hell yeah."

"Excellent. We'll get started now."

Cassie laid out additional details about the operation, emphasizing that she was the only person with clearance to listen to the recordings gleaned from the four phones, and that they wanted to avoid creating a paper trail. Jones listened closely, nodding, smiling, and asking intelligent questions.

Wiretaps on Tierney and Stryder were the only way Cassie could think of to find out if there was a plan B in the suspected plot to assassinate Dr. Michael MacDougall. Now she had to hurry over to the federal courthouse to testify against the man whose life she was trying to save.

CHAPTER 43

MARCONI HAD REFUELED DURING A WORKING LUNCH. "The prosecution calls Dr. Carole Hailes, an epidemiologist with the Washington State Department of Health." Dr. Hailes was a petite redhead with pale skin and a smattering of freckles across her nose and cheeks. Quarrington again waived the lengthy process of qualifying the witness as an expert.

"Can you tell us a bit about your job with the Department of Health?" Marconi began.

"I'm part of the state's disease surveillance team, meaning that I review statistics on physician visits, emergency room admissions, hospitalizations, the incidence and prevalence of disease, and mortality. Our team's goal is to identify trends and anomalies in health statistics to enable the state to take more effective preventive and remedial actions. Ideally, we can catch potential problems, such as epidemics, early on in ways that individual doctors or hospitals can't because they lack access to broader data sets."

"Could you give us an example?"

"Of course. Last September, we noticed a spike in reported cases of E. coli poisoning from various locations around the state. We interviewed some of the affected individuals and determined that the common link was consumption of ground beef. Our research resulted in a nationwide health alert and the removal of several brands of ground beef from the food supply chain after the problem was traced to a specific slaughterhouse in Texas."

"Thank you. Now, turning to the events at issue in this trial. We're interested in learning about the adverse health outcomes associated with the poisoning of Seattle's water supply by the toxic chemical perchloroethylene earlier this year. Did your team collect and study data on adverse health effects in the days immediately following the poisoning?"

"Yes, we did."

"And what did you find?"

"Our statistical analysis showed increases in a variety of adverse health outcomes that might be expected to occur when a community's water supply is contaminated. We found spikes in reported cases of gastrointestinal illness, emergency room visits, hospital admissions, physician visits, calls to poison control centers, and deaths in the three days immediately following the contamination event. Could I show you a series of graphs?"

"Of course."

There were several large screens positioned in the courtroom so that judge, jury, attorneys, and spectators all had a clear view. The first image showed a graph with a horizontal red line above a horizontal blue line. "The vertical axis shows the number of reported cases of gastrointestinal illness in the Seattle Metropolitan Area, and the horizontal axis covers the week of April 1 through April 7 for the ten most recent years. The lower line, in blue, shows the average number of cases of gastrointestinal illness in Seattle during that same week over the past ten years."

"And the red line?"

"The red line indicates the number of gastrointestinal illnesses reported from April 1st through April 7 of this year, following the contamination of the reservoir. As you can see, the number of cases is approximately fifteen percent higher. The second slide is basically the same but it shows telephone calls to local poison control centers. There's a seventy-six-percent rise in the number of calls in the week following the contamination event compared to the ten-year average."

"And the third slide?"

"The third slide represents the number of mortalities occurring in the Seattle Metropolitan Area for that same week this year, compared with the ten-year average. Here we see a six-percent jump in deaths occurring in that specific time period."

"What are your overall conclusions?"

"We searched for explanations that were consistent with the data, such as an influenza outbreak, a food contamination event, or a period of prolonged poor air quality. We found only one external factor that was positively correlated with the significant rise in adverse health outcomes—the contamination of Seattle's drinking water with perchloroethylene."

"So, in your expert opinion, the poisoning of Seattle's water supply led to extensive illness and even death?"

"Well, epidemiologists have to be cautious in drawing conclusions about cause and effect. There are so many confounding variables at play in any given case that we can rarely come out and say a specific factor caused a specific outcome. However, we can say with confidence that there is a positive correlation between the contamination of Seattle's drinking water and a rise in gastrointestinal illnesses, poisonings, and mortalities."

"Thank you, Dr. Hailes. No further questions, your honor." Marconi returned to her seat.

Quarrington straightened his tie and wheeled forward, smiling as though greeting a long-lost friend. "Did the Department of Health test individuals in Seattle to determine their level of exposure to PCE, if indeed they were exposed to it at all?"

"No."

"Yet the tests are very simple, are they not? PCE exposure can be measured by taking a sample of a person's breath, in the same way that police use breathalyzer tests to measure the level of alcohol in the blood of individuals suspected of drunk driving. PCE can also be measured by taking a blood sample, correct?"

"Yes."

"And yet none of the individuals whose illness you are attempting to attribute to PCE exposure were actually tested for PCE?"

"No."

"PCE is also commonly used in the dry-cleaning industry, correct?"

"Yes."

"And when an individual brings their dry-cleaning home, that is a source of exposure to PCE through the air, correct?"

"Yes."

"Can you tell us what concentration that exposure might be?"

"Not offhand, no. It would depend on the quantity of dry-cleaning, the size of the home, the layout, the ventilation system, and a host of other factors."

"Could it be in the neighborhood of eleven parts per billion?"

"I'm not sure. I suppose it's possible. But as I said, it would depend on the circumstances. We didn't test anyone in Seattle to determine their exposure to perchloroethylene."

"Thank you for clarifying those matters. Now I would like to turn your attention back to the graphs that you used to describe what you referred to as spikes in levels of gastrointestinal illness, calls to poison control centers, and deaths. You left us with the distinct impression that these spikes were anomalous, that they struck you as sufficiently distinctive as to merit investigation. Am I correct?"

"Yes."

"Good. Now do you have a similar graph showing the incidence of gastrointestinal illness in Seattle over the course of the past year?"

"Yes, I should be able to dig up that data. One minute please."

Marconi used the interruption to rise. "Your honor, is this a fishing expedition? My friend could have requested this information in advance if he thought it was relevant."

"I'm going to give Mr. Quarrington the benefit of the doubt for a minute." As if surprised by his own ruling, Klinsmann grimaced and added, "Just for a minute. If it isn't clear where he's going, then I'll shut down this line of questioning."

"Ah here we are." Dr. Hailes was immersed in searching her laptop and oblivious to the discussion swirling around her. She flashed a new graph up on the screen. It showed a jagged horizontal blue line like the profile of a mountain range.

"And this is?" Quarrington plowed ahead.

"This is the incidence of gastrointestinal illness in Seattle for the past eighteen months. The vertical axis shows the number of cases and the horizontal axis is broken down week by week."

"There is a high degree of variability, isn't there?" Quarrington asked.

"Yes." The penny dropped. "Oh." A pink blush appeared on her neck.

"Beginning from the left-hand side, let's discuss the first spike in cases of illness. What was the explanation for that jump?"

"I don't know."

"Was the reservoir contaminated at that time?"

"No."

"And yet there was a jump in gastrointestinal illness."

"Yes."

"Let's move on to the second spike on the graph. What was the explanation for that surge in illness?"

"We don't know."

"Was the reservoir contaminated at that time?"

"No." Now Hailes was blushing furiously.

"And yet there was a jump in gastrointestinal illness."

"Yes."

"Thank you. Now let's move on to the third spike."

"Objection!" cried Marconi. "Mr. Quarrington has made his point, your honor. At this point he's just harassing the witness."

"Sustained. Please move along."

"Allow me to summarize your testimony, Dr. Hailes. Surges in gastrointestinal illness occur frequently over the course of a given year and are difficult to attribute to a particular cause, is that correct?"

"Yes."

"And the same analysis would apply to calls to poison control centers, that is to say, there are significant fluctuations in the number of calls over the course of a year that cannot be attributed to identifiable external factors, correct?"

"Yes."

"And again, the same logic applies to deaths, yes?"

"Yes."

"Could we have this graph identified as an official trial exhibit, please?"

The clerk nodded.

"While we are on the admittedly distasteful subject of death, can you tell me how many of the coroner's certificates from the week following the contamination of Seattle's water supply identified exposure to perchloroethylene as the cause of death?"

"None."

"None? Not a single one?"

"No."

"What were the leading causes of death for that particular week?"

"Again, I would have to consult my records."

"Please do so."

With impressive speed, Dr. Hailes produced a summary table of deaths in the Seattle Metropolitan Area for the preceding year.

"For the record, Dr. Hailes, what were the ten leading causes of death for that week?"

"According to my records, the leading causes of death were cardiovascular disease, cancer, respiratory disease, diabetes, stroke, nervous system diseases, motor vehicle accidents, pneumonia, infectious diseases, and suicides."

"No mention of poisoning due to perchloroethylene?"

"No."

"In fact, there is not a single death in the Seattle Metropolitan Area that you can say definitely was caused by exposure to perchloroethylene, is that correct?"

"Yes."

"Thank you, Dr. Hailes, you've been very helpful. No further questions." There was an eerie silence in the courtroom as people digested Quarrington's second master class in cross-examination.

"Ms. Marconi, any redirect?" asked the judge.

Again, the U.S. attorney was faced with a key witness whose testimony seemed more helpful to the defense than the prosecution. Marconi had no choice but to give it her best shot. "Dr. Hailes, let's return to the question of death certificates for a minute, because I think Mr. Quarrington's line of questioning may have created a false impression. I'd like you to imagine a lifetime smoker with a two-pack-a-day habit who dies from lung cancer at age sixty."

"Okay." Hailes was visibly relieved that Quarrington was finished. The color had faded from her face and neck.

"Would smoking be identified as the cause of death on the coroner's death certificate?"

"No. The cause of death would be lung cancer. The cause of lung cancer might be smoking, but that would not be recorded on the death certificate."

"Thank you. Now if we could return to the list of causes of death that you showed us."

"Okay."

"Based on your knowledge of the toxicological properties of perchloroethylene, is it not true that exposure to perc is consistent with death from cancer, deaths related to the digestive system, and deaths caused by cardiovascular disease?"

"Yes, but—"

"No further questions, your honor." Marconi turned her back on Dr. Hailes and returned to her seat at the prosecution table.

"Objection!" Quarrington's sonorous bass reverberated through the courtroom. "Dr. Hailes's testimony was truncated mid-sentence. Could the court reporter read back the question for the witness?"

"I withdraw the question," said Marconi, trying to close the door.

"The rules do not permit a second sequence of cross-examination,

Mr. Quarrington. The witness is dismissed." Klinsmann had sided with the prosecution again.

Looking befuddled by the legal skirmish that closed her testimony, Dr. Hailes closed her laptop and was escorted out of the courtroom by one of the U.S. marshals.

The next prosecution witness, Terrence Mauresmo, was the FBI's forensic computer expert. He looked more like a fashion model than a computer geek. He had high, sculpted cheekbones, cerulean eyes, fleshy lips, and a square jaw. His blond hair was carefully moussed to give it a rugged, windswept appearance.

"Good afternoon, Mr. Mauresmo," said Marconi, approaching the witness. "First of all, can you provide us with some background on your involvement in this investigation."

"Yes. Subsequent to the identification of the accused as the perpetrator of the Seattle PCE poisoning, the Department of Justice obtained a search warrant for the suspect's place of residence. FBI special agents executed the search and discovered two computers, a desktop and a laptop, as well as several external memory devices. The items were tagged and taken into custody for further examination. That's where I came in."

"And what did you find that is relevant to the prosecution's case?"

"We were able to conduct a comprehensive reconstruction of the suspect's activity on the internet, using both computers, going back more than a year. There was substantially more internet and email activity on the desktop compared to the laptop. Of greatest interest was a series of Google searches conducted in the months preceding the poisoning of the Seattle water supply."

"What was the subject matter of these searches?"

"There were several distinct categories, including websites about chemical weapons, biological weapons, terrorist organizations, and bomb-making. There were documents downloaded about the toxicological properties of PCE. Finally, there were also numerous searches related to the Chester Morse Reservoir and the Seattle

Watershed Authority, including downloaded maps of the facility and surrounding region." Several jurors looked discomfited by the references to chemical weapons, biological weapons, and bombs.

Quarrington was brief but ruthless in his cross-examination. "Did Dr. MacDougall make a bomb?"

"No."

"Did he use anthrax, botulism, smallpox, tularemia, or any other form of biological weapon?"

"No."

"Did he use one of the nerve agents that are hundreds of times more potent than PCE—tabin, sarin, or VX?"

"No."

"Did he make ricin or use sodium fluoroacetate, a substance five hundred times more potent than arsenic?"

"Objection. My friend is badgering this witness, your honor."

"I agree," said Judge Klinsmann. "Do you have any other relevant questions for this witness, Mr. Quarrington?"

"Yes, your honor, I do. Mr. Mauresmo, what you really mean to tell us is that Dr. MacDougall researched a wide range of potentially deadly actions and carefully chose to use a substance that would not cause any significant adverse health effects?"

"Objection, your honor. The witness has no knowledge of the defendant's mental processes."

"Withdrawn," said Quarrington calmly. "No further questions."

Marconi had saved her star witness for the end of the day. Cassie was wearing a conservative black pantsuit and a light blue blouse. There were dark rings under her eyes. Michael was curious about Cassie's testimony. She'd struck him as an honest person, and it appeared that she'd divulged confidential information because she agreed, on some level, that Michael's arrest and prosecution had crossed a line.

To the disappointment of Marconi and the media hordes, Cassie made her testimony concise and deliberately bland. She described the EPA's role on the task force, the development of her lone-wolf theory based on previous watershed trespassing incidents, her meeting with the confidential informant who identified Michael as a potential suspect, and the physical evidence gathered at the house that pointed to his guilt. Most of the details she provided had already been reported in the media. During their preparations for the trial, Marconi tried to get Cassie to add some emotional oomph, some more sensational language, to buttress her testimony. Cassie steadfastly refused, coming across as a remarkably modest and reserved person.

The moment Cassie had been dreading arrived. Klinsmann asked Quarrington if he had any questions for the witness. Cassie looked at Michael, torn between her duty to the state and her personal convictions. He held her gaze.

Quarrington cleared his throat and said, "No questions for this witness, your honor."

"Thank you. We'll call it a day and resume proceedings tomorrow at nine a.m."

CHAPTER 44

MICHAEL SUFFERED ANOTHER LARGELY SLEEPLESS NIGHT. On the few occasions he dozed off, harrowing nightmares roused him. The usual assortment of ghosts—Laurent, dying children, dead bodies—reached out to him, chasing him, beseeching him to help them. Morning delivered a headache. So much for being well-rested for his testimony. He forced himself to choke down half a bowl of congealed oatmeal. Quarrington and Yavari met him in the holding cell. He was pleased that they looked confident and relaxed, despite their own late night. They reviewed the game plan one last time and left him with the guards. Fifteen minutes later, he joined his attorneys in the courtroom.

"We're ready for the defense case, Mr. Quarrington. Please proceed."

"Thank you, your honor. Ladies and gentlemen of the jury, as a result of Judge Klinsmann's earlier ruling, the defense will rely on just two witnesses in this case. Both of them are respected medical professionals. To begin, the defense calls Dr. Douglas Carpenter, professor emeritus at Cambridge University." Carpenter was a tall elegant man in a blue blazer and a bright yellow bow tie. His bald head reflected the ceiling lights. Patches of damaged skin on his hands and face suggested skin cancer.

Carpenter was sworn in. "Welcome to Seattle, Dr. Carpenter," started Quarrington. "I wish the circumstances surrounding your visit were more pleasant. Nevertheless, this is a very important proceeding and we are enormously pleased that you have been able to join us."

Marconi was already on her feet. "Your honor? This is a criminal trial, not an academic conference. Perhaps Mr. Quarrington could get to the point about why this witness is testifying." She had succeeded in limiting the defense to two witnesses and now sought to truncate Carpenter's testimony.

"Move along, Mr. Quarrington," Klinsmann added, with a dismissive wave of his hand.

"Of course, your honor." Quarrington began to walk Carpenter through his impressive résumé. In addition to his university affiliations, including Oxford and the Sorbonne, Carpenter had served as a special advisor to several UN health and development agencies. He was the author or co-author of more than 100 publications about the medical problems faced by children in developing countries.

Marconi stood again, shaking her head. "I have no doubt that Dr. Carpenter is a world authority on issues related to children's health. Unfortunately, I am having a difficult time seeing the relevance to the trial of a terrorist who used a chemical weapon to wreak havoc on America and blackmail the president."

"Mr. Quarrington?" A purple vein in Klinsmann's forehead throbbed.

"The connection should be clear, your honor, but I will elaborate. Dr. MacDougall is relying on the necessity defense to justify the actions for which he faces charges. Since the necessity defense requires a balancing of evils, it is imperative that the jury have a clear understanding of the magnitude of the evil that Dr. MacDougall's actions were intended to prevent."

"All right. But let me remind you, counselor, and the jury as well, that at the end of the trial, the availability of the necessity defense is a question of law for me to decide."

"We recognize the state of the jurisprudence, your honor." Carpenter was fidgeting in the witness box. "Dr. Carpenter, my apologies for that interruption. Let us proceed. Two years ago, you were the editor of a special edition of *The Lancet*, one of the world's leading medical journals. Could you please tell the court about the highlights of that special edition?"

"Certainly." Carpenter spoke in the confident tone of a professor lecturing an auditorium full of undergrads. "In recent years, I have sensed that the medical profession in wealthy nations such as the UK and the U.S. had lost touch with the global children's health crisis. This crisis is undermining the social, economic, and cultural future of dozens of countries around the world, but the situation is most pronounced in sub-Saharan Africa. Of the roughly ten million deaths of children under the age of five that occur annually in the world, mostly in Africa, at least three-quarters are preventable or treatable for mere pennies per child. The loss of human potential is devastating. Who knows how many Einsteins, Gandhis, Messis, Jordans, and Mozarts we may be losing?"

"But surely the situation is improving. Are these problems not well on their way to being solved?"

"I wish with all of my heart that that were true. We've seen the UN Year of the Child come and go. We've seen the International Children's Decade come and go. We've seen the global Convention on the Rights of the Child signed and ratified by almost every nation on Earth."

"Almost every nation?"

"Yes, well." Carpenter cleared his throat. "Every nation in the world except the USA."

"That can't be right." Judge Klinsmann glared over the tops of his glasses at the witness.

"It's an uncomfortable truth, sir, but I can provide you with a complete list of parties to the convention and you will not find the United States on that list."

"Hmmm," Klinsmann grumbled. "I remain unconvinced of the relevance of this testimony to our trial. However, I must admit your evidence is thought-provoking. Mr. Quarrington, you may continue."

"Thank you, your honor. Dr. Carpenter, I believe you were

reviewing the catalog of broken promises made to the impoverished children of the world."

"Yes. I was about to mention the UN Decade for Clean Water and Sanitation, which was the 1990s. It came and went; yet one billion people still lack access to potable water and more than two billion lack access to basic sanitation. In some places, people are still drinking out of puddles and defecating in ditches."

"That is terrible. Go on."

"Conceived on the cusp of the twenty-first century, the Millennium Development Goals sought to reduce child mortality by fifty percent, reduce poverty by fifty percent, and achieve universal primary education. All of this by 2015. That year passed, but the goals remain unmet."

"And most recently?"

"The most recent set of promises are the most comprehensive and ambitious. The United Nations identified seventeen Sustainable Development Goals, to be achieved by 2030. The SDGs include ending poverty and hunger as well as providing education, clean water, and clean energy for all."

"What stands in the way of fulfilling these commitments?"

"In one word, money. The World Bank estimates that achieving the Sustainable Development Goals would cost the world $100 billion per year."

"That sounds like an astronomical sum of money."

"To the contrary, in today's $100-trillion-dollar global economy, $100 billion is a pittance. About one-tenth of the annual American military budget. About what Americans spend every year on their pets."

"What role is the United States playing in the global war on poverty?"

"Objection. America is not on trial here." Marconi's cheeks were flushed and her voice rose an octave.

"Overruled," said Klinsmann. "Let's hear what Dr. Carpenter has to say."

"The help provided to poor countries by wealthy countries is called official development assistance, or foreign aid. The agreed-upon international target is 0.7 percent of gross domestic product. The U.S. languishes near the bottom of the rankings of donor nations at 0.2 percent."

"And can you tie these rather dry figures back to the issue of children's health?"

"Of course. It costs less than five cents per child to provide Vitamin A supplements, which can reduce mortality by up to twenty-three percent. It costs two dollars for a bed net that can reduce malaria deaths by forty-four percent. It costs less than a dollar per child to vaccinate for the most common childhood diseases, such as mumps and measles. It costs less than a dollar per child to provide oral rehydration medication or antibiotics. Yet for want of these puny sums, more than ten thousand children die unnecessary deaths every day in developing nations." Carpenter stopped talking and made an obvious show of looking at his watch.

"Are we keeping you from another engagement, Dr. Carpenter?" the judge asked.

"No. I just wanted to let you know that since my testimony commenced today, more than five hundred children have died because of preventable or treatable diseases." There was a collective gasp in the courtroom, followed by stunned silence. "This is the greatest humanitarian disaster of our time, and history will not be kind to those leaders, people, and nations who turned their backs on the world's children in this crisis."

"Deeply disturbing, but thank you for joining us today." Quarrington nodded in appreciation.

"Ms. Marconi?"

"The prosecution sees no point in pursuing the cross-examination of this witness, your honor. While his testimony may have been interesting, it was completely irrelevant to this trial."

CHAPTER 45

"THE NEXT WITNESS IS THE DEFENDANT, Dr. Michael MacDougall."
Michael took the stand. His hands, so steady in the operating room,
were trembling.

"Please state your full name for the court."

"Michael James MacDougall."

"Do you swear that the evidence you give in this proceeding will
be the truth, the whole truth, and nothing but the truth, so help
you God?"

"I do."

Quarrington, Yavari, and Michael had discussed and debated
the best approach to his testimony. This is probably where the
case would be won or lost. For the first time, the jury would hear
Michael speak. Could he connect with them? Engage their sympathy? It was a risky gambit but this was no ordinary trial.

Quarrington asked open-ended questions to walk Michael
through his background. He wanted Michael to relax into a comfortable storytelling mode, so he asked him about his father's fatal
heart attack, the event that sparked his desire to become a doctor.
Michael modestly described awards that he'd won, explained his
frustration working as an emergency surgeon at the Harborview
Medical Center, and recalled the unlikely events that led him to
become involved with IMAF.

"Tell us about your volunteer work in Africa."

"Doing aid medicine in Africa is challenging but also super
rewarding. IMAF's basic philosophy, which I share, is simple: every
human being matters, no matter how poor or how far away. A life is

a life. When I see a sick or wounded child, my heart clenches and I feel their pain. One of the most beautiful things about Africa is the small children who follow you everywhere, the bravest among them gently grasping your hand or curling a finger through your belt loop. That was really the essence of my work in the Congo, making human contact, showing that somebody cares.

"I was assigned to Goma in the Eastern Congo, a war zone where multiple militias compete for control. Ordinary citizens are routinely killed, raped, or displaced from their homes. Refugees walk hundreds of miles, barefoot, through the forest, eating roots, leaves, and stems. They carry their paltry possessions and unintentionally transport bacteria, viruses, and disease from one region to another. The damage to their feet is unimaginable. There is often little or no flesh left on their skeletal bodies. And yet some of them still manage to smile and laugh and sing. When they arrive at our clinic we do the best we can for them. But when you return on your rounds the next day, several will be gone, dead or disappeared without a whisper. Like shadows that melt into the darkness of night.

"We were treating symptoms, not problems. Malnourished children suffer from vitamin, mineral, and trace element deficiencies that increase their vulnerability to respiratory infections and diarrhea-related diseases. The most common illnesses I saw were diarrhea, malaria, malnutrition, acute respiratory infections, and measles. Children who graduated from our therapeutic feeding program were enrolled in a supplementary food course that provided high-calorie, high-protein cereal mix for their entire family. Some patients were reluctant to leave our portable tent hospital because it was safe."

"Doctor, could you please describe an average day at the clinic in Goma."

"Okay. The first thing we do when a child enters the screening area and isn't in immediate distress is attempt to determine his or her age. This may sound easy, but not in Africa. There are many orphans who have no idea how old they are. As well, malnutrition causes stunted growth, so the standardized tables and charts used to estimate age here in the U.S. are useless. What we do instead is take an upper arm measurement with these bracelets." Michael held up a thin green, yellow, orange, and red paper band. "We call them the bracelets of life. The green zone means a child is adequately nourished. Yellow means the child is at risk of malnutrition and should be closely monitored. Those whose upper arms are in the orange zone, between 110 millimeters and 125 millimeters, are suffering from moderate malnutrition. If the MUAC—sorry, the mid-upper-arm circumference—falls in the red zone (less than 110 millimeters), a child is dying of starvation and needs intensive medical care."

"Could you show us 110 millimeters on the bracelet?"

Michael adjusted the bracelet, making a tiny circle, and held it up for the jury to see. "Their upper arms are that small."

Several jurors audibly gasped.

Quarrington wheeled over to the jury box and handed out a dozen of the bracelets. "You may see for yourselves."

Michael described the chaos, madness, and sadness of a typical week working in the Congo. "The first time that you see a child die from starvation is unforgettable. It seems like such a terrible waste. You hold the light, lifeless body in your arms. Many medical professionals gradually become immune. I never did. I found the work addictive, all-consuming. You feel so alive, you're doing something useful, something good, something right. Despite the stress, the heat, the humidity, the disease, the deaths, the struggles, and the endless problems, I loved it there, loved the work, my colleagues, the country, and the people."

"Dr. MacDougall, you took photographs of your patients, is that correct?"

"Yes, with their permission."

"For what purpose?"

"I wanted to be able to remember them. All of them. Even the ones who didn't make it."

"And you kept these photographs on your laptop?" While Quarrington continued the questions, Yavari turned on the video projector.

"Yes."

"Do you recognize this USB drive?"

"Yes. It's a digital photo album of patients from my first trip to Africa."

"Could we have the lights turned down please?"

Marconi leapt to her feet. "Objection. We're here for a trial, not a slideshow. Relevance?"

"The U.S. attorney makes a good point," Klinsmann said. "Mr. Quarrington, could you enlighten us as to how photographs of African children are in any way relevant to your client's defense."

"Of course, your honor. These photographs are evidence related to the first element of the necessity defense, establishing that there is in fact a humanitarian emergency occurring in sub-Saharan Africa."

Marconi added to her objection. "We can all agree that the Congo faces major problems. There's no need to spoon-feed the court with pictures. In addition, there is no way to verify the authenticity of these photographs. They could have been taken anywhere, by anyone."

"To the contrary," Quarrington boomed, "the defendant is testifying under oath. He will aver to the authenticity of the photographic evidence and is liable to criminal prosecution for perjury if he makes any false statements. This is no different from the introduction of any physical evidence by any witness in a trial."

"I am not convinced, Mr. Quarrington," Klinsmann said. "You're on a short leash, but you may proceed." The bailiff dimmed the lights.

Quarrington handed the remote control to Michael. "Dr. MacDougall, please describe the nature of the images that you are about to present?"

"Yes. Of course I had my phone with me when I traveled to Africa. My original intention was to take photos of the places I visited and the people I met. Like a regular tourist, I guess. However, because of the intensity of the humanitarian crisis in the Eastern Congo, there were no days off, no opportunities to visit national parks or wildlife sanctuaries as I'd originally envisioned. Instead, virtually all of the photographs are of my IMAF colleagues and our patients.

"Our paper recordkeeping is very limited. We have a barebones administrative staff, so it seemed like it might be useful to take photographs of every patient that I diagnosed or treated. Some days that would be dozens of people, up to perhaps one hundred. The majority were children."

The first slide showed a dark-skinned, malnourished child, staring vacantly into the camera. "This is Amara Sembolo, the first patient that I treated after my arrival in the Congo. He suffered from diarrhea, thrush, scabies, and malaria. Amara, despite my best efforts, was too far gone." Michael's voice cracked.

"This is Edzongo Itoua. Severely malnourished but resilient. A real fighter, as you can see in his eyes. We called him 'Fast Eddie.' He gained weight and was eventually discharged."

"This is Bernadette Kabongo. Fourteen years old. Forced to work as a sex slave. She died in childbirth. Her son was stillborn."

"Arsene Malonga. Destin Tsoumou. Martine Muhindo. Francky Bhebey Ndey. Laurent Lumumba. Kaniono Lukoki." Whether they'd lived or died, for several minutes, Michael whispered their names.

Michael came to Anna's photograph of the little boy, Étienne Tshisekedi, to whom he'd given his own blood. Michael came apart on the witness stand, wracked by uncontrollable sobs.

Despite the fact that the lights were turned down, tear tracks were evident on the faces of several jurors. Two of the shadow jurors, sitting in the public gallery were openly crying. It was impossible not to be moved. These were children, no different from American children.

Michael could no longer even say the names. Photo after photo appeared on the screen in silence. Marconi stood and bravely interrupted. "Your honor, I would like to suggest that we

283

take a break. Let's give the defendant time to regain his composure before we continue."

"Excellent suggestion. We will take a fifteen-minute recess. Bailiff! Lights."

"Permission to approach the bench, your honor?" asked the U.S. attorney.

"Yes, Ms. Marconi."

Marconi and Quarrington stepped up to the dais, where the acoustics were modified to ensure that conversations between judge and counsel were out of the jury's earshot.

"I think we've seen enough, your honor. The defendant has made his point. Repeatedly. How many photographs do we expect the jury to endure?"

Quarrington had a quick answer. "The number of children who die daily in Africa due to preventable and treatable ailments numbers in the thousands, as we have heard. In my submission, that would be an appropriate range for the number of images for the jury to 'endure' as my friend put it."

"That's ridiculous," Marconi sputtered.

"Hold your vitriol, Ms. Marconi," Quarrington was unflappable. "You will be relieved to learn that the defense does not have anywhere near 5,000 photographs, let alone 10,000. I believe there are approximately 150 pictures on this CD."

Klinsmann held up a hand. "I think there's a reasonable compromise available here. In my opinion, the jury and I have seen all that we need to see to inform our judgment in this case. The disk containing all of the photographs—both viewed and unviewed—has been entered into evidence and will be available to the jury should they wish to review it as part of their deliberations. Is that satisfactory?"

"Yes, your honor." Marconi's gambit had worked. She appeared humane in seeking a respite for Michael but succeeded in her ulterior objective of stopping the defense's slideshow.

"Mr. Quarrington?" prompted the judge.

"I would like to register my objection on the record. Withholding relevant evidence from the jury constitutes a potential ground for appeal."

"So noted. Dismissed."

"I'm sorry," Michael said as Quarrington returned to the defense table.

"Absolutely no need to apologize. You were superb."

Court was called to order again and Quarrington resumed his questions. "Dr. MacDougall, please tell us about the steps you took to address the problems facing the world's forgotten children when you returned home."

"I tried to persuade the government to recognize and respond to the magnitude of preventable death, disease, and suffering, to change its approach. I set up a charitable organization called the Blue Drop Foundation. I used some of my life savings to get it started."

"Please tell us about the basic idea behind the Blue Drop Foundation."

"The idea came to me a while after I returned from Africa. It seemed so simple. I thought that if Americans paid a one-cent premium for every soda, beer, bottled water, juice, coffee, or tea, for every time they bought a beverage . . . and if you took all that money and dedicated it to providing clean water in developing countries, then one of the biggest problems facing a billion people every day could be solved within a decade. A penny per drink. Is that too much to pay to save the lives of at least one million kids a year? Can anybody in the United States answer that question 'Yes' and still look at themselves in the mirror?"

"And what was the response to your idea?"

"I presented the concept to politicians and CEOs. I approached members of Congress, governors, bureaucrats, and all kinds of corporate executives. It was like talking to lobotomy patients in a mental institution. I couldn't seem to penetrate the fog. 'Too great an impact on the bottom line.' 'Consumers will go ballistic.' 'Sure we'll do it but we don't want to be the first.' All I got was a litany of excuses.

"I went to the megacorporations. No luck. I went to the microbreweries. No luck. I reached out to every soda pop manufacturer and juice processor in the country. I got nowhere. I achieved nothing. I couldn't create even a microscopic crack in the brick wall of corporate and government indifference."

"And so you decided to pursue a different approach?"

"Yes. I realized that the humanitarian crisis warranted desperate, immediate action. I thought long and hard about the best way that I, as an individual, could get the government's attention. That's when I began to contemplate taking the extreme step of contaminating Seattle's water supply. Initially I was horrified by the very thought of it."

"But?"

"But as distasteful as the idea seemed, I couldn't come up with any viable alternatives. I witnessed too many kids dying. Hundreds of children's faces invade my brain every time I try to sleep. I lived with them. I visited with them. I listened to their stories. I gave them the best medical treatment possible in the circumstances. I did everything I could, everything, and it was light years short of being anywhere near enough.

"My goal in contaminating Seattle's water was to save people, not harm them. I planned everything extremely carefully to ensure that Americans would not die, or even become ill, as a result of my actions. If the government had listened, the outcome would have been millions of innocent children saved and not a single person hurt."

Quarrington repeated the final words: "Millions saved and not a single person hurt."

Michael was drenched with sweat when he finished, wet patches visible under both arms.

Marconi requested a recess before proceeding with her cross-examination. She was reluctant to leave the jurors reflecting on

Michael's story but wanted to consult with her superiors about the pros and cons of keeping him on the stand, where he might score even more points with the jury. They decided to keep it simple. She would ask tight, focused questions to which she already knew the answer, and would avoid letting Michael tell any more stories.

After a brief ten-minute respite, she stood in front of the witness stand. "Mr. MacDougall, I have nine simple yes or no questions for you. One, did you steal perchloroethylene from a hospital?"

"Yes."

"Two. You were well aware that perchloroethylene is a toxic chemical, were you not?"

"Yes, but—"

"These are simple yes or no questions," Marconi cut Michael off. "Three. You trespassed in an area off limits to the public and dumped PCE in the Chester Morse Reservoir, correct?"

"Yes."

"You knew that the Chester Morse Reservoir is the primary source of drinking water for the city of Seattle?"

"Yes."

"You left the country the same day that you dumped the PCE in Seattle's drinking water?"

"Yes."

"You threatened to carry out another attack on an American city's drinking water unless the government of the United States complied with your demand to spend an additional $100 billion on foreign aid, right?"

"Yes."

"You made this threat directly to the president?"

"Yes."

"Did the president comply with your demand?"

"No."

"So your plan, if I can call it that, was a failure?"

"Well—"

287

"Yes or no?"

Michael sat stone-faced, unwilling to answer. Klinsmann glared down at him and said, "You have to answer the question."

"The government—"

Marconi cut Michael off again, asking, "Did your plan succeed, yes or no?" but he ignored her. Without raising his voice, he completed his sentence: ". . . refused to do the right thing."

"Your honor, would you please instruct the witness to answer the question put to him?"

Again Klinsmann glared at Michael over the top of his glasses. "Mr. MacDougall, answer the question or I will find you in contempt of court."

"Did your plan succeed, yes or no?"

"No," said Michael.

CHAPTER 46

AFTER AN ABBREVIATED LUNCH BREAK, Marconi began her closing statement. Still not a single hair out of place. No wrinkles in her suit. Still speaking without the assistance of notes. "Most criminals have excuses for their illegal actions. This is particularly true of terrorists, who almost always justify their actions based on political or religious beliefs. In the American legal system, excuses and justifications do not qualify as defenses.

"Imagine the consequences of accepting the defendant's arguments. Grocery stores could be pillaged because somebody was hungry; hospitals could be plundered for drugs because someone was in pain; homes could be broken into because a person lacked shelter; banks could be robbed because someone was unemployed.

"There were avenues available to the defendant that preclude the defense of necessity. He could vote, write letters, lobby, circulate petitions, join like-minded citizens, or form an advocacy organization. If he wanted to take matters into his own hands, in a lawful and democratic manner, he could run for elected office.

"The defense has attempted to portray the accused as a do-gooder. In fact the accused is a terrorist. The Patriot Act defines terrorism as an activity that meets three basic criteria: intimidates or coerces either the government or the civilian population, breaks criminal laws, and endangers human life. The accused is clearly, undeniably, three for three. He blackmailed the president, stole, trespassed, used a chemical weapon, and poisoned the people of Seattle.

"American courts have consistently rejected the use of the necessity defense in comparable circumstances. Let me quote several leading cases. The Federal Court, Tenth Circuit, ruled that 'to allow the personal, ethical, moral, or religious beliefs of a person, no matter how sincere or well-intended, as a justification for criminal activity . . . would not only lead to chaos but would be tantamount to sanctioning anarchy.' The Federal Court, Seventh Circuit, ruled that 'one who elects to serve mankind by taking the law into his own hands thereby demonstrates his conviction that his own ability to determine policy is superior to democratic decision-making. Appellant's professed unselfish motivation, rather than a justification, actually identifies a form of arrogance which organized society cannot tolerate.'

"Like other terrorists who have wrought havoc on Americans, importing fear into our lives, the accused has taken it upon himself to usurp the role of the Almighty. By taking into his own hands decisions about who should live and who should die, the accused is guilty not only of terrorism but playing God. He wants you to think that he is somehow above the law, more capable than our elected president and Congress of making important fiscal and foreign policy decisions. Despite my colleague's attempts to portray the defendant as an honorable man, a humanitarian, and even, unbelievably, a hero, you must remember one fundamental point: there's no such thing as an innocent terrorist."

For his closing statement Quarrington abandoned his wheelchair and used two beautiful canes, carved from arbutus, to help him stand and face the jury.

"Dr. MacDougall is not a terrorist, a criminal, a murderer, or a madman. Comparisons to the Unabomber, Timothy McVeigh, and Osama bin Laden are grossly unfair and inaccurate. These madmen killed innocent people in pursuit of personal agendas, half-baked Luddite philosophies, and illogical religious ideas. Dr. MacDougall killed no one, injured no one, and sought to save millions of lives.

"I would like to ask each of you to think of your children, how much you love them, what they mean to you, the joy and wonder they have brought into your life, how proud you are of their accomplishments.

"Now imagine, if you will, that one of your children has become ill with a potentially deadly disease. You take your daughter or your son to a doctor, who tells you that the only available remedy is extremely expensive and not covered by your health insurance. You cannot afford to even begin the course of treatment. You watch your child waste away before your very eyes. You are helpless, incapable of providing the assistance he or she needs. One day, your child is gone. The baby you carried within you for nine months, the child who suckled at your breast, the child for whom you would willingly sacrifice your life, is dead."

Quarrington continued, with added urgency in his voice, "The loss of a young child is a devastating psychological blow from which most parents, understandably, never recover. So the toll, in human terms, is far greater than the mere total of mortalities. A circle of suffering extends outward from a dead child, like the impact zone of a bomb, with those closest to the victim most likely to be harmed by the explosion and the emotional shrapnel.

"If your son or daughter was starving to death, and you possessed the means to intervene, you would. If your neighbor's son or daughter was starving and you possessed the means to assist, you would. What about the child of a person two doors down, or in an apartment on the floor below you? What about a child living across the street or a mile down the road? Why does geographical distance materially alter the matter of your individual morality? Is it really possible that convenience trumps conscience? Is geography more important than ethics?

"District Attorney Marconi has repeatedly suggested that the evidence we put forward regarding the humanitarian crisis in sub-Saharan Africa is irrelevant to this trial. Not only is such a position egregiously lacking in principle, it is wrong in law. I shall invoke several precedents to illustrate the error of her argument.

"In Vermont, during the 1980s, protestors staged sit-ins at the office of U.S. Senator Robert Stafford based on their opposition to American policy in Central America. These actions led to their arrest on trespass charges. The court allowed a number of experts to testify about human rights atrocities in El Salvador and Nicaragua. The defendants testified they had attempted 'every reasonable manner to communicate' with the senator. The jury acquitted all of the defendants. Similar cases involving illegal activities directed at U.S. activities in Latin America took place in Massachusetts, Illinois, and other states, resulting in juries acquitting all of the defendants.

"In this very state, Washington, eight medical doctors were charged with trespassing after protests staged at the home of the South African ambassador. They were allowed to raise the defense of necessity and submit expert testimony about the adverse effects of apartheid on health, justice, and human rights. A Seattle jury acquitted after little more than an hour and made a statement supporting anti-apartheid protests. A similar case involving illegal anti-apartheid protests in Chicago produced the same result—acquittals for all defendants.

"Contrary to the hyperbolic rhetoric of the prosecution, the necessity defense cannot be used to challenge American values. For example, we value human life over property. No individual could ever justifiably take a human life merely to save some imperiled property. In the case before us, Dr. MacDougall faced a choice between insignificant harm to the health of people in Seattle and a tsunami of preventable deaths in Africa.

"Ms. Marconi cannot merely wish the necessity defense away. The leading decisions in American jurisprudence affirm its availability. Our history is replete with examples of individuals once considered terrorists whom the passage of time reveals to be heroes. The American patriots who dumped tea into Boston harbor. The Americans who built the underground railroad to free slaves. Women who broke laws in their battle for universal suffrage. The Americans who staged sit-ins and refused to sit at the back of buses, saying no to Jim Crow. Please listen to your consciences and acquit Dr. MacDougall."

CHAPTER 47

QUARRINGTON AND YAVARI WERE CAUTIOUSLY pleased with the way the trial had unfolded. But Michael had finally realized that even in the best-case scenario, an acquittal, his life was in tatters.

Klinsmann began his instruction to the jury. "There are a number of matters that I must bring to your attention prior to the beginning of your deliberations. First, the Constitution states that a person is innocent until proven guilty. Second, the burden of proof lies on the prosecution to establish all elements of the alleged crimes beyond a reasonable doubt. Third, although I would like to direct you to reach a particular verdict, it is not within my power to do so, no matter how conclusive the evidence appears to be. You must consider separately each of the charges against the defendant, after which you may find him: guilty of both charges, guilty of one charge and not the other, or not guilty of either charge.

"Through the testimony of Dr. Carpenter and the defendant, the defense presented extensive evidence about the problems currently facing sub-Saharan Africa and the shortcomings of American foreign policy. It is my obligation to advise you that from a legal perspective, their evidence is not relevant to your deliberations in this trial. All of the relevant facts involve America, not Africa."

Michael gasped. "Does that mean what I think?" he whispered, turning to Quarrington, who nodded.

Klinsmann ignored the exchange at the defense table. "To successfully rely on the necessity defense, the defendant must meet five mandatory conditions. First, the harm avoided must be greater than the harm done. Second, the defendant must have an honest and reasonable belief that his act is necessary to avoid harm. Third, there must be no legal alternatives. Fourth, the harm to be avoided must be imminent. Fifth, the defendant must not have played a part in bringing about that harm.

"The first and third elements of the necessity defense have not been met in this case. The defense has failed to demonstrate that all reasonable legal alternatives had been exhausted. There were political avenues open to the defendant, as well as economic avenues not pursued. His decision to take matters into his own hands by a series of brazenly criminal acts cannot be condoned.

"In addition, the defendant's personal opinion about the relative balance of harms is not determinative. It is up to me to carefully weigh the relative harm inflicted by the defendant and the relative harm he sought to avoid. And I find that despite his ostensibly good intentions, the defendant caused more harm than he avoided. On the one hand, poisoning Seattle's water supply caused some people to become physically ill and many people to become frightened. On the other hand, the defendant's actions did not result in any substantive change to American foreign policy.

"In conclusion, I find that as a matter of law, the defendant cannot rely on necessity to justify his unlawful acts. I consider myself bound by the precedent in a 1979 case where the Federal Court, Ninth Circuit, found that the necessity defense was not available for robberies and bombings carried out with an honest belief that the capitalist economic system needed to be overthrown to eliminate the inequality between rich and poor. Therefore, it is not open to you to reach a finding of not guilty by reason of the necessity defense. Please remember that as the presiding judge, decisions about the law are mine, and mine alone, to make, while your responsibility is to apply the law to the facts, not decide the case according to the emotional whims of your conscience."

"Objection!" Quarrington's voice reverberated around the courtroom. "Your honor, it is grossly inappropriate for you to effectively direct the jury to a particular verdict by foreclosing their only other option. The raison d'être of a jury is to act as the conscience of society in determining what is just."

"Duly noted, Mr. Quarrington, but irrelevant. Your objection is overruled." Klinsmann returned his attention to the jury. "You mustn't allow your feelings or your conscience to cloud your judgment. You have an obligation to apply the law to the facts. Nothing more, nothing less. You may now begin your deliberations."

The jury was taken to the deliberation room adjacent to the courtroom. Michael was taken to a holding cell and would be returned to the SeaTac prison if the jury's deliberations went on into the evening. Quarrington and Yavari took the elevator down to see him.

"How long do you think we'll have to wait?" Michael asked.

"Impossible to predict," Quarrington replied. "I have seen them return quickly—the jury only deliberated for four hours in the O.J. Simpson trial—and I have seen them take weeks."

"Weeks?"

"Relax. That is extremely unusual and is always the product of long, complicated trials, unlike this one. Shirin, what do you think?"

"Technically the jury should elect a foreperson and review the evidence before discussing potential outcomes. New research on the dynamics of jury deliberation indicates that there are usually three or four persuaders, four to six active participants in the discussion, and three or four people who just want to get it over with and go home. They'll go along with whatever the majority decides. I agree with Peter that predictions are purely speculative. It depends on the people in that locked room."

"So we wait?"

"Yes, and pray, if you are so inclined," added Quarrington.

"Or think positive thoughts," said Yavari.

"We are going to return to the office," Quarrington said. "The court will contact us as soon as the jury reaches a verdict."

Several hours later Michael was escorted back to SeaTac. The jury, without reaching a resolution, had returned to the Best Western.

"Stryder here."

"I listened to our jury's deliberations today," Tierney said.

"And?"

"There's a problem."

"What the fuck? You said there'd be a quick verdict. That we owned the jury lock, stock, and barrel."

"There's a holdout."

"What, someone's grown a conscience? I thought the money was supposed to take care of that."

"It's Taisha Smith, the single mother from Seattle."

"She took the first installment, right?"

"Yeah."

"Maybe she's trying to play us. Hold out for more money."

"We've used the honey. Now it's time for the stick. You have her file?"

Stryder unlocked a desk drawer and pulled out a folder. "Yup. She's got an eight-year-old daughter named Shirelle. Staying with her grandmother while the jury is sequestered. Goes to Emerson Elementary on 60th Ave. School ends at 3:10 p.m."

"It's time to send Taisha a message."

"I'm on it."

Cassie listened to the conversation between Tierney and Stryder. Alan Jones had emailed her the recording. The heads of the FBI and CIA were acting as though they were above the law. Jury tampering. Bribery. Possibly some kind of conspiracy to harm a juror's child. She had the evidence she needed and immediately made two phone calls. One to the president and one to Jack Gilhooley, Seattle's chief of police.

At the Best Western Plus Executive Inn in downtown Seattle, incoming calls to the jurors were limited to a preapproved list of family members. So when her phone rang, Taisha was excited, assuming it would be her daughter. Instead she heard a deep male voice.

"Taisha?"

"Yes? Who is this?"

"Stop jerking the jury around. Get the verdict right tomorrow, or the next time you see Shirelle's face, it will be on the back of a milk carton."

The man hung up and Taisha sat down heavily on the bed, sobbing.

CHAPTER 48

THE NEXT MORNING, AT 9:15 A.M., the bailiff delivered a message from the jury to Judge Klinsmann. They had a verdict. Phone calls were made to the lawyers and SeaTac prison. A media advisory was issued electronically.

At ten a.m., the sheriff ushered the jury back into the courtroom. All twelve jurors sat stone-faced.

Quarrington and Yavari continued to exude quiet confidence. Yavari put her hand atop Michael's on the table in front of them.

Cassie was seated in the front row of the public gallery. In the two seats flanking her were a young child with her hair braided in cornrows and Police Chief Gilhooley, an imposing figure in his uniform. Shirelle's bright smile revealed two missing front teeth. When Taisha Smith looked over at the gallery, she was unable to disguise her surprise at seeing her daughter in the courtroom and waved quickly at Shirelle.

Klinsmann cleared his throat loudly and glared at the jurors from beneath his prodigious eyebrows. "Ladies and gentlemen of the jury, have you reached a verdict?"

"Yes, your honor, we have," Rick Johanson, the foreman, replied.

"Very well." Klinsmann milked the moment. "Before we hear the verdict, I want to caution everyone to maintain order in this courtroom. Any person violating my instructions will be removed and charged with contempt."

Klinsmann turned to face the foreman. "On the first count of the indictment, using a chemical weapon, how do you find the defendant?"

"In the District Court for the District of Western Washington, Criminal Action No. 18-CR-149, United States vs. Michael MacDougall, we, the jury, upon our oaths unanimously find as follows . . ."

Yavari squeezed Michael's hand. He was holding his breath.

"We find the defendant guilty, your honor," Johanson answered.

Despite Klinsmann's warning, there was a smattering of applause and a few groans. Michael slumped forward, hands covering his face.

Meanwhile, Klinsmann beamed. "And on the second count of the indictment, committing an act of terrorism, how do you find the defendant?"

"We find the defendant guilty, your honor."

Quarrington scratched his head and blinked slowly. Yavari also looked on in disbelief. Marconi, as cool and polished as ever, merely nodded in agreement, while several of her colleagues punched the air and congratulated each other with high-fives. Journalists whispered into cellphones and typed madly on laptops.

In the clamor that followed the verdict, a piece of paper folded in half and marked with a Q was passed from the spectator gallery over the railing to Yavari. She handed it to Quarrington, who unfolded the small square of paper. The note was short and to the point.

It read, *Poll the jury!*

Klinsmann was enthusiastically thanking the jury for having completed the first step of their civic duty. "I recognize that jury duty is demanding, interferes with your daily life, and is financially unrewarding. Yet it is a cornerstone of American democracy. Members of the jury, you have determined by your verdict that the evidence established the guilt of Michael MacDougall on these charges beyond a reasonable doubt. Whether the defendant should be put to death for these crimes is a question for you to answer by serving as the conscience of the community. Although Congress has given this responsibility exclusively to the jury, the applicable statute and the Constitution command that you must exercise your discretion by following a specific procedure and giving careful consideration to information characterized as 'aggravating and mitigating factors.' These facts will be presented in a subsequent hearing that is more or less an extension of this trial."

"Your honor." Quarrington's voice had lost none of its authority despite the verdict.

"Yes, Mr. Quarrington, what is it?"

"Excuse me, your honor, but the defendant would like to exercise his right to poll the jury."

"That's a highly unusual procedure, counselor."

Michael leaned toward Quarrington. "What's going on?"

Quarrington turned to Michael, putting his finger to his lips. "It has been an unusual trial, your honor."

"Does the U.S. attorney have any objection? Any reason for not proceeding with defense counsel's request?"

Marconi looked at her team, getting nothing but bemused shrugs. "No, your honor."

"Very well. Ladies and gentlemen of the jury, at this time the court will conduct a brief exercise called polling the jury. The foreperson has delivered a verdict of guilty on both counts. I will now read the names of each individual juror, you will stand, and you will state 'Yes that is my verdict' or 'No that is not my verdict,' whichever the case might be. Let us proceed. "Elaine Renzetti?"

"Yes, that is my verdict."

Klinsmann nodded. "Rick Johanson?"

"Yes, that is my verdict."

And so it went, juror after juror. Quarrington and Yavari exchanged puzzled glances, struggling to understand who had written the mysterious note, and why. As the process of polling jurors unfolded, there were only two people in the courtroom with the slightest inkling of what was about to happen. Cassie looked on with nervous anticipation. The other person was scared to death.

Klinsmann mechanically asked the questions, working his way through the jury. "Taisha Smith?"

Taisha Smith stood with her eyes downcast. She didn't answer the judge's question. The buzzing in the courtroom stopped.

"Taisha Smith," Klinsmann raised his voice, "is this your verdict?"

All eyes in the courtroom were now glued on Smith. Her eyes lifted, scanning Michael, the judge, Quarrington, and Marconi, before resting briefly on Shirelle, Chief Gilhooley, and Cassie. Then she returned her gaze to the floor. Several other jurors began to fidget nervously.

Her answer, when it came, was so soft spoken that it was barely audible.

"Louder!" Klinsmann barked.

"I can't say yes" was Taisha's tremulous response.

The courtroom erupted in chaos. Michael grabbed Quarrington's arm. Klinsmann slammed his gavel on the polished wood of his desk with enough force to put a dent in it. "Order," he shouted. "Order in my courtroom!"

The bedlam abated but there was still an audible buzz.

"Ms. Smith, I'm going to ask you the question again, since your answer seems to contradict the foreman's statement regarding the jury's verdict of guilty. Is this your verdict?"

Again she hesitated. She looked once more toward her daughter and then spoke in a slow but clear cadence. "No, that is not my verdict."

"On what grounds?" thundered Klinsmann. "The defendant admits the actus reus and the mens rea. He committed the crime, confessed, and failed to offer a viable defense—"

"Objection." For the first time in the trial, Quarrington raised his voice to maximum volume, thundering at the judge. "Your honor, it is completely inappropriate to badger a juror. And grossly objectionable to try to bully her into a verdict that she disagrees with! We have a hung jury. A mistrial."

"Overruled!" Klinsmann shouted back. "I'm not badgering or

bullying anybody, and if you make that suggestion again I'll find you in contempt."

Taisha Smith took advantage of the sparring between judge and attorney to compose herself. "The doctor did the right thing." The courtroom quieted at her words. "He didn't hurt anybody. He was trying to save children's lives."

Mad Max was beside himself now. "I specifically excluded the necessity defense from the jury's consideration. The legal elements of the defense were not adequately made out. You, you—" Klinsmann spluttered. His hands were tied. He couldn't disqualify a juror at this point in the trial.

Marconi and her team were stunned, looking at each other in total disbelief.

The trial was over. The jury was hung. Michael, at least for now, was a free man. But Klinsmann wouldn't let go. "Why did you change your vote?"

"I can't say," said Smith.

"You must, or I'll have you jailed for being in contempt of court!"

Taisha couldn't let that happen. She needed to be with Shirelle. She weighed the severity of the moment, fearful of those who had blackmailed her and knowing her life as a single mother would never be simple again. She drew a deep breath. And another. "They said something terrible would happen to my daughter." She stood tall, refusing to be intimidated now by the judge.

"Who's 'they'? Who said that to you?"

"A man."

"Who?"

"I don't know."

The courtroom erupted again.

Quarrington jumped in. "Your honor, this is a clear case of jury tampering. It requires an immediate and full investigation. However, that is a completely separate matter. This trial is over. In light of what has transpired, I urge you to fulfill your obligation to dismiss the jury and release my client."

Klinsmann threw his arms in the air and sat, cheeks scarlet, as he reviewed his options. He looked at the jury with distaste and said, "You're dismissed." Then he turned to face Michael. "Mr. MacDougall," he spat, "the government retains the right to retry the case. Ms. Marconi, I'd like a word with you in my chambers, immediately. Mr. Quarrington, your presence is not required."

CHAPTER 49

THAT AFTERNOON, MICHAEL WAS RETURNED to his cell at SeaTac. He was waiting for Quarrington and Yavari to arrive and explain what would happen next. When summoned to the visitors' room, Michael was surprised to see Cassie Harden-Hernandez waiting to speak with him.

"Hello, Dr. MacDougall."

Michael looked at Cassie suspiciously. "What now? More bad news?"

Cassie shook her head. "There won't be a second trial. You're a free man."

Michael responded with stunned silence, then fired off a volley of questions. "How can that be? How do you know? Are you sure?"

"It's true. I'm sure. The decision was made at the top, the very top."

Michael was overcome. His knees buckled, but Cassie caught him before he fell and held him upright as he regained his balance. Their eyes met.

"Thank you," he whispered. "I need to sit down."

Cassie helped him into one of the plastic chairs.

"I can't believe it," he said.

"That's not surprising. I imagine it will take a while to sink in. Your lawyers are being served with papers as we speak. I've got to run to the airport," Cassie said. "My flight to DC leaves at 7:30. It's been too long since I saw my husband or slept in my own bed."

Michael pulled himself together. "Listen, thank you for coming here, and for doing whatever you did. There's no way for me to adequately express my gratitude."

"You can do me a favor."

"Really? What?"

"Think about going back to medicine, will you? Forget about everything else and use the special skills that God gave you. Save lives, even if it's just one at a time."

Michael sold most of his few possessions and returned to Africa. He joined an aid organization with a lower public profile and a desperate need for doctors. Assigned to the war-torn Darfur region of the Sudan, he reimmersed himself in humanitarian medicine.

Michael was back to saving lives. Not as many as he would like, but many more than if he was behind bars. The days blurred together, turning into weeks and stretching into months. Time began its slow healing process. At the medical clinic in Um Gunya, south of Nyala, the capital of South Darfur, Michael spent two hours trying to repair a boy's leg destroyed by a land mine intentionally shaped like a toy. A brightly colored, oddly shaped item lying in the dusty soil was an irresistible attraction to a Sudanese youngster but packed enough explosive punch to blow off a child's hands or feet. This boy had walked on one leg, leaning on a friend, to reach Um Gunya. He wore a faded purple T-shirt emblazoned with the image of Shaquille O'Neal and carried his lower left leg wrapped in paper like a package of meat from a butcher's shop. Michael was unable to save the severed limb. A prosthetic leg could theoretically be attached, but cash-strapped aid organizations working in the Sudan had none of those.

As was their custom, Africans improvised. Michael had seen everything from metal pipes to old rifle stocks used as artificial limbs. Perhaps the most eye-catching was a man who had a panga, a scimitar-shaped machete, attached to the stump of his severed right arm. Captain Hook paled in comparison. As for the Sudanese boy with the newly amputated leg, he would probably make do with a piece of wood scavenged from the local forest. He'd be a new recruit for the increasingly popular sport of amputee soccer. Michael finished sewing the stitches. His hands remained steady, as always. Michael leaned over the young child and gave him an awkward hug before he walked out of the surgery.

That night, with sleep elusive, Michael returned to the clinic, nodding at the Sudanese nurse monitoring the patients. He walked from person to person, some lying on tables, some on the floor, checking their charts, listening to their chests, taking their pulse, moving on. He didn't speak to anyone and moved, wraith-like, through the moonlit room.

At the last bed Michael paused. There were two tiny infants in it, twin girls. One was crying, fists clenched, while the other quietly watched the world. He had delivered them three weeks ago, prematurely, from a teenaged girl who ran away from the clinic as soon as she could stand. Michael picked up the crying baby and held her against his chest, gently rocking her back and forth as he paced the length of the tent, careful not to step on any of the outstretched hands or feet. He hummed a nursery rhyme, unable to remember the words. The baby gradually calmed down, eyelids flickering, fighting to stay awake before surrendering to the siren song of sleep.

Michael returned the baby to the bed, where she snuggled against her sister for warmth and comfort. Then he stepped outside to look at the starry sky.

ACKNOWLEDGMENTS

I WOULD LIKE TO THANK Dr. Simon Pulfrey, Dr. Elin Raymond, Dr. Amir Attaran, Dr. Kevin Chan, and Dr. Jeanette Boyd for their generous willingness to answer questions about Africa and the medical profession. I owe a debt of gratitude to many kind mentors and readers, including William Deverell, Karen X. Tulchinsky, Jack Hodgins, Ethan Smith, David Ohnona, Ken Rempel, and Paul Richardson. For the enthusiastic response of the folks at Pender Island's speakeasy I am deeply grateful. Thank you to Susan Renouf for her unwavering belief that this was a book that should be published and her yeoman editorial efforts. Finally, my everlasting appreciation to Margot and Meredith, the loves of my life.

Any factual errors, exaggerations, or inconsistencies are the author's sole responsibility.

Purchase the print edition and receive the eBook free. Just send an
email to ebook@ecwpress.com and include:

- the book title
- the name of the store where you purchased it
- your receipt number
- your preference of file type: PDF or ePub

A real person will respond to your email with your eBook attached. And
thanks for supporting an independently owned Canadian publisher with
your purchase!